# *Edmond Dantes*

*Edmund Flagg*

# Contents

# EDMOND DANTES

BY

Edmund Flagg

EDMOND DANTES.

THE SEQUEL TO

ALEXANDER DUMAS'

CELEBRATED NOVEL OF

THE COUNT OF MONTE-CRISTO.

AN ENTIRE NEW AND ENLARGED EDITION.

BY

EDMUND FLAGG

"EDMOND DANTES," one of the greatest novels ever written, is the sequel to Alexander Dumas' world-renowned chef-d'oeuvre, "The Count of Monte-Cristo," taking up the fascinating narrative where the latter ends and continuing it with marvellous power and absorbing interest. Every word tells, and the number of unusually stirring incidents is legion, while the plot is phenomenal in its strength, merit and ingeniousness. The superb book deals with the exciting career of Edmond Dantes, who first figures as the Count of Monte-Cristo, and then as the Deputy from Marseilles takes an active part in the French Revolution of 1848. Dramatic and graphic scenes abound, the reader finding startling surprises at every turn. Love, philanthropy, politics and bloodshed form the staple of the novel and are handled with extraordinary skill. Besides the hero, Haydee, Mercedes, Valentine de Ville-fort, Eugenie Danglars, Louise d'Armilly, Zuleika (Dantes' daughter), Benedetto, Lucien Debray, Albert de Morcerf, Beauchamp, Chateau-Renaud, Ali, Maximilian Morell, Giovanni Massetti, and Esperance (Dantes' son) figure prominently, while Lamartine, Ledru Rollin, Louis Blanc and hosts of revolutionary leaders are intro-duced. "EDMOND DANTES" will delight all who read it.

NEW YORK:

WM. L. ALLISON COMPANY

PUBLISHERS.


COPYRIGHT:--1884.

T. B. PETERSON & BROTHERS.

EDMOND DANTES.

AN ENTIRE NEW AND ENLARGED EDITION.

"Edmond Dantes" the Sequel to Alexander Dumas' masterpiece, "The Count of Monte-Cristo," is a novel that will delight, entertain and instruct all who read it. It has wonderful fascination, absorbing interest and rare merit, combined with remarkable power, amazing ingenuity and thorough originality. In it the narrative is taken up immediately at the close of "The Count of Monte-Cristo," and contin-ued in a style of exceeding cleverness. There is a terrible volcanic tempest on the

Mediterranean, in which Monte-Cristo and Haydee are wrecked, a vivid picture of the French Revolution of 1848 is given and the love affair of Zuleika and Giovanni Massetti is recounted in a manner unsurpassed for novelty and excitement. The central figure is Edmond Dantes, and about him are grouped Mercedes, Eugenie Danglars, Louise d'Armilly, Valentine de Villefort, Esperance (the son of Monte-Cristo), Benedetto, Albert de Morcerf, Maximilian Morrel, Ali and the other old friends of "Monte-Cristo" readers, as well as numerous political leaders famous in French history, namely, Lamartine, Ledru Rollin, Louis Blanc, Armand Marrast, Flocon, Albert and others. Thiers, Guizot, Odillon Barrot, General Lamoriciere, General Bugeaud and other noted historical characters are introduced, as well as Lucien Debray, Chateau-Renaud, Beauchamp, etc. No one can afford to miss the opportunity to read "Edmond Dantes," which is published only by T. B. Peterson & Brothers, who also issue the only correct, complete and unabridged editions of the other volumes of the great "Monte-Cristo" Series, namely, "The Count of Monte-Cristo," "The Countess of Monte-Cristo," "The Wife of Monte-Cristo, Haydee," and "The Son of Monte-Cristo, Esperance."

# EDMOND DANTES.
# THE SEQUEL TO
# THE COUNT OF MONTE-CRISTO.

## CHAPTER I.
## STORM AND SHIPWRECK.

The Count of Monte-Cristo, with the beautiful Haydee clinging lovingly about his neck, her head pillowed upon his shoulder, stood on the deck of his superb yacht, the Alcyon, gazing at the fast-vanishing isle where he had left Maximilian Morrel and Valentine de Villefort.

It was just daybreak, but by the faint glimmering light he could plainly distinguish the figures of a man and a woman upon the distant beach. They were walking arm in arm. Presently another figure, a man's, approached them and seemed to deliver something.

"Look," said the Count to Haydee, "Jacopo has given Maximilian my letter; he reads it to Valentine, and now they know all. Jacopo points toward the yacht; they see us and are waving their handkerchiefs in token of adieu."

Haydee raised her head and glanced in the direction of the Isle of Monte-Cristo.

"I see them, my lord," she replied, in a joyous tone; "they are happy."

"Yes," said the Count, "they are happy, but they deserve their happiness, and all is well."

"They owe their happiness to you, my lord," resumed Haydee, meekly.

"They owe it to God," answered Monte-Cristo, solemnly; "I was but His humble instrument, and He has allowed me in this to make some slight atonement for the wrong I committed in taking vengeance into my own mortal hands."

Haydee was silent. She knew the sad history of Edmond Dantes, and was aware of how remorselessly the Count of Monte-Cristo had avenged the wrongs of the humble sailor of Marseilles. This she had learned from her lord's own lips within the past few days. The strict seclusion in which she had lived in Paris had necessarily excluded her from all personal knowledge of the Count's subtle war upon his enemies; true, she had emerged from her retirement to testify against Morcerf at his trial before the House of Peers, but at that time she was ignorant of the fact that by causing the foe of her family to be convicted of felony, treason and outrage she had simply promoted Monte-Cristo's vengeance on Fernand, the Catalan. But, though silent, the beautiful Greek girl, with her thoroughly oriental ideas, could not realize that the man who stood beside her, the being she almost worshiped, had been guilty of the least wrong in avenging himself. Besides, she would never have admitted, even in the most secret recesses of her own heart, that Monte-Cristo, who to her mind symbolized all that was good, pure and heroic in human nature, could have been wrong in anything he did.

Meanwhile the Count also had been silent, and a shade of the deepest sadness had settled upon his pallid but intellectual visage. He gazed at the Isle of Monte-Cristo until it became a mere dot in the distance; then, putting his arm tenderly about his lovely companion's waist, he drew her gently toward the cabin.

As they vanished down the companion-way, Bertuccio and the captain of the Alcyon, followed by Ali, the Nubian, advanced to the prow of the yacht.

"Captain," said Bertuccio, "can you tell me whither we are bound? I feel an irresistible desire to know."

"Yes," answered the captain, "I can tell you. The Count ordered me to make with all possible speed for the Island of Crete."

Bertuccio gave a sigh of relief.

"I feared we were bound for Italy," he said. "But," he added, after an instant's thought, "why should we go to Rome? Luigi Vampa is amply able to care for all the Count's interests there, if, indeed, any remain now that the Baron Danglars has been attended to."

The captain, who was an old Italian smuggler, placed his finger warningly upon his lips and glanced warily around when Luigi Vampa's name was mentioned, but said nothing. Bertuccio took the hint and the conversation was dropped.

Pressing onward under full sail, the magnificent yacht shot over the blue waters of the Mediterranean with the speed of an eagle on the wing. It sped past Corsica and Sardinia, and soon the arid, uninviting shores of Tunis were visible; then it passed between Sicily and Malta, steering directly toward the Island of Crete.

Up to this time the weather had been of the most delightful description. Not a cloud had obscured the sky, and during the entire voyage the unruffled surface of the Mediterranean had resembled that of some peaceful lake. It was now the tenth of October, and just cool enough to be pleasant; the spice-laden breezes from the coast of Africa reached the yacht tempered by the moist atmosphere of the sea, furnishing an additional element of enjoyment.

The Count of Monte-Cristo and Haydee, who seemed inseparable, came on deck every morning at dawn, and each evening walked back and forth, admiring the gorgeous sunset and watching the shades of night as they gradually settled down upon the wide expanse of the waters.

It required no unusual penetration to see that they were lovers and that their delight in each other's society was unalloyed. Haydee clung to the Count, who, with his arm wound about her slender waist, looked down into the liquid depths of her eyes with a smile of perfect content, while his free hand ever and anon toyed with her night-black tresses.

One evening as they were walking thus--it was the evening of the fifteenth of October, and Crete was distant but two days' sail--Monte-Cristo tenderly took Haydee's hand in his and said to her in a tone of ineffable softness:

"Haydee, do you remember what you said to me on the Isle of Monte-Cristo just before we parted from Valentine and Maximilian?"

"Oh! yes, my lord," was the low reply. "I said I loved you as one loves a father, brother, husband--I loved you as my life."

"And do you now regret those words?"

"Regret them! Oh! my lord, how could I do that?"

"I asked you," said the Count, slowly, "because we are nearing our destination. In two days we shall land upon the shore of Crete, and, once there, it is my intention to make you my wife, provided your feelings toward me are still unchanged.

Marriage, my child, is the most important step in life, and I do not wish you to take that step without fully understanding the promptings of your own dear heart. Only misery can follow the union of two souls not in perfect accord, not entirely devoted the one to the other. I am much older than you, Haydee, and my sufferings have aged me still more than years. I am a sad and weary man. You, on the contrary, stand just upon the threshold of existence; the world and its pleasures are all before you. Think, my child, think deeply before you pronounce the irrevocable vow."

Haydee threw herself passionately upon Monte-Cristo's breast.

"My lord," she cried, in accents broken by extreme agitation and emotion, "am I not your slave?"

"No, Haydee," answered the Count, his bosom heaving and his eyes lighting up with a strange flash, "you are free, your fate rests in your own hands."

"Then," said the young girl, ardently, "I will decide it this very instant. I accept my freedom that I may voluntarily offer myself to you, my love, my husband. You have suffered. Granted. So have I. Your sufferings have aged you; mine have transformed a child into a woman--a woman who knows the promptings of her heart, who knows that it beats for you, and you alone in all the world. My lord, I resign myself to you. Do you accept the gift?"

As Haydee concluded, her beautiful eyes were suffused with tears and her whole frame quivered with intense excitement.

Monte-Cristo bent down and kissed her upon the forehead.

"Haydee, my own Haydee," he said, with a slight tremor in his manly voice, "I accept the gift. Be my wife, the wife of Monte-Cristo, and no effort of mine shall be wanting to assure your happiness."

At that moment there was a sinister flash in the heavens, that were as yet without a cloud. The livid light shot downward to the water and seemingly plunged to the depths of the Mediterranean.

The Count gave a start and drew his beloved Haydee closer to him; the frightened girl trembled from head to foot and clung to him for protection.

"Oh! my lord, my lord," she murmured, "does Heaven disapprove of our plighted troth?"

"Calm yourself, Haydee," answered Monte-Cristo. "The lightning is God's seal, and He has set it upon our betrothal."

The flash was now repeated and was succeeded by several others of increased intensity, but as yet no thunder rolled and there was not the slightest indication of an approaching storm.

Monte-Cristo took Haydee's hand and led her to the side of the yacht. Not a single wave wrinkled the surface of the sea for miles and miles; the water seemed asleep, while down upon it the moon poured a flood of silvery radiance. The stars, too, were beaming brightly. Still, however, the intense lightning shot athwart the placid sky. It had become almost incessant. Monte-Cristo could not account for the bewildering phenomenon. He summoned the captain of the Alcyon and said to him:

"Giacomo, you have sailed the Mediterranean all your life, have you not?"

"All my life, Excellency," replied he, touching his cap.

"Have you ever before seen lightning such as this on a calm night?"

"Never, Excellency."

"It certainly cannot be heat-lightning."

"I think not, Excellency. Heat-lightning has a quicker flash and is much less intense."

"What do you suppose it portends?"

"I can form no idea, Excellency."

"Oh! my lord," said Haydee, "a terrible storm is coming, I am sure; I feel a premonition Of approaching danger. I pray you, guard against it."

"Nonsense, my child," returned Monte-Cristo, with a laugh that, in spite of all his efforts at self-control, betrayed nervous agitation and an undefinable dread. "The sky is clear, the moon is shining brilliantly and the sea is altogether tranquil; if a storm were coming it would not be so. Banish your fears and reassure yourself; the lightning is but a freak of nature."

The captain, too, was disturbed, though he could give himself no satisfactory reason for his uneasiness.

Ali, with the characteristic superstition of the Nubian race, had prostrated himself upon the deck, and was making signs the Moslems of his country use to drive away malignant spirits.

The night, however, passed without accident, though the singular lightning continued for several hours.

Next morning the sun rose, encircled by a ruddy band, fringed on the outer rim with a faint yellow, while its beams had a sullen glare instead of their normal brilliancy. The lightning of the previous night was absent, but soon another and not less disquieting phenomenon manifested itself; as far as the eye could reach the sea seemed boiling, and, at intervals, a puff, as if of vapor, would filter through the waves, rising and disappearing in the heavens. Meanwhile the wind had fallen, and amid an almost dead calm the sails of the Alcyon hung listlessly, with only an occasional flapping. The yacht moved forward, indeed, but so slowly that it scarcely appeared to move at all.

Monte-Cristo and Haydee came on deck at dawn, but the young girl displayed such terror at the unwonted aspect of the sun and the sea that the Count speedily persuaded her to return with him to the cabin. There she cowered upon a divan, hiding her face in her hands and moaning piteously. Her fiance, distressed at her condition, endeavored to soothe and comfort her, but utterly without avail; her fears could neither be banished nor allayed. At length he threw himself on a rug at her feet, and, disengaging her hands from her face, drew them about his neck; Haydee clasped him frantically and clung to him as if she deemed that embrace a final one.

As they were sitting thus, the Alcyon received a sudden and violent shock that shook the noble yacht from stem to stern. Instantly there was a sound of hurrying feet on deck, and the captain could be heard shouting hoarsely to the sailors.

Monte-Cristo leaped up and caught Haydee in his arms. At that moment Ali darted down the companion-way and stood trembling before his master.

"What was that shock?" demanded the Count, hurriedly.

The agitated Nubian made a sign signifying he did not know, but that all was yet safe.

"Remain with your mistress, Ali," said Monte-Cristo. "I am going to see what is the matter."

"Oh! no, no," cried Haydee, imploringly, as the Count placed her again on the divan and was moving away. "Oh! no, no; do not leave me, my lord, or I shall die!"

Ashy pale, Haydee arose from the divan, and cast herself on her knees at Monte-Cristo's feet.

"Swear to me, at least, that you will not needlessly expose yourself to danger," she uttered, in a pleading tone.

"I swear it," answered the Count. "Ali will faithfully guard you while I am gone," he added, "and ere you can realize my absence, I shall be again at your side."

With these words he tore himself away and hastened to the deck.

There a scene met his eye as unexpected as it was appalling. The entire surface of the Mediterranean was aglow with phosphorescence, and the sun was veiled completely by a heavy cloud that seemed to cover the whole expanse of the sky. This cloud was not black, but of a bloody hue, and the atmosphere was so densely charged with sulphur that it was almost impossible to breathe. The sea was boiling more furiously than ever, and the puffs of vapor that had before only occasionally filtered through the waves now leaped up incessantly, each puff attended with a slight explosion; the vapor was grayish when it first arose from the water, but as it ascended it became red, mingling at length with the bloody cloud that each moment acquired greater density. The wind blew fitfully, sometimes amounting to a gale and then utterly vanishing without the slightest warning. Soon the bloody cloud seemed to settle of its own weight upon the sea, growing so thick that the eye could not penetrate it, and a few feet from the yacht all was inky darkness.

Monte-Cristo hurried to the captain, who was endeavoring to quiet the superstitious fears of the sailors. Drawing him aside, he said, in a low tone:

"Giacomo, we are in frightful danger. This elemental disturbance is volcanic, and how it will end cannot be foretold. No doubt an earthquake is devastating the nearest land, or will do so before many hours have elapsed. At any moment rocks or islands may arise from the sea, and obstruct our passage. All we can do is to hold ourselves in readiness for whatever calamity may happen, and make for Crete as rapidly as possible, with the hope of eventually getting beyond the volcanic zone. Do not enlighten the crew as to the cause of the disturbance; did they know, or even suspect it, they could not be controlled, but would become either stupefied or reckless. Try to convince them that we are simply in the midst of a severe electrical storm that will speedily exhaust its fury and subside. Now, to work, and remember that everything depends upon your courage and resolution."

Giacomo rejoined the sailors, who were huddled together at the stern of the yacht like so many frightened sheep. He spoke to them, doing his utmost to reassure them, and ultimately succeeded so well that they resumed their neglected duties with some show of alacrity and even cheerfulness.

Meanwhile, Monte-Cristo, with folded arms and an outward show of calmness, was pacing the deck as if nothing unusual were in progress, and his demeanor was not without its effect on the sailors, who looked upon him with a species of awe and admiration. At times he went below to cheer the drooping spirits of his beloved Haydee, but speedily returned that the influence of his presence might not be lost.

Thus the day passed. A night of painful suspense succeeded it, during which not a soul on board the Alcyon thought of sleeping. Nothing, however, occurred, save that the intense lightning of the previous night was renewed. Toward eleven o'clock the breeze freshened to such an extent that the yacht sped along on her course with great fleetness.

In the morning the sun arose amid a purple haze, and the Mediterranean presented a more tumultuous and threatening aspect than it had the preceding day. The breeze was still blowing stiffly, and the lightning continued. Giacomo informed Monte-Cristo that unless a calm should suddenly come on they would certainly arrive at Crete by noon. The sailors, he added, were in good spirits, and might be relied upon, though they were much fatigued by reason of their unceasing labor.

At ten o'clock the man at the wheel hurriedly summoned the captain to his side, and, with a look of terror and bewilderment, directed his attention to the compass, the needle of which no longer pointed to the north, but was dancing a mad dance, not remaining stationary for a single instant. To complicate the situation still further, the sun was suddenly obscured, absolute darkness invading both sea and sky. Only when the vivid lightning tore the dense clouds apart were those on board the Alcyon enabled to catch a glimpse of what was going on about them, and that glimpse was but momentary. Thunder peals were now added to the terrors of the time, while the yacht tossed and plunged on angry, threatening billows. Showers of sparks and glowing cinders, as if from some mighty conflagration, poured down into the water, striking its surface with an ominous hiss; they resembled meteors, and their brilliancy was augmented by the surrounding gloom. Rain also began to descend, not in drops, but in broad sheets and with the roar of a cataract; in a moment everybody on the Alcyon's deck was drenched to the skin.

Haydee had not ventured from the cabin since the first day of the elemental commotion; in obedience to his master's commands, Ali constantly watched over her whenever the Count was facing the strange storm with Giacomo and the sailors.

As the captain approached the man at the wheel, Monte-Cristo fixed his eyes upon the old Italian's countenance and saw it assume a deathly pallor as he noticed that the needle of the compass could no longer be depended on.

In an instant the Count was beside him and realized the extent of the new evil that had befallen them.

"We can steer but by guess now," said Giacomo, in a low, hoarse whisper. "God grant that we may be able to reach our destination."

As he spoke, a loud crash was heard, and the rudder, torn from its fastenings by the violence of the tempest, swept by them, vanishing amid the darkness. The man at the wheel gazed after it, uttering a cry of despair.

"We are completely at the mercy of the wind and waves!" said Monte-Cristo, in an undertone. "Can nothing be done?" he added, hurriedly.

"Nothing, Excellency," returned the captain. "A temporary rudder might be rigged were the sea calmer, but, boiling and seething as it is, such a thing is utterly impossible."

A panic had seized upon the sailors as they witnessed the catastrophe that rendered the Alcyon helpless, but this immediately gave place to stupor, and the men stood silent and overwhelmed.

Bertuccio, from the time the dread storm had broken forth, had been gloomy and uncommunicative; he had held persistently aloof both from Monte-Cristo and the crew. In the general turmoil and confusion his bearing and behavior had passed unnoticed even by the vigilant eye of the Count.

The steward now approached his master, and, taking him aside, whispered in his ear:

"Heaven's vengeance is pursuing the Alcyon and all on board because of my crimes! I feel it--I know it!"

The steward's face was as white as a sheet, but his eye betokened fixed resolution.

"Not another word of this," cried Monte-Cristo, sternly. "Should the superstitious sailors hear you, they would demand with one voice that you be cast into the boiling sea."

"And they would be right," rejoined Bertuccio, doggedly. "If I remain where I am, the Alcyon's doom is sealed. On the other hand, the moment you are rid of me the storm will cease as if by magic, and you will be saved."

"Be silent!" commanded Monte-Cristo. "You are a Corsican--show a Corsican's courage!"

"I will!" was the determined reply, and the steward walked with a firm tread to the side of the yacht.

"What do you mean?" said the Count, hurrying after him and placing his hand on his shoulder.

"You shall see!" answered Bertuccio.

Shaking off Monte-Cristo's grasp, he leaped upon the bulwarks and suddenly sprang far out amid the seething waves. The Count uttered a cry of horror that was echoed by the captain. As for the crew, so utterly stupefied were they that they did not seem to comprehend the suicidal act. For an instant Monte-Cristo and Giacomo saw the steward whirling about amid the tumultuous flood; then he was swept away, and vanished in the impenetrable darkness beyond.

The force of the wind had meanwhile augmented until a perfect hurricane was raging about the Alcyon; the noise was deafening, and the sails swelled to such an extent that they threatened to snap asunder. Suddenly they gave way, and the tattered shreds flew in all directions, like white-winged sea-fowl. Simultaneously the mast toppled and went by the board. The yacht, now a helpless wreck, pitched and tossed, but still shot onward, impelled by the wild fury of the gale. Gigantic waves at intervals swept the deck, each torrent as it retreated carrying with it all it could tear away, and making huge gaps in the bulwarks, to which the sailors were clinging with all the energy of desperation. Monte-Cristo had grasped the stump of the mast, and the captain clung with all his strength to the remains of the wheel. The lightning had become terrific, and the almost continuous roar of the thunder was sufficient to drown the mad din of the waters.

All at once the jagged outlines of a gigantic rock loomed up, directly in the course of the fated vessel; in another instant the Alcyon struck and remained fast, while a vivid flash of lightning revealed what appeared to be an island, about a quarter of a mile away. But though the wreck of the yacht was motionless, the furious sea continued to break over the deck, and it seemed only a question of a few moments when the battered and torn hull of the Alcyon would go to pieces. The boat the vessel carried had long since been wrenched from its fastenings and swept into the whirlpool.

Monte-Cristo, quitting the stump of the mast, darted down the companion-way into the cabin, and quickly returned to the deck bearing in his arms the swooning form of his adored Haydee. Ali followed him. The Nubian seemed to have entirely recovered from his fear, and manifested both alertness and decision.

Shifting his lifeless burden to his left arm and grasping her firmly, Monte-Cristo advanced to the side of the Alcyon. Pausing there for an instant, he said, addressing Giacomo and the crew:

"The yacht cannot hold together much longer; if we remain where we are we shall inevitably be ground to powder on the rock with our vessel. There is an island some distance to the right of us, and, sustained by Providence, we may succeed in reaching it by swimming. For my part, I shall try the venture and endeavor to save this lady. You, men, are untrammeled and stand a better chance of success than I do. I advise you all to follow my example; to cling further to the wreck is death!"

With these words the Count made his way to a gap in the bulwarks and, grasping Haydee tightly, leaped with her into the midst of the angry sea. Ali followed his master, and soon they were seen far in the distance, struggling and battling with the waves.

# CHAPTER II.
# THE ISLAND.

It was the month of December, but on the little Island of Salmis in the Grecian Archipelago the temperature was as mild and genial as that of June. The grass was rank and thick, while the blooming almond trees filled the atmosphere with fragrance. On a narrow strip of sandy beach three or four fishermen were preparing their nets and boats for a fishing expedition to the waters beyond. They chatted as they toiled. The eldest of them, a man about sixty, with silvered locks and a long gray beard, said:

"You may talk of storms as much as you please, but I maintain that the most severe tempest ever experienced in this neighborhood was the one I witnessed ten years ago last October, when we had the earthquake and the strange man, who now owns this island, was washed ashore."

"The Count of Monte-Cristo you mean?" remarked one of the party.

"Yes, the Count of Monte-Cristo, who has done so much for us all and whose wife is nothing less than an angel of goodness and charity."

"You rescued him, did you not, Alexis?"

"I found him lying upon the beach, with the lady who is now his wife tightly clasped in his arms, so tightly that I had no end of trouble to separate them. Both were unconscious at the time, and no wonder, for the sea was furious and they must have been dashed about at a fearful rate. It was a miracle they escaped with their lives. Near them lay that dark-skinned African, their servant, who styles himself Ali, as well as the corpses of several sailors. The African, however, revived just as I approached him. He's a man of iron, I tell you, for he immediately leaped to his feet and helped me to restore his master and mistress. When they came to, I took the whole party to my hut and cared for them. The next day I rowed the Count and the African out to the wreck of their vessel on that rock you see away over there, and they brought back with them a fabulous amount of money and jewels that they found in the strangest closets I ever saw in the cabin. Then the Count bought this island and has lived here ever since. He took the lady to Athens and was married to her there, and on his return he had the palace they now occupy built in the midst of the palm grove."

By this time the fishermen had completed their preparations and, leaping into their boats, they started on their expedition.

The palace in the palm grove to which old Alexis had alluded was, indeed, a magnificent dwelling, suitable in every respect for the residence of an oriental monarch. It was built in the Turkish fashion and its exterior was singularly beautiful and imposing. Huge palm trees surrounded it; they were planted in regular rows upon a vast lawn that was adorned with costly statues and fountains, while at intervals were scattered great flower beds filled with choice exotics and blooming plants of endless variety. A wide graveled walk and carriage-road led to the palace, the main entrance to which was flanked on either side by columns of dark-veined marble. The edifice itself was of green stone, and sparkled in the sunlight like a colossal emerald. It was surmounted by three zinc-covered domes, above each of which towered a gilded crescent.

Within all was elegance and luxury. There were immense salons, with marble floors, and walls covered with Smyrna hangings of the most beautiful description that of themselves must have cost a fortune. These salons were furnished with rich divans, tables of malachite, cabinets of ebony, and oriental rugs of the most artistic and complicated workmanship. There were dazzling reception rooms filled with exquisite statues and superb paintings, the works of the greatest sculptors and artists of the east and west, of the past and the present. Figures by Thorwaldsen, Powers and other modern celebrities of the block and chisel stood beside antique masterpieces framed by the genius of Phidias and his brother sculptors of old Greece and Rome, masterpieces that had been torn from the ruins of antiquity by the hand of the untiring and enterprising excavator. Among the paintings were fine specimens of the skill of Albert Duerer, Murillo, Rubens, Van Dyck, Rembrandt, Sir Joshua Reynolds and other votaries of the brush whose names are immortal. These paintings did not hang on the walls, for they were covered with rich tapestry from the looms of Benares and the Gobelins, but rested on delicately fashioned easels, themselves entitled to a high, rank as works of art. In the salons were statues by Michael Angelo, Pierre Puget and Pompeo Marchesi, and paintings by Claude Lorraine, Titian, Sir Thomas Lawrence, Correggio and Salvator Rosa.

The vast library was encircled by lofty bookcases of walnut and ebony, filled with rare and costly volumes from the curiously illuminated missals of monkish days to the latest scientific works, together with a liberal sprinkling of poetry and fiction; upon tables, stands and mantels were superb ornaments in brass repousse work and grand old faience, including some wonderful specimens of ancient Chinese crackle ware, the peculiar secret of the manufacture of which had been lost in the flight of ages.

At an exquisite desk of walnut, carved with grotesque images, sat the Count of Monte-Cristo; he was busily engaged in writing, and beside him lay a huge pile of manuscript that was ever and anon augmented by an additional sheet, hastily scrawled in strange, bewildering Semitic characters.

The Count showed but small trace of the passage of years; he did not look much older than when he left the Isle of Monte-Cristo with Haydee on that voyage which was destined to result so disastrously for the Alcyon and her ill-fated crew. To be sure, his hair was slightly flecked with gray, but his visage still retained its full outline, and not a wrinkle marred its masculine beauty. He was clad in an exceedingly picturesque costume, half Greek and half Turkish, while upon his head was a red fez from the centre of which hung down a gilt tassel.

As he wrote his eyes sparkled and he seemed filled with enthusiasm. At length he threw aside his pen, and rising began to pace the vast apartment with long strides. "Alas!" he muttered, "perhaps after all I am only a vain dreamer, as hosts of others have been before me. But no, my scheme is feasible and cannot fail; it is based on sound principles and a thorough knowledge of mankind; besides, the immense wealth that an all-wise God has placed at my disposal will aid me and form a mighty factor in the cause. In the past I used that wealth solely for my own selfish ends, but now all is different; I have no thought of self--the philanthropist has replaced the egotist; I have aided the poor, relieved the stricken and brought joy to many a sorrowing home, but hitherto I have acted only in isolated cases; now I meditate a grand, a sublime stroke--to give freedom to man throughout the entire length and breadth of the Continent of Europe. If I succeed, and succeed I must, every down-trodden human being from the coast of France to the Ural Mountains, from the sunny Mediterranean to the frozen Arctic Ocean, will reap the benefit of my efforts and shake off the yoke of tyranny. Where shall I begin? Ah! with France, my own country, the land that gave me birth. I shall thus return good for evil, and Edmond Dantes, the prisoner of the Chateau d'If, will free the masses from their galling chains. My most potent instrument will be the public press; by means of journals I will found, or buy, the minds of all Europeans shall become familiarized with the theory of universal liberty and ripened for sweeping revolutions and the establishment of republics; I will also call fiction to my aid; struggling novelists and feuilletonists shall receive liberal subsidies from my hand on condition that they disseminate my ideas, theories and plans in their romances and feuilletons; thus will I reach thousands upon thousands who hold themselves aloof from politics, and almost insensibly they will be transformed into zealous, active partisans of the order of things that is to be; poets, too, shall sing the praises of freedom louder and more enthusiastically than ever before; in fine, no instrument, no means, however humble and apparently insignificant, shall be neglected when the proper moment

arrives, but until it does arrive I must wait, wait patiently, wait though while waiting an internal fire consume me, and my veins throb with anxiety and expectation
to the point of bursting."

He sank into a chair, and, burying his face in his hands, was lost in profound
thought.

Meanwhile, a lovely woman, leading a beautiful girl of eight years and a handsome boy of nine, had noiselessly entered the apartment. It was Haydee, the wife of
Monte-Cristo, Haydee grown mature and more beautiful than ever. Her night-black
tresses were gathered in two wide braids at the back of her shapely head, so long
that they reached below her waist. Her eyes were as bright as stars, and her slender hands, tipped with their pink nails, as white as the lily; her tiny feet, encased
in Cinderella slippers of rose-hued satin, peeped out from beneath ample Turkish
trousers, which were semi-transparent and disclosed the outlines of her beautifully
turned limbs; she wore a close-fitting gilet of pearly silk, adorned with gilt fringe
and cut low, displaying her snowy neck and magnificent shoulders; her arms were
encompassed but not hidden by flowing sleeves of filmy gauze as fine as the tissue
of a spider's web; about her neck flashed a collar of brilliant diamonds of enormous
value, and on her tapering fingers were rings of emerald, ruby and sapphire; on her
head was a red fez, precisely similar to her husband's; her countenance, a perfect
revelation of angelic beauty, was wreathed in sunny smiles that betokened thorough happiness and contentment.

The little girl, Zuleika, the daughter of Monte-Cristo, was her exact image, a
reproduction of her lovely mother in miniature, a promise of rare delight for the
future. The child's costume was also modeled after Haydee's, but with modifica-
tions suited to her tender years. Zuleika was of a gentle, loving disposition, but a
vein of romance and poetry had already developed itself in her notwithstanding
her extreme youth. She sighed for the unknown delights of the sea, and the wail
of the surf sounded to her like the most delicious of mysterious harmonies. Her
infant imagination peopled the watery realm with spirits of good and evil always
in contention, and the great ships, with their huge white sails, that she saw in the
distance from the sandy beach of the Island of Salmis, were in her eyes the mighty
birds of Arabian story.

The boy, Esperance, the son of Monte-Cristo, resembled his father both in disposition and appearance; his youthful soul was full of noble aspirations, while his daring and bravery filled even the hardy fishermen of the coast with wonder and amazement. He was a very manly and handsome child; quick, enthusiastic and energetic; his father's hope and his mother's idol; though Haydee saw, with extreme uneasiness, that the little lad was wise beyond his years, and was already devoted to Monte-Cristo's somewhat visionary schemes, which he appeared to grasp in all their complicated details. His attire was that of a Greek fisher boy; his trousers, rolled up above his knees, displayed his naked legs and bare feet; in one hand he held a rough sea cap that he had removed from his head at the door of the library. Esperance loved, above all other things, to be with the fishermen on the beach, and his joy knew no bounds when he was permitted to accompany them on their fishing expeditions to the waters beyond.

Haydee remained silently gazing at Monte-Cristo for a moment; then, advancing into the middle of the room, she stood beside him with the children. Zuleika, dropping her mother's hand, sprang lightly upon her father's knees, and, clasping him about the neck with her chubby arms, kissed him rapturously.

The Count started from his deep reverie and returned his daughter's kiss; then, looking up, he perceived Haydee and Esperance.

"Ah! my loved ones," said he, "so you are all here!"

"Yes, papa," returned Zuleika, in a clear, crystal voice, that sounded like the tinkle of a fairy bell, "we are all here--mamma, Esperance and 'Leika!"

Monte-Cristo smiled faintly, and patted the little girl tenderly on the cheek.

"Haydee," said he, "fortune favors us in our children; they are, indeed, a blessing to us."

"A veritable blessing, my lord," answered the lovely Haydee, "but still I cannot help feeling some terror at the thought that Esperance may one day be drawn into those political struggles you have so often foretold, and in which it is your intention to act a prominent part."

"Papa will lead the people to victory, and I will fight by his side!" cried Esperance, proudly.

Haydee gazed sadly at the enthusiastic boy, and tears came into her gazelle-like eyes.

"Oh! my lord," she said to her husband, "teach Esperance the arts of peace, implant in his boyish bosom, while there is yet time, the love of home and domestic joys."

The Count glanced admiringly at the little lad, who stood with dilated nostrils and eyes flashing fire; then, turning to Haydee, he said in an impressive tone:

"My beloved wife, Esperance is but an infant, and it may be years ere Europe shall awake from her lethargy and strive to overturn the thrones of her despots; before that period, the period of revolution and bloodshed, our son may change his opinions and cease to be the ardent Republican he is now."

"No, no," protested the enthusiastic boy; "I will be a Republican all my life!"

Monte-Cristo smiled sadly, and, drawing the lad to his knee, said to him:

"Esperance, my son, you are yet too young to know the ways of the world and the snares that monarchs set for the inexperienced and unwary. There are temptations at their command capable of winning over even the most zealous enemies, and they never hesitate to use them when the opportunity offers. At the proper time I will instruct you fully about all this; now, you cannot understand it."

As Monte-Cristo ceased to speak, Ali entered the library, followed by three native servants attached to the palace. The Nubian bowed low before his master and reverently kissed Haydee's hand; the servants did likewise. Then Ali handed the Count a sealed letter, making signs to the effect that he had found it tied with a cord to one of the palm trees on the lawn.

Monte-Cristo opened the letter and glanced at the signature; as he did so a look of surprise and annoyance settled upon his face.

The note was written in the French language, and read as follows:

COUNT OF MONTE-CRISTO: I am in hiding on the Island of Salmis and must see you without delay. Meet me at midnight in the almond grove near the eastern shore. Be sure to come alone.

BENEDETTO.

"Humph!" said the Count to himself as he finished reading this singular epistle. "I thought I was rid of that scoundrel forever, but it seems that the galleys at Toulon cannot hold him. Well, I suppose I must meet him; otherwise he may take a notion to come here, which would be both inconvenient and disagreeable. I imagine he wants a little money to enable him to escape to the east; if that is all, I will gladly give it to be rid of his presence, on the island. I prefer not to have as a neighbor a thief and an assassin, even if he did shine so brilliantly once in aristocratic Parisian society as the Prince Cavalcanti!"

"What is the matter, my lord?" asked Haydee, noticing the expression on Monte-Cristo's countenance. "From whom is the letter?"

"Oh! it is nothing," answered the Count, with a smile. "A poor fellow wishes my assistance, and is too modest to ask it in person; that's all!"

Haydee was not satisfied with this indefinite reply; she knew that the contents of the letter so strangely conveyed to her husband had vexed and troubled him; but she also knew that Monte-Cristo could be as silent as the tomb about anything he wished to keep secret, and, therefore, judged it useless to attempt further questions. Besides, a singular presentiment of evil had taken possession of her at the sight of the ominous note, and she felt certain that some disaster was threatened; hence, she determined to be watchful and keep strict guard over her children until the mystery, whatever it was, should be cleared up.

As the clock in his library struck the quarter before midnight, Monte-Cristo arose from the chair in which he had been sitting; donning his fez and a light cloak, he prepared to go to the almond grove on the eastern portion of the island, the spot Benedetto had appointed for their meeting; prior to setting out he slipped into his pocket a well-filled purse, and thrust a loaded revolver into the belt he wore about his waist.

"The scoundrel was anxious that I should come alone, but he did not prohibit me from arming myself," muttered he, with a grim smile, "and I have seen too much of Signor Benedetto to care to leave the game entirely in his hands!"

Quitting the palace by a private door, after making sure that everybody was asleep and that he was unobserved, Monte-Cristo bent his steps in the direction of the almond grove. It was a moonless night and very dark; the air was rather chill, while the roar of the surf sounded louder than usual in the crisp, bracing atmosphere. The Count gathered his cloak tightly about him and walked steadily onward, notwithstanding the thick darkness. At length the heavy odor of the almond blossoms warned him that he was approaching his destination, and he paused to survey the scene.

About fifty yards away the almond grove loomed up, casting a denser shade upon the surrounding blackness. The Count hastened his steps and in a few seconds stood among the trees. As he paused the figure of a man emerged from behind a huge fragment of rock and thus hailed him:

"Are you the Count of Monte-Cristo?"

"I am," was the firm reply.

"And are you alone, as I recommended?"

"Entirely alone. Now, if you have finished your questions, pray who are you?"

"Why do you ask?"

"Merely for form's sake."

"Well, then, I am Benedetto."

"Of course. As it was too dark for me to distinguish your features, I simply wanted to identify you. Now, state your business as briefly as possible."

"I escaped from Toulon long ago, and, after wandering all over Europe, settled in Athens, where I remained until a week since, when the result of a difficulty compelled me to quit the city."

"An assassination?"

"Yes, an assassination!"

Monte-Cristo shuddered to hear the cold-blooded villain talk so calmly of his foul crime, but, conquering his aversion, he said between his teeth:

"Proceed."

"I fled from Athens under cover of the night and the next morning hired a fisherman to bring me here in his boat, thinking that the island was inhabited only by a few poverty-stricken wretches who gained a scanty subsistence from the sea. On my arrival I was filled with terror at beholding your magnificent palace, which I was told belonged to a great lord. I naturally imagined that no one could inhabit such a dwelling save some high official of the Greek Government, and, without making further inquiries, again secured the services of the fisherman, who took me to the neighboring Island of Kylo. There I was in safety, for I fell in with a band of stout-hearted men, of whom I eventually became the chief."

"Bandits, no doubt!"

"Yes, bandits, if you will, but valiant men all the same. We prospered exceedingly and imagined that our career could be continued with impunity as long as we might desire; in this, however, we were sadly mistaken, for one fatal night the Greek soldiery suddenly descended upon us and hemmed us in on every side ere we were aware of their presence. We fought none the less desperately on that account, and in the sanguinary conflict all my companions were slain. I was grievously wounded and left for dead, but the following day managed to crawl to the beach and contrived to be conveyed hither, having learned by accident that the great lord of the Island of Salmis was no other than my old friend of happier days, the Count of Monte-Cristo, in short, yourself. Now, you know my story. I am a fugitive here as in France, and need your aid to enable me to escape."

"You want money?"

"Yes."

"How much?"

"A million of francs!"

"Man!" cried Monte-Cristo, breathless with astonishment at Benedetto's audacious demand, "you are out of your senses! I will give you a thousand francs, but not a sou more!"

"Beware how you trifle with a desperate man!" hissed Benedetto.

"What have I to fear?" said Monte-Cristo, calmly. "You are alone."

"I am not alone, Count of Monte-Cristo; my stout-hearted friends of the Island of Kylo are with me, and ready to support my demand!"

"Then you lied to me; your story was a base fabrication."

"Partly, Count; but enough of this--I want the million of francs; it is a small sum for you to spare an old friend, who did you as much service as Prince Andrea Cavalcanti! Are you going to give me the money?"

"I am not!" replied Monte-Cristo, drawing his revolver from his belt and cocking it.

"Ho! ho!" laughed Benedetto, mockingly, "that's your game, is it? Again I tell you to beware how you trifle with a desperate man!"

At the repetition of this phrase, as if it had been a preconcerted signal, a dozen stalwart figures started up from the darkness and surrounded Monte-Cristo, who instantly discharged his weapon right and left among them. Several of the bandits fell, pierced by the balls, and Benedetto, with a loud oath, leaped at the Count's throat, brandishing a long, keen-bladed dagger above his head.

Raising his empty revolver, Monte-Cristo with a hand of iron struck his on-coming assailant full in the face, stretching him instantly at his feet; but scarcely had he accomplished this when three of the bandits sprang upon him and hurled him to the earth beside Benedetto.

"Now," cried one of the miscreants with a frightful curse, at the same time placing the muzzle of a pistol at the Count's temple, "now, my lord of Salmis, your time has come!"

As he was about to fire, there arose a tremendous shout, and, headed by Ali, who swung aloft a Turkish yataghan, the entire force of Monte-Cristo's servants, armed to the teeth, swept down upon the astonished bandits. At the same instant a pistol-shot rang out, and the man who had threatened to take the Count's life fell to the ground a corpse. As Monte-Cristo regained his feet he saw Esperance standing a short distance away, the smoking weapon with which he had just killed his father's would-be murderer still clenched in his boyish hand. The struggle that ensued was of short duration, for the bandits, finding themselves outnumbered, speedily fled to their boats, leaving their wounded comrades behind them.

When the Count realized that Esperance, his beloved son, had saved him from death, he rushed to the heroic lad, took him in his arms and bore him beyond the reach of danger; this done, he returned to aid Ali and the servants, but they were already victors and in full possession of the field.

A search was made for the body of Benedetto, but it had disappeared.

# CHAPTER III.
# THE CONFLAGRATION.

As the Count of Monte-Cristo, Esperance, Ali and the servants approached the palace on their return from the struggle with the bandits in the almond grove, their ears were suddenly saluted by loud cries of terror. They came from the library and thither Monte-Cristo hurried, followed by his son. On the floor in the centre of the apartment Haydee lay in a swoon, and bending over her mother was Zuleika, screaming and wringing her little hands. The Count raised his wife and placed her upon a divan, while Esperance brought a water-jar and bathed her temples with its cool, refreshing contents, Zuleika meanwhile holding her mother's hands and sobbing violently.

At last Haydee recovered consciousness, and opening her eyes gazed wildly around her; seeing her husband, Esperance and Zuleika safe beside her, she uttered a faint sigh of relief. It was several moments longer before she could speak; then she exclaimed in a tremulous voice:

"Oh! my lord, did you meet that terrible man?"

"What man, Haydee?" asked the Count. "Do you mean Benedetto?"

"I do not know his name; I never saw him before," answered Haydee; "but his face was all battered and bleeding; on his uncovered head the locks were matted and unkempt, and his garments were torn as if in wrenching his way through a thicket of tangled briers."

"Benedetto, it was Benedetto!" cried Monte-Cristo. "You do not mean to say he was here, in this room?"

"He was here and only a short time ago," replied Haydee, with a shudder. "I was standing at the window with Zuleika when he rushed by me like a whirlwind, and going to your secretary endeavored to open it, but in vain; then with a cry of rage he ran to the window, leaped out into the darkness and was gone! I know nothing further, for as he vanished I fell to the floor in a swoon."

Monte-Cristo touched a bell and almost immediately Ali stood bowing before him, as calm and unmoved as though nothing unusual had occurred.

"Ali," said the Count, "post all the servants within and without the palace, and let the strictest watch be kept until dawn. The chief of the bandits, who is no other than the former Prince Cavalcanti, was here in our absence and must yet be hovering in the vicinity. See that he does not effect another entrance, as his purpose is robbery if not murder!"

Ali signified by his eloquent pantomime that he had already taken it upon himself to station the servants as his master directed, and that it would be utterly impossible for any one to approach the palace without being seen and seized.

As the faithful Nubian turned to retire, Monte-Cristo noticed that his right hand was bandaged as if wounded, and inquired whether he had been hurt in the conflict with the bandits. Ali explained that a dagger thrust had cut his palm, but that the wound had been properly cared for and would soon heal.

When the Count and his family were once more alone together, Haydee threw herself at her husband's feet and humbly demanded pardon.

"What have you done to require pardon?" asked Monte-Cristo, in astonishment. "Speak, but I forgive you beforehand.'

"Oh! my lord," said Haydee, still maintaining her kneeling posture despite her husband's efforts to raise her, "oh! my lord, I have been guilty of a despicable act, but my love for you and fears for your safety must be my excuse. You left the letter you received so strangely this morning lying upon your secretary. I opened it and hurriedly made myself acquainted with its contents, for I had a premonition that some terrible danger threatened you. Oh! my lord, pardon, pardon!"

Monte-Cristo raised her to her feet, and imprinted a kiss upon her pallid brow.

"So then, it is to you, Haydee, that I owe my timely rescue from the hands of Benedetto and his band of cut-throats! Had you committed even a much more serious fault than peeping into my correspondence, that would be more than sufficient to secure my full forgiveness. But do you know that Esperance shot and killed the miscreant who held his pistol to my temple and was about to blow out my brains?"

"Esperance?" said Haydee in bewilderment. "Did he not remain behind with Zuleika and myself?"

"No, mamma," said the boy, holding his head proudly erect. "I could not remain behind. I knew papa was in danger, and, taking a pistol that I had seen Ali load this morning from the cabinet of fire-arms, I followed the servants, arriving at the almond grove just in time."

Haydee ran to her son, and, taking him in her arms, pressed him fondly to her heart, kissing him again and again.

"Oh! Esperance," she cried, "had I known you were in the midst of those blood-thirsty cut-throats I should have died of terror! But you have saved your father's life, my son, and I bless you for it!"

"He is a little hero," said Monte-Cristo, impressively.

Zuleika had thrown herself upon the divan, and, utterly worn out by the excitement through which she had passed, was already wrapped in a deep slumber. The Count, Haydee and Esperance, however, could not resign themselves to sleep, and when the gray light of dawn appeared in the eastern sky, they were still in the library and still watching.

Benedetto had not been seen again, and a diligent search of the entire island, made by Ali and the servants, failed to reveal even the slightest trace of him. He had evidently succeeded in finding some fisherman's skiff and in it had made his escape.

This view of the case was confirmed a few hours later, when old Alexis came to the palace and informed Monte-Cristo that his smack had vanished during the night, having, in all probability, been carried off by thieves.

"I knew," said the fisherman, "that the Island of Kylo was infested by bandits, but I had no idea they would venture here. Now, however, I thought I had better put you on your guard."

"I am much indebted to you, Alexis," said the Count; then, slipping a purse of money into his hand, he added: "Take that and provide yourself with a new boat."

Alexis touched his cap, bowed and was about to withdraw when Monte-Cristo said to him, assuming a careless tone:

"By the way, my good fellow, have you ever chanced to meet any of the bandits you mentioned?"

"Often, Excellency," replied Alexis.

"What kind of men are they?"

"Bold, bad wretches, whose hands have been more than once stained with innocent blood."

"What is their strength?"

"They number about fifty."

"Do any women dwell among them?"

"Yes, Excellency, their wives and sweethearts."

"Who is the leader of the band?"

"A strange, morose man, who has not been long in their midst."

"Is he a Greek?"

"No, Excellency, he is a foreigner."

"A Frenchman?"

"Quite likely, though I am not sure."

"What is his name?"

"He calls himself Demetrius."

"Did he ever question you about me?"

"Yes, Excellency."

"And what did you reply?"

"I told him you were the Count of Monte-Cristo."

"Ah! What did he say then?"

"He said he had heard of you before."

"That will do, Alexis; I have all the information I require."

The fisherman again touched his cap, and, making a low bow, took his departure.

Under ordinary circumstances Monte-Cristo would not have been disturbed by the presence of bandits so near the Island of Salmis, but it became an altogether different thing when those bandits were led by Benedetto.

A month passed, but in it nothing occurred calculated to break the tranquillity of the Count and his family. The bandits had not reappeared and Benedetto had given no sign of life. The faithful Ali no longer deemed it necessary to maintain his precautions against surprise, and the strict watch that had been kept up day and night ever since the conflict in the almond grove was abandoned. Haydee, Zuleika and Esperance resumed their usual mode of life, having apparently dismissed the robbers from their minds, while even Monte-Cristo seemed free from all uneasiness.

One night, while the Count was writing at a late hour in the library, he yielded to fatigue and fell asleep over his papers. His slumber was troubled with a strange and vivid dream.

A man in the picturesque garb of a Greek peasant, and wearing a mask on his face, suddenly stood before him, with his arms folded upon his breast. Monte-Cristo saw him distinctly, though unable to stir either hand or foot. The singular visitant surveyed the Count long and steadily. There was something vaguely familiar about him, but as to his identity the sleeper could form no idea. At last he slowly removed the mask, and recognition was instantaneous. The man was Danglars. He raised his right hand, and, pointing with his forefinger at the Count, said deliberately, with a hiss like some venomous serpent:

"Edmond Dantes, there is a bitter account open between us, and I am here to force you to a bitter settlement!"

The light of the huge lamp, suspended from the ceiling, fell full upon Danglars' countenance; it was as bloodless as that of a corpse, and the eyes shone with a remorseless, vindictive glare. The banker continued in the same hissing tone, his words penetrating to the very marrow of the slumberer's bones:

"Count of Monte-Cristo, for by that name it still pleases you to be called, listen to me. By the most ingenious and fiendish combinations possible for a human being to contrive, you wrecked my fortune and with it my hopes. You drove me ignominiously from Paris; in Rome you caused me to be starved and robbed by Luigi Vampa and his brigands; then with the malevolent magnanimity of an arch-demon you sent me forth into the world a fugitive and an outcast. Count of Monte-Cristo, Edmond Dantes, low-born sailor of Marseilles, modern Mephistopheles as you are, I will be even with you! You have had your vengeance; now you shall feel mine! Here in the Grecian Archipelago, on the Island of Salmis, I will torture you through your dearest affections, and grind you to dust beneath my heel!"

As Danglars finished, his features changed and became those of Villefort, while his Greek peasant's garb was transformed into the sombre habiliments of the Procureur du Roi. Villefort's face wore the look of madness, but there was a freezing calmness in his voice as he said:

"Edmond Dantes, Count of Monte-Cristo, gaze upon the ruin you have made. Through you I was dragged down from my high position, exposed, humiliated and deprived of reason. But although the mere wreck of my former self, I am not utterly powerless, as you shall learn to your cost. You raised up my infamous son, Benedetto, to be the instrument of my destruction. Now, he shall work yours, and avenge his unhappy father!"

The apparition paused, sighed deeply, and then resumed in a tone of still greater menace:

"Count of Monte-Cristo, look well to your beloved wife, Haydee, look well to your heroic son, Esperance, look well to your darling daughter, Zuleika, for this night they are in frightful danger! Look well to your fabulous riches, for they are threatened; look well to your stately and magnificent palace, for already the element that shall devour it is noiselessly and stealthily at work! Count of Monte-Cristo, farewell!"

A heart-rending shriek rang in the sleeper's ears, a mighty flash dazzled his eyes, and, with a grim smile upon his pallid countenance, Villefort vanished.

Monte-Cristo awoke with a quick start and passed his hand across his forehead, as if dazed; then he leaped to his feet and glanced breathlessly about him. Danglars and Villefort had been only the idle coinage of his brain, but the heart-rending shriek, the mighty flash, they were, indeed, stern realities--the shriek was Haydee's, and the flash was fire!

"My God!" cried Monte-Cristo, standing for an instant rooted to the spot, "can it be possible that this dream is the truth after all, and that I am even now to feel the vengeance of those two men?"

He sprang into the spacious hall that was as light as day, and, as he did so, the figure of a man rushed by him--it was Benedetto, and in his hand he held a long knife dripping with blood. The Count turned and pursued him, snatching a dagger from a table as he ran. At the door leading to the lawn, he grasped him firmly by the shoulder and held him.

"Murderer!" he shouted, "whose blood is that upon your knife?"

"The blood of Haydee, the Greek slave!" hissed Benedetto, with a glare of ferocious triumph, "the blood of Haydee, your wife! Edmond Dantes, I am even with you!"

Monte-Cristo struck at the assassin with his dagger, but Benedetto eluded the blow, and raising his own weapon inflicted a frightful gash upon the Count's cheek.

A terrible struggle ensued. Monte-Cristo was possessed of wonderful strength and activity, but in both these respects the two desperate antagonists seemed fairly matched. Three times did the Count bury his dagger in Benedetto's body, but, though the assassin's blood gushed copiously from his wounds, he continued to fight with the utmost determination. At length the men grappled in a supreme, deadly effort, but Monte-Cristo, making a false step, slipped on the blood-spattered marble floor, and Benedetto, with the quickness of thought, hurling him backward, freed himself and bounding through the open doorway vanished in the darkness beyond.

The Count uttered a groan of despair as he saw Haydee's self-confessed murderer escape him, and staggered to his feet; the fierce conflict with Benedetto had exhausted him, and he stood for an instant panting and breathless. The shrieks had now grown fainter and the hall was full of smoke. During all this time neither Ali nor any of the servants under him had appeared, a circumstance that, to Monte-Cristo, seemed inexplicable. He, however, did not pause to give it thought, but dashed up the stairway and strove to reach his wife's apartment; blinding, stifling clouds of smoke, through which penetrated the glare of the conflagration, drove him back again and again, but he renewed his attempts to force a passage with undaunted energy and courage. Finally, compressing his lips and holding his nostrils with the thumb and forefinger of his right hand, he gave a headlong plunge, and succeeded in reaching Haydee's door; it was open, displaying a scene that caused the Count's heart to sink within him; the whole chamber was one sea of flame; fiery tongues, like so many writhing and hissing serpents, were licking and consuming the costly tapestry, the richly carved furniture and the magnificent objects of art; the curtains of the bed were blazing, and upon the couch lay the senseless form of the wife of Monte-Cristo, the pallor of her faultless countenance contrasting painfully with the ruddy glow of the devouring element. In Haydee's breast was a gaping wound, from which her life blood was slowly oozing in ruby drops.

Rendered utterly reckless by the terrible sight, the Count madly rushed to the couch, tore his beloved Haydee from it, and, clasping her tightly against his bosom, staggered into the corridor with his precious burden. There the smoke had increased in volume and density, but, summoning all his resolution and endurance to his aid, he plunged through it, and finally was successful in reaching the library.

Then, with the swiftness of a flash of lightning, the husband was replaced by the father, and Monte-Cristo, for the first time since Haydee's shrieks had awakened him from his dream, thought of his children. Where were they and what had happened to them? The Count felt a cold perspiration break out upon his forehead, and a feeling of unspeakable dread took entire possession of him. Haydee demanded immediate attention, but Esperance and Zuleika must instantly be found and rescued. At the top of his voice Monte-Cristo shouted for Ali, but no reply was returned. Fearing to leave Haydee for even a moment, the Count strode about the library like a caged wild animal, still holding her in his arms. He shouted again and again until he was hoarse, calling distractedly upon Esperance, Zuleika and all the servants in turn.

At last an answering shout came suddenly from the lawn, and old Alexis, followed by several fishermen, leaped into the library through an open window.

Resigning Haydee to Alexis, the Count, accompanied by the fishermen, fairly flew to the apartment of his children, situated on a corridor in another portion of the palace. There Esperance and Zuleika were discovered gagged and bound; they lay upon the floor of their chamber, while Ali, who had been treated in like manner, was extended near them. To release the prisoners was but the work of a moment, and then it was learned that all the servants under Ali were confined in their dormitory. They, as well as Monte-Cristo's children and the Nubian, had been suddenly seized by a party of rough-looking Greeks, evidently a portion of Benedetto's band.

Meanwhile the flames had spread from Haydee's chamber to the adjoining quarters of the edifice, and the entire palace seemed doomed, for to check the conflagration appeared impossible, but so happy had the Count been made by the recovery of his son and daughter, unharmed, that he gave himself no concern about the probable destruction of his magnificent property.

Seizing his children, he directed Ali and the fishermen to release the captive servants, and hastily returned to the library. As he entered the room Haydee uttered a low groan and opened her eyes; she was lying on a divan, where old Alexis had placed her. Esperance and Zuleika sprang to her side; she took each by the hand, and as she did so they saw the wound in her breast. Zuleika burst into tears. Esperance compressed his lips and grew deadly pale.

"My loved ones," said Haydee, faintly, "I feel that I am about to leave you forever, perhaps in a few moments. Be good children and obey your father in all things. Esperance, Zuleika, stoop and kiss me."

They did as she desired; her lips were already purple and cold; the stamp of death was upon her features. Suddenly her frame was convulsed and her eyes assumed a glassy look.

"Monte-Cristo, my husband, where are you?" she said, in a broken voice.

"Here, Haydee," answered the Count, approaching.

He strove to appear calm, but could not control his emotion.

"Nearer, nearer, Edmond," said Haydee, growing weaker and weaker.

The Count sank on his knees beside his dying wife and put his arms about her neck.

"Oh! Haydee, Haydee," he sobbed; "thrice accursed be the infamous wretch who has done this!"

"Edmond, my children, farewell," gasped Haydee; "I am going to a better land!"

The death rattle was in her throat; she raised herself with a mighty effort, gazed lovingly at her husband and children, and strove to speak again, but could not; then a flickering shade of violet passed over her countenance, and she fell back dead.

Esperance and Zuleika stood as if stunned; Monte-Cristo was overwhelmed with grief and despair.

"The whole palace is in flames! Save yourselves, save yourselves!" cried a fisherman, rushing into the library, followed by his companions, Ali and the servants.

Monte-Cristo leaped to his feet, seizing the corpse of Haydee and raising it in his arms. Ali grasped Esperance and Zuleika, and the entire party hastened from the burning edifice. They were not an instant too soon, for as they quitted the library the tempest of fire burst into it, accompanied by torrents of smoke. The fishermen and servants, commanded by the Nubian, had made every effort to save the doomed mansion, but in vain.

Monte-Cristo and his children found refuge in the hut of Alexis, to which Haydee's body was reverently borne.

The wife of Monte-Cristo was buried on the Island of Salmis, and over her remains her husband erected a massive monument.

Shortly afterwards the Count, Esperance and Zuleika, attended by the faithful Ali, quitted the Island and took passage on a vessel bound for France.

# CHAPTER IV.
# THE NEWS FROM ALGERIA.

Beauchamp, the journalist, sat at his desk in his editorial sanctum early one bright morning in the autumn of 1841. He had gone to work long before his usual hour, for important movements were on foot, the political atmosphere was agitated and Paris was in a state of feverish excitement; besides, Beauchamp had that day printed in his journal a dispatch from Algeria that would be certain to cause a great sensation, and, with the proper spirit of pride, the journalist desired to be at his post that he might receive the numerous congratulations his friends could not fail to offer, as the dispatch had appeared in his paper alone.

The sanctum had not an attractive look; in fact, it was rather dilapidated, while, in addition, the disorder occasioned by the previous night's work had not been repaired, and all was chaos and confusion.

Beauchamp was busily engaged in glancing over the rival morning papers when Lucien Debray entered and seated himself at another desk. The Ministerial Secretary smiled upon the journalist in a knowing way, and the latter, nodding to him with an air of triumph, silently pointed to the pile of journals he had finished examining. Lucien took them up, and without a word began scanning their contents.

"Glorious news that from the army in Algeria!" cried Chateau-Renaud, rushing into the sanctum.

"Glorious, indeed!" replied the editor, looking up from the paper over which he was hurriedly skimming. On the huge table at his side, as well as beneath it, and under his feet and his capacious arm-chair, nothing was to be seen but newspapers.

"Take a chair, Renaud, if you can find one, and help yourself to the news. You see I have Lucien similarly engaged yonder."

The Ministerial Secretary glanced up from his papers, returned his friend's salutation and resumed his reading. He was dressed with his customary elegance and richness, but his form and face were fuller than when last before the reader, and his brown hair was besprinkled with gray.

"I congratulate you, Beauchamp, on being the first to give the news," continued Chateau-Renaud. "Not a paper in Paris but your own has a line from the army this morning."

"Rather congratulate me and my paper on having a friend at court."

"Ha! and that explains the fact, otherwise inexplicable, that an opposition journal has intelligence, which only the Bureau of War could have anticipated! Treason--treason!"

The editor and the Secretary exchanged significant smiles.

"Oh! I don't doubt that your favors are reciprocal," continued the young aristocrat, laughing. "I've half a mind to be something useful myself--Minister--editor-

-anything but an idler and a law-giver--just to experience the exquisite sensation of a new pleasure--the pleasure of revealing and publishing to the world something it knew not before. Why, you two fellows, in this dark and dirty little room, are the two greatest men in Paris this morning--or were, rather, before your paper, Beauchamp, laid before the world what only you and Lucien knew previously. Oh! the delight, the rapture of knowing something that nobody else knows, and then of making the revelation!"

"And this news from Algeria is really important," remarked the editor.

"Important! So important that it will be before the Chambers this morning," replied the Secretary.

"So I supposed," said the Deputy, "and called to learn additional particulars, if you had any, on my way to the Chambers."

"We gave all we had, my dear Lycurgus, and for that were indebted to an official dispatch, telegraphed to the War Office, and faithfully re-telegraphed to us by our well-beloved Lucien."

"It's true, then, as I have sometimes suspected, that the wires radiate from the Minister's sanctum to the editor's?" was the laughing rejoinder.

"It must be so, or there's witchcraft in it. There's witchcraft, at any rate, in this new invention. Speed, secrecy, security and surety--no eastern genius of Arabian fiction can be compared to the electric telegraph; and how Ministers or editors continued to keep the world in vassalage, as they always have done, without this ready slave, seems now scarce less wonderful than the invention itself. Instead of detracting from the power of the press, the telegraph renders it more powerful than ever."

"But affairs in Algeria--is not the news splendid!" cried the editor. "Why did we not all become Spahis and win immortality, as some of our generals have?"

"As to immortality," said the Secretary, "we should have been far more likely to win the phantom as dead men than as living heroes."

"Debray was at the raising of the siege of Constantine," said Beauchamp laughing, "and knows all about the honors of war."

"Yes, indeed, and all about the raptures of starvation, of cold and hunger, after victory, and the ecstatic felicity of being pursued by six Bedouins, and after having slain five having my own neck encircled by the yataghan of the sixth!"

"And how chanced it that you saved your head, Lucien?" asked the Count.

"Save it--I didn't save it; but a most excellent friend of mine--a friend in need--galloped up and saved it for me."

"Yes," replied Beauchamp, "our gallant friend, Maximilian Morrel, the Captain of Spahis--now colonel of a regiment, and in the direct line of promotion to the first vacant baton--eh, Lucien? A lucky thing to save the head of one of the War Office from a Bedouin's yataghan. Up--up--up, like a balloon, has this young Spahi risen ever since."

"You are wrong, Beauchamp. Not like a balloon. Rather like a planet. Maximilian Morrel is one of the most gallant young men in the French army, and step by step, from rank to rank, has he hewn his own path with his good sabre, in a strong hand, nerved by a brave heart and proud ambition, to the position he now holds."

"His name I see among the immortals in the dispatch of this morning. Well, well, Morrel is a splendid fellow, no doubt, but it's a splendid thing to have friends in the War Office, nevertheless, who will give that splendor a chance to shine--will plant the lighted candle in a candlestick, and not smother its beams under a bushel."

"Morrel has now been in Africa five whole years," said the Secretary--"a few months only excepted after his marriage with Villefort's fair daughter, Valentine, (as was said) when he was indulged with a furlough for his honeymoon."

"She is not in Paris?" asked Beauchamp.

"No; she leads the life of a perfect recluse with her child, during her husband's absence, at his villa somewhere in the south--near Marseilles, where the department forwards her letters."

"Yet she is said to be a magnificent woman," remarked the Count.

"Wonderful!" cried Beauchamp. "A magnificent woman and a recluse!"

"Oh! but it was a love-match of the most devoted species, you must remember."

"True; she was to have married our friend, Franz d'Epinay."

"And died to save herself from that fate, I suppose--and afterwards was resurrected and blessed Morrel with her hand and heart, and the most exquisite person that even a jaded voluptuary could covet. Happy--happy--happy man!"

"Apropos of dying," said the Secretary, "do you remember how fast people died at M. de Villefort's house about that time?"

"Horrible! A whole family of two or three generations, one after the other! First M. and Madame de Saint-Meran--then Barrois, the old servant of M. Noirtier--then Valentine, and, last of all, Madame de Villefort and Edward, her idol. No wonder that M. le Procureur du Roi himself went mad under such an accumulation of horrors! By the by, Debray, is M. de Villefort still an inmate of the Maison Royale de Charenton?"

"I know nothing to the contrary," replied the Secretary, who had resumed his paper, and to whom the subject seemed not altogether agreeable. "He is an incurable." Then, as if to turn the subject, he continued: "Apropos of the immortals of Algeria, here is a name that seems destined even to a more rapid apotheosis than that of the favored Morrel."

"You mean Joliette?" said the editor. "Who, in the name of all that is mysterious and heroic, is this same Joliette? I have found it impossible to discover, with all the means at the command of the press."

"And I, with all the means at the command of the Government. All we can discover is this--that he is a man of about twenty-five; that he enlisted at Marseilles, and in less than three years has risen from the ranks to the command of a battalion. His career has been most brilliant."

"And to whose favor does he owe his wonderful advancement, Beauchamp?" asked the Deputy, laughing.

"To that of Marshal Bugeaud, Governor-General of Algeria."

"Ah!"

"Who has indulged him with an appointment in every forlorn hope!"

"Excellent!" cried the Count. "What more could a man resolved to be a military immortal desire? Immortality the goal--two paths conduct to it--each sure--death--life!--the former the shorter, and, perhaps, the surer! But there is one name I never see in the war dispatches. Do you ever meet with it, Messrs. editor and Secretary--I mean the name of our brilliant friend, Albert de Morcerf? The rumor ran that, after the disgrace and suicide of the Count, his father, he and his mother went south, and he later to Africa."

"I have hardly seen the name of Morcerf in print since the paragraph headed 'Yanina' in my paper, about which poor Albert was so anxious to fight me."

"Nor I," said Debray. "But where now is Madame de Morcerf? Without exception, she was the most splendid specimen of a woman I ever saw!"

"High praise, that!" cried the Count, laughing. "Who would suppose our cold, calculating, ambitious, haughty, talented and opulent diplomat and aristocrat had so much blood in his veins? When before was he known to admire anything, male or female--but himself--or, at all events, to be guilty of the bad taste of expressing that admiration?"

"Debray is right," replied the journalist, somewhat gravely. "Madame de Morcerf was, indeed, a noble and dignified woman--accomplished, lovely, dignified, amiable--"

"Stop!--stop!--in the name of all that's forbearing, be considerate of my weak nerves! You, too, Beauchamp. Well, she must have been a paragon to make the conquest of two of the most inveterate bachelors in all Paris! But where is this marvel of excellence--pardon me, Beauchamp," perceiving that the journalist looked yet more grave, and seemed in no mood for bantering or being bantered--"where is Madame de Morcerf at the present time?"

"At Marseilles, I have heard."

"And is married again?"

"No. She is yet a widow."

"And is a recluse, like Morrel's beautiful wife?"

"So says report. They dwell together."

"How romantic! The young wife, whose hero-husband is winning glory amid the perils of war and pestilence, pours her griefs, joys and anticipations into the bosom of the young mother, who appreciates and reciprocates all, because she has a son exposed to the same perils--and both beautiful as the morning! A charming picture! Two immortals in epaulets and sashes in the background are only wanted instead of one. But I must to the Chambers. M. Dantes is expected to speak in the tribune this morning upon his measure for the workmen."

"Do you know, Count, who this M. Dantes really is?" asked Debray.

"There's a question for a Ministerial Secretary to ask a member while a journalist sits by! I only know of M. Dantes that he is the most eloquent man I ever listened to. I don't mean that he's the greatest man, or the profoundest statesman, or the wisest politician, or the sagest political economist; but I do mean that, for natural powers of persuasion and denunciation--for natural oratory--I have never known his rival. If Plato's maxim, 'that oratory must be estimated by its effects,' is at all correct, then is M. Dantes the greatest orator in France, for the effect of his oratory is miraculous. There is a sort of magic in his clear, sonorous, powerful, yet most exquisitely modulated voice, and the wave of his arm is like that of a necromancer's wand."

"You are enthusiastic, Count," observed Beauchamp, "but very just. M. Dantes is, indeed, a remarkable man, and possessed of remarkable endowments, both of mind and body. His personal advantages are wonderful. Such a figure and grace as his are alone worth more than all the powers of other distinguished speakers for popular effect. 'The eyes of the multitude are more eloquent than their ears,' as the English Shakespeare says."

"I never saw such eyes and such a face," remarked Debray, "but once in my life. Do you remember the Count of Monte-Cristo, Messieurs?"

"We shall not soon forget him," was the reply. "But this man differs greatly from the Count in most respects, though certainly not unlike him in others."

"True," replied the Secretary; "in manners, habits, costume and a thousand other things there is a marked difference. Besides, the Count was said to be incalculably rich, while the Deputy has every appearance of being in very moderate circumstances. But he leads a life so retired that he is known only in the Chambers and in his public character. I allude to the Deputy's person, when I speak of resemblance to that wonderful Count, who set all Paris in a fever, and, more wonderful still, kept it so for a whole season. There is I know not what in his air and manners that often recalls to me that extraordinary man. There are the same large and powerful eyes, the same brilliant teeth for which the women envied the Count so much, the same graceful and dignified figure, the same peculiar voice, the same good taste in dress, and, above all, the same colorless, pallid face, as if, to borrow the idea of the Countess of G----, he had risen from the dead, or was a visitant from another world, or a vampire of this. Her celebrated friend, Lord B----, she used to say, was the only man she ever knew with such a complexion."

"But, if I recollect rightly," said Beauchamp, "the Count of Monte-Cristo was somewhat noted for his profusion of black hair and beard. The Deputy Dantes is so utterly out of the mode, and out of good taste, too, as to wear no beard, and his hair is short. His face is as smooth as a woman's, and he always wears a white cravat like a cure."

"But he is, nevertheless, one of the handsomest men in Paris," added the Count--"at least the women say so. You might add, the Deputy has many gray hairs among his black ones, and many furrows on his white brow, while Monte-Cristo had neither. Besides, M. Dantes has a handsome daughter and a son who resembles him greatly, both well grown, while the Count was childless."

"Well, well, be his person and family what they may," said the Secretary, rising, "I wish to God the Ministry could secure his talents. I tell you, Messieurs, that man's influence over the destinies of France is to be almost omnipotent. His powerful mind has grasped the great problem of the age--remuneration for labor. The next revolution in France will hinge upon that--mark the prediction--and this man and his coadjutors, among whom Beauchamp here is one, are doing all they can to hasten the crisis. The whole soul of this remarkable man seems devoted to the elevation of the masses--the laboring classes--the people--and to the amelioration of their condition. His efforts and those of all like him cannot ultimately succeed. But they will have a temporary triumph, and the streets of Paris will run with blood! These men are rousing terrible agencies. They are evoking the fiends of hunger and misery, which will neither obey them nor lie down at their bidding."

"And the magicians who have summoned these foul fiends will prove their earliest victims!" said Chateau-Renaud, in some excitement.

"Messieurs, listen a moment!" cried Beauchamp, rising. "Pardon me, but this discussion must cease, at least here. It can lead to no good result. As the conductor of a reform journal, I entirely differ with you both. But let not political differences interfere with our personal friendship. Come, come, old friends, let us forsake this place, redolent with politics, having a very atmosphere of discussion, and repair to the Chambers, taking Very's on our way."

"Agreed!" cried the Deputy and the Secretary, and the three left the journalist's sanctum arm in arm.

# CHAPTER V.
# EDMOND DANTES, DEPUTY FROM MARSEILLES.

Beauchamp, Lucien Debray and Chateau-Renaud were not the only persons puzzled with regard to the enigmatical M. Dantes; all Paris was more or less bothered about him; his entire career prior to his appearance at the capital as the Deputy from Marseilles seemed shrouded in impenetrable mystery, and this was the more galling to the curious Parisians as his wonderful oratorical powers and his intense republicanism rendered him the cynosure of all eyes and made him the sensation of the hour. The Government had instituted investigations concerning him, but without result; even in Marseilles his antecedents were unknown; he had come there from the east utterly unheralded, attended only by a black servant, and bringing with him his son and daughter, but almost immediately he had plunged into politics, winning his way to the front with startling rapidity. From the first he had ardently espoused the cause of the working people, and such was his personal magnetism that he had made hosts of admirers, and had been chosen Deputy with hardly a dissenting voice. Some of the inhabitants of Marseilles, indeed, remembered a youthful sailor named Edmond Dantes, but they asserted that he had been dead many years, and that the Deputy was unlike him in every particular.

As the young men passed the Theatre Francais, on their way to the Chamber of Deputies, after a glass of sherry and a biscuit at Very's, their attention was attracted by a crowd gathered around an immense poster spread upon the bill-board. There seemed no little excitement among the throng, a large proportion of whom appeared to be artisans and laborers, and loud expressions of admiration, accompanied by animated gestures, were heard. Nor were there wanting also words of deep denunciation and of significant threatening.

"Down! down with the tyrants! Bread or blood! Wages for work! Food for the laborer!" and other cries of equally fearful significance were audible.

"Do you hear that, Beauchamp?" said Debray, quietly.

"Undoubtedly," was the equally quiet reply.

"Those laborers have deserted the daily toil which would give them the bread they so fiercely demand, in order to discuss their imaginary misery, and denounce those who are richer than themselves."

"But what brings them to the theatre at this hour?" asked Chateau-Renaud.

"The new play," suggested Beauchamp.

"Ah! the new play. 'The Laborer of Lyons,' is it not?"

"Yes," said Debray, "and one of the most dangerous productions of the hour."

"It is evidently from the pen of one unaccustomed to dramatic composition, yet familiar with stage effect," added the journalist. "And yet, without the least claptrap, with but little melodramatic power, against strong opposition and bitter prejudices, and without claqueurs, its own native force and the popularity of the principles it supports have carried it triumphantly through the ordeal of two representations. It will, doubtless, have a long run, and its influence will be incalculable in the cause it advocates--the cause of human liberty and human right."

"No doubt it will exert a most baneful influence," bitterly rejoined Debray. "Without containing a syllable to which the Ministry can object, at least sufficiently to warrant its suppression, it yet abounds with principles, sentiments and theories of the most incendiary description, well calculated to rouse the disaffection of the laboring classes to frenzy. Its inevitable effect will be to give them a false and exaggerated idea of their wrongs and their rights, and to stimulate them to revolution. Oh! these men have much to answer for. They are drawing down an avalanche."

"They are the champions of human liberty," said Beauchamp, warmly, "and will be blessed by posterity, if not by the men of the present generation."

"Truce to politics, Messieurs!" cried the Deputy, observing that his friends were becoming excited. "I had heard of this play and its powerful character. Who's the author, Beauchamp?"

"The production is attributed to M. Dantes, the Deputy from Marseilles, with what truth I know not; but he is fully capable of composing such a drama. To-morrow night, it is supposed, the author, whoever he may be, will be compelled by the people to appear and claim the laurels ready to be showered on him in such profusion. But it is nearly three o'clock," continued Beauchamp, "and M. Dantes is expected to speak in the early part of the sitting."

"To the Chamber, then," said the others, and the trio mingled with the crowd hurrying in the same direction.

"What a glorious thing is popularity!" exclaimed the Count.

"What a glorious thing to be the champion of the people!" rejoined Beauchamp.

"And how glorious is that champion's glorious career!" cried the Secretary. "Let the hydra alone. Like the antique god of mythology, it eats up its own children as soon as they get large enough to be eaten. It is a fickle beast, and the idol of to-day it crushes to-morrow."

The hall of the Chamber of Deputies was crowded when the three friends entered. Although the hour for the President to take the chair had not yet arrived, the benches were full, and the galleries, public and private, were overflowing. Strong agitation was visible among the Ministerial benches of the extreme left. The Premier himself was present, although his cold countenance, like the surface of a frozen lake, betrayed neither apprehension nor the reverse. Self-reliant, self-poised, calm, seemingly insensible to surrounding objects and events, this man of iron, with a heart of ice and a brain of fire, glanced quietly and fixedly around him, with his cold, dark eye, which, from time to time, rested on the Communist benches of the extreme right, unmoved by the stern glances hurled at him by his many fierce opponents and the almost tumultuous excitement by which they were agitated.

At length President Sauzet took the chair. The house came to order, and the sitting opened with the usual preliminary business. A large number of petitions from the workmen of Paris for employment by the Government were presented and referred, and one immense roll containing a hundred thousand names, which came from the manufacturing districts, was brought in on the shoulders of two men and placed in the area before the President's chair, escorted by a deputation from the artisans; it was received with an uproar of applause from the centre of the extreme right of the benches, and from the throngs of blouses in the galleries. The tumult having, at length, subsided, the order of the day was announced to be the discussion of the bill introduced by M. Dantes, having for its purpose the general amelioration of the condition of the industrial classes in the Kingdom; and M. Dantes was himself announced to be the first on the list to occupy the tribune. A deep murmur of anticipation ran around the vast hall at this announcement. The multitudes in the galleries leaned forward to gain a better view of this idol, and to catch every syllable that might fall from his lips; and every eye among the members was turned to the seat of M. Dantes, on the centre right of the benches.

A tall figure in black, with a white cravat, rose and advanced to the tribune slowly, amid a stillness as hushed and breathless as the prior excitement had been noisy. In age, M. Dantes seemed about fifty or fifty-five. His form was slight and his movements were graceful and dignified. His face was livid and as calm as marble; but for the large and eloquent eye, dark as night, one might have thought that broad white brow, that massive chin, those firmly compressed lips and that color-less mouth were those of a statue. Yet in the furrows of that forehead and the deep lines of that face could be read the record of thought and suffering. The busy plow-share had turned up the deep graves of departed passions. No one could gaze or even glance at that face and not perceive at once that it was the visage of a man of many sorrows--yet of a man proud, calm, self-possessed, self-poised and indomitable. His hair, which had been raven black, now rested in thin waves around his expansive forehead and was sprinkled with gray, while his intellectual countenance wore that expression of weariness and melancholy which illness, deep study and grief invari-ably trace.

Mounting the steps of the tribune with slow and deliberate tread, he drew up his tall figure, and resting his left hand, which grasped a roll of papers, upon the marble slab, glanced around on the turbulent billows of upturned and excited faces, as if at a loss how to address them. Having read the bill, after the usual prefatory remarks, he began by laying down the platform which he proposed occupying in its advocacy and support, consisting, of course, of abstract, self-evident propositions, which none could have the hardihood to gainsay, yet, when once admitted, the de-ductions inevitably flowing therefrom none could resist. The propositions seemed safe and indisputable, but the deductions evolved from those propositions were as frightful to the legitimist as they were delightful to the liberal. That each man is born the heir to the same natural rights--that each man, alike and equally with all others, has a birthright of which he cannot be divested and of which he cannot di-vest himself, to act, to think and to pursue happiness wherever he can find it with-out infringement on the rights of his fellow beings--none were disposed to deny. That each human animal, as each animal of inferior grade, has, also, the right of subsistence, drained from the bosom of the earth, the great mother of us all, which without his foreknowledge or wish gave him being, seemed, also, indisputable. But when from these propositions were deduced that crime is rather the result of misery than depravity, and that the office of government is more to prevent crime by creating happiness than to punish it by creating misery, and that for the natural rights resigned by the individual in entering into and upholding the social system human government is bound to afford employment and subsistence to each of its members, that labor and its produce should be in partnership, that competition should be abolished, and work and wages so distributed by the State as to equalize the condition of each individual in the community, and, finally, that the claims of labor are not satisfied by wages, but the workman is entitled to a proprietary share in the capital which employs him, inasmuch as all the woes and miseries of the laborer arise exclusively from the competition for work--when these deductions were advanced the opulent and the conservative started back in terror and dismay. Distribution of property, universal plunder, havoc, bloodshed, sans culottism, a red republic and the ghastly shapes of another Reign of Terror rose in frightful vividness before the fancy. As the speaker proceeded to illustrate and sustain his positions, which were those of the Communist, Socialist, Fourierist, call them which we may, and poured forth a fiery flood of persuasion, invective, denunciation and shouts of applause, mingled with cries of rage and dismay, rose from all quarters of the hall. Unmoved and undaunted, that marble man, livid as a spectre, his dark eyes blazing, his thin and writhing lip flecked with foam, his tall form swaying to and fro, rising, bending--now thrown back, then leaning over the marble bar of the tribune--continued to pour forth his scathing sarcasm, his crushing invective, his eloquent persuasion and his unanswerable argument in tones, now soft and tuneful as a silvery bell, then sad and pitiful as an evening zephyr, then clear, high and sonorous as a clarion, then hoarse and deep as the thunder, for a period of four hours, unbroken and continuous, without stop or stay.

The effect of this speech, as the orator, pale, exhausted, shattered, unstrung, with nerves like the torn cordage of a ship that has outridden the tempest, descended from the tribune, baffles all description. Fearful of its influence, the Minister of Foreign Affairs at once arose, and in order to divert the attention of the Chamber asked leave to lay before it the late dispatches from the seat of war, setting forth the glorious triumphs of the French arms in Algeria. This intelligence, which, at any other time, would have been received with rapturous enthusiasm, was listened to under the influence of a counterirritant already at work, with comparative calmness, and its only effect was to cause a postponement of the vote on the laborers' bill upon the plea of the lateness of the hour, although not without strenuous opposition from the extreme right. The rejoicing of the galleries at the triumph of their champion and their fierce applause knew no bounds at the close of the sitting, and their idol escaped being borne in his chair to his lodgings only by gliding through a private exit from the hall to the first carriage he could find.

"What think you?" cried Beauchamp, triumphantly, to the Ministerial Secretary, as they were pressed together for an instant by the excited throng on the steps as they left the hall.

"Think, Monsieur!" was the bitter rejoinder of the Secretary, whose agitation completely overcame his habitual and constitutional self-possession, "I think Paris is on the eve of another Reign of Terror!"

Beauchamp laughed, and the friends were drawn apart by the conflicting billows of the crowd.

# CHAPTER VI.
# THE MYSTERY THICKENS.

M. Dantes' wonderful speech was the principal topic of conversation in every quarter of Paris, exciting comment of the most animated description. Of course, the workmen and their friends were delighted with it, and could not find words strong enough to adequately express their enthusiastic admiration for the gifted orator. Those belonging to the Government party, on the other hand, denounced the speaker as a demagogue and the speech as in the highest degree incendiary and dangerous. Strange to relate, whoever spoke of the oration always mentioned the new play, "The Laborer of Lyons," attributing its authorship to the mysterious Deputy from Marseilles, and the drama received cordial endorsement or scathing censure, according to the political opinions of those who alluded to it.

For these reasons curiosity in regard to M. Dantes ran higher than ever, but instead of decreasing as he became more prominent, the mystery surrounding him seemed only to thicken. Nevertheless, the Deputy was the lion of the hour, or rather would have been, had he permitted himself to be lionized, but this he persistently declined to do, holding aloof from society and mingling with none save his political associates, though even to them he was a problem they could not solve; they, however, recognized in him a powerful coadjutor, and with that were forced to be content.

"THE HALL OF THE CHAMBER OF DEPUTIES was last evening thronged to

overflowing. It had been understood that M. Dantes was to advocate the People's Bill, and, as usual, it had but to be known that this distinguished orator was to occupy the tribune to draw out all classes of citizens. Nor was the vast multitude disappointed. A more powerful speech has never been heard within those walls. More than four hours was the audience enchained by the matchless eloquence of this remarkable man, which was received with thunders of applause. A report of this speech will be found under the appropriate head."

"THE NEW PLAY entitled, 'The Laborer of Lyons,' recently produced at the Theatre Francais with triumphant success, and which has caused such a deep and universal sensation, is repeated to-night. There is reason to anticipate that the author, who is supposed to be a celebrated orator of the opposition, may be induced to comply with the call, which will be again renewed, to avow himself."

Such were two paragraphs which the following morning appeared in Beauchamp's journal, and similar notices of both speech and drama were published in every other opposition sheet in Paris. In the Ministerial organ, on the contrary, and in all the papers of like political bias, appeared the following and similar paragraphs:

"THE SPEECH OF M. DANTES, last evening, in the Chamber of Deputies, was one of the most dangerous diatribes to which we ever listened--dangerous for the insidious and sophistical principles it advanced, and the almost fiend-like eloquence with which they were urged. Where are these things to stop? At what terrible catastrophe do these men aim? What crisis do they contemplate?"

"THE NEW DRAMA at the Theatre Francais, called 'The Laborer of Lyons,' which is to-night to be repeated, is calculated and seems to have been designed by its reckless author to produce the very worst effects among the laboring classes. We deeply regret that it has been suffered by the censors to be brought out."

The multitude called forth by paragraphs like these to witness the new play was, of course, immense. Long before the time for the curtain to rise, the vast edifice was crowded to its utmost capacity with an eager and enthusiastic assemblage. Not only were the galleries, parquette and lobbies filled with blouses, but the boxes were glittering with a perfect galaxy of fashion, loveliness and rank. Conspicuous in the orchestra stalls were the three friends--the Secretary, the journalist and the Deputy. In a small and private loge in the second tier, concealed from all eyes by its light curtain of green silk, and its position, but himself viewing everything upon the stage or in the house, sat the author of the play, calmly awaiting the rising of the curtain.

The performance at length began, and the piece proceeded to its termination amid thunders of applause, which, as the curtain finally descended on the last scene of the last act, became perfectly deafening, accompanied by cries for the author. But no author appeared behind the footlights or in the proscenium box; and, at last, the uproar becoming redoubled, the manager came forward, and, in the author's behalf, tendered grateful acknowledgments for the unprecedented favor, even by a Parisian audience, with which the production had been received, but, at the same time, entreated the additional favor that they would grant the author's request, and permit his name, for the present, to remain unknown. He would, however, venture to reveal this much, that the author was a distinguished friend of the people. The earthquake of applause which succeeded this announcement was almost frightful, and while the scene was at its height, the three friends with great difficulty managed to extricate themselves from the multitude which wedged up the lobbies, and to make their escape.

"A friend of the people!" cried Debray, bitterly, as his coupe, containing himself and companions, drove off to Very's. "From such friends let the people be saved, and they may save themselves from their foes."

"And the play, what think you of that?" cried Beauchamp.

"That it is a most able and abominable production, eminently calculated to cause exactly the evils which we have this night perceived--to excite and rouse the worst passions of the mob, and render the masses dissatisfied with their inevitable and irredeemable lot, and as dangerous as wild beasts to all whose lot is more favored."

"Man has rights as man, and men in masses have rights, and one of those rights is to know actually what those rights are," said Beauchamp. "The most melancholy feature in the oppression of man is his ignorance that he is oppressed. Enlighten him as to those rights, elevate his mind to appreciate and value them, and then counsel him firmly and resolutely to demand those rights, and quietly and wisely to obtain them."

"Aye! but will he obey such counsel?" exclaimed Chateau-Renaud. "Will not the result of such enlightenment and excitement prove, as it ever has proved, anarchy, revolution, guilt, blood? Who shall restrain the monster once lashed into madness?"

"But you can surely perceive no such design in this play, and no such effect," rejoined Beauchamp.

"In the abstract," replied the Count, "this production is unexceptionable--most beautiful, yet most powerful. How it could have been the work of an unpracticed pen, embodying as it does passages of which the first dramatists of the romantic school might be proud, I cannot imagine. Besides, there seems familiar acquaintance with stage effect and the way in which it is produced. But that might have been, and probably was, the result of some professional player's suggestions."

"And, then, the profound knowledge of the human heart evinced--its passions, motives and principles of action," added the journalist. "There seems an individuality, a personality in the production, which compels the idea that the author is himself the hero, that he has himself experienced the evils he so vividly portrays, that the drama is at once the effusion of his own heart and the embodiment of his own history. Can that man be M. Dantes?"

"If it be he," cried the Secretary, "there is more reason than ever to call him the most dangerous man in Paris. What with his speeches in the Chamber and his plays at the theatre, all tending to one most unrighteous end, and all aiming to inflame such an explosive mass as the workmen of Paris, he may be regarded as little less than the very agent of the fiend to accomplish havoc on earth!"

"Yet, strange to say, my dear Secretary," said the journalist, laughing, "you have not yet estimated the tithe of this man's influence for good, or, as you think, for evil. Rumor proclaims him to be as immensely opulent as appearances would indicate him to be impoverished. That his whole soul, as you say, is devoted to the people, with all his wonderful powers of mind and person, is undoubted. That he has availed himself of that grand lever, the press, to accomplish his purposes, be they good or bad, seems equally certain. 'La Reforme,' the new daily, is undoubtedly under his control, if not sustained by his pen and his purse, for it has a wider circulation than all the other Parisian papers put together. It goes everywhere--it seeks the alleys, not the boulevards, finds its way to the threshold of all, whether paid for or not."

"Ah!" cried Debray, in great agitation. "Is it so?"

"And, then, not only is the public press subsidized by this man, if report is not even false than usual, but a whole army of pamphleteers, journalists, litterateurs and students await his bidding, as well as some of the most distinguished novelists and dramatists of the nation and age!"

"My God!" exclaimed the Count. "Can this be so?"

"Nay--nay," replied Beauchamp, "I make no assertions, I merely retail rumors. But what cannot uncounted wealth achieve, directed by genius and intelligence?"

"But is this man actually so wealthy?" asked Debray, pale with agitation. "His manners, dress, equipage, residence and mode of life would indicate just the reverse."

"I know not--no one knows," said Beauchamp. "It is only known to myself and to a few others that he dwells in the mansion No. 27 Rue du Helder, formerly the residence of the Count de Morcerf, and that his private apartment is that pavilion at the corner of the court, where at half-past ten, on the morning of the 21st of May, 1838, we breakfasted with our amiable friend Albert, and were met by that remarkable man, the Count of Monte-Cristo."

"I remember that morning well," said Chateau-Renaud.

"Everything, it is said, remains in that once splendid mansion precisely as when it was deserted by the Countess and her son, at the time of the suicide of the Count--everything except that glorious picture of the Catalan fisherman by Leopold Robert, in Albert's exquisite chamber, which alone he took with him."

"It is strange that a man so opulent as you represent M. Dantes to be, should adopt his magnificence at second hand," observed Debray, coolly.

"But I do not represent him as opulent, my dear Lucien; and he certainly is the last man either to invent magnificence or to adopt it. Why, he is as plain in manners and mode as St. Simon himself. His dress you have seen; as to equipage his only conveyance is a public fiacre; as to diet, household arrangements and everything else of a personal nature, nothing can be more republican and less epicurean than is witnessed at his house. His study, Albert de Morcerf's pavilion, is said to be the only sumptuous apartment in the whole establishment; and that sumptuousness is of a character entirely literary and practical. His retinue consists of three servants, called Baptistin, Bertuccio and Ali, the latter being a Nubian, although fame gives him a perfect army of servitors prompt to execute his bidding. But I will not indulge your skeptical and sarcastic nature, Lucien, with a detail of all that rumor says of this wonderful man. I will only say that all he is, and has or hopes for seems devoted to one single object--the welfare of his race."

"Has he a wife?" asked Debray.

"He is a widower, with two children, a young girl, called Zuleika, and a youthful son, called Esperance. But my acquaintance with him is wholly of a public character. I have never been in his house, and very few there are who have been. But here we are."

And the coupe stopped at Very's.

# CHAPTER VII.
# DANTES AND HIS DAUGHTER.

Even in the immediate vicinity of the Morcerf mansion, No. 27 Rue du Helder, no one was aware that its new tenant was M. Dantes, the famous Deputy from Marseilles. All the neighbors knew was that the palatial edifice had been purchased by a stranger, who said he was acting for his master, a man of great wealth lately arrived from the east. No repairs or alterations had been made, while the Morcerf furniture was bought with the house, the only new articles making their appearance being several huge bookcases and a number of large boxes evidently containing books, together with a host of traveling trunks filled, as was to be presumed, with the wardrobe of the family. The servants took possession during the day and were duly noted, but how or when the proprietor came could not be ascertained, while after his installation glimpses of him were exceedingly rare.

Occasionally, however, a beautiful girl, with an oriental look notwithstanding her tasteful and elegant Parisian attire, would be seen for a moment at the windows, but she invariably vanished on realizing that she was observed. Sometimes, a handsome young man stood at her side, but he also seemed anxious to avoid the scrutiny of the curious, although he evinced less timidity than his companion, always withdrawing slowly and with great deliberation.

It was after midnight. On the second floor of the pavilion once inhabited by the Viscount Albert de Morcerf was now a spacious library. The walls were lined with tall book-shelves, mounting to the lofty ceiling, and groaning under ponderous piles of volumes, from the huge black letter folio of the Middle Ages to the lightest duodecimo of the day; while in all parts of the chamber, on the floor, tables and chairs, and in the deep embrasures of the windows, were scattered huge masses of papers, pamphlets, manuscripts and charts. Over the bookcases stood marble busts of Danton, Mirabeau, Napoleon, Armand Carrel, the Duc de St. Simon and other great men whose names are identified with France; between the windows looking out on the garden, shrouded in shrubs and creeping plants, hung a full-length and magnificent picture of Fourier. Near the centre of the apartment stood a vast table covered with books, papers, manuscripts and writing materials, beside which stood one of those sombre and massive arm-chairs, on the possession of which the former proprietor had so felicitated himself, bearing on a carved shield the fleur-de-lis of the Louvre, and in whose sumptuous and antique embrace had, perhaps, reposed a Richelieu, a Mazarin or a Sully. The windows were hung with heavy tapestry of ancient pattern and rich dye, and also the walls, save where covered with books. A soft and summery atmosphere, the warmth of which emanated from concealed furnaces, neutralized the chill of an autumnal night, and the mellow chiaro-oscuro of a vast astral diffused its lunar effulgence on all around.

Within this chamber was a man, who, with arms crossed upon his bosom and eyes fastened in profound and seemingly mournful contemplation upon the floor, slowly paced from one extremity of the spacious apartment to the other.

This man was M. Dantes, representative of Marseilles in the French Chamber of Deputies.

"At last, at last," he murmured, "the avenging Nemesis ceases to gnaw! At length the angel Peace begins to smile! The tempest, which, for nearly thirty years, has raved and swelled in my heart, begins to lull! At length I commence to live-- at length I realize and pursue life's true end. Let me reflect," he continued, after a pause, "let me review the past. The past! alas! my past is a painful blank! At twenty, from the very marriage-feast, from the side of her whom more than life I loved, I was torn by the envy of one man and the jealousy of another, and then, by the ambition of a third, to whom nothing was crime if it but ministered to that unhallowed impulse, I was plunged into a dungeon, whose counterpart only the vaults of hell can furnish. For fourteen long years I was the tenant of a sombre tomb. The agony, the despair of those awful years--oh! God! oh! God!" and he shuddered and clasped his hands over his head as if to crush the recollection.

After a pause he resumed: "And then those daily vows of vengeance! oh! vain and impotent vows as then they seemed! vows of awful agony, of fiendish retribution, though at that time I knew not all! I knew not that a venerable father had pined and died of starvation through the wrong done to me! I knew not that the woman I loved had become the bride of my destroyer! Yet those vows, awful and blasphemous as they were, those vows of vengeance have been terribly, dreadfully fulfilled! As the destroying angel of God's retributive providence, I was endowed with superhuman powers to walk the earth, to administer His justice and to execute His decrees. For fourteen years was that vengeance prepared, yet delayed. At last, it fell--it fell. All who had wronged me met their dreadful doom. Ambition was changed to madness. Avarice was tortured with bankruptcy. Falsehood sought refuge in self destruction; and all--all--all--even the meanest of those who had contributed to blight my life--perished miserably at my will! And did the guilty suffer alone? Alas! impious, remorseless, horrible revenge! The innocent and the criminal suffered alike. A might approaching omnipotence was vouchsafed me, but no power of omniscience to direct my hand or stay its effects. Blind and mad I knew not what I did. Those I most loved fell beneath the blow which crushed those I most abhorred, and shared the same fate. The terrible agencies I had summoned as my slaves became my masters. The fiends which, as ministers of God's justice, garbed in the guise of angels of light, I had, by hideous necromancy, evoked to aid me in righteous retribution, proved the dark demons of hell and derided all orders to accomplish my bidding. The awful engines I had set in motion I found myself powerless to arrest or control. Effects ceased not with the causes in which they had their origin. The stroke of vengeance, aimed at foes, recoiled on friends--recoiled on myself. And when I fain would stop, when I would arrest the awful havoc which my will had commenced, the dark ministers I had called up howled in my ears, 'On! on! on! vengeance is thine! vengeance is thine!' They mocked my terror and laughed at my apprehensions.

"At last there seemed a pause. Fate appeared to have done her worst, to have executed her decrees. The blind agencies of vengeance blasted no more, because there seemed no more to blast. The misery I had caused I strove to alleviate, the innocent hearts I had crushed I endeavored to heal; rejoicing in the joy I had created and the affection I gratified, once more I loved--loved, but, oh! not as I first had loved--not with that deep, adoring, delirious passion of my youth, and yet with a subdued, fraternal feeling I loved; in the calm and sweet seclusion of a favored clime, parted from the world with all its miseries and its crimes, environed by all that man or nature could contribute to human bliss, I began to dream of happiness, in the happiness I had created. But, alas! I forgot that man's happiness lies not in his own hand, but in the hand of his Maker. I forgot that an omniscient eye pursued me, that a blasphemed and omnipotent Power was over me. The blow paused--

hovered--fell, not upon me, not on the guilty, but again it fell on the innocent; and she, who was my only hope, my beloved Haydee, my wife, was snatched from my heart, ruthlessly murdered by that fiend, Benedetto!"

The unhappy man pressed his hand to his forehead, and for some time paced the chamber in silence; then, approaching a small alcove at one extremity of the apartment, he raised the heavy and sumptuous hangings and revealed a small silver casket of exquisite workmanship and appointments, that sparkled as the mellow light poured in upon it. M. Dantes knelt beside the ebony table on which this casket rested, and for some moments seemed absorbed in prayer; then, rising and taking the casket in his hands, he touched a spring, when the lid flew open, disclosing a miniature portrait of Haydee, set in a frame of gold, ornamented with flashing diamonds and emeralds; he gazed long and lovingly at this portrait, that seemed designed to show how exquisitely fair God's creatures may be, after which he kissed it reverently, closed the casket, restored it to the table, and slowly dropped the hangings to their place. Resuming his walk, he said, mournfully: "But the deepest wound will close; the heaviest grief, the bitterest woe, becomes assuaged. Time, the comforter, soothes and consoles. From this stroke of bereavement I at length awoke, and, at the same moment, awoke to the conviction that my whole past had been an error; that my life had been a lie; that the years which had succeeded my imprisonment had been more utterly lost than those passed within my dungeon itself; and there came to me the conviction that time, talent, power and wealth had been worse than wasted--that the wondrous riches, undreamed of save in the wildest flights of oriental fiction, and by a miracle bestowed upon me, were designed for nobler, holier purposes than to subserve a fiendish and blasphemous vengeance for even unutterable wrongs, or to minister to the gratification of pride, and the satisfaction of selfish tastes and appetites, however refined and sublimated.

"I looked around me--the world was full of misery--and the same disposition which had plunged me into a dungeon was crushing the hearts and hopes of millions of my race. My bosom softened by bereavement yearned toward my suffering fellows, and the path of duty, peace and happiness seemed open to my desolate and despairing heart. Resolution followed conviction; the world was my field; liberty, equality and fraternity were my objects. Not France alone, with her miserable millions, but Russia with her serfs, Poland with her wrongs, the enslaved Italian, the oppressed German, the starving son of Erin, the squalid operative of England, the priest-ridden slave of Jesuit Spain, and the oppressed but free-born Switzer. Great men and good men I found had already, with superhuman skill, constructed a system, a machine for the amelioration of mankind's condition, which needed only the co-operation of boundless wealth to set it in motion. That wealth was mine! The common house for the laborer, the asylum for the insane, for the orphan, the Magdalen, the destitute, the sick, the friendless, the deserted, the bereaved, or the asylum for the victim of his own vices, or the vices of others, for the depravity which originates in misery, ignorance or fate--all these my riches could sustain. Around me, in the accomplishment of this design, the uncounted wealth intrusted to my stewardship has already gathered the mightiest minds in every department of intellect, and the best hearts; and if but a few years are vouchsafed us to carry out the system we have adopted, all Europe, despite her throned and sceptred tyrants, impiously claiming the right to oppress by the will of God, shall be free! Silently but surely, the principle of human liberty is ceaselessly at work, undermining thrones and overthrowing dynasties. The hush that precedes the tornado even now broods over Europe; nations slumber the heavy sleep that preludes the earthquake. The hour of revolution is at hand--of social regeneration, disenthrallment, redemption, over all the world. In every capital of Europe the mine is prepared--the train laid to be lighted, and from this solitary chamber the free thought on the lightning's pinion flies to Vienna, St. Petersburg, Rome, Madrid, Berlin, London, over mountain and plain--over sea and land--through the forest wilderness and the thronged city; taken up by the press, it makes thrones totter and tyrants tremble--tremble at an influence which emanates they know not whence and contemplates a purpose they know not what--an influence whose mystery they are impotent to penetrate, and whose shadowy but awful right they are powerless to resist!"

At that instant the silvery tinkle of a bell was heard at the table, and a low and continuous whizzing as of clockwork at once commenced. The Deputy advanced hastily to the table. The register of the electric telegraph like a living thing was unfolding the secrets of events at that moment transpiring at the furthest extremity of the Kingdom! Eagerly seizing the slip of paper which was gliding through the machine, he glanced over the cabalistic cipher there traced. "Lyons--Marseilles--Rome--Algeria," he murmured. "All goes well." And while the wonderful register, like a thing of life, still whizzed, clicked and delivered its magic scroll, covered with characters unintelligible to all but him for whose eye they were designed, he touched a spring, and a row of ivory keys resembling those of a piano-forte was revealed. Then rapidly touching them with the fingers of one hand, while he held up before him the endless slip of paper in the other as it was evolved, he transferred its cabalistic contents, character by character, to their distant destination.

And when the day dawned on Paris, Berlin, Vienna and Madrid, the intelligence thus concentrated, and thus distributed in that solitary chamber, was laid by the press before a hundred thousand eyes, in a language which each could comprehend, for in every capital of Europe unbounded wealth had established a press which groaned in unceasing parturition for human rights, causing princes to tremble and ministers to wonder and grow pale; over each press, thus set in motion as if literally by an electric touch a thousand miles away, presided men of the greatest powers and most varied attainments which philanthropy or covetousness could enlist, while the result of their labors was sown broadcast among the poorest and humblest, without price or compensation, pouring light upon their darkened understandings and giving them knowledge of their rights.

Nor was the newspaper press alone active. The feuilleton press was also at work; and magazines, reviews, pamphlets, whole libraries of volumes, were flung like Sibylline leaves on the four winds of heaven. Fiction, the drama, religion, art, literature, moral and mechanical science--all departments of intellect--silently, unseen, yet surely exerted their omnipotent influence for the attainment of one single glorious end--the happiness, rights, freedom of man; all this was under the guidance of one powerful mind and benevolent heart, wielding the resistless necromancy of countless and exhaustless treasure! Not a point in all Europe whence influence could radiate and be distributed was there at which this man, in one brief year, had not set in motion the press and the telegraph, those tremendous levers of the age to move the world, and all the more powerfully to move it because oft unseen. Not a court was there of emperor or prince, czar or kaiser, king, duke or potentate in which dwelt not his emissary, who suspected, least of all, knew everything that occurred, and, on the lightning's wing, dispatched it to its destination, so that the most important decrees of the cabinet-council of Vienna were exposed to the whole world by the Parisian press long before they had been communicated by Metternich to his sovereign. And thus, often, the ruler first learned the purposes of the Minister. Not a city or village was there in all Europe which nourished not in its bosom the germ of reform and revolution, while the great principle of association combined, embodied, and concentrated into a focus energies and influences which would otherwise have proved comparatively powerless.

The click and buzz of the register ceased--the engine had revealed its secret--the shadowy tale had been caught up as it fell and given to the press of all Europe, thence to be laid before men's minds.

Exhausted by the severe mental toil, and by the lateness of the hour, the Deputy sank back into his arm-chair and clasped his hands. "Glorious, omnipotent science!" he exclaimed in low and trembling, yet eager and enthusiastic tones. "Wealth must yield in power to thee, for what wealth can rival thy achievements or secure thy results? Thou hast girt the earth with web-work, forced the lightning to syllable the unspoken thought and made man's mind ubiquitous like God's; ere long, thou wilt have knit together with thy magic spells a world of mankind into one vast brother-hood!"

M. Dantes ceased and, closing his eyes wearily, continued to think over the possibilities of the future. As he sat there motionless and seemingly asleep, a light footfall was heard in the apartment and his daughter stood before him. Zuleika was now sixteen, tall and matured beyond her years; she greatly resembled her dead mother, Haydee, the beautiful Greek, and the half-oriental costume she wore helped to render the resemblance still more striking; her abundant hair was the hue of the raven's wing, her feet and hands were those of a fairy, while her large and expressive eyes flashed like diamonds, and her parted lips, as red as rubies, disclosed perfect teeth of the whiteness of pearls. A shade of anxiety settled upon her hand-some countenance as she bent over her weary father. The Deputy opened his eyes and glanced at her.

"Why are you up so late, my child?" he asked, fondly. "I thought you were sleeping soundly long ere this."

"I was waiting for you, papa," replied Zuleika, in a low, musical voice, that sounded like a chime of tiny bells; "I could not retire to my couch while you were toiling."

M. Dantes pointed to a stool; the young girl brought it and seated herself at his feet; he drew her to his knee, smoothing her tresses gently and affectionately.

"So you would not desert me, darling?" he said, with a glad smile.

"No, indeed, dear papa," answered she, nestling closer to him.

"Will you always love me as you do now, Zuleika?" asked the father, looking down into the liquid depths of her eyes.

"Oh! papa, what a question, what a singular question!" said the girl, springing to her feet, throwing her arms around his neck, and kissing him again and again.

"But love of another kind and for another will come along after awhile," said the Deputy sadly, "and then you will forget your father."

Zuleika blushed and hung her head in maidenly modesty; then she exclaimed:

"No, no, papa; never will I forget you whatever may happen!"

"Ah! my darling, you know not what you are saying; it is only natural for a woman to cast her father aside and cleave unto her husband."

"But, papa, I have not even a lover yet, and, besides, I am not a woman; I am merely a little girl and your own, true, loving daughter."

"Yes, yes, but you must remember that last year, young as you were then, you attracted marked attention from several youthful Romans of the best families in the Eternal City, and that one of them, the Viscount Giovanni Massetti, went so far as to ask me for your hand."

At the mention of Massetti's name the blush upon Zuleika's cheek deepened. She trembled slightly, but said nothing; her heart fluttered painfully, but the pain was not altogether disagreeable. The young Viscount was evidently not unpleasing to her.

M. Dantes resumed, looking at her fixedly the while:

"My daughter, as you were then attending the convent school I felt it my duty to deny Giovanni Massetti's solicitation, nay, his ardent, impetuous prayer, but I did not deprive him of all hope; I gave him permission to urge his suit with you personally after a year from that time had elapsed. Did I do right?"

Zuleika maintained silence, but blushed and trembled more than ever, while her heart fluttered so that she placed her hand upon her breast to still it.

"Come, come, my daughter, answer me," said the Deputy, kindly, "did I do right? Tell me what your little heart says."

"I do not know, oh! I do not know!" cried Zuleika, bursting into tears.

"There, there now," said her father, soothingly; "I did not mean either to frighten or wound you. If the Viscount is displeasing to you I will answer his letter to-morrow and tell him as gently as possible that he has no hope of winning your hand."

"What! have you received a letter from Giovanni?" exclaimed Zuleika, with sudden interest, her tears vanishing instantly and her pretty face brightening up.

"Ho! ho!" said M. Dantes to himself, "Mademoiselle has waked up in earnest now." Then he added aloud: "Yes, one came this afternoon. The Viscount is in Paris, and has claimed the privilege I accorded him a year ago, provided you interposed no objection. However, the matter can speedily be settled. Young Massetti is a man of honor, and will not for an instant think of troubling with his attentions a lady to whom they cannot prove acceptable."

"Oh! papa, papa, don't tell him that; he wouldn't come here if you did; besides, did--did--did I ever tell you that Giovanni's attentions would prove unacceptable to me?"

"No, not in so many words," answered M. Dantes, archly, "but I inferred as much from your manner and tears just now. So I am to understand that you do not want me to reply to the Viscount's letter, am I?"

"Oh! yes, I want you to reply to his letter, but--but----"

"But what, darling?"

"I do not wish you to tell him there is no hope!"

"You think there is hope, then?"

"I--I--am afraid so, dear papa!"

"Yet a moment ago you told me you had no lover, and were merely a little girl!"

"I did not know then that Giovanni was in Paris, and I--I--thought he had forgotten all about me."

M. Dantes smiled as he said:

"That makes all the difference in the world, doesn't it, Mademoiselle?"

"Yes," answered Zuleika, innocently; then she added in a tone of great earnestness: "Write to Giovanni in the morning, and--and tell him I shall be delighted to see him."

"I will write and inform him that, so far as I have been able to discover, my daughter does not object to receiving a visit from him."

"Oh! that would be too cold and formal, and Giovanni is such an old friend."

"Well, well," said M. Dantes, "I will so frame my reply as to give entire satisfaction both to you and him. Now, my child, kiss me and retire to your couch, for it is very, very late."

Zuleika embraced her father and kissed him repeatedly; then, with beaming eyes and a countenance overflowing with happiness she ran lightly from the apartment.

As she tripped joyously away, M. Dantes arose from his arm-chair and gazed after her with a look of the utmost sadness.

"Oh! my daughter, my daughter," he murmured, "soon will you also quit me, and then I shall be alone, indeed! True, Esperance will remain, but, generous, manly and heroic as he is, he can never fill the void Zuleika will leave. Oh! Haydee, Haydee, my beloved wife, why were you torn so ruthlessly from your husband's heart!"

Zuleika's dreams that night were rose-hued and delicious, and in all of them the central figure was the youthful Roman Viscount.

When day dawned M. Dantes was still pacing his library.

# CHAPTER VIII.
# A VAST PRINTING HOUSE.

A street somewhat famous in Paris is the Rue Lepelletier, famous not for its length, for its breadth, for the splendid edifices it exhibits, or for the scenes and events it has witnessed, but famous for the exploits beheld by its neighbors, and the magnificent structures by them displayed. Not that the Rue Lepelletier can boast no fine edifices, for the grand opera-house would give the loud lie to such an assertion. And then there is the Foreign Office near by, the Hotel of the Minister of Foreign Affairs at the corner of the Boulevard and the Rue des Capucines, and other noted places.

But there is one structure on the Rue Lepelletier not very noticeable save for its immense size and its ancient and dingy aspect, which has witnessed more scenes and events, and is more important than all its more splendid neighbors put together.

This edifice is of brick, five stories in height, and, as has been intimated, is time-stained, storm-stained, smoke-stained and stained, it would seem, by all other conceivable causes of stain, so begrimed and dingy, yet so venerable and imposing, does it seem.

This vast and ancient pile can be said to represent no order of architecture. Architectural elegance appears not to have been thought of when it was designed, and yet the facade of the old building seems to bear the same relation to the building itself as the face of an old man bears to his body, and that face is full of character, as are the faces of some men--sombre, sedate, serious, almost sinister in aspect. This old face, too, seemed full of apertures, through which unceasing and sleepless espionage could be kept up on the good citizens of the good City of Paris. Doors, and especially windows, numberless, opened and looked upon the street, and on a cul de sac at one end of the edifice.

One of the doors opening on the cul de sac, at its further extremity, was broad, low, dark and sombre; like the gates of hell, as portrayed by the English bard, it "stood open night and day." If you entered this door and advanced, you would immediately find yourself ascending a narrow, gloomy and winding flight of stairs. Having with difficulty groped your way to the top, without having broken your neck, by having first reached the point from which you started, to wit, the bottom; or your shins, by stumbling against the steps--having, I say, accomplished the ascent to the first landing, your further passage is effectually stopped by a massive door, which resists all your efforts to open it; and, as you are contemplating the dangerous descent which you now think you are immediately and inevitably forced to make, an ivory bell-handle against the wall, beside the door, arrests your attention, with the words around it, which, with difficulty, you decipher by the dim light, "Editor's Room--No Admittance," followed by the encouraging, but somewhat contradictory word, "Ring," which, doubtless, means this: "If you are a particular friend of the editor, or have particular business with him as a journalist, ring the bell, and perhaps you may be admitted." Supposing either of these positions yours, you "ring the bell," and immediately you are startled by the tinkling of a small bell in the darkness close beside you, and the ponderous door, firm as a barricade till then, is now opened by unseen hands--by the same hand, indeed, and by the same action of that hand which caused the bell to tinkle.

You enter the door, and find yourself in a corridor or passage, long and dark, for everything in this building is dark, and gaslight is the only light eighteen hours in the twenty-four; you find yourself in a corridor, I say, running the entire depth of the building, and bringing you back again toward the Rue Lepelletier, which you left on entering the cul de sac, to seek the low entrance below. As you traverse the endless gallery, your attention is arrested by a deep hum, as of many voices at a distance, with which the entire structure seems pervaded, accompanied by a heavier sound, which rises and falls with measured stroke. This mysterious hum might have been heard when you first approached or entered the building; but the silence and solitude of the corridor have caused you to notice it now for the first time, and to wonder at its cause.

Now had you the power of those magicians, necromancers, clairvoyants and demi-devils, whether of the flesh or the spirit, who, at a glance, can gaze through massive walls and peer down the chimneys of a great city, and who, almost without glancing at all, can see through partitions, key-holes and iron doors, your wonder at the cause of these unknown sounds would instantly cease, while it would be yet more excited by those causes themselves, for the vast building all around you, and through which you are passing, and which envelops you in its ceaseless hum, like the voice of a great city, would seem to you nothing less than a leviathan of life and action--a Titan--a Frankenstein--a mental and material giant, with its acoustic tubes, like veins and arteries, running all over the structure, just beneath the surface of the walls, and uniting in every apartment; with its electric wires, like bundles of nerves, which, having webbed the whole body with network, converge into a focus-tube, and thence pass down into the vaults, through the massive foundations, and beneath, the pavements of the thronged streets of the metropolis, and thence, rising again to the surface, branching on distinct, diverse and solitary routes without the suburbs all over Europe. You would see, too, the mighty heart of this Titan, whose heavy heavings you have felt, heard and wondered at--THE PRESS--in its subterranean tenement, amid smoke and flame. THE PRESS; which, like the animal heart, receives eventually all that the veins convey to it, and flings forth everything in modified form through lungs and arteries. Tireless and untired in its action, never ceasing, never resting, for as well might a man think to live when his heart had ceased to beat, as a printing office exist when the throbbings of its press were no longer felt; and as well could a man be supposed to live without breath as a printing-office of the nineteenth century without its lungs, the steam engine, or its breath of life, the subtle fluid by which it is moved.

But to drop metaphor. In the basement of the building you would find the press-room, with its steam engine, its furnaces, its presses, its dark demi-devils, and ghostly and ghastly gnomes and genii groping or flitting about amid the glare and gloom, begrimed and besmoked, seemingly at work at unhallowed yet supernatural toil, which toil, as if a punishment for sin, like that of Sisyphus, or the daughters of Danae in the heathen Tartarus, was eternal. The press never stops.

On the first floor you would perceive the financial and publishing department in all its endless ramifications, with the separate bureaus for folding, enveloping, mailing, etc.

On the second floor--but that you will shortly behold, and it will describe itself.

On the third floor you would discover immense magazines of material--paper, ink, of every hue and quality, and type of every known description; and all in quantities seemingly as useless as incalculable.

On the fourth and fifth floors you would find the composition rooms, whence fly the winged words all over the world, peopled by its whole army of compositors; while from the long platoons of cases, "click--click--click" is heard, the sole and unceasing sound which alone in those apartments is ever suffered to fall on the ear. If we add that the entire structure is warmed in winter by heated air, conveyed in tubes from the furnaces of the press, our description will be complete, and we may say such is the printing office of the nineteenth century in Paris. How changed from that of German Guttenberg or English Caxton, three hundred years before! Such is it by daylight. Flood every object and apartment with gaslight, and you have the scene at night--through all the night, for couriers and dispatches never cease to arrive--and the journal issues with the dawn--and the workmen are relieved by constant and continuous relays. Such an office gives employment to hundreds and bread to thousands. It demands twenty editors, exclusive of their chief, twenty reporters, exclusive of the same number in the commercial and mercantile corps; twenty-five clerks and bureau agents, sixty carriers, twenty mechanicians and mar-gers, sixty folders, twenty pressmen, seventy correctors and compositors and five hundred distributors, besides a numberless and nameless army of attaches and employes too numerous to be specified. The aggregate compensation of this army is ten thousand francs per day, the annual income is nine millions of francs, the circulation is ninety thousand copies daily, and each number is read by half a million people, and through their influence by half a million more.

The daily tax of the Government is nine thousand francs. The press has been called the Third Estate of France. It is not! Nor is it the second--nor is it the first! It combines all three. Nay, the power of all three united equals not its tithe; and its position--its rank!--royalty itself bows to the press! Ask the history of the past ten years. Point to the man of power or position in the court or State, who owes it not to the press! Where is the statesman who is not, or has not been, a journalist, or the savant, the philosopher, the philanthropist, the poet, the orator, the advocate, the diplomat, even the successful soldier? The sword and the pen are emblems of the power of France--its achievements and its continuance; Sir Bulwer Lytton says,

"The pen is mightier than the sword!"

But I have left you, dear reader, perambulating the dim corridor--so dim that your eyes can hardly decipher, although it is now high noon, the various signs upon the series of doors in the wall on your left, designating the various rooms of the editorial corps, for to the editorial department is devoted the second floor of this extensive edifice. The last door in this prolonged series bears the name of the chief journalist. You ring a bell, are bid to enter, and the apartment is before you. Immense windows, rising from the floor to the ceiling, and opening upon a balcony, which overhangs the Rue Lepelletier, afford abundance of light for your eye to detect everything in the room by day, and an immense chandelier with gas-burners and opaque shades, pouring forth its flood of mellow radiance, would facilitate the same investigation yet more at night. Beneath the chandelier is spread the immense oval slab of the table. At it sits a man writing. Well, let him write on, at least for the present. Beside him, pile upon pile, pile upon pile, rise papers, wave after wave, flood upon flood, nothing but papers; on the floor beneath his feet, on the table and under the table, before him, behind him, and all around him, naught but papers, papers, rising, rising, as if in wrathful might and stormy indignation, while the very walls are lined with papers in all languages, from all climes and governments, and of every age and dimension, deposited in huge folio volumes and arranged in huge closets, along one whole side of the room. From the four continents, yea, and from the islands of the sea likewise, has this vast army come. In those tall closets extending from floor to ceiling might be found the full files for years of every leading paper in every part of Christendom, affording a treasury of reference, universal, unfailing, exhaustless, of knowledge of every conceivable description, rapidly found by means of exact and copious tables of contents.

Upon the other side of the apartment extend ranges of shelves, from floor to ceiling, filled with ponderous tomes in black substantial binding, seeming to belong to that class of standard works chiefly valuable for reference as authorities, and bearing ample testimony in their wear and tear, and their soiled appearance, to having been faithfully fingered. No thin, delicate and perfumed duodecimo is there, resplendent in gold and Russia, with costly engravings on steel, and letter-press in gilt or hot-pressed post. No, the books, the table, the journalist and the whole chamber bear the dark, stern, toil-soiled aspect of labor, the severe air of practical utility. The only ornaments, if such they can be styled, are busts--the busts of the silver-tongued Vergniaud and a few of his political brothers--the victim Girondins of '92 being conspicuous. Here, too, in a prominent niche is the noble front of Armand Carrel, the brave, the knightly, the chivalric, the true Republican, the true statesman, the true journalist, the true man--Armand Carrel, who, with Adolphe Thiers, his associate, sat first in this apartment as its chief--Armand Carrel, who fell years ago before the pistol of Emile de Girardin, a brother journalist, the founder of the cheap press, the hero of scores of combats before and since, yet almost unscathed by all.

Such are some of the ornaments of the chief editor's sanctum. At the further extremity of the apartment, the wall is covered with maps and diagrams, as well as charts of the prominent cities and points in Europe; and a large table beneath is heaped with books of travel, geographical views, and historical scenes arranged with no regard to order, and seeming to lie precisely as thrown down after having been used.

In a word, the whole room bears unmistakable evidence of stern, practical thought. In it and about it display is everywhere scrupulously eschewed. Practical utility is the only question of interest as touching the instruments of an editor, as of those of a carpenter; and the workshop of the journalist bears no inconsiderable similarity to that of the artisan in more respects than one. To each a tool is valuable, be that tool a book or a chisel, only for its usefulness, and the facility and rapidity with which it will aid the possessor to accomplish his ends, and not for its beauty of form, or costliness of material or construction.

In one respect only was there variance from this settled custom to be perceived, and that was in that delicate mechanism embodying the triumphs of modern science, which facilitates transmission of thought, and which, by skillful adaptation, made this one chamber a focus to which ideas and feeling in every other apartment of that vast establishment converged, and which enabled one man, without rising from his chair, to issue his orders to every department, from press-room to composing-room, from foundation stone to the turrets of that tall pile, everything being governed by the will and impulse of a single mind. Indeed, to such an extent is labor-saving carried in the Parisian printing office that the compositor may never have seen the journalist whose leaders he has spent half his life in setting up, for copy, proof and revise glide up or down as if by the agency only of magic, and the real actors rarely meet.

# CHAPTER IX.
# ARMAND MARRAST.

The journalist who now occupied the editorial chair was seemingly about thirty-five years of age, and one whom the ladies would call "a fine-looking man." His stature was about the average, his shoulders broad and his form thick-set. His face was long and thin, his forehead full and capacious, though not high, and was furrowed by thought. His beard, which, like his hair, was black, encircled his chin, and a moustache was suffered to adorn his lip. His dress was black and a plain stock, without a collar, surrounded his throat. His eyes were large, black, and piercing, and the expression of his countenance was contemplative and sad.

Such is a hasty limning of the personal outlines of the first journalist in Paris, the chief editor of the chief organ of the democracy in Europe, Armand Marrast, of "Le National."

An air of depression, exhaustion and regret was upon his face as he sat beside the table, with a pen in his hand and paper before him, in a thoughtful mood, as if planning a leader for his journal, of which but a single line was written. Whatever were his reflections, they were evidently far from pleasant; but the single line traced at the head of the paper indicated the source of his uneasiness. It read:

"Again the House of Orleans triumphs!"

Throwing down his pen, he folded his arms, and began hastily pacing the chamber.

"Again the House of Orleans triumphs!" he bitterly exclaimed. "Aye, again and again! It is thus forever, and thus forever seems likely to continue. Every measure, however imperative, of the opposition, ignominiously fails--every measure of the Government, however infamous, succeeds. And so it has been for twelve years. Ah! what a barren sceptre did the Three Days of '30 place in the hands of the French people! The despotism of a Citizen King has been as deadly as that of the Restoration, and more insulting. For twelve years his acts have been but a continuous series of infringements upon the rights, and insults to the opinions, of the men of July. The Republican party is trampled on. Freedom of the press, electoral reform, rights of labor, restriction of the Royal prerogative, reduction of the civil list, all these measures are effectually crushed. The press is fettered, and its conductors are incarcerated. Out of a population of thirty-three millions, but two hundred thousand are electors. Out of four hundred and sixty deputies, one-third hold places under the Government, the aggregate of whose salaries would sustain thousands of starving families at their very doors. Paris, despite every struggle of freedom, is, at this hour, a Bastille. The line of fortification is complete. Wherever the eye turns battlements frown, ordnance protrudes, bayonets bristle. Corruption stalks unblushingly abroad in the highest places, and the frauds of Gisquet all Paris knows are but those of an individual. The civil list, instead of being reduced, is every year enlarged. A Citizen King receives forty times the appropriation received by the First Consul, while his whole family are quartered on the State. The dotation to the Duke of Orleans, on his marriage, would have saved from starvation hundreds of thousands whose claim for charity far exceeded his. Thank God, his own personal unpopularity defeated the dotation designed for the Duke of Nemours. But the appanages were granted because the King's life was attempted by an assassin. A Citizen King, indeed! This man cares only for his own. He would be allied to every dynasty in Europe. His policy is unmixed selfishness. His love for the people who made him their monarch is swallowed up in love for himself. Millions have been wrung from the sweat of toil to accomplish a worse than useless conquest, thousands of Frenchmen have been sacrificed on the burning sands of Africa, and all for what?--that a throne might be won for a boy--a boy without ability, or experience, and now the Duke of Aumale is Governor-General of Algeria, while hundreds of brave men are forgotten."

As these last words, which indicated the cause of the present agitation, were uttered by the excited journalist a door at the further end of the apartment softly opened, and a young man of very low stature and boyish in aspect entered. He seemed, at a first glance, hardly to have attained his majority, though actually he was ten years older. His face was round, yet pale, his lips full, his brow commanding, his eye large, dark and thoughtful, and His characteristic expression mild and benevolent. He wore a dark frock coat, buttoned to the chin, and a plain black cravat was tied around his neck.

The journalist was so deeply absorbed in his meditations that for some moments he seemed unaware that he was no longer alone, and he might have remained yet longer in that ignorance had not the guest approached and exclaimed:

"Algeria!"

The journalist raised his head and hastily turned.

"Ah! Louis, is it you?" he said, cordially extending his hand; "I'm glad you've come. But why did I not hear you?"

"For two reasons, my dear Armand," said the visitor, seating himself in an editorial chair: "one, that I came in by the private entrance, and the other, that you were too zealously engaged in cursing the recent appointment of the King to hear anything short of a salvo of artillery."

"Ah! that cursed appointment! What next I wonder? Thank God, the old man has no more sons to make governors, although he'll never be satisfied till each one of them has a crown on his head, by his own right or the right of a wife."

"And what care we whom the boys marry, so long as marriage takes them out of France? Montpensier can find favor in the eyes of the Spanish Infanta, Christina's sister, and thus balk England; be it so, yes, be it so, especially since it can't be helped or prevented."

"But this affair of Algeria, Louis--"

"Is a very different affair you would say. No doubt, no doubt. As to Algeria, I have always viewed it as a very costly bauble for France, 'an opera-box' as the Duke of Broglie once said, 'rather too expensive for France.'"

"But then it has been a splendid arena for French valor. It has given the rough old Bugeaud a Marshal's baton, and has made the gallant Lamoriciere, his sworn foe, a general officer, thanks to his own intrepid conduct and the court influence of his brother-in-law, Thiers."

"In the late dispatch appear the names of some new candidates for advancement, I perceive."

"You allude to Morrel and Joliette among others, I suppose. Morrel has received a regiment, and Joliette is Chef d'Escadron of Spahis. Luckily for aspirants, and thanks to disease and slaughter, there is no lack of vacancies."

"The name of Morrel I have seen before in the 'Moniteur,' but Joliette--who is he?"

"A sort of protege of Bugeaud, 'tis said. He is reported to have enlisted at Marseilles, and in three years has risen to his present position from the ranks. He is of a good family, rumor says, but, suddenly reduced by some calamity, he became a soldier."

"He must be a brave fellow, Armand! As I said before, Algeria has been a fine field for the development of military genius. My chief objections to French conquests are these--they have drained millions from France which should have been devoted to the cause of labor, and have tended to dazzle the masses with the glory of the achievements of French valor abroad; thus while thousands of the young and enterprising have been lured away to fill up the ranks, and to seek fame and fortune, the minds of those remaining have been withdrawn from their own wrongs, oppression and suffering, and from efficiently concerting to sustain the measures of their friends for their relief. There is not a race in Christendom so fond of military glory and achievement as the French. Dazzled by this, the people, the masses--"

"The people, the masses!" impatiently interrupted the journalist. "You know me, Louis; for years you have known me well, for years have we devoted every energy of heart and soul to the cause of the people, and for years, ever since we came to man's estate, have we been equal sufferers in the same cause--"

"Sufferers in the cause of the people of France, in the cause of man, we both, doubtless, have been, but not equal sufferers. What have been my sacrifices or sufferings, my dear Armand, compared to yours? In that dark hour when Armand Carrel fell--fell by an ignoble bullet in an ignoble cause--fell in bitterness and without a hope for liberty in his beloved France--I felt impelled to come forward and exert myself for the welfare of my race, and endeavor to aid others in filling the gap created by his loss. To France, to my country, did I then, though but a boy, devote myself--France, my country!--for such I feel her to be, though I was born in Spain and my mother was a Corsican. Since that hour my pen has been dedicated to the cause of the people, the dethronement of the Bourgeoisie and the organization of labor. As to sacrifice or suffering, I have sacrificed only my time and toil at the worst. I have not been deemed worthy of suffering even a fine for a newspaper libel, and my paper has never been thought worth suppression!"

"And what have I accomplished, Louis?" asked Marrast, gloomily. "My life seems almost a blank."

"With Armand Carrel, you have for fifteen years been the champion of Republicanism in France, and with you, as leaders, has all been accomplished that now exists. When Carrel died, on you fell his mantle. As editor of 'La Tribune,' your boldness and charging Casimir Perier and Marshal Soult with connivance in Gisquet's scandalous frauds brought upon you fine and imprisonment. Your boldness and patriotism during the insurrection of the 5th and 6th of June, 1832, once more caused your paper to be stopped and your presses to be sealed. In April, '34, your press was again stopped, and you, with Godefroi Cavaignac, were thrown into Sainte Pelagie, whence you so gallantly escaped, though to become an exile in England. Again, in '35, you were sentenced to transportation. So much for sufferings; as to sacrifices--why, you have been utterly ruined by fines!"

"Well, Louis, well," was the sad answer, "granting all this, my sacrifices and sufferings are only the more bitter from the fact of having been utterly in vain, entirely useless. You, Louis, have been wiser than I. Your journal is well named 'Bon Sens.'"

"Possibly wiser," was the reply, "and possibly less bold. But does not discretion sometimes win what boldness would sacrifice? In rashly struggling for all we sometimes lose all. Prudence and perseverance, my dear Armand, are invaluable."

# CHAPTER X.
# THE COMMUNISTS.

At this moment the private door opened, and three men entered the editorial sanctum.

Marrast quickly turned, and his friend was silent.

"Ha! Albert, Flocon, Rollin!" he cried. "Welcome, welcome! Our friend, Louis Blanc, was just about wasting on me a sermon upon patience, but now he'll have an audience worthy of the subject. Be seated and listen!"

"Patience!" exclaimed Flocon. "Well, I'm sure we need it."

"That we do, in our present low estate," echoed Rollin.

Albert said nothing, but smiled with sarcastic significance.

When the salutations were over and the party, all but Marrast, who restlessly paced the room, were seated, Louis Blanc looked around on his friends with a sad smile, and continued:

"Marrast is right, Messieurs. I was, indeed, preaching patience. I was endeavoring to soothe his irritation and chide his depression with a sermon; since we are all old friends and fellow-sufferers in the good cause and have a common interest in knowing the reasons of failure and the means of triumph, I will by your leave proceed."

"Aye, dear Louis, go on!" cried Marrast, kindly. "But you are the most youthful sage I ever listened to."

"Yes, Louis, proceed; you look like a cure," said Rollin, laughing.

"I subscribe to Louis Blanc's creed, be it what it may," added Flocon, briskly.

"And so do I," said Albert, gravely, in a deep tone.

Of the new visitors, Ledru Rollin was a man of medium stature, about thirty-five years of age and dressed in the extreme of the mode. His complexion and hair were light, his eyes large, blue and protruding, his mouth prominent, and his full cheeks covered with whiskers, which like those of Marrast, were closely trimmed and met beneath his chin. His head and shoulders were thrown back, and his air was bold and independent. He was a lawyer of talent, who had gained celebrity as advocate of the accused on many occasions of State prosecutions.

Flocon was an older man than Rollin, and his countenance bore the wary, vigilant and suspicious look which experience alone gives. He was low in stature, thick-set and close-knit in figure; his eyes seemed always half closed; his brow was broad and massive; his face was long; a moustache was on his lip, and his hair was closely cut. The outline of his head and the expression of his face seemed those rather of one born on the banks of the Rhine than on the banks of the Seine, so calm and passionless did they appear. His dress was plain but neat. Flocon was the chief editor of "La Reforme," the name of which indicates its character. It was this man who, in February, 1833, repressed the violence of his partisans and saved the office of the "Gazette de France," yet the very next day published his celebrated letter to the Legitimists, which, for audacity, force and pungency was only equaled by the paralyzing effect it produced. The fines, imprisonments and civil incapacities to which this man had been subjected for assaults upon a government he deemed corrupt, for the ten years preceding, had been literally numberless.

Albert was a man of fifty or more, with a large head, square German face and forehead, a large hazel eye, fixed and unexcitable, hair closely cut, and beard upon his chin and lip. His dress was a long iron-gray frock coat, buttoned closely to his chin. His face was rather thin, and his complexion bronzed. His name had for years been identified with reform; and though a manufacturer himself, of the class of workmen, being proprietor and chief engineer of a large machine factory at Lyons, he had established and sustained in that city a paper to advocate his principles, named "La Glaneuse," the prosecution of which by the Government for libel and the fining and imprisonment of its editor formed an originating cause of the revolt in Lyons of April, 1834. For the part played by this man in the revolt thus arising, he was sentenced to transportation, a penalty afterwards commuted to fine and imprisonment. He was a man of few words, remarkably few, but of deep thought and prompt action, and, in moments of crisis and emergency, a man of unshaken and inflexible nerve. To the casual observer, he seemed only a silent man, or a sullen one, astute or stolid; in times of peril he was a man of iron, but a man of action and passion, too, moving with resistless might. To rouse his powers, mental or physical, demanded, indeed, circumstances of unusual import, but once roused they were irresistible.

Such were the personages now assembled in the office of "Le National;" and, of those five men, all were connected with the press, directly, as editor or proprietor, save only Ledru Rollin, and he was a writer for "La Reforme," as well as an advocate.

The name of Louis Blanc's paper was, as has been said, "Le Bon Sens."

But to return to the narrative.

"And you really wish a sermon from me, old comrades, with patience as the text?"

"Aye--aye--aye!" exclaimed all.

"Suppose I add to it this line I find on the paper before me on the table, that our good Marrast had just written as the text for a paragraph which would probably have cost him another fine and imprisonment, had the paragraph been completed and published?"

"Read! read!" cried Rollin.

"With your permission, Armand?"

"Certainly," replied the editor, still continuing his promenade.

"'Again the House of Orleans triumphs!'" read Louis Blanc, aloud.

"And is it not true--the accursed tyrants?" vociferated Rollin.

"Aye, true!" was the mild answer; "alas, too true! That perfidious House does triumph, and for that very reason the fact should never be acknowledged by its opponents."

Rollin shook his head, and, throwing himself back in his capacious chair, folded his arms, sunk his chin upon his breast and closed his eyes.

Marrast continued his walk.

Flocon remained silent and thoughtful.

Albert gave a significant smile.

"Oppose ceaselessly, but quietly, every act of despotism this Bourgeois Government may attempt; but, be the result what it may, never admit yourselves discouraged, depressed, dismayed, defeated. From every fall rise like Antaeus, with renewed vigor. Nor is it wise or prudent in those engaged in a great and glorious cause to provoke danger, to brave penalty, when nothing of good to that cause can reasonably be expected. Prudence, policy, patience and perseverance accomplish more than rashness, yet are not inconsistent with intrepidity, boldness, patriotism and philanthropy the most exalted. Comrades, what says the past, the past ten years, in whose events we have all so intimately mingled? Shall I tell you?"

"Aye! 'L'Histoire de Dix Ans,'" said Flocon.

"We are all sure of being immortal there, in that same book of yours! Eh! Louis?" cried Rollin, opening his large blue eyes.

Louis Blanc smiled and continued:

"Shall I convince you, comrades, by the history of the past ten years, the scenes we have all witnessed, the events we have all deplored, the defeats we have all sustained, the insulting ovations we have all been forced to behold and the unceasing triumphs and tyranny of the House of Orleans that, had patience and prudence been our motto, these defeats and triumphs would never have been witnessed, because these premature revolts would never have been made?"

Albert bowed and gave his peculiar smile.

"Our friend Albert smiles, and well he may. He has had a sad experience in this error of premature outbreaks. In April, 1834, he exerted every energy to restrain the revolt in Lyons, as chief of the Societe des Droits de l'Homme, and as the undoubted friend of the operatives. But his efforts were futile. Exasperated, urged on by less experienced leaders, they were in full tide of revolution, and could no more be restrained in their unwise rising than could the mountain cataract in mad career be dammed. The result was, of course, defeat--most disastrous defeat. Hundreds of the people perished, and our friend was imprisoned and fined for taking part in a movement, which he had in vain attempted to quell, and then, with the certainty of defeat, had joined, rather than desert the people who trusted and relied on him."

"A noble act!" cried Marrast, as he paced the room.

Albert quietly smiled, but otherwise his countenance remained unmoved.

"And was it not a most noble and a most wise act," continued the author of "The Ten Years," "when our friend Flocon, by an energetic and eloquent harangue, restrained the indignant people from razing to the ground the office of the 'Gazette de France,' the organ of the Duchess of Berri, and his bitter foe? Terribly would that rash act have recoiled on us, and yet, at the same time, with this most patriotic and prudent deed before us, a wilder measure than even that was adopted, and it was quelled only by force. You all remember the events. In February, '33, Eugene Brifault, in his 'Corsair,' alluded jestingly to the mysterious pregnancy of the mother of Henry V., Duke of Bordeaux, as did every one, she then being imprisoned at Baye because of her prior conspiracy to place her son on the throne, and her secret marriage in Italy being unrevealed. The Legitimists of 'Le Revenant' challenged; the allusion was repeated, and a second trial and a death ensued. 'Le National' and 'La Tribune,' regarding these repeated challenges as a menace to the Republicans, hurled defiance at the Legitimists, and demanded twelve distinct rencontres in behalf of as many names of our friends posted at their offices, among which those of Armand Carrel, Godefroi Cavaignac and Armand Marrast were conspicuous. The challenge is accepted--the names of twelve Legitimists are furnished--Armand Carrel selects Roux Laborie--they fight, and Carrel is dangerously wounded--the police then interfere--the affair ends with Flocon's terrific and audacious defiance flung down at the whole Legitimist and Orleans parties in the columns of 'La Reforme.' Now, what to Republicans were the quarrels of Legitimists and Orleanists? If we were to be ruled by a king, what cared we whether that king were Henry V. or Louis Philippe? How would the sacrifice of Carrel, Marrast, Cavaignac, or of any of those twelve brave men have been repaid, or made up? And afterwards, alas! in July of '36, when Armand Carrel, causelessly assuming a quarrel not his own, because of a fancied attempt to degrade the press, by rendering its issues accessible, by cheapness, to the masses, was slain in the Bois de Vincennes by the vulgar bullet of Emile de Girardin, of 'La Presse.' What reparation to our cause was it that our champion had died like a hero, and Chateaubriand, Arago, Cormenin and Beranger wept around his grave? Alas! that inestimable life belonged to his country and his race, and not to himself, to fling away in an obscure quarrel."

"But we are not all of us Armand Carrels," said Rollin.

"And yet, to the great cause of human liberty, and the amelioration of man's condition, to which each of us stands sworn, are pledged our lives. To hazard that cause, by the sacrifice of those lives, or by rashly and unwisely attempting its advancement, makes us violators of our vows, quite as much in reality as if we had become traitors."

"But the instances you cite are those only of individual rashness, Louis, and not of the people, or of their leaders acting in concert," remarked Marrast.

"True, concert of action has been chiefly needed, but I have only to recall the dates and places of our repeated attempts and defeats, for the past ten years, to convince you all that those attempts were premature, and had they not been so, they might have been successful--that they have frittered away energies which, properly concentrated and directed, might have achieved a revolution; and that while they have betrayed our designs and depressed our friends, have enabled our foes insultingly to triumph and caused them to be on the constant qui vive to anticipate our movements. What but premature and undigested uprisings were the conspiracy of the bell-tower of Notre Dame, in January of '32, when 'Le National' was seized--or the disturbances in La Vendee--or those in Grenoble--or those in Marseilles--or those in the Rue des Prouvaires--or those in April, during the cholera, when Casimir Perier died--or those of the 5th and 6th of June, on the occasion of General Lamarque's funeral, on pretence of avenging upon the Government the affront offered during the obsequies of Casimir Perier, the victim-Premier of the cholera? For the part taken by 'La Tribune,' then conducted by Marrast, in this revolt, its press was seized and sealed. The same was the fate of 'La Quotidienne,' and the same would have been the fate of 'Le National,' but for its barricades. Well do I remember the meeting of our friends in this very apartment on the night after General Lamarque's funeral. The great shade of the venerable warrior seemed among us, repeating for our counsel and imitation his last impressive words, 'I die but the cause lives!' But, alas! we observed it not. Doubt, dissension, dismay and despair were in our midst. All was dark--all was defiance and denunciation, crimination and recrimination--brother's hand raised against brother. Armand Carrel that night sat in this chair, but he was not the man to command his own will or opinions; how could he then bring to obedience and concert the conflicting impulses of others? Armand Carrel was a wonderful man. His motto, like that of Danton, was this: 'Audacity, audacity, always audacity!' Yet with all the audacity of Danton, he had little of his firmness. An officer under the Restoration, a conspirator at Bifort, in arms in Spain against the white flag, three times a prisoner before a council of war--in 1830 he was with Thiers, the founder of this journal; but everywhere he carried the exactitude of the camp; even in dress, manner and bearing he was a soldier--lofty, haughty, seemingly overbearing, yet, at heart, noble and generous, and to his friends accessible in the extreme. To his military notions, nothing could be accomplished without soldiers, and for the people to carry a revolution against soldiers seemed to him absurd."

"Armand Carrel would have been, nevertheless, a good revolutionist, Louis," said Marrast; "but he was a bad conspirator. He had no faith in the people, no confidence in the efforts of undisciplined and unarmed masses."

"And therein," said Rollin, "he greatly erred."

"Although we can as yet boast of having accomplished but very little by them, Ledru," added Flocon, with a meaning smile. "The masses are easily roused, but they don't stay roused, and then they often get unmanageable, even by those by whose summons they were stirred up. They fight well, but, somehow or other, they always get beaten; they succumb at last, and bow their necks to the yoke lower than ever."

"It is not the people," said Louis Blanc, "it is we the leaders, who are to be blamed. We rouse them before we are ready for them--before we have prepared them or anything else for a result; and then it is not strange that they only rush bravely on to death and defeat. We seize on the occasion of a funeral for an outbreak without organization, and the cuirassiers of the military escort trample our ranks beneath their horses' hoofs. But for unusual efforts, such would have been the case at the funeral of Dulong, the Deputy who fell in a duel with General Bugeaud, in January of '34."

"What were the circumstances?" asked Rollin.

"Armand recollects them better than I," replied Louis Blanc.

"The circumstances were these, as I remember them," said Marrast. "General Bugeaud remarked in the course of a speech in the Chamber that 'obedience is always a soldier's duty.' 'What if the order be to become a turnkey?' asked Dulong, in allusion to the General's position in relation to the Duchess of Berri, during her pregnancy and confinement at Baye. Armand Carrel endeavored to pacificate, but the effort failed. They met in the Bois de Boulogne at ten o' clock in the morning; the weapons were pistols; the distance forty paces. Bugeaud fired almost as soon as he turned, advancing only a few steps; his ball entered above Dulong's right eye, and at six o'clock that evening he was dead."

"There was a splendid ball at the Tuileries that night, was there not?" asked Flocon.

"There was, and this, with other things, excited in the masses the idea that their champion was the victim of a Royalist conspiracy, which all the influence of Armand Carrel and Dulong's uncle, Dupont de l'Eure was hardly sufficient to suppress. But Dupont immediately resigned his seat in the Chamber. He would sit no longer in a body one man of which he deemed the murderer of a beloved nephew. The obsequies were grand. Armand Carrel pronounced the eulogy, and two hundred and thirty-four deputies wet the grave with their tears. The people were greatly excited, and, as has been said, were with great difficulty restrained by Carrel and Dupont. Had they been suffered to revolt, the only result which could have followed would have been a terrific outpouring of their blood, furnishing another instance, I suppose, of the evil of impatience; is it not so, Louis?"

"Undoubtedly," was the reply; "and only two months after that other instance actually occurred, for our warning, in the revolt at Lyons, with which we are all familiar, and in which we were all actors, most of us to our sorrow. This was in April. Albert's journal, 'La Glaneuse,' had been seized for libel on the Government, and the editor fined and imprisoned. Next a reform banquet of the operatives was forbidden, although but a year before Garnier Pages had been suffered to banquet the Lyonnese to the number of two thousand, and although at no period had so many gorgeous festivities and public balls been given by the rich Royalists, as if in premeditated scorn of the banquet prohibited to the poor Republicans. The result was so prompt as to seem inevitable; there was a strike of the operatives, an insurrection of the people. Albert was sent to Paris as an envoy, to find a man to lead the revolt. MM. Cabet and Pages were deemed too moderate. Cavaignac would go only with Cabet. Lafayette was too feeble, but gave his name and letters. Carrel and Marrast were not members of the Societe des Droits de l'Homme, and Albert had been cautioned that Carrel was too moderate. Thiers had denounced 'La Tribune,' and Marrast's friends were hiding him from the police. In despair concerning his mission, the envoy was about returning home, when he was sent for to Armand Carrel's house, and Carrel offered to go to Lyons and lead the revolt, provided Godefroi Cavaignac would accompany him. Now these friends had long been at feud, but all private grievances were forgotten in this crisis of the cause, and Albert is just about preceding them in the post-chaise, to announce their coming, when, lo! the telegraph says, 'Order reigns in Lyons!' Here, then, after a terrific slaughter, was recorded another fruitless revolt, because a premature one. Nay, it was infinitely worse than fruitless. Not only did the Republicans utterly fail in their attempts, not only were they cruelly crushed by the Royal mercenaries, but they were openly derided in their defeat, and the cause was gloomier than ever. The slaughter of women and children in the streets of Lyons, and on their own hearthstones, in the course of this insurrection, was hideous, and is graphically portrayed in the memorial of our friend Ledru Rollin, as advocate in the matter. But, as if all this were not enough for our persecuted cause, the decease of the great and good Lafayette, the idol of freemen all the world over, took place in the following May. Alas! his sun went down in clouds. His end was dark. Bitter maledictions quivered on his dying lips. He had lived to mourn that July day, only three years before, when, on the steps of the Hotel de Ville, he had, with his own hands, been called to invest a cold-blooded, perfidious, selfish, and most ungrateful tyrant with Royal robes. Alas! there was order in Lyons--Lafayette was in his grave--peace reigned in Paris--the House of Orleans triumphed!"

"Those were dark days," said Marrast, sadly.

"They were, dear Armand, dark, indeed, for you and your friends, for your journal had been suppressed, and you were an inmate, with Cavaignac, of Sainte-Pelagie."

"Whence you both, bravely and boldly effected your escape more than a year afterwards and fled to England, to the most glorious discomfiture of the knaves who put you there!" cried Rollin. "Vive la Republique! yet, Messieurs! We've all seen dark days, and the present is none of the brightest; and we've all come together at these old headquarters of liberty just to be unhappy together, just to help each other be miserable, which, in fact, is vastly happier unhappiness than being miserable alone. At all events, that's what I want. But it can't always be right. I predict a revolution before another ten years shall have rolled round, which shall make immortals of us all--that revolution for which we have been waiting, watching, toiling and writing, lo! now these thirteen years and upward, for the which waiting, watching, toiling and writing we have some of us been fined, who had money enough to pay a fine, and others imprisoned and hunted about and persecuted. Why, there's Albert and Flocon haven't been able to get a franc cleverly warm in their pockets these ten years, before forth it was drawn in the form of a fine; while as for Marrast, he has the perfect air and bearing of a bandit, so often has he seen the inside of a dungeon; and our friend Albert isn't much better looking. As for Louis and myself, why, we never knew what it was to have a franc get warm in our pockets, so we escaped having any drawn forth by Ministers, and they have never thought us worth prosecuting or imprisoning. But they may change their minds when Louis' book, that is to make us all immortal, comes out. Eh, Louis?"

Louis Blanc smiled, but made no answer.

"Well, it is only meet, I suppose, that I should receive my share of the blows," said Marrast. "I'm sure I'm not very delicate or very ceremonious in bestowing them. Besides, every one of my predecessors has endured the same--Carrel, Thomas, Bastide; while poor Rouen, the proprietor, would have been ruined, indeed, a dozen times with fines, but for his enormous profits. Why, this old office has been a perfect butt for Ministers to fire at--it has received a dozen fusillades, at least; but it stands yet, and, strange as may have been the scenes it has witnessed, it will witness yet other and stranger ones, and we shall all be witnesses thereof, and actors in them, too, or greatly do I err."

"So be it, with all our hearts!" was the general shout.

"Apropos of State prosecutions against 'Le National,'" said Louis Blanc, "that was a most exciting time when Rouen was brought by Thiers before the Court of Peers, for a libel on that most august and erudite body."

"Aye! and a most, liberal, honest and honorable conclave--the thrice-sodden and most solemn knaves and mules!" cried Rollin.

"Rouen at the bar demanded Armand Carrel for his defence," continued Louis Blanc. "To refuse was impossible, but a bitter pill must it have been to Thiers and Mignet to consent. They must have foreseen what came. Both, now in the Ministry, only four years before both had been in 'Le National'--Thiers as the colleague of Carrel, and Mignet as a collaborateur. The files of the journal were produced, and, lo! there stood paragraphs proven to have emanated from the pens of the prosecutors far more libelous and venomous on the august peers than anything Rouen had published. You all remember the scene that ensued and won't forget it soon."

"No; nor shall we soon forget that noble passage in Armand Carrel's defence," said Flocon, "in which he evoked the shade of Marshal Ney, and from the wild excitement that followed, one would suppose that it had really risen in the hall, bleeding and ghastly, and pointing to its wounds, like the ghost of Banquo, to blast his hoary, jeweled and noble assassin, who, seated on those very seats, had sentenced him to an infamous doom. Carrel was instantly stopped, but General Excelmens rose in his seat and pronounced the charge true. It was then reiterated with tremendous applause from the galleries. How Carrel escaped punishment for contempt is not known. Rouen was convicted of libel on the peers, of course; his sentence was a fine of ten thousand francs and imprisonment for two years."

"But of what words did this famous libel actually consist?" asked Ledru Rollin.

"Louis can tell you better than I," said Flocon.

"Why, the words were severe enough, no doubt," replied Louis Blanc, "but Thiers and Mignet had themselves expressed the same ideas a hundred times, though in less powerful and pointed language. The passage which seems particularly to have given offence was this, that in the eyes of eternal justice and those of posterity, as well as in the testimony of their own consciences, these renegades from the Revolution, these returned emigrants, these men of Ghent, these military and civil parvenus, these old Senators and spoiled Marshals of Bonaparte, these Procureur Generals, these new-made nobles of the Restoration, these three or four generations of Ministers sunk in public hatred and contempt, and stained with blood--all these, seasoned with a few notabilities, thrown in by the Royalty of the 7th of August, on condition they should never open their lips save to approve their master's commands--all this farrago of servilities was not competent to pronounce on the culpability of men seeking to enforce the results of the Revolution of July!"

"It was not until the commencement of 1835, I think," said Marrast, "that Ministers opened a general onslaught upon the Parisian press. 'Le Republicain' was interdicted that year. It was then, too, that the laws against public criers and newspaper hawkers were instituted. As far back as '33, however, Rodde had braved all such prohibitions by selling and with impunity, too, his own paper in the streets. In May of '35 came on the general prosecution of the press. Rollin was advocate in the defence. There were warm words between Armand Carrel and his friend Dupont, the lawyer, and there was at one time apprehension of a duel."

"The position of Armand Carrel with Thiers, his former colleague, was, at that time, a singular one," remarked Rollin. "Each seemed to be on the constant search for opportunities to exasperate the other. The editor assailed the Minister in his columns, and the Minister retaliated by an arrest. Carrel censured and ridiculed Thiers, though he respected his abilities, and Thiers feared and hated Carrel, though he admired his talents."

"It was about this time that Fieschi exploded his infernal machine at the King, was it not?" asked Flocon. "Thiers arrested Carrel then, I know."

"It was on the 28th of July of '35, at ten in the morning, on the Boulevard du Temple. This was the second attempt on the King's life, the first having been that of Bergeron, in November of '33. Carrel was arrested as an accomplice, it was pretended, for every one of these attempts has been attributed to the whole body of the Republicans, while they were utterly ignorant of them until they took place, and then bitterly denounced them. But the Government has made capital out of all these insane attempts, and against the opposition, too."

"I've heard it asserted," said Rollin, "that the Government got up some of those little exhibitions of fireworks for that very purpose. They are quite harmless, so far as the old man is concerned--wonderfully so--and Fieschi was made a perfect fool of, so ridiculously lionized was he by King, Court and Ministers. Our friend Marie was advocate for that wretched old man, Pepin, Fieschi's accomplice, more a ghost than a living creature."

"You are entirely right, friend Rollin," said Louis Blanc, "in the idea that every one of these attempts strengthens the Government and recoils on the opposition. No one should so vigilantly and vigorously watch for and suppress such attempts as we. Heaven defend the old despot from the assassin's weapon, as it seems well inclined to do, or the deed will surely be attributed to us. Every unsuccessful attempt at assassination is viewed like an unsuccessful attempt at revolt on the part of the opposition, and injures our cause accordingly. Better never to attempt than never to succeed."

"Do you think it true, Louis, as was reported," asked Marrast, "that as soon as the smoke of Fieschi's explosion swept off, and the old man found himself standing unharmed amid a heap of slain and mangled, Marshal Mortier and Colonel Rieussec being among the killed, his first exclamation was this, with, ill-concealed gratification, 'Now I shall get my appanages and the dotations for the boys.'"

"Nothing is more probable," said Louis Blanc. "That old man has but one impulse--selfishness, and but one attachment--to his family--his family, because it is his. His purse and family have for years been his sole objects of love. To aggrandize his own has been for years his sole end and aim. He parcels out the thrones and kingdoms of Europe among his children as if it were but a family estate."

"What thoughtful selfishness!" exclaimed Flocon; "and at a moment, too, when he had but just escaped an awful death, and all around him flowed the blood and lay scattered the lacerated limbs of his faithful servants, either dead or dying with groans and shrieks of most agonizing torture, and all because of himself; how disgraceful that, at such a terrible moment, his first thought should have been of the few more francs his trembling hand was striving to tear from a people by whom he had already been made the richest man in Europe, and which the occurrence of this dreadful event might serve to win for him."

"Well," said Rollin, "whether this event aided to win the appanages and dotations, and was so designed, or not, it is very sure the aforesaid appanages and dotations were secured. No wonder that such attempts succeed each other so rapidly-- one every year, at the least! When was the next, Louis--that of Alibaud, I think?"

"That took place about sunset on the 25th of June, '36," was the reply. "Alibaud discharged a walking-stick-gun at the King, as he left the Tuileries, on his way to Neuilly, at the corner of the Porte Royale. That Alibaud was a mere boy, and a very interesting and intelligent boy, too; but for some mysterious cause he did not find favor with the court, as did Fieschi. He evidently attempted the assassination from conviction, from a feeling of manifest destiny. After his failure, he only wished to die, and to die at once. All who have succeeded Alibaud have been but vulgar cutthroats."

"In what year was the insurrection of Armand Barbes and Martin Bernard?" asked Flocon. "That proved most disastrous to our cause."

"That was in '39, May, I think," answered Rollin. "Barbes, Blanqui and Bernard were arraigned as leaders. Marie and myself were advocates for Barbes. Blanqui was sentenced to death and Barbes to the galleys for life. But we obtained commutation of penalty for both."

"And where is to be the end of all these things?" asked Marrast, gloomily, as he continued pacing the chamber with folded arms, his head resting on his bosom. "Are the ten years on which we have now entered to be characterized by the fruitless efforts of the past? Are the people of France again, and again, and again to strike for freedom, only to be stricken into the dust and trampled beneath the armed heel of a despot's myrmidons? Are the streets of Lyons, Paris and Marseilles again to be drenched with the life-blood of their dwellers, poured out as freely as water and as fruitlessly? Are we all again, for full ten years, to toil, strive, struggle and suffer; to be hunted down like the vilest criminals, and, like criminals, plunged into the most pestilential dungeons; to be stripped like slaves of our hard-won earnings, and to be deprived of the most humble franchises of men claiming at all to be free; to be treated with scorn and contumely, and to be debarred the exercise of those common rights, which, like air and water, belong to all; I say, brothers, are all these scenes to be repeated during the ten years on which we have now entered, as they have been witnessed during the ten years now past?"

"You speak sadly, Armand," observed Rollin.

"Not so sadly as I feel. I have listened with attention to the recapitulation of the political events of the past ten years in France; and most plainly, and as sadly as plainly, does the result prove that every movement in our cause has been as premature as it has been unsuccessful."

"May we not gather wisdom, which shall conduct us to success in the future, from the very errors and disasters of the past?" remarked Flocon.

"Alas!" despondingly replied Marrast, "what is there in our present to promise a bright future more than was in our past to promise us a bright present? Our great leaders of another generation have all left us, one after another--all have dropped into their graves. The cold marble has closed over their venerable brows, and they rest well. Yet they died and made no sign of hope. On us, young, inexperienced and rash, has devolved their task; but the mantle of their power and virtue has not, alas! descended with that task to aid in its momentous accomplishment. General Lamarque's sun went down in clouds. Midnight, deeper than Egyptian darkness, brooded over the delirious deathbed of Lafayette. Armand Carrel fell without hope; and are we wiser than they? How often, oh! how often have I listened to the words of wisdom that fell from those eloquent lips, even as a boy reverently listens to a parent--for such was Armand Carrel to me. Upon this very spot have I stood, in that very chair has he sat, that chair, which, with mingled shame and pride, I reflect is now filled by me--shame, that it is filled in a manner so unworthy of him--pride, that I should have been deemed fit, after him to fill it at all--in that very chair, I say, has his noble form reclined, when he for hours, even from night till the next day's dawn, dwelt with sorrowful eloquence upon his country's present, and looked forward with gloomy foreboding and prediction for the future. It almost seems to me that this mighty shade is with us now!"

"And why was all this despondency, my dear Armand?" remarked Louis Blanc, mildly. "Was it not because our noble and gifted friend was essentially a soldier, not a civilian, not a statesman, not a revolutionist? Had Armand Carrel gone to Algeria, he would have died--if died he had not in an unknown duel, with an unknown bravo--he would have died a Marshal of France--a Bugeaud, a Chaugarnier, a Bedeau, a Cavaignac, a Clausel, a Lamoriciere. Carrel had no faith in the masses to achieve a revolution. He never believed that they could even withstand a single charge of regular troops, much less repel and overcome it."

"Not even with barricades?" asked Rollin.

"Not even in defence of barricades," continued Louis Blanc.

"Regular troops have much to learn," added Rollin, with a significant smile. "They will see the day--aye! and we all shall see it and rejoice at its coming, despite all melancholy prognostications, when the people of Paris will dictate abdication to the king of the barricades, from the top of the barricades, the people's throne! Nor will that event tarry long!"

"I doubt it not, I doubt it not, Ledru!" exclaimed Louis Blanc, rejoiced that one of the youngest and least stable of their number appeared free from the apprehensions of one of the most influential and seemingly most reliable. "I accept the omen indicated by your enthusiasm. But I accounted for the vacillation and distrust of our lamented friend, Armand Carrel, by reverting to the fact that he relied entirely on regular troops, military skill, scientific tactics and severe subordination. Now, all of these belonged to our oppressors and none of them to us; and, inasmuch as he could not perceive that enthusiasm, passion for freedom, love of country and family, and the very wrath and rage of desperation itself sometimes not only supply the place of discipline, arms and the knowledge requisite to use them, but even enable vast masses to break down and crush beneath their heel the serried ranks of veteran troops, he could only despair at the prospects apparently before him. Besides, Armand Carrel, like all military men, was a man of action, not reflection--of execution, not contrivance--a soldier, not a conspirator. At the head of ten thousand veteran troops, he would have charged on thrice their number without discipline, with the confident assurance of sweeping them from his path as the chaff of the threshing floor is swept before the blast; but, with an undisciplined mob, as he contemptuously called the masses, he would have moved not a step. The larger the multitude, the less effective and the more impossible to manage he would have deemed it. A revolution accomplished by means of the three arms of the military service--artillery, cavalry and infantry--horse, foot and dragoons, he could readily conceive; but a revolution conducted to a successful issue only by means of pikes, axes, muskets and barricades, never, to the hour of his death, despite the victory of the Three Days, could Carrel comprehend."

"Besides," said Flocon, "it must not be forgotten that Armand Carrel, though a most devoted friend to Republicanism, was never a member of the Societe des Droits de l'Homme--was never, as we all now are--a Communist, a Socialist, a Fourierist, a friend to the laborer. No wonder he hoped so little for the people, and trusted to accomplish so little through them."

"There can be no doubt that the social principle which Republicanism is now unconsciously assuming all over France," mildly remarked Louis Blanc, "is lending to the cause incalculable strength. How terribly impressed with a conviction of the justice of the cause in which they perished must have been the unhappy insurgents of Lyons, when, with this motto on their banner: 'To live toiling or die fighting,' they marched firmly up to the cannon's mouth and fought, and, thus fighting, fell. Yet this conviction is not peculiar to the workmen of Lyons. It pervades all Paris, all France, and needs only to be roused to act with an energy which no human power can resist. Social Republican will be the type of the next revolution in France--it must be. The French people have been dazzled by the mirage of liberty ever since '89,--but it has been only a mirage. On the last three days of July, '30, the people of Paris drove out one Bourbon to enthrone another. True, 'The State is myself,' was not the despotic motto he assumed, as did one of his successors, but it was 'Me and my family,' which has proved equally selfish, if not so absolute, and far more dangerous to freedom. With Lafayette and Benjamin Constant, the Citizen King they had made, quarreled as soon as on his throne, and Lafitte and Dupont de l'Eure, his supporters, were banished from the Court. Casimir Perier was called to crush the Liberals. Armand Carrel assailed the act, and urged a republic. 'Le National' was prosecuted, and insurrections followed. Thus was the Revolution of the Three Days won by the people to be seized and enjoyed by the Bourgeoisie. The next revolution will be won by the people, too, but the people will enjoy it!"

"And how progresses our principles, Louis, among the people?" asked Marrast, who had listened attentively to every word that had been uttered.

"Never so gloriously as now, Armand, never! Never has there been such a diffusion of information upon the subject of the rights of labor as now. Pagnerre tells me every day that volumes, tracts and pamphlets on this topic disappear like magic from his shelves."

"Has not the Minister a hand in this mysterious disappearance of Communist literature?" asked Rollin. "We all know he is quite frantic on the topic of popular education."

"Oh! yes, we all understand Guizot's love for the people! His system of education promulgated in 1833 was so very beautiful that it was almost a pity it was utterly impracticable. But Guizot has very little to do with Pagnerre's book-shelves, or with Pagnerre in any way, except to prosecute him from time to time for publishing Cormenin's withering tracts designed for the Minister himself, and yet it would almost seem there was a design to exhaust the market of the publications of our friends; only the great mass of them go to the provinces and large quantities abroad. My own little brochure, 'The Organization of Work,' after having fallen stillborn from the press, died a natural death and been laid out in state for a year or two on Pagnerre's shelves, all at once is resurrected, runs through half a dozen large editions, and is translated into half a dozen languages. The same is true of Lamartine's 'Vision of the Future,' and the same of Cormenin's tracts, and of the ten thousand brochures on this same subject of Communism in all its different shades and phrases, and in every variety of size, form and style of writing and appearance. These publications are adapted to every taste and comprehension. The workman is suited as well as the savant. All this savors of magic. Even my most sanguine anticipations are surpassed by reality. There will never long lack a supply for a demand, be that demand what it may. A demand for Fourier literature has turned all the pens in Paris hard at work upon it--novelists, essayists, pamphleteers--while the Porte St. Antoine, the Porte St. Martin and all the minor theatres, where are found the masses, swarm with melodramas, farces and vaudevilles on the same subject, and none of you have forgotten the powerful play, entitled 'The Laborer of Lyons,' attributed to M. Dantes, recently produced with such success on the boards of the Francais itself."

"And who is this M. Dantes," asked Ledru Rollin, "if you will suffer me to interrupt?"

"Decidedly the most remarkable man in the French Chamber of Deputies," replied Marrast. "In powers of natural eloquence I never saw his rival."

"Nor is that all," added Louis Blanc. "Unlike most men noted as mere orators, he is a sound logician, as well as a polished rhetorician. As a political economist he has few equals. To that subject he seems to have devoted much study, while his familiarity with the political history of France and of the times generally all over Christendom seems boundless. In debate, you observe he is never at a loss for fact or argument, let the discussion take what direction it may."

"And he has celebrity also as a writer, has he not?" asked Ledru Rollin.

"The author of 'The Laborer of Lyons' must be a man of distinguished literary genius," was the reply.

"Better than all," said Flocon, "he is devoted heart and soul to the good cause."

"Such devotedness to a cause I never witnessed," said Marrast. "He puts us all to the blush. With him it appears a matter of direct individual interest. He is perfectly untiring. He is like one impelled by his fate. Love or vengeance could not force onward a man to the attainment of an object more irresistibly than he seems forced, and that, too, without the slightest apparent stain of personal interest or ambition. That man appears to me a miracle--a pure philanthropist. He strives, struggles, suffers, sacrifices, and all with the sole object of ameliorating the condition of his race."

"It is, indeed, wonderful," said Rollin, thoughtfully. "Do you know, Marrast, anything of his past history?"

"Little, if anything. Of himself he never speaks, and I can gather nothing from others. Even his constituents had known nothing of him but a few months before he became their representative in the Chamber. His popularity with them he owes to his efforts to ameliorate their condition. At his own expense he established among them a Phalanstrie, which is now in most successful operation."

"He is rich, then?" asked Flocon.

"Seemingly not, to judge from his habits of life," replied Marrast. "Not a man in the Chamber is more Republican in garb, manner, equipage or residence than he, and yet he may be rich."

"Is he married?" asked Rollin.

"He has been, I am told," said Marrast. "But we interrupt you, Louis. You were alluding to the unusual influences now at work for our cause."

"I was about speaking of the newspaper press," said Louis Blanc. "Never has there been known such a revolution in favor of Reform and Communist journals, and to none is this better known than to some of ourselves. There's Flocon's new journal, 'La Reforme,' that has leaped at once into a circulation never before achieved but by long years of toil and enterprise. The old 'National,' we need but to look around us to be sure, was never more prosperous than now, while I am free to confess that my journal, 'Le Bon Sens,' which has been a sickly child ever since its birth, has, within three months, tripled its number of readers, or, at least, its payers. The same is in the main true of 'Le Monde,' by La Croix, 'Le Journal du Peuple,' by Dubose, 'Le Courier Francais,' by Chatelain, 'La Commerce,' by Bert, 'La Minerve,' by Lemaine, 'La Presse,' by Girardin, and all the journals in Paris which diffuse true ideas upon labor and the rights of the people, be they in other respects what they may. Even the 'Charivari,' which views the old King and his Ministers as fair butts of ridicule, perceives a marked increase in its patronage since it commenced that course, which sudden popularity naturally excites it to increase of zeal in the same path. Besides all this, an army of new papers, aiming to aid the great cause, have not only sprung up of late, like mushrooms, in Paris, but all over France, and even all over Europe; and so far appear they from interfering with each other's prospects that the more there are the better they seem sustained and the more ably conducted. A swarm of new and unknown writers for the press on this great subject seems all at once to have appeared from unseen hiding-places."

"This is very strange, Louis," said Marrast, "and yet it is, doubtless, very true. I had observed what you remark myself, although I have viewed the movement less hopefully for the cause of the Republic than you."

"Depend upon it, Armand," said Louis Blanc, smiling, "that Republicanism and Socialism are identical terms, as much so as Communism and despotism are antagonistic terms."

"But how do you account for this wonderful change, this unprecedented fever for Fourierism?" asked Flocon.

"I don't pretend to account for it at all. The merits of the cause have, perhaps, begun to be properly appreciated. Unusual efforts have been made by our friends of late. Whole nations and epochs are sometimes seized with a contagious mania for peculiar species of literature, as for everything else. But I will hint to you a suspicion which I have recently entertained, namely, that, after all, the rapid sale and ready market for every species of Fourier literature is not an unerring indication of the amount of reading of such literature, or the demand that actually exists of buyers as well as readers--individual ones at least. As for the journalistic literature, that I have learned is, without doubt, gratuitously distributed, to a great extent, among the masses."

"But can the masses read the papers?" asked Marrast.

"Each family, house, neighborhood, cafe or cabaret, at any rate, has, at least one reader," said Rollin; "and all the men, women and children have ears to hear, if not power to comprehend. But some of these papers, which I have seen, come down in style to the very humblest comprehension."

"Can it be," asked Flocon, "that there is such a club as a society for the diffusion of social knowledge in Paris, after the form of that in London, instituted by Lord Henry Brougham and his Whig coadjutors, for the diffusion of general information, and so opposed by the Tories."

"If there be such an association," said Louis Blanc, "it has managed to elude all my vigilance thus far, and that of the Government, too, for Guizot can perceive, if no one else can, the inevitable effect of all this, and he has no idea that the dear people of France shall be educated by any one save himself. But, actually, there seems to me to exist too much unity of purpose and action in this enterprise for it to be the work of an association. I should rather suppose one powerful and philanthropic mind at the head of the movement, were there not two things so plainly opposed to it as to forbid the idea--the first being that there is no one man in Europe who is rich enough to expend such immense sums upon such an enterprise, if he would, and the second that there is no man who has the subject sufficiently at heart to do it, if he could."

# CHAPTER XI.
## "WAIT AND HOPE."

Just then a light rap was heard at the private door, which Marrast immediately hastened to open, as if in anticipation of the arrival of a friend.

A brief and rapid colloquy ensued; then M. Dantes, the Deputy from Marseilles, was introduced. He seemed acquainted with, and to be held in high regard by all present. His dress, as usual, was black, with a white cravat, and his manner and bearing had all that magnetism and dignity which so deeply impressed those he met.

"I find you in private conference, do I not, Messieurs?" asked he, glancing around with a smile. "I pray you let me not interrupt. I have called but for a moment to speak with M. Marrast respecting a measure in the Chamber, and have consented to enter only at his solicitation."

"You are right, M. Dantes," replied Marrast, "in supposing us engaged in a private conference, and upon matters of deep import, though conferences in this office can never be so private or so important as not to derive benefit from the presence and counsel of the Deputy from Marseilles."

"Most true," observed Louis Blanc; "and so far from intrusion do we view your arrival that we can but consider it most opportune that we have the privilege of referring to you a question on which, between us, especially between our friend Marrast and myself, there seems some little diversity of sentiment."

"It would, I fear," said M. Dantes, "be unpardonable arrogance in one so young as I am in the great cause of human liberty to offer counsel to you, who are all veterans, and most of you little less than martyrs to your enthusiasm. But no good citizen will shrink from the responsibility of declaring the results of his reflections on all topics which have reference to the general weal."

"We differ mainly in this," said Marrast: "Louis Blanc attributes the Republican failures of the past ten years to prematurity and want of preparation in our attempts, and contends that all those reverses may be retrieved by patience and prudence in future, while, to my mind, there is nothing to indicate for the future, from the same causes, different results than those experienced in the past."

"Concert of action," said M. Dantes, mildly, "is always an indispensable requisite in the accomplishment of every enterprise which relies for its success on association, or the combined efforts of individuals laboring for a common end; yet, with all the concert of action which can possibly be attained, the best arranged and best digested scheme in the world may be ruined by premature movement. Of this we surely have sad proof in the history of the past ten years alluded to. There is something of truth in the declaration so frequently made that the French people are not yet prepared for freedom. If this be so, then it is the duty of their friends to prepare them. It is folly to suppose that the masses should, at first, intuitively know all their rights and the best mode of vindicating them. This they must be taught; and, to this end, the press should be unceasingly at work, not only all over France, but all over Europe, in diffusing correct views upon life and labor, and political rights and powers. There should be, also, concert of action among the friends of freedom, and clubs should at once be instituted in every city, town and village in France, which should be in private and intimate correspondence with similar clubs at Paris and in all the capitals of Christendom. There should, likewise, be unity of action introduced among the masses themselves. In a city like Paris, and among a people like the French, secret signals can easily be arranged, by which, at any hour of the night, or of the day, fifty thousand laborers in their blouses might be concentrated at any point where their presence is required, and that, too, with arms in their hands furnished from secret arsenals; and thus would those pitiable slaughters of helpless insurgents, like those of sheep in the shambles, we have so often witnessed, be avoided, if nothing besides were gained. The people are ever but too ready to pour out their blood, and the most difficult and delicate task in our enterprise is, after all, to restrain them--to impress upon them the all important maxim, without which nothing great, good or enduring is achieved, those three words in which all human wisdom is contained, 'Wait and hope.'"

"And for what are we to wait and hope, for which we have not already in vain waited and hoped the past ten years?" asked Marrast.

"The true hour to strike!" was the firm answer.

"And that hour, when will it come?"

"It may come quickly, as it will come surely, soon or late! It cannot be that the

Revolution of July should continue much longer to result in the solemn mockery it has. It cannot be that its friends should much longer be withheld from those by whom it was achieved, only to aggrandize one old man and his sons. It cannot be that the unmitigated and disgusting selfism of Louis Philippe, and his efforts to ally himself with every crowned head in Europe--not for the glory of France, but for his own--will much longer be overlooked or their perils masked. The appanages grasped by himself--the dotation and bridal outfit of the Duke of Orleans--the dotation sought for the Duke of Nemours, and his appointment as Regent during the minority of the Count of Paris--the Governorship of Algeria bestowed on the youthful and inexperienced Aumale, to the insult of so many brave and victorious generals--the naval supremacy, to which has been exalted the ambitious Joinville, and his union to the opulent Brazilian Princess--the effort to unite the young Montpensier with the Infanta of Spain--the environment of Paris with Bastilles, with the avowed purpose of fortifying order by turning the ordnance which should protect into enginery of destruction--an immense standing army--the notorious corruption of officials, and the audacious dabbling of Ministers in the stocks, if not the King himself, by means of information obtained by the Government telegraph, and withheld from the people, or of information manufactured by the telegraph designed to affect the Bourse--the unprecedented number of placemen occupying seats in the Chamber of Deputies, yet receiving exorbitant salaries as incumbents of civil offices, one man being often in receipt of the salaries of several offices, though performing the duties of none--the fact that Ministers have maintained majorities by unblushing bribery in elections--that hardly one man in two hundred is an elector--the profligate arts of corruption by which every able man is bought by the Court--the disgraceful censorship of the press and the drama--the enormous appropriations for the civil list, wrung out by grinding taxes from the toil and sweat of millions--the absurd assumption, yet the monstrous power, over the press and its conductors, of that conclave of hoary dotards called the Chamber of Peers--the utter and most impious disregard of the deprivation and misery of the operative and laborer, although arrayed side by side with the insolence and wealth pampered by the taxes torn from themselves--the total forgetfulness of the self-evident truth of the right of all men to labor, unrestricted by the baleful influences of the competition of capitalists--these facts, properly urged and set forth by the press, from the tribune and in the clubs, in connection with due enlightenment of the masses upon their rights as to labor and its reward and the duty of government thereupon could not fail to prepare the popular mind, all over France, and all over Europe, for reform--for revolution."

"Unquestionably," cried Louis Blanc, "such would be the effect; and it would not only prepare the people for reform, and stimulate them to obtain it, but it would make them Republicans--true Republicans--American Republicans! The Americans do not plume themselves on the title citizen, but they work; they dispute little about words, but clear their lands; they do not talk of exterminating anybody, but they cover the sea with their ships, they construct immense canals, roads and steamers without jabbering at every stroke of the spade about the rights of man. With them, labor, merit, talent and honest opulence are honored and rewarded aristocracies. Such Republicans would furnish France more Washingtons, Jeffersons and Madisons, and fewer Robespierres, Dantons and Marats!"

"There can be no doubt," remarked Flocon, "that the paramount interest in a republic is that of those who work, that the labor question is of supreme importance, that the profound problem now submitted to the industrial nations of Christendom demands satisfactory solution, and that the long-enduring and most iniquitous miseries of those who toil must cease. Reform, revolution and government which achieve not these, achieve nothing! They would be worse than useless. The measures suggested by our distinguished friend seem to me eminently calculated to attain the consummation we desire."

"A good government must and always will systematically uphold the poor, and ever interpose to protect the weak against the strong," said Louis Blanc. "The state should be tutelary for the ignorant, the poor and the suffering of every description. We must have a guardian government--a government that will accord the aid of that mighty engine, credit, not to the rich only, but also to the poor. It must interpose likewise in the matter of industry, and exclude that antagonistical principle of competition--the poisoned fount of so much virulence, violence and ruin. Our maxim is, brothers, and in this do we all concur, 'Human Solidarity,' and our motto, 'Unity, Liberty, Equality and Fraternity.' All men are of one family, and once thoroughly sensible of this kindred, discord, hate and selfism will no longer be possible."

"The views advanced," said Ledru Rollin, "so far as they tend to the elevation of the masses and to popular preparation for reform, Republicanism or revolution, have my most cordial approval; but I would beg to ask how long are the people to 'wait and hope?' When is to come the hour to strike?"

"Who can tell," said M. Dantes, in his low, clear and musical tones, "at what moment the breath will come which may hurl on its errand of devastation the avalanche which the snows and suns of centuries, perchance, have been preparing for its awful mission? In the stillness of the night-time, beneath the clear blue sky of summer, or amid the ravings of the midnight tempest, its dread march is ordered, and in resistless, crushing sublimity it begins to move on to accomplish its terrible errand. Who may predict the precise moment when the earthquake shall rock, the tornado sweep, the red lightning scathe, or the lava flood desolate? And who shall tell the day or the hour when the people, in their majesty and might, shall rise to avenge their wrongs? The snow-flake falls fleecily on the mountain's top through many a long and silent night; a land green as Eden smiles over the volcano; through many a calm and sunny day the electric flame gathers in the firmament! At length, when least expected, the avalanche sweeps, the volcano bursts, the red bolt strikes. France is the victim of many wrongs. Which one of them shall prove the last drop in her cup of bitterness we know not. France is divided into many political sects, and all but one aim at revolution. Which one of all shall it be to set the ball of revolution in motion? The Legitimists, who consider the Duke of Bordeaux the rightful heir, and Louis Philippe a usurper; the Bonapartists, who think they evoke the great shade of Napoleon in the person of his unworthy descendant; or the old Republicans? As for the Conservatives, let them with Guizot at their head, uphold themselves if they can, and let the dynasties under Barrot and Thiers overthrow and succeed their factional foes. Their petty quarrels we care not for. Nor shall we, the Communists, ever suffer ourselves to be deemed the revolutionary party; but the revolution once commenced, let us throw ourselves into its torrent, and with our thorough, perfect and secret organization, we cannot fail to shape it most successfully to our own, our righteous ends. The hour when revolution may commence we cannot predict, as it is not our policy to start or precipitate it; but that hour may come quickly. It must come on the demise of Louis Philippe, which event cannot be long delayed, and it may be precipitated before. Nor will France alone be convulsed.

As the news of that old man's death, on the lightning's wing, spreads over Europe, the electric wire will prove but a train passing through repeated mines, which, one after the other, will explode with awful devastation. Berlin, Vienna and St. Petersburg, the strongholds of despotism in Europe, each will totter--all but the last will fall. The press is powerless on the Russian serf. Russia will be the tyrant's last citadel. Italy will throw off the Austrian yoke and be free. Gregory XVIII. will shortly die. A wise, far-seeing and benevolent priest, named Giovanni Maria Mastai Ferretti, born at Sinigaglia, and now a cardinal, with the title of SS. Peter and Marcellinus, will succeed to the Papal See, and Italy will be a republic; Genoa, Venice, Naples, Lombardy, Piedmont and Sardinia will be sister yet sovereign states, forming one union--the constellation of freedom, the favorite scheme of Napoleon's better days at last achieving reality. Switzerland, with her green hills and her field Morgarten, her priestly despots expelled, shall also be free. But I weary you, Messieurs."

"By no means," cried Marrast, cordially clasping M. Dantes by the hand. "I have listened in silence to your earnest exposition of the policy you suggest, and so truly do I subscribe to it that, henceforth, I am your disciple and adopt your motto, 'Wait and hope' for my own. But it is nearly two o'clock. In an hour the Chamber sits."

"And, meanwhile, Messieurs," interrupted M. Dantes, "I know not that we can better employ ourselves, after so protracted a seance, than to repair to Vefour's. This talking is hungry work, and listening and thinking, which are by far more tedious, are still more so. So to Vefour's."

"The seance 'National' is closed!" cried Ledru Rollin, laughing, as the whole company descended the gloomy stairs.

# CHAPTER XII.
# THE MYSTERIOUS PRIMA DONNA.

All fashionable Paris was excited over the announcement of a new prima donna, whose wonderful achievements in Italian opera had set even the exacting critics of Italy wild with enthusiasm and delight.

This great artiste was no other than the renowned Louise d'Armilly. She had never before sung in the presence of a Parisian audience, but her fame had preceded her, and it was accepted as certain that her triumph at the Academie Royale would be both instantaneous and overwhelming.

She was to assume the role of Lucrezia Borgia, in Donizetti's brilliant opera of that name, a role in which the enterprising director of the Academie Royale assured the expectant public that she possessed no equal.

For weeks every Parisian journal had been sounding her praises with unremitting zeal, and now her name was as familiar as a household word in all the high society salons, where the ladies and their gallants could talk of nothing but the approaching operatic event, while in the cafes and on the boulevards an equal degree of interest was exhibited.

Even the masses, notwithstanding the political agitation in which they were involved, had caught the prevailing excitement, and the leaders of the contending parties themselves paused amid their heated discussions to talk of Louise d'Armilly.

The career of this young and beautiful artiste had been remarkable. Her debut had been made at Brussels, about two years before, in company with her brother, M. Leon d'Armilly, and there, as well as at all the theatres of Italy, La Scala, Argentina and Valle, they had roused a perfect storm of operatic enthusiasm.

The origin of this young artiste was veiled in the deepest mystery. Rumor ascribed to her descent from one of the oldest and most respectable families of France; and domestic trials, among which was a matrimonial misadventure, no less than the arrest of an Italian Prince whom she was about to wed, on the bridal night, as an escaped galley slave, were assigned as the cause which had given her splendid powers to the stage.

At an earlier hour than usual--for Parisian fashion never fills the opera-house until the curtain falls on the second act--the Rue Lepelletier was crowded with carriages, La Pinon with fiacres, and the Grande Bateliere and the passages to the Boulevard des Italiens with persons on foot, all hastening toward that magnificent edifice, constructed within the space of a single year by Debret, to replace the building in the Rue de Richelieu ordered to be razed by the Government because of the assassination at its door of the Duke of Berri, in 1820--that magnificent structure which accommodates two thousand spectators with seats.

Among the first in the orchestra stalls were Beauchamp and Debray, whose attention was divided between the stage and the arrivals of splendidly attired elegantes in the different loges, during the overture. All the elite of Paris seemed on the qui vive.

"It will be a splendid house," observed Debray.

"The debutante, be she whom she may, should feel flattered by such an unexampled assemblage of all the ton of Paris."

Orchestra, balcony, galleries, amphitheatres, lobbies and parterre were packed; every portion of the vast edifice, in short, was thronged except a few of the loges and baignoires, into which every moment brilliant companies were entering.

"Who is that tall, dark military man, with the heavy moustache, now making his way into the Minister's box?" asked Beauchamp, after a pause.

"That man is no less a personage than the Governor of Algeria, Eugene Cavaignac, Marshal of Camp," said Debray. "He reported himself at the War Office this morning, and is the lion of the house."

"Ah!" cried the journalist; "and that is the hero of Constantine! What a frank, open countenance, and what a distingue bearing and manner!"

"You would not suppose all that man's life passed in a camp, would you?"

"His career has, I understand, been remarkable," said Beauchamp.

"Very. His father was a Conventionist of '92, a famous old fellow, who, among other terrible things laid at his door, is said to have pawned an old man's life, old Labodere, for his daughter's honor; somewhat, you remember, as Francis I. spared St. Valliar's life for the favor of the lovely Diana of Poitiers, his only child. His aged mother is yet living, a woman of strong mind, though seventy, and he does nothing without her advice. His brother Godefroi's name was notorious as that of a powerful Republican leader for years before his decease. At eighteen Eugene entered the Polytechnic School. At twenty-two he was a sub-lieutenant in the engineer corps of the second regiment. In '28 he was first lieutenant in France; in '29 he was captain; in '34 he was in Algeria; and, in '39, his cool, bold, decided but discreet conduct had made him chef de bataillon, despite the fact that he had incurred the Royal displeasure some years before by a disloyal toast at a banquet. In '40 he was lieutenant-colonel; in '41 marshal of camp, and first commander of division of Tlemeen; in '43, he was conqueror of Constantine, at the first siege of which I so nearly lost my own valuable head, and he is now Governor of Algeria, after service there of fourteen years."

"And the tall and sinewy man beside him, presenting such a contrast to Cavaig-nac, with his light complexion, gray hair, and sullen and not very intelligent ex-pression?"

"Oh! that is General Bugeaud, by some deemed the real conqueror of Algeria. But he's not at all popular with the army. His manners are simple and excessively blunt. He is a perfect despot with his staff, 'tis said; yet he is quite a wag when in good-humor, and, at Ministerial dinners, can unbend and make himself as agreeable as need be wished. His voice is as harsh as a Cossack's, and in perfect contrast to that of Cavaignac, which is the richest and most musical you ever heard, yet distinct, emphatic and impressive."

"Bugeaud incurred intense odium with the opposition for his unwarranted se-verity as jailor of the Duchess of Berri, in '34, and his killing Dulong in a duel, be-cause of a deserved taunt on the subject."

"Bugeaud did his duty," said the Secretary, "though a man of his nature could hardly perform such a duty with gentleness. Bugeaud is not a gentleman; he knows it, and don't try to seem one. He is only a soldier. But there comes his very par-ticular foe; General Lamoriciere. That magnificent woman on his arm is his wife and the sister of the lady who follows, with her husband, the ex-Minister, Adolphe Thiers."

"What a contrast!" cried Beauchamp. "The tall and elegant figure of Lamoric-iere, in his brilliant uniform of the Spahis, half oriental, half French, with his lovely wife, and the low, swarthy little ex-Minister in complete black, with his huge round spectacles on his nose nearly twice the size of his eyes, and a wife on his arm nearly double his stature. Why, Thiers reminds me of a Ghoul gallanting a Peri."

"And yet that same dark little ex-Minister has perhaps, in many respects the most powerful mind--at all events, the most available mind--impelled as it is by his restless ambition, in all France. Do you observe how incessantly his keen black eye flashes around the house, beneath his huge glasses?"

"He seems perfectly aware that every eye in the house is directed toward his loge. But is it true that his brother-in-law owes his rapid rise to his influence at Court?"

"By no means," replied Debray. "If there is a man in the French army who has achieved his own fortunes, that man is Lamoriciere. He went to Algeria a lieutenant, and bravely and gallantly has he attained his present brilliant position. It was he who proposed the creation of a corps of native Arab troops, like the Sepoys of British India; and he was appointed colonel of the first regiment of Spahis. Our quondam friend, Maximilian Morrel, has a command in this regiment, and is a protege of his illustrious exemplar."

"The hostility between Lamoriciere and Bugeaud arises, I suppose, from the latter's detestable disposition, his overbearing and dictatorial temper. Lamoriciere is not a man, I take it, to be the slave of any one."

"Rivalry in Africa is thought to have originated the feud," remarked Debray, "and political differences in Paris to have inflamed it. Bugeaud is a Legitimist, and Lamoriciere a Republican."

"Silence!" cried the musical connoisseurs in the orchestra. "The curtain rises."

As the curtain rose a hush of expectation reigned over the audience. The hum and bustle ceased, and silence most profound succeeded. The appearance of the fair cantatrice was the signal for such a reception as only a Parisian audience can give, and the first strains that issued from her lips assured them that their applause was not misplaced.

And surely never was the dark Duchess of Ferrara more faithfully personated than by the present artiste. This vraisemblance, which is so seldom witnessed in the opera, seemed to strike every eye. Her figure was tall and majestic, and voluptuously developed. Her air and bearing were haughty, dignified, and queen-like. Her complexion was very dark, but perfectly clear; her forehead broad and high; her brows heavy, but gracefully arched; her eyes large, black and flashing; her hair dark as night, and arranged with great simplicity in glossy bands; and her mouth large, but filled with teeth of pearl-like whiteness, contrasted by lips of coral wet with the spray. The entire outline of her face was Roman, and exhibited in its contour and lineaments even more than Roman sternness and decision; and its effect was still more heightened by a large mole at one corner of her mouth and the velvet robes in which she was appropriately costumed.

The scene between the Duchess and the Spaniard, Gubetta, was received with the utmost applause, and the pathos of that between the son and his unknown mother, which succeeded, touched the audience to tears; but when the maskers rushed in and her vizard was torn off, and her true name proclaimed, and, amid her heart-rending wailings, the curtain fell on the first act, the shouts were perfectly thunderous with enthusiasm. The role of Gennaro was performed by the brother of the cantatrice, Leon d'Armilly, a young man of twenty, of delicate and graceful figure, and as decidedly blonde as his sister was brunette. Nature seemed to have made a great mistake in sex when this brother and sister were fashioned. Indeed, it seemed hardly possible that they could be brother and sister, a remark constantly made by the audience, and the kindred announced on the bills was generally viewed as one of those convenient relationships often assumed on the stage, but having no more reality than those of the dramatis personae themselves.

"A second Pasta!" cried Chateau-Renaud, entering the stalls immediately on the descent of the curtain. "Heard you ever such a magnificent contralto?"

"Saw you ever such a magnificent bust?" asked Beauchamp.

"Were it not for a few manifest impossibilities," thoughtfully remarked Debray, "I should swear that this same angelic Louise d'Armilly was no other than a certain very beautiful, very eccentric and very talented young lady whom we all once knew as a star of Parisian fashion, and who, the last time she was in this house, sat in the same loge where now sit the African generals."

"Whom can you mean, Debray?" cried Beauchamp.

"A certain haughty young lady, who was to have married an Italian Prince, but, on the night of the bridal, in the midst of the festivities, the house being thronged with guests, and even while the contract was receiving the signatures, the Prince was arrested as an escaped galley-slave, and at his trial proved to be the illegitimate son of the bride's mother and a certain high legal functionary, the Procureur du Roi, now at Charenton, through whose burning zeal for justice the horrible discovery transpired."

"Ha!" exclaimed Chateau-Renaud. "You cannot mean Eugenie Danglars, daughter of the bankrupt baron, whom our unhappy friend Morcerf was once to have wed?"

"The very same," quietly rejoined the Secretary; "but this lady cannot be Mlle. Danglars, I say absolutely, for many sufficient reasons," he quickly added; then, as if to turn the conversation, he hastily remarked: "Ah! there are M. Dantes and M. Lamartine, as usual, together."

"M. Dantes!" exclaimed the Count, in surprise, looking around. "Impossible!"

"And yet most true," observed Beauchamp; "in the third loge from the Minister's to the right. What a wonderful resemblance there is between those men--the poet and the Deputy! One would suppose them brothers. The same tall and elegant figure, the same white and capacious brow, the same dark, blazing eye, the same raven hair, and, above all, the same most unearthly and spiritual pallor of complexion."

"No wonder M. Dantes is pale," said the Count. "Have you not heard of the occurrence of this evening in the Chamber? M. Dantes was in the midst of one of his powerful harangues against the Government, when suddenly, in the middle of a sentence, he stopped--coughed violently several times, and pressed his handkerchief to his mouth; then taking a small vial from his vest pocket, he placed it to his lips, and instantaneously, as if new life had entered him, proceeded more eloquently than ever to the conclusion of his speech."

"I heard something of this," said Beauchamp.

"As he descended from the tribune his friends thronged around him, anxious about his health. He quieted their apprehensions with his peculiar smile of assurance, but I observed that his white handkerchief was spotted with blood, and he almost immediately left the Chamber."

"That man will kill himself in the cause he has espoused," remarked Debray. "See how ghastly he now looks. But so much the better for the Ministry. He is a formidable foe. Indeed, that loge contains the two most powerful opponents of the Government."

"And who are those men just entering the box?" asked Beauchamp.

"None other than the two rival astronomers of Europe," said Debray, "and yet most intimate friends. The taller and elder, the one with gray hair, a dark, sharp Bedouin countenance, and that large, wild, black eye, with a smile of mingled sarcasm and humor ever on his thin lip, is Emanuel Arago. The other, the short, robust man, with fair complexion, sandy hair, bright blue eye and vivacious expression, is Le Verrier, the most tireless star-gazer science has produced since Galileo. But hush! the curtain is up."

"Oh! it matters not," said the Count; "only Gennaro and the Spaniard appear in the second act, and I have neither eyes nor ears save for the Duchess to-night. But who are those, Beauchamp?"

"Where?"

"In the loge on the first tier, next to the Minister's and directly opposite to that of M. Dantes?"

"Ah! two officers of the Spahis and two most exquisite women!" exclaimed Debray. "They belong, doubtless, to the African party in the Minister's loge. Your lorgnette, Count. What a splendid woman!"

Hardly had the Secretary raised the glass to his eyes before he dropped it with the exclamation:

"A miracle! a miracle!"

"What?" cried both of the other young men, turning to the box at which Debray was gazing.

"Messieurs, do you remember the fair Valentine de Villefort, whose untimely and mysterious demise all the young people of Paris so much bewailed, some two or three years ago, and whose lovely remains, we, with our own eyes, saw deposited in the Saint-Meran and de Villefort vault at Pere Lachaise, one bitter cold autumn evening, and there listened most patiently and piously to a whole breviary of mournful speeches, declarative of the said Valentine's most superlative excellence?"

"Undoubtedly, we remember it well," was the reply.

"Then behold, and never dare to doubt the reappearance of the dead again to the ocular organs of humanity."

"Valentine de Villefort!" exclaimed the Count, after a careful and scrutinizing survey, "by all that's supernatural; and more exquisitely lovely than ever!"

"Then it was true, after all, the strange story we heard," said Beauchamp, "of the young lady's resurrection and marriage to Maximilian Morrel, somewhere far away in parts unknown?"

"No doubt," replied the Count, "for, if I mistake not--and I'm sure I don't mistake, now that I look more closely--that stalwart, splendid fellow, with the broad forehead, black eyes and moustache, and the order of the Legion of Honor on his breast, to set off his rich uniform of the Spahis, and on whose arm the fair apparition is leaning, is no other than Maximilian Morrel himself--the identical man who saved my worthless neck from a yataghan in Algeria."

"How dark he's grown!" said Debray.

"No more so than all these African heroes--for instance, Cavaignac and Lamoriciere."

"But what a splendid contrast there is between the young Colonel of the Spahis and his lovely bride, if such she be! He, dark as a Corsican; she, fair as an English-woman--he, upright as a poplar; she, drooping like a willow--his hair and eyes black as midnight, while her soft, languishing orbs are as blue as the summer sky, and her glossy ringlets as brown as a chestnut!"

"On my word," said Beauchamp, "the Count grows poetical! Morrel had better keep his beautiful wife out of the way! But have you discovered who are the other couple in the box?" he added to the Secretary, who had his lorgnette in most vigilant requisition. "Any more discoveries, Debray?"

A sigh might have been heard as the Secretary took his glass from his eye, and replied simply:

"Yes."

"And who now?" asked Chateau-Renaud. "There seems no end to discoveries to-night."

"The young man who, by his decorations, seems a chef de bataillon of the Spahis," replied Debray, "I cannot make out. But, be he whom he may, he is effectually disguised from his most intimate friends by his luxuriant beard and moustache. As for the lady--there is but one woman in the world I have ever had the good fortune to behold who could be mistaken for her."

"And that is?" said Beauchamp.

"Herself."

"And who is herself, Lucien?" asked Chateau-Renaud.

"Have you forgotten the Countess de Morcerf?"

"The Countess de Morcerf?--the wife of the general who was convicted by the peers of felony, treason and outrage in the matter of Ali Tebelen, Pacha of Yanina?" said Beauchamp.

"And who blew his brains out in despair?" added the Count.

"The same," said Debray. "She returned to Marseilles with her son Albert. You remember Albert and his strange conduct in the duel with the Count of Monte-Cristo?"

"One could hardly forget such chivalric generosity, such magnificent magnanimity and such sublime self-control as were exhibited by the young man on that occasion!" said Beauchamp. "It is to be hoped he was not equally forbearing toward the Arabs in his African campaigns, although, as his name has never been seen or heard since he entered the army, in all probability he was."

"Well, well," cried the Secretary, impatiently, "the Countess retired to Marseilles, and there she is said to have resided in utter seclusion, in company only with Morrel's beautiful wife, devoting the vast wealth of the deceased Count to philanthropic objects, having received it, as his widow, only with the understanding it should be thus bestowed."

"But the rumor was," said Beauchamp, "and indeed I was so assured by M. de Boville himself, Receiver-General of the Hospitals, at the time, that the Countess gave all the Count's fortune to the hospitals, and that he himself registered the deed of gift."

"Oh! that was only some twelve or thirteen hundred thousand francs," said Debray. "Three months after her settlement at Marseilles, in a small house in the Allees de Meillan, said to be her own by maternal inheritance, a letter came to her from Thomson and French, of Rome, stating that there was a deposit in their house, to the credit of the estate of the late Count, of the enormous sum of two millions of francs, subject to her sole control and order, as the Count's only heir, in the absence of his son."

"Two millions of francs!" cried the two young men in a breath.

"Even so, Messieurs," said Debray. "The story does sound rather oriental; but I have reason to know that it is entirely true, for I made diligent inquiry about it when last at Marseilles."

"And what took you to Marseilles, Lucien?" asked the Count significantly.

"The Ministry," replied Debray, with evident confusion, coloring deeply.

"But why does not the Countess marry again?" asked Chateau-Renaud, surveying her faultless form and face through his glass. "In the prime of life, rich, and, despite her past troubles, most exquisitely beautiful, it is strange she don't make herself and some one else happy!"

"Especially as no one could ever accuse her of having very desperately loved her dear first husband," added the journalist. "Why don't she marry, Lucien?"

"How the devil should I know!" replied the Secretary in great confusion. "You don't suppose I ever asked her the question, do you?"

"Upon my word," exclaimed the Count, laughing, "I shall begin to think you have, if you take it so warmly. But, hist! the bell! The curtain rises. We mustn't lose the third act of Donizetti's chef d'oeuvre, with such a Lucrezia, for any woman living."

But it was very evident that much of the magnificent performance of the debutante and her companion, in the thrilling scene between the Duke and Duchess of Ferrara and the young Captain Gennaro, was lost to the Secretary.

"Do you observe, Beauchamp, how strangely fascinated with the new cantatrice seems the young officer of the Spahis who accompanies the Countess?" he whispered. "Do but look. He sits like one transfixed."

"And the Countess seems transfixed also, though not by the same object," was the reply. "How excessively pale, yet how beautiful she is! That plain black dress, without ornament or jewel, and her raven hair, parted simply on her forehead, enhance her voluptuous charms infinitely more than could the most gorgeous costume. Heavens! what a happy man will he be who can call her his!"

"Amen!" said Debray, and the word seemed to rise from the very depths of his heart. "But she will never marry. Some early disappointment, even before her union with Morcerf, has withered her heart, and the terrible divorce which parted her from him, although she never loved him, will keep her single forever. Her first and only love is either dead or--worse--married to another."

"See, see, Lucien!" cried Beauchamp, hurriedly; "at whom does she gaze so intently, and yet so sadly? It cannot be Lamartine, for there sits his lovely young English wife at his side; nor can it be old Arago, nor young Le Verrier; and yet some one in that box it surely is."

"M. Dantes?" cried Debray.

"Impossible! That man seems hardly conscious that there are such beings as women. His whole soul is in affairs of state."

"His whole soul seems somewhere else just at present," exclaimed the Secretary, bitterly. "Look!"

"How dreadfully pale he is!" said Beauchamp; "and yet his eyes fairly blaze. Is it the Countess he gazes at?"

"Is it M. Dantes she gazes at?"

At that moment, amid the wild farewell of the mother to her son, upon the stage, the curtain came down, and at the same instant, M. Dantes hastily pressed his white handkerchief to his lips, and, leaning on the arms of Lamartine and Arago, hastily left the box.

"Ha! the Countess faints!" cried Debray, as the door closed on M. Dantes. "Do they know each other, then?"

# CHAPTER XIII.
# THE ITALIAN LOVER.

It was early in the evening succeeding the day on which M. Dantes had answered Giovanni Massetti's letter. Zuleika was seated in the vast, sumptuously-furnished salon of the magnificent Morcerf mansion, now, as the reader already knows, the residence of the famous and mysterious Deputy from Marseilles. She sat upon a superb green velvet-covered sofa, half reclining in an indolent, picturesque attitude; behind the sofa and leaning over its back stood a young Italian, a perfect model of manly beauty; his ardent black eyes were riveted on Zuleika's blushing countenance with a look of the most profound and enthusiastic adoration, while his hand held the young girl's with a gentle, loving pressure, which was returned with unmistakable warmth. The apartment was dimly lighted and huge, sombre patches of shadow lay everywhere. Zuleika and her lover were alone together; for some time they seemed too full of happiness to speak, but finally Giovanni said, in a soft, flutelike whisper, as if unwilling to break with loudly uttered words the delicious spell of his love-dream:

"Zuleika, darling Zuleika, so you did not once forget me during our long, cruel separation?"

"Never for a single instant, Giovanni," answered the young girl, the flush upon her cheek deepening as she spoke, her hand tightening about her lover's and her lovely eyes filling with a soft fire. "But I sometimes feared you had forgotten me!"

"You were always present in my mind and in my heart," replied the Italian in a tone that thrilled her through and through. Stooping, he placed his lips to her forehead and imprinted upon it a long and silent kiss; then, flushing in his turn, he added, still holding his head against hers: "From the very moment of our first meeting you have reigned in my bosom, my own, my love, the queen of my destiny and my life!"

"Oh! Giovanni, Giovanni," murmured the young girl, "I am happy, so happy!"

He kissed her again, this time upon her upturned lips that with a slight movement almost imperceptibly returned the kiss, sending his blood tingling through his veins and causing him to tremble with delight from head to foot. No longer able to restrain himself, he hastily quitted the back of the sofa, threw himself down beside her and clasping her in his arms drew her unresistingly upon his bosom. Once there she did not offer to stir, but even nestled closer to him and pillowed her head on his broad shoulder. The tumultuous beating of both their hearts was audible amid the unbroken silence that ensued. With one hand the Viscount tenderly smoothed her silken tresses, and his arm tightened around her waist as if he had determined never to release her again.

"Your father, in his letter of this morning," said Giovanni finally, "told me there was hope, that you did not look upon my addresses with aversion, and that I had his leave to pay court to you and ascertain your wishes from your own dear lips. I hastened here this evening, and M. Dantes himself bade me seek you in this salon. I came on the wings of love and found all my fondest hopes realized; that I possessed your heart as you possessed mine. Oh! tell me, Zuleika, that this is not all a dream, for it seems too delicious to be true!"

"It is reality, Giovanni, blessed reality," answered the young girl in a low voice.

"And do you really love me with all your soul?"

"With all my soul, Giovanni!"

The ardent Italian showered a flood of burning kisses upon her forehead, cheeks and lips, and she quivered like a leaf in his embrace. Then he said, with a shade of anxiety in his tone:

"And your brother Esperance, is he disposed to look upon me with approval? You know that in Rome he did not see fit to include me in the number of his friends. We had a little difference, you will remember, and ever afterwards he was cold toward me."

Zuleika shuddered as she recalled the fact that the little difference alluded to had been a violent quarrel that had nearly resulted in a duel between the two young men. She had never known the details, for both her brother and Giovanni had studiously concealed them from her; indeed, Esperance had carefully avoided all mention of the Viscount's name ever since the day they had become embroiled. Was M. Dantes aware of the trouble between his son and the youthful Italian? She did not know, but, at the same time, felt firmly persuaded that her father had fully investigated the doings, character and family of her suitor, and would not have sanctioned a renewal of his addresses to her had he not been perfectly satisfied in every respect. She, therefore, answered:

"I am altogether ignorant as to what Esperance thinks of you, and cannot say whether he still harbors resentment against you or not; but, whatever may be his opinion and feelings, rest assured that he will never interfere to cause his sister an instant of unhappiness, more especially as he knows that my father looks upon you with a favoring eye."

"But how about the coldness existing between us?"

"Does it still exist on both sides?"

"Not on mine, Zuleika, not on mine. I forgave and forgot all long ago."

"Forgave and forgot! Then Esperance must have wronged you!"

"He did, Zuleika, and with the proverbial hot blood and headlong impulses of the Roman youth I resented that wrong. But I could not remain at enmity with the brother of the girl I loved, so when I became cooler I sought him out and endeavored to apologize."

"And he accepted your apology?"

"He did not accept it, but turned on his heel and left me without a word. He evidently thought me a coward and attributed my efforts toward effecting a reconciliation to a desire to escape fighting him."

"But why did you quarrel in the first place? What was the cause of the difference between you?"

The young Italian hung his head and did not answer. Zuleika saw that he had grown deadly pale, and she felt his hand tremble nervously.

Freeing herself from his embrace, the young girl sprang to her feet and faced him.

"Giovanni," said she, firmly, "tell me the whole story of this painful affair. It is imperative that I should know it!"

"Do you doubt me, Zuleika, do you doubt me?" he asked, bitterly, and he buried his face in his hands.

"Do I doubt you, Giovanni? No. But, if you love me, tell me all the details of the trouble between my brother and yourself!"

"I cannot, I cannot, Zuleika!" he cried. "Command me to shed the last drop of blood in my veins for you and I will do it without an instant's hesitation, but I cannot tell you that terrible tale of deceit, treachery and bloodshed!"

He had arisen and was walking excitedly about the salon; his pallor had increased and he trembled in every limb.

Zuleika stood with folded arms and gazed at him; she was calm and her eyes had a look of determination the young man had never before beheld in them; it filled him with dismay. A few moments ago she had been all love and tenderness, a yielding, trusting maiden in her lover's arms; now, she resembled a beautiful Amazon bent on achieving a victory, whom nothing but unconditional surrender would satisfy.

"The story, the story," she repeated, "tell me the story!"

Her face was as white as marble and her faultless lips seemed chiseled from stone. She looked so beautiful and tempting as she stood there, her surpassing loveliness enhanced by the picturesque half-oriental, half-Parisian dress she wore, that the Viscount felt his passion for her redoubled. He flung himself at her feet and seizing the hem of her superb robe kissed it rapturously.

"Oh! Zuleika, Zuleika," he cried, utterly unable to restrain himself, "I am your slave! Place your tiny foot upon my neck and crush me where I lie! I shall expire adoring you!"

"Giovanni," replied Zuleika, greatly moved by this display of devotion, "rise and be a man!"

The Italian sprang up as if he had been struck by a thunderbolt; then he endeavored to clasp her in his arms, but she quietly repulsed him.

"Zuleika," cried he, sadly, "you do not love me; you never loved me; I have been the victim of a cruel deception!"

"If you think so," answered the young girl, quietly, "there is but one course you can pursue as a man of honor--spurn the deceiver from you and never look upon her face again!"

The young man gazed at her reproachfully.

"What have I done to turn you thus against me?" he asked, his tone suddenly becoming humble.

"What have you done? You refuse to reveal this mystery to me, which, as you yourself admit, involves deceit, treachery and bloodshed, and which, for aught I know, has set an indelible stain upon your life! I love you truly, love you with all the passion of a woman's nature, but I must know this history that I may judge whether you are worthy of my love!"

"I assure you, Zuleika, that there is no stain upon my life, that there is nothing in this history that tends in the least to dishonor me, but still I cannot speak."

"Then we must separate."

"Oh! Zuleika, Zuleika, do not be pitiless! You will drive me mad!"

The young girl touched a bell and Ali, the Nubian, appeared.

"Monsieur is about taking his departure," said she to the faithful servant. "I leave him in your hands."

And without a word of farewell to Giovanni, she swept from the salon like a queen.

The Viscount gazed after her with indescribable sadness pictured upon his handsome countenance. Then he followed Ali, put on his overcoat and hat and regretfully left the house.

# CHAPTER XIV.
# THE MINUTE VIALS.

Even to the Communists, with whom he had come into such close contact, M. Dantes, the Deputy from Marseilles, remained as much of a mystery as ever. Marrast, though now devotedly attached to him, admitted that he was totally unable to fathom either his designs, or his methods of accomplishing them, while Lamartine, who was in his company a large portion of the time, when questioned concerning him, replied that all he knew of M. Dantes was that he was a firm friend of the cause and an untiring worker in the interest of the weary and oppressed masses.

Debray, though he had no tangible foundation for it, could not get rid of the idea that the dangerous Deputy and the Count of Monte-Cristo were one and the same individual, but Beauchamp, with the usual incredulity of journalists, scoffed at the notion, and Chateau-Renaud derided it whenever it was mentioned in his presence.

That M. Dantes had great wealth was, however, generally admitted, though whence it was derived or in what manner it was invested no one could tell. It was now no longer a secret that he had purchased and resided in the magnificent mansion formerly owned by the Count de Morcerf, in the Rue du Helder, and this circumstance, while it vastly augmented the interest attaching to him, did not in the least detract from the enthusiasm felt for him by the working classes.

It was night. In a large chamber, richly furnished, but dimly lighted, in the mansion in the Rue du Helder, the same apartment once inhabited by the Countess de Morcerf, motionless, and seemingly lifeless, with a countenance as pale as alabaster, and as still, lay M. Dantes, the Deputy from Marseilles. Although, in the ashy pallor of the lips and brow, and the fixed, serene, almost stern aspect of the immovable face, might be read unmistakable evidence of an exhausting and dangerous constitutional shock to the system, yet none of that emaciation, over which broods the shadow of the angel of death, resulting from protracted illness, was there to be seen. The broad white forehead--the raven hair, sparsely sprinkled with silver--the round temples--the delicately penciled brow, encircling, like a sable arch, the large and almond-formed eye--the full calm lip, and the chiseled chin and nostril--all these were as perfect now as when last before the reader. The cheek was, perhaps, slightly sunken, but it could not be more pallid than when last beheld; and but for that nameless quietude--that "rapture of repose," as Lord Byron well expresses it--that placid languor which sleeps on the features, which illness always creates and which spiritualizes and intellectualizes the most common features, the invalid might be supposed to be enjoying the most quiet slumber.

Excepting the invalid, there was no one in that chamber save the faithful Ali, who moved noiselessly about, from time to time, or sat immovably upon the floor and gazed on his master's pallid face.

As the silvery tones of the chamber clock tinkled forth the third quarter after ten, the door opened, and a small, dark, thin man, with large whiskers, keen, penetrating eyes, broad, bald forehead, thinly covered with gray hair, and apparently about fifty years of age, briskly entered. It was Dr. Orfila, a name somewhat known in medical science. Approaching the bed, he placed his fingers upon the sick man's pulse, and gazed earnestly on his face for some time in silence.

"Strange!" he at length muttered; "the most powerful drugs in the most un-heard-of quantities are powerless! Who, then, is this man, whose nature so differs from that of every one else? Can he so have accustomed his system to poisons, that, as with the King of Pontus, they are ineffectual to help or to harm him? His constitution must be iron! The vitality of a dozen men is in him, or he'd have been dead a month ago. Well, it's plain he's no worse, if he's no better. Drugs are useless, and he must be left to nature and his amazing constitution. This stupor, this utter death of all the faculties and senses for so long a time, is wonderful. Fever, delirium, anything but this death-like trance. It seems as if this man had been sleepless all his life before, and that now his overwrought brain and heart were compensating themselves for the toil and wakefulness of years. Could I but excite the nerves!"

For some time the physician gazed in deep thought at the pale face of the un-conscious slumberer. Suddenly turning to the Nubian, he said to him:

"Ali, where does your master keep the drugs he has been for years accustomed to take?"

The Nubian stared in mute amazement, but moved not from his rug.

"Ali," said Dr. Orfila, sternly, "unless I see and know those drugs, this night your master dies."

The Nubian looked anxiously into the face of the physician, and then, as if satisfied with the scrutiny, rose, and, with noiseless steps, left the room. In a few moments he re-entered and placed in the physician's hands a small casket of ebony, exquisitely worked and studded with gems. Taking it hastily to the shaded lamp upon a table at the extremity of the chamber, he attempted to open it, but his at-tempts were vain. Indeed, to all appearances, it was a solid block of ebony, and its extreme heaviness, compared with its dimensions, seemed to favor the idea.

"Well?" said the doctor, returning the casket, after a close scrutiny, to the Nu-bian, who had followed him.

Ali took the casket, and instantly a portion of the top flew up, disclosing within the centre of the cube of ebony a cavity lined with crimson velvet, and a dazzling array of minute vials of crystal, each filled with a fluid--pink, blue, green and yellow in hue, while the contents of several were colorless. The Nubian had touched a spring concealed in the carving, and known only to his master and himself.

The physician removed the minute vials one after another from their receptacles, and held them up to the light; on each was a cipher, and on no two was the same. Most of them were quite filled with the fluid contained, but some were only half full, while one was nearly empty. Dr. Orfila looked closely at the cipher upon each vial as he removed it from the casket. He then held it to the light to determine its particular hue or shade, and sometimes withdrew the crystal stopper ground into the deep mouth, touching it cautiously and quickly to his nostril or the tip of his tongue. "Morphia, cinchonia, quinia, lobelia, belladonna, narcotina, bromine, arsenicum, strychnos colubrina, brucoea ferruginea," muttered the savant, as he examined one vial after the other and replaced it. "Brucoea ferruginea--ha! brucine! I thought as much," exclaimed he, holding up the vial, which showed, by being nearly empty, that its contents had been used more frequently than those of any of the others.

"How many drops of this is the greatest number your master has ever taken?" asked Dr. Orfila.

The Nubian, who, it will be remembered, was a mute, held up both hands with the fingers outspread, and then two other fingers of one of his hands.

"Twelve drops!" cried the astonished physician. "Impossible!"

Ali insisted on the assertion.

"And yet it must be so," the doctor added. "That would explain all."

Taking the vial and a minute crystal vessel, which he found in the casket, he hastily but carefully dropped into the latter thirteen drops. Then filling the vessel with water, he approached the patient, who still slumbered heavily on, and placed it to his lips. For an instant he seemed conscious of the wish of the physician, and with an effort the mixture was swallowed. Then he lay as still and motionless as before.

Returning the vials and the vessel to their places, Dr. Orfila closed the casket and gave it to the Nubian. He then gazed long and anxiously at the torpid slumberer, standing at the bedside and watching that marble face.

At length the clock struck eleven. Dr. Orfila started and hastily glanced at his repeater; then, turning to the Nubian, who had carried away the casket, and, having noiselessly returned, stood silently beside him, he said:

"Ali, in one hour your master will be in high fever; in two hours he will, probably, be delirious. He will then sleep soundly, and toward morning will wake, I hope, in his right mind, but terribly exhausted and profusely perspiring. At daylight I shall be here. You must not leave him for a single instant as you value his life."

The Nubian clasped his hands above his head and bent his forehead almost to the floor.

"If you think necessary, however, Ali, send for me before morning."

The physician gave one more look at his patient, pressed his fingers on his pulse, placed his palm on his forehead, and then, taking his hat and cane, left the chamber.

# CHAPTER XV.
# THE UNKNOWN NURSE.

When the rumor that M. Dantes had been taken seriously ill was first circulated throughout Paris, it caused excitement in every quarter of the city, filling the Communists and workmen with dismay and greatly elating their opponents.

In the midst of the excitement a strange lady, very plainly attired, but whose language and bearing gave unmistakable evidence of refinement and aristocratic associations, made her appearance one morning at the office of Dr. Orfila and humbly asked permission to nurse his distinguished patient. The physician, somewhat surprised at such a request from such a woman, immediately grew suspicious and demanded an explanation, when the lady informed him that she had known the sick man in his youth and was still deeply interested in his welfare. She refused to give her name, but solemnly assured the doctor that, should he grant her petition, M. Dantes on his recovery would be ready to thank him on bended knees.

Convinced at length that no harm was intended, the physician gave his permission and the unknown lady was duly installed as nurse. She discharged her duties with unflagging devotion and energy, satisfying even the exacting Nubian, with whom she divided the watch at the bedside of the unconscious deputy. Dr. Orfila was delighted, while Esperance and Zuleika were overjoyed.

On--on--the sleeper still slumbered on! One--two--three--four quarters after eleven tinkled in silvery numbers upon the delicate bell of the clock, yet the closed eyelids and fixed lips moved not, gave no sign; but for the light, though regular undulation of the chest, life itself might seem to have fled forever. Yet life was still there!

How strange the bond which connects vitality with consciousness--the body with the soul! And yet more strange is that phase of existence in which the one moves on without the other. The mind sometimes is all life when the body is dead, and oftener still is the body all life when the mind seems gone. Mind, too, may frequently act independently, not only of the body, as in dreams, but, also, of consciousness and of the heart; while the body, as in somnambulism, may act altogether alone.

On--on--the slumberer breathed on, but he thought not, felt not, perceived not. A revolution, an earthquake might heave around him, but the convulsive throes of man or of nature would have been as nothing to him. The brow would have remained as calm and as cold, and the cheek as pale and as still, while, in all human probability, the faithful Nubian would have sat as immovable upon his rug at the bedside of his beloved master, and have gazed upon him as untiringly with his dark and sleepless eye.

As the last quarter after eleven sounded, followed immediately by the hour of midnight, a small door beside the bed noiselessly opened, and a female figure in white silently entered the room; but not so noiselessly was the entrance effected as to escape the ear of the vigilant Ali. He glanced hurriedly around; then, as if familiar with the apparition, and anticipating its approach, he rose, and, taking his rug to the further extremity of the chamber, again laid himself down, like a faithful dog, though not now to watch.

Meanwhile the lady, quietly approaching the bed, gazed long and mournfully at the slumberer's pale yet noble visage; then, kneeling, she buried her face in her hands amid the coverings.

She was, probably, forty; yet, in the full and faultless perfection of her form--in her graceful and yielding motions--in her statuesque bust, rounded cheek and night-black hair, she would, to the casual observer, have indicated hardly the half of that age. Her figure was tall and dignified, yet mobile as a willow; her eyes were dark and luminous, and, in their profound depths, slept a world of melancholy meaning. Her hair was simply parted on a broad forehead, and was gathered in heavy masses low on the neck. Her lips were full and red, and, when parted, exhibited teeth of dazzling whiteness, while her complexion, which was very dark, was yet clear and pure as the hue of the magnolia's petal. But that face was pale, very pale, almost as colorless as that of the quiet sleeper at its side, and upon it rested an expression of love unutterable, mingled with the sadness of death.

Such was the unknown nurse, the Countess de Morcerf, as she again was an inmate of that apartment of which she had once, under circumstances how different, been mistress; such was Mercedes, the Catalane of Marseilles, again at the side of the man whom all her life she had loved, with none to gainsay or forbid!

Upon that pale and motionless countenance she gazed long and deeply, and, oh! the world of memory that passed through her mind!--the world of thought and feeling that centred in that fixed gaze! At length, clasping her hands upon her forehead, her eyes streaming with tears, she bowed her face upon the bed, from which she had just raised it, and long seemed absorbed in prayer.

Roused from this position by some movement of the slumberer, she started up and watched him.

The shaded rays of the dim and distant lamp threw a faint glimmering of light upon the pale countenance, but the quick eye of love instantaneously detected a change. A slight flush was mounting the cheek, and gentle perspiration was distilling upon the brow, while a smile played on the mouth. Suddenly, as she gazed, those pallid lips moved. Astonished, she listened.

"Marseilles! beautiful Marseilles!" said the sleeper. "Home of my boyhood, home of my heart. I come!" Then quickly and sternly came the order, "Let go the anchor--furl the sails--mate, take charge of the ship!" Then the tones changed, and a joyful light shot over the face as the lips exclaimed, "Now for my father! now for my love! Mercedes! Mercedes!"

Amazed, the fair watcher retained her position, and gazed and listened so silently and breathlessly that the quick and audible beatings of her heart might have been numbered.

"Mine--mine at last!" continued the dreamer. "The marriage-feast--the marriage-feast!" But instantly the expression of the voice and the countenance altered.

The light of joy was shrouded in clouds. "Arrest--arrest me?" was the exclamation--"me! at my marriage-feast! A dungeon for me! Mercedes! Mercedes! My love--my wife! Oh! God! it is the Chateau d'If! Despair--despair!"

Shocked, terrified at the terrible energy of these words, and the expression of unutterable woe that rested on the countenance of the sleeper, the affrighted woman, who comprehended but too well the fearful significance of the abrupt and disjointed syllables, hastily arose as if to rouse the slumberer from his dream or to call on the Nubian for aid.

But, before she could carry the purpose into execution, the aspect of the Deputy's visage again had changed. A dark frown settled on the brow, a spirit of fixed resolve contracted the firm lip and dilated the nostril, and the word, "Vengeance--vengeance!" in whispers scarcely audible, but repeatedly and rapidly pronounced, was heard.

A longer silence than before succeeded. At length another change swept over the face, and the words, "Free--free--I am free!" burst from the lips; then they murmured, "Treasure untold! wondrous wealth!--diamonds--pearls--rubies--ingots of gold! The mad abbe's dream was reality!" Again the countenance darkened. "Fourteen years in a dungeon for no crime!--a father dead of starvation!--a bride the bride of the fiend who has done all this--and he a peer of France--and his friends a millionaire of Paris and the Procureur du Roi! Vengeance--vengeance--vengeance!" There was a pause, and the dreamer exultingly continued, "It is done! The peer of France is a disgraced suicide! The Procureur du Roi is a madman! The banker is a bankrupt!" The dreamer again paused, and his countenance once more changed. "Alas! alas! man is not God! 'Vengeance is mine, I will repay, saith the Lord!' The innocent suffer with the guilty. To avenge a wrong has been sacrificed a life, and only misery has been the recompense! No more--no more--no more of this! Man and man's happiness be henceforth the aim! To that be devoted wealth untold!"

The lips ceased to move. Gradually the high excitement of the features passed away and was succeeded by an expression of sadness and love. "Haydee--gone--gone to a better world. Mercedes--Mercedes--oh! does she love me yet? The long lost idol of my heart!--the adored angel of my life!--come! come! come!"

As the dreamer spoke, he spread wide his arms; when his eyes opened, and his long slumbering senses returned, Mercedes, his own Mercedes, was, indeed, clasped to his breast.

"Mercedes! Mercedes?" he faintly whispered. "Ah! it was no dream, for you are, indeed, beside me and mine--mine forever!"

"Thine--thine--forever!" was the reply, and she clasped his feeble form to her heart as she would have clasped that of a child.

# CHAPTER XVI.
# A NOTABLE FETE.

On the night of Monday, February 21st, 1848, all Paris was at the house of M. Gaultier de Rumilly, in the Avenue des Champs Elysees. M. Gaultier de Rumilly was well known as one of the leaders of the extreme left, though the confidential friend of M. Odillon Barrot, and the fete was perfectly understood to be a political reunion, rather than a social one. All the accompaniments of the most splendid society events of the season were in requisition. Even the brilliant balls given by the opulent citizens of New York were eclipsed in luxury and splendor. There was the streaming of lamps and chandeliers, the swell of enchanting music, the whirl of the fascinating polka, redowa or mazurka, while throngs of richly attired and lovely women were constantly enhancing the magnificence of the scene by their arrival. The brilliancy of the occasion was also richly diversified by the presence of an unusually large number of officers of the Municipal and National Guards in full uniform, as well as of several belonging to the Line or the regiments of Algeria.

It was about ten o'clock. Within, all was light, life and loveliness; without, the winter wind moaned drearily through the leafless trees of the Boulevard, and the drifting sleet swept along the deserted streets. It was a wild night. Throughout all Paris seemed going forth a portentous murmur, like that mysterious moaning of the ocean, which, with mariners, is the prelude of a storm. An ominous whispering, as of many voices, seemed to sink and swell on the sweeping night blast; then all was still. Again, in the distance, would rise a sharp shout, or the stern, brief word of military command. At intervals, also, one might imagine he heard a deep rumbling, as of heavy ordnance and its tumbrels over the pavements, accompanied by the measured tread of armed men and the clattering hoofs of cavalry horses. Then these sounds died away, and along the narrow streets of Paris again the night wind only swept, the bitter blast howled and the ominous whispering, as of spirits, rose and fell.

It was a strange and stormy night--murky and chilly--while at intervals the cold rain dashed down in cutting blasts. But within the magnificent mansion of Gaultier de Rumilly all was light and loveliness, as has been said. The splendid salons were already thronged, yet crowds of richly-attired guests were constantly arriving.

"Ha! Beauchamp, just come?" cried Chateau-Renaud to his friend, as he entered.

"By the grace of God, yes!" said the journalist. "What a night!"

"What a throng of men and women say rather!" was the reply.

"Very true. Who's here?"

"Ask who's not here, and your question may be easily answered. All Paris is here! Women of every age and station, and men of all political creeds--Conservatives, Dynastics, Legitimists, Republicans and Communists. Indeed, this soiree seems to me, and I shouldn't wonder if it were designed so to be, a general reunion of the leaders of all the great parties in France, to compare notes and learn the news."

"And there is news enough to learn, it would seem. Is M. Dantes here?"

"He is, or was, and his beautiful wife, too, the most magnificent woman in Paris. Morrel also is here with his fair bride."

"And who is that dark, dignified man in the Turkish costume, around whom the ladies have clustered so inquisitively?" asked the Deputy.

"Why, that's the Emir of Algeria, the famous captive of the Duke d'Aumale," was the reply.

"What! Abd-el-Kader! How comes he here?"

"Oh! as a special favor, I suppose; he has a respite from his sad prison."

"What a splendid beard, and what keen black eyes!"

"No, his eyes are decidedly gray, but so shaded by his extraordinary lashes that they seem black. They say that he was more distinguished as a scholar, in Algeria, than as a soldier, statesman or priest. In fact, he is as erudite as an Arab can be, and his library, which is contained in two leathern trunks, accompanied him in all his wanderings prior to his submission."

"And what think you really induced him to surrender himself?"

"Policy of the deepest character, and worthy of Talleyrand, Metternich or Nesselrode, if we are to rely on the eloquent speech of Lamoriciere in the Chamber, the other day."

"I remember. Bugeaud spoke first, and Lamoriciere followed. He thought that the Arab Curtius leaped into the gulf because, by so doing, he was convinced he could injure French interests more than by his freedom. Well, perhaps he was right. He bids fair to be a hard bone of contention between the opposition and the Ministry."

"If I mistake not, Lamoriciere disclaimed all responsibility for accepting the surrender, and placed it on the Governor-General, the young Duke, for whom the Ministry is liable?"

"Yes; and Guizot announced that he would send the Emir back to Alexandria, could security be given against his return to Algeria."

"As to the Emir's surrender, at which you wonder, the real cause is said to have been not policy, but the universal passion--love."

"He is an Antony, then, instead of a Curtius."

"So it seems. At the moment when, with incredible efforts, he had effected the passage of the Moorish camp, and was off like an ostrich for the desert, the firing of the French, who had reached his deira, struck his ear. Back he flew like the lamiel. Twice his horse fell under him dead--twice he was surrounded and seized, and twice, by his wonderful agility, he regained his freedom. At last, perceiving that all was lost, he turned his face again toward the desert, and, for two days and nights, continued his flight. But his heart was behind him. Certain of escape himself, he preferred hopeless captivity with her he loved, and he returned."

"Quite poetical, on my word! Worthy of Sadi, the Arab Petrarch, himself!" said Chateau-Renaud.

"He is decidedly a great man, that Abd-el-Kader. They say he bears his misfortunes like a philosopher--or, better, a Turk--unalterably mild and dignified, while his wives and his mother wail at his feet. Every morning he reads the Koran to them, and during the orisons all the windows are open, and a large fire blazes in the centre of the room."

"He is a decided godsend to the quidnuncs of Paris."

"So would be a Hottentot, or a North American savage," replied Beauchamp.

"Rather a different affair this from the Ministerial soiree a week ago, I fancy," remarked the editor.

"Rather. I will confess to you, Beauchamp, I attended that soiree from curiosity to see whether M. Guizot retained his habitual placidity of manner amid the clouds every day thickening around him."

"And what was the result?"

"Why, this. He was as polite and courteous as ever, and the same cold, imperturbable smile was on his thin lip; but he looked careworn, and upon his countenance was an expression of solicitude, when it was closely watched, which I never saw there before. Ah, Beauchamp, I envy not the Premier!"

"And the guests?" asked the journalist.

"Of guests there were but few; and the spacious salons of the Hotel des Affaires Etrangeres looked dismal and deserted."

"The lovely Countess Leven--"

"Even she was absent."

"And the Countess of Dino?"

"Absent, too."

"The soiree must have been, indeed, dull without those 'charming queens of intrigue,' as Louis Blanc courteously calls them. But tell me, Count, is the Minister really the husband of the beautiful Leven, or is she only his par amours?"

"No one knows. It is certain, however, that the great man devotes to the enchantress every moment he can steal from the State, though to look at him one would hardly suppose him a lover, in any meaning of the term. But who knows? To read his writings can one imagine a purer man? But, then, the affairs of Gisquet, Cubieres, Teste, and, last and worst, Petit, whose case was before the Chamber, do they not betray deplorable lack of firmness or morality? But no more of this. Who is that dark, splendid woman to whom young Joliette seems so devoted? I have seen them together before!"

"Why, you surely have not forgotten Louise d'Armilly, the charming cantatrice! She has recently left the boards, to the irreparable loss of the opera, having come into possession of an immense inheritance--some millions, it is said, left by her father, who was once a banker of Paris. She is asserted to be very accomplished and very ambitious, and, as the young African paladin is thoroughly bewitched by her, and she by him, they will, doubtless, be matched as well as paired."

"Has Lucien been here?" asked the Deputy, after a pause, during which the young men surveyed the brilliant throngs that passed before them and returned the salutations of their acquaintances.

"I think not. We have not met, at least," replied the journalist.

"He can hardly be spared to-night, I fancy. The Ministry have had a stormy day, and are, doubtless, preparing for one still more stormy to-morrow."

"There was a perfect tempest in the Chamber this evening, I understand."

"Call it rather a hurricane, a tornado!"

"Ah! give me the particulars; here, come with me into this corner. Unfortunately, I was not present. I was busy on the General Committee for the Banquet of the Twelfth Arrondissement, to-morrow, at Chaillot. To avoid all possibility of collision with the police, we resolved, you know, not to have the banquet within the walls of Paris, and so there is to be a procession to the Barriere de l'Etoile. I have been there since morning, and reached the city only in time to come here. So, you see, I am edifyingly ignorant of the latest news."

"Then I have to inform you that there is to be no banquet after all."

"No banquet! Why, I thought it was compromised between Guizot and Barrot that the banquet should be allowed to proceed under protest, in order that the question might be brought before the Supreme Court."

"Such was the purpose, but a manifesto of the Banquet Committee, drawn up by Marrast, it is said, and, at all events, issued in 'Le National' this morning, declaring the design not only of a banquet, but of a procession, changed everything. The address sets forth that all invited to the banquet would assemble at the Place de la Madeleine to-morrow at about noon, and thence, escorted by the National Guard, and accompanied by the students of the universities, should proceed by the Place de la Concorde to the Arc de Triomphe, at the extremity of the Avenue des Champs Elysees, and thence to the immense pavilion on the grounds of General Shian. Only one toast, 'Reform, and the right to assemble,' was announced to be drunk, and then a commissary of police could enter a formal protest against the whole proceeding on the spot, on which to base a legal prosecution, and the multitude would disperse."

"A very sensible mode of procedure," quietly remarked the journalist, "and one eminently calculated to relieve your friend Guizot and my friend Barrot from the awkward dilemma of a direct issue."

"But so thought not my friend Guizot. Like his oracle, the sage Montesquieu, he thought, 'Who assembles the people causes them to revolt.' He took fright at the manifesto, as he was pleased to dignify the simple programme in this morning's 'National,' and so, early in the sitting, it was announced that the reform banquet was utterly prohibited by M. Delessert, Prefect of Police, on the express injunction and responsibility of M. Duchatel, Minister of the Interior, by and with the advice of M. Hebert, Minister of Justice."

"Ha! and what said Odillon Barrot?" cried the journalist.

"He--why he said nothing at all, but immediately retired at the head of the opposition from the Chamber."

"To consult?"

"Of course. An hour after, they returned in a body two hundred and fifty strong, with Barrot at their head, who at once mounted the tribune and denounced the despotism of the Ministry in forbidding the peaceful assembling of the citizens, without tumult or arms, to discuss their political rights. Duchatel replied, under great excitement.

"'Shall reform committees dare to call out the National Guard at their pleasure?' he asked.

"'Will you dare to call out the National Guard?' retorted De Courtais, fiercely. 'Only try it!'

"'The Government of France will never yield!' rejoined the Minister, pale with fury.

"'Speak in your own name, Monsieur!' shouted Flocon.

"'I shall never speak in yours!' was the answer.

"'You play the game of menace!' cried Lesseps.

"'The Government will never yield!' again vociferated Duchatel.

"'Those were the very words of Charles X.!' observed M. Dantes, sternly. The entire left responded in a terrific roar.

"'There is blood in those words!' shouted Ledru Rollin.

"'The Government will never yield!' the Minister of the Interior for the third time vehemently exclaimed, and the right gathered around him. 'This is worse than Polignac or Peyronet!' vociferated Odillon Barrot, his trumpet tones rising above all others like a clarion in a tempest. Those hated names were greeted by a yell of abhorrence perfectly savage from the left; then all was uproar--a dozen voices simultaneously shouting at their loudest--denunciation--menace--defiance--retort--clenched hands--extended arms--furious gesticulations--every one on tip-toe--fiery eyes--stamping feet--shouts of 'Order! order! order!'--and, amid all, the incessant tinkling of old Sauzet's little silver bell, which was just about as effective in restoring peace as it would be to quiet the tempest now howling through the streets of Paris. At length, in utter consternation and dismay the old President put on his hat, and, pronouncing the seance ended, rushed from his chair amid a hurricane of uproarious shouts."

"And Odillon Barrot?"

"Odillon Barrot led the opposition members immediately from the Chamber to his own house, where they have been ever since in deliberation. It was six o'clock when the sitting closed, and they must be in consultation now, or Barrot would surely be here, if but for a moment, out of respect to his bosom friend, our host. Ah! there he is, just entering, surrounded by a perfect army of Republicans--De Courtais, Marrast, Lesseps, Duvergier, Flocon, Lamartine, Dupont and a whole host besides."

"How excited they look!" exclaimed the journalist. "Ah! Thiers approaches them from the other end of the salon!"

"M. Thiers, like the worldly-wise and selfish man he is, has held himself aloof from the banquet, and even declined the invitation accepted by a hundred of his party; to-day he was absent from the Chamber and to-night from the conclave, all with the aspiring, yet vain hope, that the King will send for him to form a Ministry."

"And yet, in the Chamber, a few days ago, he said that he was of the party of the revolution in Europe."

"True, but he added that he wished the revolution carried on by its moderate supporters, and that he should do all he could to keep it in the hands of the moderate party."

"'But if it should pass into the hands of a party not moderate,' continued the crafty ex-Minister, 'I shall not abandon the cause of the revolution. I shall be always of the party of the revolution.' But see, he singles out Marrast, of all others!"

"And his old colleague of 'Le National' seems to give him no very cordial reception," added the Deputy. "But let us move up and hear the determination of the opposition relative to the banquet."

"That's the very question the little historian has just propounded to the great journalist. Now for the answer."

"The opposition decide, Monsieur, to abandon the banquet," was the angry reply of the editor to the ex-Minister.

"Indeed!" was the bland rejoinder; "and has a manifesto of this decision been issued to the people?"

"It has; and it instantly called forth a counter manifesto from the electoral committee of the Twelfth Arrondissement, expressing very natural astonishment that, at the same time the opposition abandoned the banquet, they had not abandoned their seats in the Chamber, and inviting them so to do at once."

"And the Ministry?" anxiously asked M. Thiers.

"Will to-morrow be impeached, Monsieur!"

"Ah! indeed! indeed!" cried the smart little aspirant, gleefully rubbing his hands.

At that moment General Lamoriciere, the brother-in-law of Thiers, who owed so much to the house of Orleans, hastily approached.

"I come straight from the Tuileries," he said, with considerable excitement. "General Jacqueminot has just issued an order of the day, as commander-in-chief of the National Guard, appealing to them as the constitutional protectors of the Throne to take no part in the banquet. Orders have, also, been issued for the rappel to be beaten at dawn, in the Quartier St. Honore, the scene of the contemplated procession. But it's all folly to rely on the National Guard. They are of the people. Only the Municipal Guard and the troops of the Line can be relied on in the civil conflict, which is sure to come to-morrow."

"And the Ministers, what do they?" asked Thiers.

"Oh! they are not idle," replied the soldier. "The bastilles are armed, and those of Montrouge and Aubervilliers are provisioned. The horse-artillery at Vincennes are ready, on the instant, to gallop into the capital. Seventy additional pieces of ordnance are now entering the barrieres. The Municipal Guard are supplied with ball-cartridges. The troops concentrated at sunrise to-morrow will not be less than one hundred thousand strong. With these men in the forts and faithful, the city can be starved in three days, National Guard and all, if rebellious. Now is the crisis in which to test the remarkable admission of M. Duchatel, in May, '45, that the bastilles of Paris were designed to 'fortify order.' We shall see, we shall see!"

"And the Marshal Duke of Islay--where is he?" quietly asked Marrast, with a significant shrug and smile.

At this mention of his bitter foe, a frown lowered on the fine face of Lamoriciere, as he briefly and sternly replied:

"With the King, Monsieur--General Bugeaud is with the King. But they mistake, Monsieur. Eugene Cavaignac is the man for this emergency. Bugeaud is a soldier--a mere soldier--Cavaignac is a statesman--a Napoleon! Paris will discriminate between the two one day, and that shortly."

And with an abrupt military salute the conqueror of Algeria walked away, followed by his little brother-in-law, who seemed yet shorter and more insignificant at the side of his towering and graceful form. At the same moment, Ledru Rollin entered in great agitation, and, having glanced hastily around, as if in search of some one in the assemblage, advanced straight to the journalist and grasped his hand.

"By heavens, Armand, I think the hour has arrived!"

"Whence do you come?" was the quick question.

"From the Boulevards, where I left Flocon, Louis Blanc and M. Dantes, with the people. I tell you, Armand, the people are ripe--ripe! The Ministerial ordinances prohibiting the banquet have kindled a flame wherever they have gone. The pitiful manifesto of the opposition and the counter manifesto of the Twelfth Arrondissement have only served to fan this flame into fury. It has been our care to restrain and direct, not to excite. It is dark and cold without, Armand; the winter wind howls dismally along the streets, the sleet freezes as it falls and the furious blast almost extinguishes the torches by which, at the corners and at the cafes, the different manifestoes of the day are being read to the eager throngs, on whose faces, in the flare of the blood-red light, can be perceived the fury of their hearts. The people, at length, are ripe! To-morrow all Paris will be in arms!"

While Ledru Rollin was thus speaking, Louis Blanc entered and quietly approached, courteously saluting his acquaintances on his way, and stopping to exchange a few words with Madame Dantes, who inquired with considerable anxiety for her husband.

"I have this moment left him, Madame," said Louis Blanc. "Be assured, he is safe and well. Ah! how glorious to be an object of solicitude to one like you!" he added, with a smile.

The lady smiled also, and offered an appropriate jest in reply to the gallantry of the distinguished author, as he moved on to join his friends.

"The Ministry provokes its fate!" he said, in a low tone, as he approached. "'Whom the gods would destroy, they first make mad.' These men suffered seventy reform banquets all over France. The seventy-first one they prohibit, and that, too, by the exhumation of an old despotic edict of 1790. This is exactly what we would have. It was the first, not the last banquet they should have suppressed. Barrot was right to-day, in the Chamber, when he said that had this manifestation been suffered the people would have become tranquil."

"Tranquil, indeed!" cried Ledru Rollin. "That's exactly what we have apprehended! No--no--it is too late! This Reform Banquet was, at first, but an insignificant thing. In it we now recognize the commencement of a revolution. The various announcements and postponements of this banquet have caused an agitation among the masses favorable to our wishes, and the threats and obstinacy of the Ministry have completed the work. The hopes, fears, doubts and disappointments attending this affair have put the mind of all Paris in a ferment, and excited passions of which we may take immediate advantage."

"Aye!" cried Louis Blanc, "we may now do what I have always wished and counseled--we, the Communists, may now take advantage of a movement, in the origin or inception of which we had no hand."

"True, most true!" observed Marrast; "this is the work of the Dynastics--Thiers, Barrot and the rest--the commencement of a reform under the law which we design to make a revolution paramount to all law."

"They begin to fear already that they have gone too far, those discreet men!" said Louis Blanc, smiling bitterly. "Did you observe how they shuffled to-night at M. Barrot's, and finally resolved to abandon the banquet, but, as a sop to the people, pledged themselves to impeach the Ministry?"

"Ah! ha! ha!" laughed Ledru Rollin; "just as if their abandonment of the banquet is to keep the people away from it to-morrow, any more than the Ministerial ordinances! Why, not one man in ten thousand knows of the existence of these manifestoes! But the faubourgs have been promised a holiday for a fortnight past, and they don't intend to be put off again."

"Whether the Dynastics designed or wished to be compromised in this affair," remarked Marrast, "they certainly are committed now, and it is too late for them to get out of the movement. Indeed, I view it as nothing less than a union of all the oppositions against the Crown--aye, against the Crown, and for a republic! We comprehend this--they don't. They have not, like us, waited seventeen years for a signal for revolution;--and now, before God, I believe the hour is at hand! This is no accidental insurrection of the 5th and 6th of June, '32--no outbreak at a funeral--no riot of operatives--no unmeaning revolt, as in '39. It is a reform, with the first names in France as its advocates and supporters, which we will make a revolution if we can secure the National Guard."

"The National Guard is secured already," said Louis Blanc. "Are they not of the people? At least twenty thousand of the National Guard are Republicans. Of the remaining forty thousand, nearly all are well disposed or neutral in feeling. Have I studied the National Guard for twenty years in vain, and have all the measures of the Communists to secure them, when the crisis came on, proved utterly ineffectual? On the National Guard we may rely. The Municipal Guard are picked men, and well paid to support the Throne--they will fight even better than the Line. With the Line and the National Guard the people must seek to fraternize from the beginning--with the other troops they have solely to fight--but, after all, general facts and principles only can be laid down. Circumstances utterly beyond human control must direct and govern, and vary and determine results when the period of action arrives; and arrive it may at any hour of the day or night. At this moment Paris sleeps on a volcano, the fires of which have long been gathering through many a fair and sunny day! God only knows when the volcano will burst; but, when the hour comes, let the people be prepared!"

As these enthusiastic words were uttered, the dark eye of the speaker flashed and his lip quivered. The silver clock on the mantel, beside which the conspirators stood, struck the first quarter after two. The night was waning, but the festivity seemed rather to increase than diminish within the salons of the magnificent mansion, while the storm howled even more drearily without, and the rain, at intervals, in heavy blasts, beat even more fiercely against the northern casements.

As Louis Blanc ceased speaking, M. Flocon entered the salon, and, as if by some preconcerted arrangement, at once sought his political friends.

"What of the night, watchman?" cried Ledru Rollin, as the editor of "La Reforme" approached. "The latest news! for 'That of an hour's age doth hiss the speaker,' as the English Shakespeare says. The news! good or bad!"

"As I entered," said Flocon, "the house trembled with the jar of a train of heavy ordnance, attended by tumbrels and artillery caissons, and escorted by a regiment of horse, which rolled along the pavement of the Champs Elysees."

"Good!" answered Marrast, with enthusiasm.

"All night," continued Flocon, eagerly, "through darkness and storm, whole regiments of infantry have thronged the line of boulevards which stretch from the Tuileries to Vincennes, and each soldier bears upon his knapsack, in addition to all his arms, an axe to demolish barricades. The garrisons of the arrondissements of Paris are already seventy thousand strong; and the troops of the Line are concentrating around the Palais Bourbon and the Chamber of Deputies."

"Excellent--most excellent!" joyfully exclaimed Louis Blanc. "The affront will not be wanting! But where is M. Dantes?"

"He is still with the chiefs of the faubourgs and the committees of the Freemasons and workmen, in the Rue Lepelletier, issuing his last instructions for the morrow. Messieurs, that man is a magician! His zeal in the good cause puts the boldest of us all to the blush. By most indefatigable energy and indomitable perseverance, he has brought about a systematic, almost scientific organization and fraternity, through various modes of rapid intercommunication between the innumerable classes of operatives of every description throughout the whole capital and its faubourgs, so that, within six hours, he can have in military array an armed mass of one hundred thousand blouses upon the boulevards. The workshops alone, he tells me, can furnish fifty thousand. The rapidity with which he conveys intelligence through this immense army and their utter subservience to his will and subordination to his orders are all so wonderful that it is impossible to determine which is most so. To control a Parisian populace has hitherto been deemed a chimera. With M. Dantes it is an existing reality. Not an army in Europe is so obedient or so prompt as his army of workmen. The secret is this--they know him to be their friend. All over Paris are to be seen his workshops, savings banks, hospitals and houses of industry and reform, and, in the suburbs, his phalansteries and his model farms. That he has the command of boundless wealth is certain; but whose it is, or whence it comes, no one can divine; and never did man make use of boundless wealth to attain his ends more wisely than he does! Why, I am told that the pens of half the litterateurs and feuilletonists of Paris have for years past been guided by his will and compensated from his purse to accomplish his purposes. 'The Mysteries of Paris' and 'The Wandering Jew' are but two of the triumphs of his policy. And his system of philanthropy seems not bounded by France, but to embrace all Europe. The Swiss Protestant and the Italian patriot have each felt his effective sympathy as well as the French workman; and in the same manner as with the operatives so has he obtained influence and weight with the National Guard, and to such an extent that of the sixty thousand one-half would obey his orders with greater alacrity than those of Jacqueminot himself. I tell you, Messieurs, he is a magician!"

"Hush! hush!" cried Marrast; "he is entering now!"

"He pauses and looks around him!" said Louis Blanc.

"He looks for us; I will go to him!" remarked Flocon.

"He looks for his wife," replied Louis Blanc. "There, he catches her eye. See how eagerly she flies to him!"

"That is the finest pair in Paris," remarked the journalist.

"And the most devoted," added Ledru Rollin. "They have been man and wife for some time, it is said, and any one would take them for lovers at this moment."

"Have they children?" asked Flocon.

"No; but M. Dantes has by a former wife a son and daughter, who rival in good looks the celebrated children of our friend Victor Hugo," returned Louis Blanc.

"I met Arago, Lamartine, Sue, Chateaubriand and some other celebrities at his mansion in the Rue du Helder one night, recently," continued Marrast, "and I thought I never saw a house arranged with such perfect taste. The salons, library, picture-gallery, cabinet of natural history, conservatory, and laboratory were superb--everything, in short, was exquisite."

"And then one is always sure to meet at Madame Dantes' soirees," added Louis

Blanc, "exactly the persons who, of all others, he wishes to see, and whom he would meet nowhere else, poets, painters, authors, orators, statesmen and artists of every description--in fine, every man or woman, whether native or foreigner, distinguished for anything, is certain to be met with at M. Dantes' house."

"I once met there," said Flocon, "Rachel, the actress, and Van Amburgh, the lion-king."

"M. Dantes is a perfect Maecenas in encouraging merit, as every one knows," remarked Marrast; "and he manifests especial solicitude to show that he appreciates worth more highly than wealth--genius than station. Poverty and ability are sure recommendations to him."

"Madame Dantes is, I am told, as devoted to the good cause as her husband," remarked Flocon.

"She is a second Madame Roland!" exclaimed Louis Blanc. "France will owe much to such women as she and her friend Madame Dudevant!"

"She differs greatly from Madame George Sand in some respects, I fancy," said Marrast; "but, if she at all rivals that wonderful woman in devotedness to the cause of human rights, whether of her own sex or ours, she deserves well of France. In her charities, it is notorious, she has no rival. Half the mendicants of the capital bless her name, and she is at the head of a dozen associations and enterprises for the amelioration of the condition of the destitute, suffering and abandoned of her sex."

"Upon my word, Messieurs," cried Ledru Rollin, "your praises of M. Dantes and Madame, his beautiful wife, are perfectly enthusiastic--so much so, that, in your zeal, you utterly forgot another matter quite as momentous. I am so unfortunate as to know M. Dantes only as one of the great pillars of our noble cause, and a man who, for nearly six years, has proven himself an apostle of man's rights, and ready, if need be, to become a martyr! That's enough for me to know of him!"

"But who really are M. Dantes and his wife?" asked Flocon.

"Who really are any of us?" laughingly rejoined Louis Blanc.

"Who really is any one in Paris," continued Marrast, "the blood-royal always and alone excepted?"

"Of M. Dantes this only is known," said Louis Blanc, "that for five or six years past he has been a Deputy from Marseilles, Lyons and other southern cities, all of which have been eager to honor themselves by returning him as their representative, as one of the boldest and most eloquent Republicans in all France; as for Madame Dantes, we know her to have once been the Countess de Morcerf, but now the wife of our friend, and one of the noblest and most lovely matrons in Paris. What need have we to know more? But our friend comes."

While this conversation was proceeding, Dantes and Mercedes had joined each other, and their hands were quietly clasped.

"Is all well, Edmond?" was the anxious inquiry of the fond wife, in low, soft, musical tones, as she fixed upon his pale face her dark eyes, beaming with the tenderest solicitude.

"All is well, love," replied the husband. "You will pardon my protracted absence, when I tell you it has been unavoidable--will you not, Mercedes?"

"Will I not? What a question! But I have been so anxious for your safety, knowing the perilous business in which you are engaged; and the night is so tempestuous."

"You forget that I have a constitution of iron, dear," replied Dantes; "you forget that I was a sailor once, and the storms were my playthings!"

"But you will go home with me now, Edmond, will you not?" she anxiously asked, placing her little white hand on his arm and gazing beseechingly into his eyes.

"Have I ever passed one night from your arms, my Mercedes, since we were wed?" was the whispered response. "Ah! love, any pillow but thy soft bosom would be to me a thorny one! You have spoiled me forever!" he added, smiling.

"And shall we go now, Edmond?" eagerly asked the delighted woman. "Oh! I'm so weary of this fete!"

"I must exchange a few words with our friend Louis Blanc, whom I see yonder, with others of our party, and then, dear, we will to our pillow. We are both weary. Au revoir!"

"Edmond--Edmond!" cried the lady, as her husband was going, "do you see Joliette and Louise in the redowa yonder?"

Dantes looked and, with a well pleased smile, nodded assent; a more brilliant and well-matched pair could hardly have been found, Joliette in the splendid uniform of an officer of the Spahis, and she in her own magnificent beauty, fitly garbed.

M. Dantes was received with marked respect by the knot of Republicans as he approached.

"I am delighted to meet you all, and to meet you to-night, or, rather, this morning," said Dantes, warmly, "in order that I may render you an account of my stewardship for the past six hours. They have been hours big with fate; and the first day of Republican France has already commenced. Messieurs, we can no longer remain blind to the fact that the long looked for--hoped for--expected hour has come--the hour to strike--strike home for liberty and for France! To-morrow the streets of Paris will swarm with blouses!--the Marseillaise will be heard!--barricades rise!-- the Ministry be impeached! Next day the National Guards will fraternize with the people!--blood will flow!--the Ministry resign! On the third, the King abdicates!-- the Tuileries are surrendered!--a Regency is refused!--a Republic is declared! And this day, two weeks hence, liberty will be shouted in the streets of Vienna and Berlin, and every throne in Europe will tremble! The honors of prophecy are easily won," continued the speaker, with a significant smile that lighted up his features, pale with enthusiasm and exhaustion, "when the problem of seventeen years approaches solution with mathematical certainty!"

"Are our plans all complete?" asked Louis Blanc.

"So far as human forethought or power could render them so, our efforts have, I trust, been effectual," was the reply. "Yet the events of every hour will induce changes, and render indispensable policy now undreamed of. Ah! Messieurs, we must none of us sleep now! Not a moment must escape our vigilance! Not an advantage must be sacrificed! We can afford to lose nothing! Without leaders, the people are blind! Not, for an instant, must they be abandoned! To-morrow, let the masses gather at different points! Next day let barricades choke the Boulevards; and, if the conflict come not, be it precipitated--provoked! Thursday, an hundred thousand men must invest the Tuileries, and a Provisional Government be declared in the Chamber of Deputies! The Bourbons will then be in full flight, and France will be free! And now, Messieurs, will you permit me to suggest the propriety of our separation? Yonder Ministerial Secretary has had his eye upon us ever since he entered."

The expediency of the suggestion of M. Dantes was at once perceived; the conspirators parted and one after the other, by different routes, shortly disappeared. As for M. Dantes, he threw himself carelessly in the way of the Ministerial Secretary to whom he had alluded, who was no other than our friend Lucien Debray, and saluted him with most marked and winning courtesy.

"Will the Ministerial Secretary suffer me to compliment him upon his indefatigable industry and exertions to-night to fortify order in Paris and sustain the administration?"

Debray bowed somewhat confusedly at this remark, and having returned a diplomatic reply, from which neither himself nor any one else could have elicited an idea, M. Dantes continued the conversation.

"Let me see, it is now nearly three o'clock," he said, consulting his repeater; "at half-past two you received an order, signed by the Duke of Montpensier, and directed to the War Ministry, commanding that seventy-two additional pieces of artillery be transported from Vincennes to Paris before dawn. That order was issued, and the ordnance is now on the boulevard!"

"How!" exclaimed the astonished Secretary.

"At Vincennes, the horses of the flying artillery stand harnessed in their stalls! All night infantry have been pouring into Paris, and, obedient to midnight orders, every railway will disgorge, at dawn, additional troops!"

"Are you a magician?" asked the astonished Secretary.

"Shall I reveal to you the Ministerial tactics for the morrow's apprehended insurrection?" coolly asked Dantes, with a smile. "The salons of the Tuileries have not been deserted to-night. 'Can you quell an insurrection, General?' asked the King of the Marshal Duke of Islay. 'I can kill thirty thousand men,' was the humane answer. 'And I, sire, can preserve order in Paris without killing a score,' said Marshal Gerard, the hero of Antwerp, 'if I can rely on my men.' 'What is your plan, Marshal?' asked the King. Shall I give you the Marshal's reply, my friend?"

"You were present--you know all!" exclaimed Debray.

"Not quite all," thought Dantes, "but I shall before we part. Well," continued he, aloud, "the Marshal's strategy was this--exceedingly simple and exceedingly efficacious, too, provided, to use the Marshal's own words, he can rely on his men. It is this: Occupy the Tuileries, the Hotel de Ville, the Halles, the Louvre and other prominent points with a heavy reserve of infantry and artillery, and sweep the boulevards, and the Rues St. Honore, de Rivoli, St. Martin, St. Denis, Montmartre and Richelieu with cavalry. A simple plan, is it not? Almost as simple as that of the insurrectionists themselves--a barricade on every street and one hundred thousand men in the Place du Carrousel!"

"The Government will not yield, Monsieur!" said Debray, firmly. "The Minister is unshaken. To crush an unarmed mob cannot severely tax the most skillful generals in Europe."

"True, they are unarmed," returned Dantes, with apparent seriousness. "Their leaders should have thought of that--arms are so easily provided--but then they can rely on their men!"

"We have yet to see that!" replied Debray, with some asperity.

"True, we have yet to see it. It is only a matter of belief now; then it will be a matter of knowledge. Seeing is knowing," added M. Dantes, with his peculiar smile. "But, pray, assure me, M. Debray, are the Ministry and their advisers, indeed, sanguine of the issue to-morrow!"

"They are certain!" replied the Secretary, with energy. Then, feeling that he had, perhaps, made a dangerous revelation, he quickly added: "I have the honor, Monsieur, to wish you a very good night! It is late!"

"Say, rather, it is early, Monsieur!" replied Dantes. "I have the honor to wish you a very good morning!"

The Secretary returned the courtesy, turned away, and, after exchanging a few words with M. Thiers, disappeared.

"They are certain, then!" soliloquized M. Dantes, as Debray quitted the salon. "I was sure I should know all before he left."

Then, rejoining Mercedes, who was patiently awaiting him, they stepped into their carriage, as the drowsy tones of the watchman rose on the misty air, "Past four o'clock, and all is well!"

# CHAPTER XVII.
# THE REVOLUTION BEGINS.

Tuesday, the 22nd of February, the birthday of the immortal Washington and the first of the Three Days of the French Revolution of 1848, broke darkly and gloomily on Paris. The night had been tempestuous, and the wind still drove the sleet through the leafless trees of the Champs-Elysees and howled drearily along the cheerless boulevards.

The streets were dismal, desolate and deserted. Here and there, however, through the gray light of the winter dawn, could be caught the semblance of a figure closely muffled, whether for concealment, disguise, or protection from the biting blast was doubtful, stealing along; these figures often met and exchanged ominous signs of recognition.

"Is the procession still to take place?" asked one of another of these persons, pausing for an instant as they hurried along.

"Yes!" was the emphatic answer. "Dupont, Lamartine and the sixteen others who are faithful are resolute."

"And the rendezvous?"

"Is the Place de La Concorde."

"And the hour?"

"Twelve."

Whereupon the conspirators parted.

Gradually the number of persons in the streets increased as the morning advanced. Chiefly, these were artisans, lads, blouses and workmen.

"Whither so early this disagreeable morning?" cried a peaceable-looking shopman of the Rue de Rivoli, who was taking down his shutters for the day, to a friend who was hurrying by.

"I don't exactly know where I am going," was the reply. "We were all roused at daybreak in the Quartier St. Honore by the rappel, and so I happen to be awake."

"And are the National Guard turning out in good numbers?"

"No. They don't turn out at all. The drummers are followed by a crowd of gamins in blouses, who shout Vive la Reforme and sing the Marseillaise."

"The National Guard don't turn out!" cried the alarmed shopman; "then I'll not take down my shutters!"

And as his friend moved on to the Madeleine, he took the precautionary measure he had spoken of.

At nine o'clock troops were in motion all over Paris, and the roll of the drum was heard in every street.

At ten o'clock ten thousand men were assembled at the Madeleine.

"Is there to be a banquet?" asked one of another, as they met on the Rue Royale.

"No. It is a procession. The people are to march to the Chamber of Deputies and sing the Marseillaise."

All the avenues to the Palais Bourbon and part of the Place around the Madeleine were now occupied by the 21st Regiment of the Line and mounted Municipal Guards. Before the Chamber of Deputies was marshaled a squadron of dragoons, and a battalion of the 69th Regiment of Cuirassiers stood ready to charge on the throng.

At eleven o'clock two thousand students in blouses from the Parthenon were joined by an immense column of workmen from the faubourgs, and, having fraternized in the Place de la Concorde, advanced in perfect order in procession, led by National Guards, shouting the Marseillaise and the Hymn of the Girondins. Slowly and solemnly moved the vast mass up the Rue Royale to the Pont de la Concorde, leading to the Place of the Chamber of Deputies.

At twelve o'clock the vast arena between the Chamber of Deputies and the Madeleine contained thirty thousand people. Along the railing of the church was drawn up a regiment of horse. A man in a tri-colored sash three times read the summons and ordered the crowd disperse.

The order is disregarded! The charge is sounded! The dragoons rush with sheathed sabres on the mass! Again and again they charge, but they cut down none!

All at once a heavy cart with a powerful horse is discovered--the people seize it--the horse is lashed into fury--he rushes on the double line of dragoons and chasseurs--a breach is made--the crowd dash through--some rush up the steps of the Chamber of Deputies--they force the gates--they even enter the hall--then, suddenly panic-stricken at their own audacity, they rush back! At this moment, along the Quai d'Orsay, gallops up a strong detachment of the mounted Municipal Guard, led by General Peyronet Tiburce Sebastiani, brother of the Marshal and uncle of the unhappy Duchess of Praslin. A charge was ordered, the crowd was driven over the bridge, and the Municipal Guard, a company of dragoons and a squadron of hussars took up a position at the foot of the Obelisk of Luxor. "Long live the dragoons!"

shouted the people. "Down with the Municipal Guard!" accompanied by hootings, groans, shouts and showers of stones. The troops, with sheathed sabres, charged. One of the immense fountains afforded the gamins a place of shelter. Suddenly the flood of water was let on and they fled.

Thus began the revolution.

One o'clock tolled from the tower of the Madeleine. The area was clear. Cavalry patrolled the boulevards. Infantry, bearing, besides their usual arms, implements for demolishing barricades--axes, adzes and hatchets--each soldier one upon his knapsack, followed.

At two o'clock, at the Hotel des Affaires Etrangeres, at the corner of the Rue des Capucines and the Boulevard, an immense mass of men ebbed and flowed like tides of the sea, and a tempest of shouts, groans and choruses to national songs arose.

A commissary of police in colored clothes, and with the tri-colored sash, led a body of Municipal Guards into the court. Deliberately they charge their muskets with ball. "In the name of the Law!" shouted the commissary. "Vive la Ligne!" responded the people, as they slowly retired.

"Away," cried a trooper to a blouse, in the Place de la Concorde, at the corner, near the Turkish Embassy; "Away, or I'll cut you down!"

"Will you, coward!" replied the artisan, calmly, with folded arms. At that moment a body of the people rushed on the Municipal Guards and drove them for safety into their barracks; then they fled themselves to avoid the fusillade of the enraged troops.

On the Pont de la Concorde the people stopped the carriage of a Ministerial Deputy and saluted him with groans. The next moment Armand Marrast, of "Le National," approached and was most rapturously cheered.

The money-changers, those seers of Napoleon, scented not yet the revolution. On Friday, the three per cents. were 75f. 85c. On Tuesday they opened at 73f. 90c. and closed at 74f.

The day advanced. The Republican and Communist power augments in its systematized order. Paris swarms with insurgents. Bakers' and gunsmiths' shops are plundered. Barricades are thrown up. A column rushes down the Champs-Elysees, and, having been repulsed at an escalade of the railings of the Chamber of Deputies, retires, shouting the Marseillaise and a chorus from the new opera of the Girondins,

"Mourir pour la Patrie." At dusk a deputation of students, at the office of "Le National," presents a petition for the impeachment of the Ministry.

That impeachment had already taken place!

"What news?" shouted a student to a workman, as he hurried along.

"There has been fighting in the Faubourg St. Marceau; half a dozen Municipal Guards have been carried wounded to the hospital of Val-de-Grace and a captain was killed."

"And is it true that the Guard has been disarmed on the Rues Geoffroi and Langevin, and a gunmaker's shop near the Porte St. Martin broken into and rifled?"

"I hadn't heard of that," was the hurried reply. "But I hear this, that the guard-houses in the Champs-Elysees have been taken, and the troops driven off, and that lamps and windows have been torn down."

At that moment another workman rushed along.

"The news!" shouted the student and the first workman.

"The railing of the Church of the Assumption has been torn away by the people to supply arms; two women of the people have been crushed by a charge of the Municipal Guard; the shop of Lepage, the armorer, in the Rue Richelieu, has been entered by means of the pole of an omnibus used as a battering ram; and barricades rise on the Rue St. Honore."

At three o'clock a column of the people dashed down the boulevards, smashing lamps and breaking shop windows. In the Rue St. Honore and the Rue de Rivoli an omnibus and two carriages were seized to aid in erecting a barricade. A guard-house in the Champs-Elysees was burned. The troops at the Ministry of Foreign Affairs were increased. No one was suffered to pass. A Municipal Guard was dismounted and nearly killed by the people. The crowd in the Rue Royale had become so dense that it was impossible to pass to the Place de la Concorde. The troops charged. The people gave way. Some were wounded badly; but still rose the shouts, "Vive la Ligne! Down with the Municipal Guard!"

In the Place Vendome stood a regiment of the Line. There was the hotel of M. Hebert, the Minister of Justice, and M. Hebert was hated by the people. "Down with Hebert, the inventor of moral complicity!" yelled the populace, but they made no attack.

It was ten o'clock at night. Many of the shops were closed, but the cafes and restaurants were thronged. From time to time the shouts, "Down with Guizot!" and "Vive la Reforme!" were heard and, also, the roll of drums as a body of troops passed along; knots of individuals gathered around the doors of bakers' shops, and, while they eagerly ate their bread and sausage, as eagerly denounced Guizot and the Ministry.

But all was comparative order in Paris.

# CHAPTER XVIII.
# THE MIDNIGHT CONCLAVE.

It was twelve o'clock at night, on the 22nd of February, 1848.

Lights still gleamed in the vast edifice of "Le National" printing office, and in the editorial chamber were assembled the chiefs of the revolution.

"All goes well," said Louis Blanc. "The blow is struck; let it only be followed up, and the efforts of the past ten years will not prove vain!"

"How true was the opinion of M. Dantes respecting the National Guard!" said Marrast.

"How true also respecting the workmen!" said Albert.

"How true respecting the Ministry!" said Ledru Rollin. "But where is M. Dantes? Why is he not here?"

At that moment the private door opened, and M. Dantes, Flocon and Lamartine entered.

"The news from the Chambers!" cried Marrast, as they approached.

"Three impeachments of the Ministry have been proposed," said Lamartine.

"By whom--by whom?" asked Louis Blanc. "By whom presented?"

"One by Odillon Barrot, one by Duvergier d'Hauranne and one by M. de Genoude, Deputy from Toulouse."

"And what said Guizot?" asked Marrast.

"Nothing. He only laughed when the papers were handed him by old President Sauzet."

"Ah!" cried Ledru Rollin.

"Few deputies were there," continued Flocon. "The opposition benches were vacant. Guizot was there early, pale and troubled, but stern and unbending. All the Ministers followed him."

"What was discussed?" asked Marrast.

"The Bordeaux Bank Bill."

"Ah!" cried Ledru Rollin again.

"Yes," continued Flocon, "until five o'clock that bill was discussed. Barrot then ascended the tribune and deposited a general proposition to impeach the Ministry."

"And what was done with it?" asked Louis Blanc.

"The President raised the sitting without reading it, but announced that the bureaux should have it for examination on Thursday."

"Infamous!" cried Ledru Rollin.

"It is all as it should be," said M. Dantes, calmly.

"And the peers--what of them?"

"The Marquis de Boissy made an effort to get a hearing on the state of Paris, but, of course, it was in vain."

"Is it true," asked Flocon, "that the rappel has been beaten to-day?"

"It was beaten in the Quartier St. Honore, at dawn," said Louis Blanc, "and this evening, at about five o'clock, in several of the arrondissements. But no reliance need be placed on the National Guard. They are with us--they are of the people-- they shout, 'Vive la Reforme!'"

"But the Municipal Guard and the Line? I am told that an immense body of them was this evening, at about eight o'clock, reviewed by the King and the Dukes of Nemours and Montpensier, in the Place du Carrousel," said Flocon.

"That's true," said Ledru Rollin; "I witnessed it myself in passing, and I could not help saying, 'It is the last.'"

"Six thousand troops of the Line are on the boulevards, from the Madeleine to the Porte St. Martin," said M. Dantes. "The Hotel de Ville, the Places de la Bastille, de la Concorde and du Carrousel, and the Quays frown with artillery. To-morrow will be a warm day!"

"It has been rather warm to-day in some parts of Paris," said Louis Blanc, smiling. "Was there ever a grander spectacle than that in the Place de la Concorde at noon? At least one hundred thousand men were there assembled. Rushing across the bridge, they gathered around the Chamber of Deputies--then from the south-ern gate of the Tuileries issued two bodies of troops, one of mounted Municipal Guards, the other infantry of the Line, and, pressing on the dense mass, they drove them over the bridge. Only a few old fruitwomen were crushed beneath the horses' hoofs, and a few of the troops were wounded by pebbles, however."

"At the same time," said Flocon, "all the chains in the Champs-Elysees were in requisition for a barricade, as well as all the public carriages, and the people sang the Marseillaise, the Parisienne and the Hymn of the Girondins. A guard-house was also consumed."

"Have you heard Bugeaud's remark at noon, when looking upon the Place de la Concorde?" asked Marrast.

"We have been too busy to-day to hear anything," said Ledru Rollin.

"'Ah! we shall have a day of it,' said the bloodthirsty old hero. 'I care not for the day,' said the pale Guizot, 'but the night!'"

"The people made quite a demonstration about Guizot, I hear," said Flocon. "They assailed him with a shower of groans, it is said, and some of the gamins flung pebbles at his gates."

"The most significant shout before the office of Foreign Affairs was this," said Ledru Rollin--"'Countess of Leven, where is the Minister?'"

"And the very moment this was occurring," said Flocon, "I understand that M. Thiers, on his return from the Chamber, in passing through the Champs-Elysees, narrowly escaped a most unwelcome ovation from the people. The two rivals were duly and simultaneously honored it seems."

"Thus much for to-day," said Marrast; "what of to-night?"

"Barricades rise all over Paris," said M. Dantes. "But we can do no more. Let us each retire to his home. To-morrow the National Guard will fraternize with the people, and the Ministry will resign."

A few words of parting salutation passed, and all departed.

M. Dantes and Lamartine left the office in company.

"What say you, Edmond," asked Lamartine, "will your wife spare you long enough from her pillow to make with me a brief tour of the town?"

"Mercedes is rather exacting," said Dantes, with a laugh; "but if your fair lady will suffer your absence, mine must do the same, I fear."

"Well, then, let us first to the Hotel de Ville, that grand centre of Paris in all that is revolutionary."

As the two friends passed along, conversing on the events of the day and the anticipations of the morrow, they were met, from time to time, by knots of men at the corners, eagerly recounting the incidents of the hour; the roll of drums was heard in the distance, and occasionally there came the heavy and measured tread of infantry, the clatter of cavalry and the lumbering of artillery, as they passed on their way. All the shops and cafes were closed. Many of the lamps were demolished, and others were not lighted, the gas being shut off. A fearful gloom brooded over the city. The winter wind swept sharply and cuttingly along the deserted streets, and rain, which froze as it fell, at intervals dashed down.

The Hotel de Ville was encompassed by troops as the friends approached it.

"Is that a cannon?" asked Lamartine, pointing to a dark object that protruded from an embrasure of the edifice.

"It is!" replied Dantes.

"Then the revolution has, indeed, begun! Artillery in the streets of Paris!"

"Behind each column of the portico of the Chamber of Deputies this day frowned a concealed cannon!" was the significant response.

The friends turned off from the Hotel de Ville, and, crossing the right branch of the Seine, were under the deep shadows of Notre Dame. But all was tranquil and still. Only the howlings of the wintry blast were heard through the towers and architectural ornaments of the old pile. Up the Rue St. Jacques, into the Quartier Latin, they then proceeded, but the students and the grisettes seemed to be fast asleep. Turning back, they passed the Fish Market, and here a large body of cavalry had bivouacked. Patrols marched to and fro; officers in huge dark cloaks smoked, laughed and chatted, regardless of the morrow. The friends went on. All was dark in the faubourg which succeeded. Not a light gleamed, save, in some lofty casement, the fainting candle of the worn-out needlewoman or of the overtasked student.

"Ah!" exclaimed Lamartine, as they passed one of these flickering lights, "who knows what plotting head and ready hand may be beside that candle? Who knows of the weapon burnished, the cartridge filled and the sabre sharpened by that light for the morrow?"

"The morrow!" exclaimed M. Dantes; "that morrow decides the fate of

France!"

And the friends parted.

# CHAPTER XIX.
# THE SECOND DAY.

The 23d of February dawned on Paris as a city under arms. Artillery frowned in all the public places; the barricades of the preceding night had been thrown down as fast as erected; National Guards thronged the thoroughfares; the people swarmed along the boulevards. In the neighborhood of the Porte St. Denis and the Porte St. Martin, barricades rose as if by magic, but were as if by magic swept away. Cavalry bivouacked in the streets, and ordnance was leveled along their entire extent. The avenues were closely invested, and even old men and women were arrested on their way to their own thresholds. From time to time single shots or volleys of musketry were heard in the distance, and wounded men were carried past to the hospitals.

The Government had ordered all public carriages to be cleared from the stands, that material for new barricades might not exist when the old ones were demolished; but the people were busy, too, for the iron railings at the hotel of the Minister of Marine, in the Place de la Concorde, and at the churches of the Assumption and St. Roch had been torn away to supply weapons of attack or defence, or implements with which to tear up the huge square paving stones of Paris for barricades.

At eleven o'clock the National Guard of the Second Arrondissement gathered at the opera house in the Rue Lepelletier, and near the office of "Le National." "Vive la Reforme!" "Vive la Garde Nationale!" "Long live the real defenders of the country!"--these were the shouts, intermingled with the choruses of national songs, that now rose from the people and the National Guard.

At twelve o'clock the 2d Legion of the National Guard was at the Tuileries to make a demonstration for reform. Its colonel, M. Bagnieres, declared to the Duke of Nemours that he could not answer for his men. At one o'clock, accompanied by an immense multitude, with whom they fraternized, they were again on the Rue Lepelletier. A squadron of cuirassiers and one of chasseurs advanced to dislodge them.

"Who are these men?" cried the chef d'escadron.

"The people of Paris!" replied the officer of the National Guard.

"And who are you?"

"An officer of the 2d Legion of the National Guard."

"The people must disperse!"

"They will not!"

"I will compel them!"

"The National Guard will defend them!"

"Vive la Reforme!" shouted the people.

The National Guard and the cuirassiers united. The officer, chagrined, turned back to his men and vociferated in tones of thunder:

"Wheel! Forward!"

And the whole body resumed its march down the Boulevard.

An hour afterwards a still larger body of troops, Municipal Guards mounted and on foot, cuirassiers and infantry of the Line, came down the Boulevard and made a half movement on the Rue Lepelletier, but, seeing the hostile attitude of the National Guard, continued their march amid shouts of "Vive la Reforme!" "Vive la Garde Nationale!" "Vive la Ligne!"

Twice, within an hour afterwards, the same thing occurred.

It was plain that the National Guard fraternized with the people.

The 3d Legion deputed their colonel, M. Besson, to demand of the King reform and a change of Ministry. The colonel presented the memorial to General Jaqueminot, who promised to place it in the Royal hands.

The 4th Legion marched to the Chamber of Deputies and presented a petition for reform.

Col. Lemercier, of the 10th, arrested a man for shouting "Vive la Reforme!" The man was liberated by his own troops, with shouts of "Vive la Reforme!" The colonel withdrew.

The cavalry legion, the 13th, in like manner repudiated Col. Montalivet.

The Municipal Guard was ordered to disarm the 3d Legion. Both advanced--bayonets were crossed--blood was about to flow. At that moment Col. Textorix, of the National Guard, rushed up and exclaimed:

"Brothers, will you slay brothers?"

The effect was electrical. The muskets were instantly shouldered and the combatants separated.

All over Paris the same scenes took place, with a few exceptions.

"Vive la Republique!" cried Ledru Rollin to Albert, who was hurrying down the Rue Lepelletier, at about noon.

"Vive la Republique!" was the hearty response. "What of the National Guard?"

"The Guard fraternizes with the people," replied Ledru Rollin. "What of the blouses and the barricades?"

"Last night, the barricades of yesterday were swept from the streets, and even the material of which to build them also, the pavements only excepted; yet, at dawn this morning, the whole space between the Quartier Saint-Martin des Champs, the Mont de Piete and the Temple, and all the smaller streets were choked with barricades."

"And they were at once assailed?"

"By the troops of the Line, the Municipal Guard and the chasseurs of Vincennes."

"Who were repulsed?"

"With most obstinate bravery. At the Rue Rambuteau, the 69th Regiment was three times driven back; also at the corner of the Rue St. Denis and the Rue de Tracy. In the Rue Philippeaux a ball passed through the face of a soldier of the 21st of the Line infantry, and then through the head of a voltigeur behind him. Sixteen soldiers fell in the attack on the barricade of the Rue Rambuteau. A blouse pointed a pistol at an officer of the Municipal Guard; the pistol hung fire, and the officer passed his sword through his assailant's body. From this you can infer that we have had close fighting."

"I have heard that an assault was made on the armory of our friends, the Leparge Brothers, for weapons; is it so?"

"There was an assault at about ten o'clock; but the windows were too strong to be carried. There has been fighting in the Rue de Petit Carrel, and the neighborhood of the Place Royale, I learn. Achmet Pacha, son of Mehemet Ali, is fighting for us with the most wonderful intrepidity. A chef de bataillon of the 34th was slain by a shot from a window, and some offices of the Octroi have been burned. Three men were killed at the Batignolles, and their bodies were accompanied by an immense throng to the Morgue."

"Have you heard that the 5th Regiment, as in 1830, has joined the people, and that, on their way to the Prefecture of Police to liberate some of the people who had been arrested, they stopped at the office of 'La Reforme,' and were eloquently addressed by our friend, Louis Blanc?"

"What did he say to them?"

"He told them the fight was not yet over; that there must still be a banquet; and that this time there must be no mistake--the workmen must have the freedom they won!"

"Vive Louis Blanc!" cried Albert, and, in a higher state of excitement than he had ever before been known to exhibit, he hurried off.

"I am for the Tuileries," said Ledru Rollin, as they parted.

"And I for the Palais Royal," said Albert.

"We meet to-night at the office of 'Le National?'"

"Without fail, at midnight!"

It was on the square at the south end of the Palais Royal that most blood was spilled between the people and the troops. The Chateau d'Eau was furiously assailed and obstinately defended--assailed by the people and defended by six thousand picked troops. The people triumphed! Of the troops, at least a thousand perished, and the remnant fled.

At three o'clock M. Rambuteau, Prefect of the Seine, waited on the King and informed him that the National Guard demanded reform, and the Municipal Guard a change of Ministry.

The King in dismay convened the Ministry.

"Can the Ministry maintain itself?" asked Louis Philippe.

"That question brings its own answer to your Majesty," replied Guizot. "If you doubt the stability of your Ministry, who can trust them?"

"I have thought of the Count Mole," observed the King.

"He is an able man, sire," replied Guizot; "and his political connections with M. Barrot and M. Thiers may aid him to form a Ministry. But, sire, not an instant is to be lost. Your faithful Ministers will do all they can, but a Ministerial crisis cannot be delayed; and, if your Majesty will permit the suggestion, the emergency demands that to Marshal Bugeaud be given the command of Paris."

"You will proceed to the Chamber to announce that M. Mole is entrusted with the formation of a new cabinet," said the King.

And the council closed.

At four, an officer of the staff passed along the boulevards, announcing the fall of the Ministry.

Instantly, with the speed of the telegraph, the intelligence flew to the obscurest parts of Paris. Its effect was, at first, most cheering. Barricades were deserted and arms thrown down; faces brightened, hands, almost stained with each other's blood, were clasped; troops and people, unwillingly fighting, embraced; all was triumph, joy and congratulation.

"All now is over--all is right at last!" was the exclamation of one man of the people to another.

"Guizot has fallen, but the King has sent for Count Mole," replied a third, with a dissatisfied air.

"No matter," cried the first speaker, "the system is overturned! What care we who is Minister?"

"It is too late," replied the other. "Guizot has been forced away by the people--Mole may be forced away, too--so may the King! No more tricks! The people now know their power. There shall be no mistake this time!"

And the insurrectionists parted.

As the day closed, barricades rose in the Quartier du Temple, and there was fighting between the people and the Municipal Guard. But the National Guard came to the rescue, and the latter surrendered.

At nine o'clock Paris was illuminated. White, red, blue--yellow, orange, green--these were the tri-colors of the lamps that poured their rich effulgence from every window on the gloomy scene without. The streets were thronged and the cafes crowded; men of all nations and Parisians of all classes were in the streets; the rattle of musketry had ceased; the troops were in their barracks and the people at their homes.

At the corner of the Boulevard and the Rue des Capucines, Flocon and Louis Blanc met.

"Guizot has fallen!" cried the first.

"And the most intimate friend of the King has succeeded him! What have we to hope for from the change?"

"What are we to do?" asked Flocon.

"In one hour the people will sing the Marseillaise before the Hotel des Affaires Etrangeres!"

"The 14th Regiment of the Line is there," replied Flocon.

"So much the better! Blood will flow! The revolution will not stop!"

And the conspirators separated.

At ten o'clock, before the official residence of M. Guizot, himself then absent, and probably in full flight for the coast, an immense crowd of the people with torches was assembled. Their purpose was to sing the Marseillaise. The 14th Regiment barred the way--the street was dimly lighted--a single row of lamps along the courtyard wall was all the illumination--a double line of troops was the defence.

"Let me pass!" cried the officer of the National Guard who led the people to the officer who led the troops.

"Impossible!"

"In the name of the people, I demand to pass!"

"In the name of the Law, you shall not!"

"The people command! Forward!" cried the National Guard.

"Present! Fire!" shouted the officer.

There was a roll of musketry--a shrill shriek rang along the Boulevard--the vast mass recoiled--the smoke floated off--sixty-three of the people of Paris lay weltering in their gore!

"The blow is struck at last!" cried M. Dantes, rushing across the Boulevard, pale and excited. "To arms, people of Paris, to arms!"

"To arms, to arms! Vengeance for our brothers!" was now the terrible cry that burst from the infuriated populace. The congratulation--the illumination--all was lost in the wild wish for vengeance.

At eleven o'clock that night an immense multitude, composed chiefly of workmen from the faubourgs, was coming down the Boulevard des Capucines. It was the largest and most regular throng yet seen. In front marched a platoon of men bearing torches and waving tri-color flags. Immediately behind walked an officer in the full uniform of the National Guard, with a drawn sword in his hand, whose slightest command was implicitly observed. Next came a tumbrel bearing the naked corpses of the slain, whose faces, mutilated by their wounds and disfigured by blood, glared horribly up, with open eyes, in the red torchlight that flared in the night blast around! Behind this awful display marched a dense mass of National Guards, succeeded by a countless mass of the people armed with, guns, swords, clubs and bars of iron, chanting forth in full chorus, not the inspiring Marseillaise or the Parisienne, but in awful concert sending upon the night air the deep and dreadful notes of the death-hymn of the Girondins, "Mourir pour la Patrie," intermingled with yells for vengeance.

Down the boulevards approach the multitude--more distinct becomes the dirge--more redly glare the torches--and, amid all, more deeply rumble the wheels of the death-cart on the pavement!

The funeral column reaches the corner of the Boulevard and the Rue Lepelletier--the death-hymn rises to a yell of fury--the officer of the National Guard turns the head of the column to the right--before it is an edifice conspicuous by its illumination of huge and blood-red lamps--it is the office of "Le National"--the crowd halts--one long loud shriek of "Vengeance!" goes up--it is succeeded by the thrilling notes of the Marseillaise from ten thousands lips, and "Marrast! Marrast!" is the shout that follows.

The windows of the front office were thrown up, and the editor, surrounded by friends, appeared. His speech was brief but fervid. He exhorted the people to be firm--to secure their rights beyond recall--and promised them ample retribution for past wrongs and security for future rights.

M. Garnier Pages, who stood at the side of Marrast, next addressed the people in the same strain, amid thunders of applause.

Making a detour to the office of "La Reforme," the multitude were addressed by M. Flocon, its editor; then, proceeding to the Place de la Bastille, the corpses were deposited at the foot of the Column of July, and the crowd dispersed.

The night that succeeded was an awful one. The streets, which an hour before blazed with the illumination, were dark. Barricades rose in every direction. At every corner shopmen, workmen, women, clerks and children were at work. The crash of falling trees, the clank of the lever and the pickaxe, the rattle of paving stones--these were the significant sounds that broke the stillness. Every tree on the whole line of the Boulevard was felled and every lamp-post overthrown; a barricade of immense strength rose at the end of the Rue Richelieu; the troops offered no resistance; they piled their arms, lighted their fires and bivouacked close beside the barricades. At the Hotel de Ville the troops of the Line and the Chasseurs d'Afrique quietly ate their suppers, smoked their pipes and laid themselves down to sleep. On the Boulevard des Italiens appeared three regiments of the Line, a battalion of National Guards, a regiment of cuirassiers, and three field-pieces, with their caissons of ammunition. The horses were unharnessed by the people, the caissons opened, the ammunition distributed and the guns dragged off. The troops, guards and cuirassiers fraternized.

# CHAPTER XX.
# ANOTHER MIDNIGHT CONCLAVE.

Again it was midnight. Again the chiefs of the revolution of '48 assembled in conclave. The second of the Three Days had passed, but the streets of Paris were all alive with excitement.

Every leader of the reform was there--Ledru Rollin and Flocon excited and fiery, Louis Blanc exhausted and agitated, Albert stern and collected, Lamartine pale and troubled, Marrast sanguine and confident--all of them more or less disturbed but M. Dantes. As for him, the same calm smile was on his lip, the same mild light in his eye and the same unchanging resolution upon his countenance.

"Who attended the Chamber of Deputies to-day?" asked Marrast. "Did you, Lamartine?"

"I did," was the reply, "and witnessed a somewhat stormy sitting. At three o'clock, as usual, old Sauzet took the chair. Our friends were there in large numbers; the Ministerial benches were also filled. Immediately after, M. Guizot entered. He had been saluted with groans by the 10th Legion, stationed on guard without, and with cries of 'Down with Guizot!' Calm, undisturbed, stony in aspect, though strangely pallid, he entered and took his seat. M. Vavin, Deputy for the Seine, instantly mounted the tribune. As Deputy of Paris he had, he said, a solemn duty to fulfill. For twenty-four hours Paris had been in insurrection. Why was this? He called on the Minister of the Interior to explain."

"And what said Guizot?" asked Louis Blanc, eagerly.

"He said he thought the public interest did not demand, nor was it proper for the Chamber at that time, to enter into debate on the subject. The King had called M. le Comte Mole to form a new cabinet."

"And then the left cheered?" exclaimed Flocon.

"Most emphatically," was the reply.

"And what said Guizot then?" asked Ledru Rollin.

"He calmly said that no such demonstrations could induce him to add to or withhold a single syllable of what he designed to say, or to pretermit a single act he had designed to do. As long as his Ministry remained in office he should cause public order to be respected, according to his best judgment, and as he had always done. He should consider himself answerable for all that might happen, and should in all things act as conscience might dictate for the best interests of the country."

"A noble answer!" exclaimed M. Dantes, with enthusiasm.

Ledru Rollin and Louis Blanc assented.

"And what next?" pursued Flocon.

"After considerable confusion," continued Lamartine, "M. Odillon Barrot rose and demanded, in consequence of the situation of the cabinet, a postponement of the proposition for its impeachment, fixed for to-morrow."

"Ah! And what said the Chamber?" asked Flocon.

"The demand was so loudly reprobated that M. Barrot immediately said he made the proposal in entire submission to the majority."

"And what said Dupin?" asked Ledru Rollin, eagerly.

"Dupin said the first thing necessary for the capital was order. Anarchy must cease. The Ministry could not at the same time occupy themselves in re-establishing order and in caring for their own safety. He demanded the adjournment of the impeachment and of all business."

"And what did Barrot reply to that?" asked Louis Blanc.

"M. Barrot was silent; but the Minister of Foreign Affairs at once rose and said with much energy that as long as his cabinet remained entrusted with the public interest, which would probably be for some hours, it would cause the laws to be respected. The cabinet saw no reason for the suspension of the labors of the Chamber. The Crown was at that moment exercising its prerogative, and it must be respected.

So long as his cabinet was on those benches, the Chamber need not suspend its labors."

"What was the vote on the question to postpone consideration of the impeachment?" asked Flocon.

"Some of the opposition supported the motion, but the whole centre opposed it, and it was lost. The Chamber immediately rose in great agitation, and M. Guizot disappeared."

"It seems to me that the position of M. Odillon Barrot is a somewhat peculiar one at this moment," observed Louis Blanc. "He is neither with the Crown nor with the people, and yet both seem to confide in him."

"As I passed his house this evening, at about eight o'clock," said Flocon, "a large multitude were in his courtyard shouting, 'Long live Odillon Barrot!' A deputation of the people penetrated, I understand, even to his private apartment, where he was in consultation with Thiers and Dupin. Barrot then urged them to be moderate in their triumph and to retire. M. Garnier Pages, who chanced to be there, urged them to do the same, and they went off shouting louder than ever."

At that moment one of the reporters of "Le National" hastily entered and handed Marrast a note.

"Whence do you come, Monsieur?" asked the editor.

"From the Tuileries, Monsieur," was the reply, and the reporter left.

The editor opened the note and read aloud:

"One o'clock--Count Mole, unable to form a cabinet, has this moment resigned, and the King has sent for M. Guizot, M. Thiers and Marshal Bugeaud.

"Half-past one o'clock--Marshal Bugeaud's commission as Commander-in-chief of the National Guard and of the troops of the Line, in place of Generals Jaqueminot and Peyronett Tyburce Sebastiani, has just been signed by M. Guizot and his colleagues, the Ministers of War and the Interior, and will appear in the 'Moniteur' of this morning. Bugeaud's plan is this: Instant attack with an overwhelming force of artillery, cavalry and infantry of the Line, (which, he asserts, he has now all ready in position in anticipation of this event, and well disposed to act,) on all the barricades. He promises to sweep away every obstruction from the streets before dawn, though at the cost of fifty thousand lives."

"Ha!" exclaimed all the conspirators, instantly springing to their feet.

"This, indeed, is resistance!" said M. Dantes. "But Bugeaud can concentrate no more troops upon us. Every avenue to Paris will be effectually closed before morning and even the telegraph stopped!"

"If this be true, we have not an instant to lose!" said Louis Blanc.

"I had a hint of this," began M. Dantes.

"Stay--stay, Messieurs!" cried Marrast, as the whole company was rushing to the door. "Here is another and later dispatch."

"Two o'clock--Marshal Bugeaud has gone to complete his arrangements for instant attack. M. Thiers has arrived, and, with Odillon Barrot, Duvergier de Hauranne and de Remusat, has formed a cabinet. General Lamoriciere supersedes Marshal Bugeaud--the latter is        recalled and forbidden to fire on the people. He protests with  violence, and sheathes his sword in despair."

"To be sure he does, the old cut-throat!" cried Ledru Rollin. "The idea of being let loose with his mastiffs on the people of Paris, like sheep pent up in a fold, was to him a source of rapturous anticipation, and his rage at the disappointment is proportional!"

"Messieurs!" cried M. Dantes, "this last step of the Government was all that we required to insure our success. Thiers and Barrot mistake if they think there is sufficient magic in their names to quell a revolution. In fact, neither of them are trusted by the people. It is too late! Yesterday this might have been done; but now the demand is not reform, but a republic--not 'down with the Ministry,' but 'down with the dynasty!'"

The conspirators looked at each other and then at M. Dantes in amazement and doubt. It was apparent they were as yet unprepared for language so plain.

"M. Dantes is right!" cried Flocon. "To-morrow night when we meet we shall all admit it!"

It was now nearly three o'clock, and the Republicans repaired to their homes for a few hours' sleep before the exciting scenes anticipated for the morrow.

As Louis Blanc and M. Albert passed up the Rue Lepelletier, and came opposite the Hotel of the Minister of Foreign Affairs, which, but a few hours before, had been the scene of so much confusion and bloodshed, they paused and looked around. The pavement was still dark and wet with the gore of the slaughtered citizens, but the whole street was deserted and silent. Here and there a solitary light might be detected in the attic windows of the immense hotel; but no other sign of life or human occupation was to be perceived. True, there was an ominous sound of rising barricades in the Boulevard beyond--the crash of trees, the click of steel on stone, the lumbering of wheels--and, at intervals, a distant shout. But this excepted, all was as quiet in Paris as if the old city had never known of insurrection.

"This spot will be noted in the future history of France," said Louis Blanc. "Do you know the exact facts of the case, M. Albert? There are so many rumors that we can with difficulty get near the truth."

"I was not present when the 14th delivered their fire," was the reply, "but I learned from M. de Courtais, who hastened to the spot, that the colonel of the regiment, now in prison, asserts that, at the moment of the arrival of the crowd, a ball from a musket which accidentally went off, broke the leg of his horse, and he, thinking this the signal for an attack, at once gave orders to fire. Another story is that one of our young blouses blew out an officer's brains with a pistol."

"Many of the troops must have fired in the air," said Louis Blanc, looking around him, "for there were two hundred of them in line, I understand, and their discharge was delivered across the whole breadth of the Boulevard swarming with people."

"It was unfortunate for M. Guizot," rejoined M. Albert, with a sardonic smile, "that his hotel should have witnessed such a scene."

"But fortunate for the cause, nevertheless," replied Louis Blanc. "This last movement is called the movement of the journalists, I understand."

"If suspicions are always as correct," said M. Albert, "there will be fewer false ones, I fancy."

Louis Blanc made no reply, and the friends walked on up the Boulevard, reconnoitering every spot.

At the Rue du Faubourg Montmartre they were stopped by a barricade, which was rapidly rising under the united and vigorous exertions of several hundred men.

Steadily, sternly and silently, all that night they toiled, and when the barricade was completed the tri-color flag was planted on its summit, and a citizen-soldier stood beside its staff to defend it. On the other side of the Boulevard, in the Rue Montmartre, rose another barricade entirely finished.

"These men are resolved," said Louis Blanc.

"Desperate, rather," replied Albert. "They have counted the cost and prepared to go on with the attempt they have begun at all hazards. It is better to fight than starve, they think."

"But do you observe how few of them are armed?" asked Louis Blanc.

"We have provided for that deficiency. You will see arms enough for all tomorrow," replied Albert. "Barricades first, arms afterwards!"

And, indeed, while he was yet speaking, a tumbrel loaded with arms of every description drove silently up, and each man supplied himself with a weapon that suited his fancy. In some instances the taste exhibited was ludicrous in the extreme; there were swords without scabbards and bayonets without guns--a towering helmet on the head of one man, and broad white leather cross-belts on the shoulders of another--daggers and knives, sabres and pikes mingled in grotesque confusion. But each individual was armed with something, and, to crown all, a small piece of ordnance, borne on the shoulders of four stout men, who staggered beneath its weight, was now brought up and placed in battery.

"From such men what may we not hope!" exclaimed Louis Blanc. "But it is near morning; let us proceed."

"I stop here," quietly said Albert.

"What! Pass the night here?" exclaimed his companion.

"The night is nearly passed now," replied Albert, with a smile. "I will sleep a few hours with my men of the barricades, and be ready to help them defend their work in the morning."

"You are devoted to the cause, Albert," said Louis Blanc, warmly grasping his hand.

"Oh! no more than yourself," was the reply. "We are all devoted to it, but each in his own way. You are an author, I am a workman. It is a light thing for me to pass a night with only the sky for a canopy. It is a light thing for you to pass a night in your study. A change of positions would possibly kill us both!"

The friends grasped each other warmly by the hand and parted, the author going to his study and the workman to his barricade.

# CHAPTER XXI.
# THE THIRD DAY.

The next morning the following placard attracted general attention:
"CITIZENS OF PARIS:
Orders have been given to cease firing everywhere.
We have just been charged by the King to form a new Ministry.
The Chamber will be dissolved and an appeal made to the country.
General Lamoriciere has been appointed Commandant of the National Guard.

Liberty! Order! Union! Reform!
ODILLON BARROT. THIERS."

Such was the placard which appeared at every corner in Paris on the morning of Thursday, February 24th. At three o'clock it had been hastily struck at the offices of "La Presse" and "Le Constitutionnel," and given into the hands of the bill-posters. At daylight it was read by the early passers, and, as soon as read, indignantly torn down with the significant murmur, "It is too late!"

At eight o'clock a proclamation to the National Guard, signed by Lamoriciere and countersigned by Odillon Barrot, was similarly received.

At nine o'clock the 45th Regiment of the Line fraternized with the National Guard, the 30th resigned its arms to the people, and the five companies of Compiers yielded their quarters with all their arms and ammunition at the first summons.

At ten o'clock a proclamation was posted up at the Bourse, signed by Odillon Barrot and Thiers, ordering the troops not only to cease firing, but to retire to their quarters. Immediately the trumpets sounded a retreat, and the most important positions hitherto held by the Line were yielded to the people. The men of the barricades could now concentrate and advance. Magic there was none in the names of

Barrot and Thiers to restrain them. Both were viewed as deserters from their cause. The latter was openly insulted by the populace wherever he appeared, and the former, though at first respectfully listened to, was, at length, assailed with murmurs of disapprobation on his way to the Tuileries.

In his editorial sanctum sat our friend Beauchamp, of whom for some time we have lost sight, but who has, meanwhile, been most industriously at work in his paper, "Le Charivari," in concert with "Le National" and other larger sheets, in forwarding the cause of reform and, finally, of revolution.

The door opened and Chateau-Renaud appeared.

"Farewell, Beauchamp!" he exclaimed, "I've not a moment to lose! A post-chaise is at the door! Farewell!"

"Off!" cried the journalist, in astonishment. "And whither--and why?"

"Yes, off for England--Italy--America--anywhere but France!" exclaimed the young noble.

"And why?"

"Why?" cried the indignant Deputy. "Look around you and then ask what there is left in France for me! Beauchamp," continued the young man hurriedly and in low tones, "France will have no King at this hour to-morrow! Mark the prophecy! The National Guard fraternizes with the populace; the Line fraternizes with the Guard. The Government is, of course, paralyzed. All is over; six hours hence the Tuileries will be ransacked by a drunken mob!--Farewell!"

"One moment! Why do you leave in this way? Why do you not go to Boulogne by the cars?"

"And do you not know--you, a journalist--that for three leagues around, in every direction, every railway radiating from Paris has been torn up? Do you not know that every public conveyance, even to the Mail Diligences, has been stopped, and that all the telegraph stations have been dismantled--all to prevent the further concentration of troops in Paris by the Government?"

"I did hear of this, indeed," said Beauchamp.

"At dawn I was at the railway depot, having late last night, with extreme difficulty, procured a passport. And whom think you, among crowds of others, I encountered there? You would never guess, and I haven't time for you to try. Lucien Debray, and with him--but that's impossible for you to divine--she who was Madame Danglars, wife of the rich banker years ago. Well, the banker is dead and she is immensely rich, and I suppose Lucien's spouse into the bargain."

"And where go they?"

"Oh! to England of course--that grand reservoir of all emigrant royalists, that asylum for all who love kings! But farewell, farewell! If I am not off soon I may have to go without my head! And if you are not massacred by your detestable party, I hope to hear of you yet as a Cabinet Minister. Despite your abominable principles, you have my best wishes! Farewell!"

And with a hearty shake of Beauchamp's hand, the young noble was off for an atmosphere more congenial to monarchists than was that of Paris.

Nor was he alone. Thousands fled from Paris in like manner that same day, and the only cry that followed them was this:

"Let them go! Let them go!"

The streets of Paris were now choked with barricades--not the mere temporary breastworks of the first and second days, which a single charge of heavy dragoons would sweep away, but regular systematic, scientific structures, erected apparently under the direction of military engineers, and calculated upon every principle of art to insure resistance. Some of them were of immense size--that, for example, at the corner of the Rue Richelieu; some had port-holes from which protruded the mouths of ordnance in battery; all were surmounted by a flag, tri-color or red, and all were defended by desperate men. Some other thoroughfares were crossed by many barricades--the Rue St. Martin, for instance, by thirty or forty. The troops assailing these structures were mowed down, throughout the day, in a manner which even their opponents deemed most merciless. Instances of individual bravery on both sides were frequent. In the Rue Mauconseil, a young man exposed himself on the top of the barricade, time after time, firing with fatal aim, and every time a shower of balls from the troops assailing whistled around him. But he stood untouched, and, at length, the officer ordering the troops to fire at him no more, he retired at once behind the breastwork. A boy in the Rue St. Honore mounted the barricade, enveloped in a tri-color flag, and dared the troops to fire on their colors. He descended unharmed. An officer of the Line was summoned to yield his sword. He did so, but first broke it in twain across his knee. The same demand was made to a lieutenant of the Municipal Guard, with a musket at his breast; he was bidden also to shout "Vive la Republique!" but he only cried "Vive le Roi!" as the weapon was wrenched from his grasp! Yet he was spared. Arms were demanded from every householder, and when given, the gift was endorsed on the door in these words: "Here we were given arms." One man received a sword splendidly decorated with gems upon its scabbard and hilt. "I want only the blade!" he said, tearing it away from its ornaments and grasping the naked steel!

At ten o'clock M. Odillon Barrot, General Lamoriciere and Horace Vernet, the great marine artist, proceeded on horseback to the barricades to induce the people to disperse, but all their eloquent entreaties were received only with insults. "No truce--no tricks--no mistake this time!" were the decisive shouts with which they were greeted. A second time, in the Rue Richelieu, General Lamoriciere, accompanied by Moline Saint Gru bearing a palm-branch, was equally unsuccessful. "It is too late!" was the terrible response from the heart of the barricades, followed by a shower of stones, one of which wounded General Lamoriciere on the hand. A third time, in the Rue Rohan, General Gourgaud, who even promised the abdication of the King, met with the same utter defeat, and hastily fled from the fury of the monster now thoroughly roused.

At twelve o'clock the rumor sped with lightning rapidity through the streets of Paris that the troops, who had ostensibly been ordered to their quarters, were, in fact, concentrated around the palace. Instantly rose the shout, "To the Tuileries! To the Tuileries!" and a hundred thousand men from all sections of the city marched toward the Palais Bourbon and the Tuileries!

The rumor of the concentration at the palace was true. The Place du Carrousel was crowded with troops of every arm, including several squadrons of cuirassiers, and six pieces of ordnance were in position, with their ammunition caissons and their provisions and baggage wagons, as if for a siege. The King, attended by his staff and accompanied by the Dukes of Nemours and Montpensier, now descended into the court to pass the troops in review. The Line shouted "Vive le Roi!" as the King rode along. The National Guards, with tones and looks of menace and defiance, cried "Reform!" The King replied, "Yes, my friends, you shall have reform," and sad and dispirited turned away to his apartments; as he retired the bitter murmur was heard from his aged lips, "Like Charles X."

A deputation of the people had been admitted within the limits of the Place du Carrousel to announce the terms they would accept, but after a brief parley had retired dissatisfied. The men of the barricades now invested the Tuileries and the Palais Royal on every side.

Such was the scene without. Within, all was confusion and dismay. The salons were thronged by deputies, peers, generals and marshals; Bugeaud, Lamoriciere, Dupin, Thiers, de Lasteyrie and many others were there, together with all of the Royal family then in the capital, whether male or female.

Meanwhile, the rattle of musketry, broken by the occasional roar of ordnance, in the direction of the Palais Royal, indicated the severe struggle then going on between the people and the troops; from time to time, the furious shout of "To the guillotine with Louis Philippe!" reached the ear.

"Does your Majesty hear that?" asked the Duke of Nemours coldly of his dismayed father. Alas! the old man was no longer the hero of July 3d!

"I do, my son," was the trembling reply. "Do you advise abdication?"

"Is there any other course left?" asked the Duke of Montpensier.

"Any other course!" cried the Queen, indignantly. "Oh! are you my son--are you a son of Orleans, and can you talk thus of degradation? Are you a soldier and do you fear? Mount!--mount!--charge on the rebels!--cut them to the earth!--drench the pavement with their blood!--perish, but yield not ignominiously thus!"

"Madame," said M. Thiers, solemnly, "it is too late! There must be an abdication in favor of the Count of Paris, and the appointment of the Duchess of Orleans as Regent, or all is lost!"

"Then if this must be, let it be done with dignity becoming a monarch," said the noble Queen. "Let us all retire to St. Cloud. There may be dictated terms of honorable capitulation. There--"

At that instant in rushed a man breathless, bearing a sheet of paper in his hand, and exclaiming:

"Sire--Sire--your troops are delivering their arms to the people! In a moment they will stand where you now stand! Sign this paper, or your life and the lives of all your family will be sacrificed!"

That man was Emile de Girardin, the editor of "La Presse," and the murderer of Armand Carrel, and that paper was an act of abdication.

"Ah! this is a bitter cup," said the old King as he placed his signature to the sheet, "and doubly bitter presented by such a hand! Like Charles X.!"

At one o'clock, at the Bourse and at the corners of all the principal streets, was posted this proclamation:

"CITIZENS OF PARIS: The King has abdicated in favor of the Count of Paris, with the Duchess of Orleans as Regent.

A General Amnesty.

Dissolution of the Chamber.

Appeal to the Country."

But the people were now in the midst of the assault on the Palais Royal, and to check them was impossible.

The Palais Royal consisted of two portions--the Chateau d'Eau, or palace, and the other part, which though the property of the Orleans family was yet rented by private persons, and was occupied for cafes, shops, dwellings and places of entertainment--adorned by colonnades and arcades, and by trees, statues and fountains in the magnificent quadrangle. The property of the citizens was respected--that of the King only was assailed. For two hours did the 14th Regiment pour forth its fire from the numerous windows of that edifice and from the court below. At length, a band of bold Republicans, headed by the chivalric Etienne Arago, musket in hand, charged from the side of the Cafe de la Regence, followed by a detachment of the National Guard, and, driving the troops into the building, surrounded it with straw which they set on fire. The vast edifice was instantly filled with smoke and flame. The defence ceased. The soldiers rushed out and were instantly slain. The commander of the detachment was pierced by a bayonet. The multitude rushed in, and the building was sacked. The richest and most costly furniture and decorations were at once torn down, dashed to pieces and thrown from the windows by the infuriated populace.

Within the Palace of the Tuileries is a subterranean passage, constructed for the infant King of Rome and his nurses, which, plunging beneath the pavements, and passing along the whole length of the gardens, under the terrace beside the river bank, suddenly emerges at the gate of the Place du Carrousel, in front of the obelisk. Into this passage, in wild panic, descended the King and Queen of France, with all their children and grandchildren, immediately upon the signing of the abdication, and just as the doors were about to be forced. Emerging from the passage, the King, leaning on the arm of his faithful wife, Marie Amelie, and followed by the Royal party, crossed the Place de la Concorde as far as the asphalt pavement. The Royal party now consisted of the King and Queen, the Duchess of Nemours and her children, the Princess Clementine and her husband, the Duke Augustus of Saxe-Coburg, and the Duke of Montpensier with his young and lovely Spanish bride, now enceinte and far advanced. Ignorant of the language, only sixteen years of age, a stranger to the customs and people of the country, and in her delicate situation, the position of this young creature was peculiarly trying. At one moment she clung with terror to her young husband's arm, which she refused for an instant to resign, and the next laughed at her own terror, saying that one who in her infancy had twice, in Madrid, been saved by being carried off in a sack ought not now to fear when she had feet to carry herself away and was suffered to use them! It is said that the fair Senora was forgotten in the hurry of the flight and almost left behind!

As soon as the Royal party were perceived, they were surrounded by a troop of National Guards as an escort, and a large number of officers of the Line in various uniforms. The King leaned on the Queen, as if for support, while she boldly advanced with a firm step and stern look. Both were in deepest mourning for the recent death of the beloved sister of the King, the Princess Adelaide.

Upon this melancholy procession the people gazed with mingled curiosity, amusement, gratification and regret.

"They are going to the Chamber of Deputies to complete the abdication!" cries one.

"Vive la Reforme!" shouts another.

"Vive la France!" shouts a second.

"Vive le Roi!" in suppressed tones falters a third.

"See the poor young Duchess!" cried a woman, who was availing herself of her peculiar rotundity as a battering-ram to force her way through the crowd.

"She had better have remained at home!" sneered a Dynastic bitterly.

"The poor little children!" exclaimed a young woman more remarkable for prettiness than neatness, and more remarkable still for the scantiness of her attire, nearly all of which had been torn from her rounded shoulders in the throng.

The spirit which pervaded the mass was, evidently, by no means unfriendly to the Royal family, and it was as evidently misunderstood by them, for, suddenly, as if by fatality, on the very spot where Louis XVI. was beheaded, just beyond the Pont Tournant, on the pavement of the Obelisk of Luxor, the whole party, with no apparent necessity, came to a dead and complete halt. Instantly the multitude was crowded upon them, and this augmented their terror. The King dropped the Queen's arm and hastily raising his hat cried, "Vive la Reforme!" All was in a moment uproar and confusion. The Queen in terror at finding her husband's arm was gone turned hurriedly on every side.

"Fear not, Madame," said a mild voice beside her. "The people will do you no harm."

This was M. Maurice, editor of "Le Courrier des Spectacles."

"Leave me, leave me, Monsieur!" she exclaimed, in great excitement, evidently mistaking the words. Then regaining her husband, she again grasped his arm, and the mass at the same time opening its ranks, the two hastened on to a couple of those little black one-horse vehicles, chancing there to stand, which run to St. Cloud. In one of these already sat the Duchesses of Montpensier and Nemours with two of the children. In the other stood the two remaining children. Into the latter hurriedly stepped the Royal pair. The door was instantly closed and the vehicle drove off at a furious rate, surrounded by an escort of dragoons, cuirassiers and National Guards, two hundred in number, taking the water-side toward St. Cloud. The other carriage, similarly escorted, followed at a like rapid pace, the children standing at the windows, their faces pressed to the glass, gazing eagerly, with the innocent curiosity of infancy, on a scene from which their future fate would take shape.

"He is gone!" shouted a stentorian voice, breaking the momentary stillness as the carriages, surrounded by their escort, swept from the view.

"Let him go! Let him go!" was the stern and significant response. "We are not regicides!"

"To the Tuileries! To the Tuileries!" was now the tremendous shout which rose from the multitude, as they rushed toward the deserted palace.

But the Tuileries had already fallen. It was no longer the dwelling-place of kings.

Even before the Royal abdication was declared, even before it was signed, the troops of the Line in the courtyard of the palace--infantry, artillery, dragoons--to the number at least of twenty-five thousand, were summoned to surrender their posts, while the fraternal shout, "Vive la Ligne!" elicited from the lips of many of the soldiers the answering cry of "Vive la Reforme!" In vain was it that Marshal Bugeaud, the veteran of a hundred battles, menaced and blasphemed. In vain did his old protege and subaltern, but now bitter foe, General Lamoriciere, dashing from one end of the line to the other on his white horse, entreat and persuade with his eloquent tongue. The people insisted--the National Guard fraternized--the Line wavered. And yet most imminent at that moment was their own peril.

The 1st, 2d, 3d, 4th, 6th and 10th Legions of the National Guard invested the Tuileries, and others were on the march, accompanied by countless masses of the people. Within the courtyard were twenty-five thousand of the best troops in the world of every arm, and a park of ordnance charged to the muzzle frowned upon the dense masses which swarmed the Place du Carrousel. The watchful artilleryman stood at his cannon's breech, with the lighted linstock in his hand, which he kept alive by constant motion. He awaited but a word from the pale, firm lips of General Lamoriciere, and that vast and magnificent space now swarming with life would have been swept as if by destruction's besom. Death in all its most horrid forms would have been there. That pavement would have run with gore! The facades of those splendid edifices would have been polluted with shreds and fragments of human flesh, and spattered with human blood. Yet dreadful would have been the sure retribution! Indiscriminate massacre of all unfortunate souls within that Royal palace would have been inevitable and instantaneous. Yet, such a catastrophe might be precipitated by a single word!--the avalanche might be started by a single breath; and blood once shed, Paris would be deluged!

"In the name of the people I demand to speak with the commandant of the Tuileries!" shouted a young man in the uniform of an officer of the National Guard, advancing to the iron railing of the court near the Rue de Rivoli.

It was Lieutenant Aubert Roche. The commandant was sent for and immediately arrived.

"Monsieur, you are lost!" cried the young man.

"You are surrounded by sixty thousand men of the National Guard, and one hundred thousand of the people of Paris!"

"What is demanded?" was the trembling response.

"That you evacuate the Tuileries!--resign it to the National Guard!"

"The troops shall be withdrawn, Monsieur. Orders for their retirement to the palace shall be issued instantly."

"That will not do! The palace must be evacuated," insisted the Lieutenant, "or the people will raze it to the ground!"

"Come with me, Monsieur," said the commandant.

The gate was immediately opened, and Lieutenant Roche, accompanied by M. Leseur, chef de bataillon, bearing a flag of truce, followed the commandant to the Pavillon de l'Horloge, where stood the Duke of Nemours, pale with excitement, surrounded by generals.

"Monseigneur," said the commandant, "suffer me to present a deputation from the people."

"Messieurs, what do the people demand?" asked the Duke in trembling tones.

"The evacuation, this instant, of this palace, and its delivery to the National Guard!"

"And if we do not comply?" asked Marshal Bugeaud, calmly.

"Then, Monsieur, you all are lost!" was the bold answer. "This palace is surrounded by one hundred and sixty thousand men. The combat once begun must be exterminating--must be a massacre! The 5th Legion of the National Guard, to which I belong, is, at this moment, sacking the Palais Royal. It may be here before we part!"

"The troops shall retire, Monsieur," said the Duke; and on the instant orders for the retreat were issued.

The artillery went by the railing of the palace, and the staff and the Duke of Nemours by the Pavillon de l'Horloge, their well-trained horses descending the flight of steps. The cavalry followed, succeeded by the infantry.

The National Guards were then introduced by Lieutenant Roche, and entered the court of the Tuileries by the gate of the Rue de Rivoli, their muskets shouldered, with the stock in the air. At the same moment the abdication of the King was declared. General Lamoriciere had resigned. The Ministry was dissolved. There was a tremendous shout, and the conquerors of the Palais Royal rushed in to take possession of the Tuileries!

# CHAPTER XXII.
# THE LAST SESSION OF THE
# CHAMBER OF DEPUTIES.

The usual hour for the opening of the Chamber of Deputies was three o'clock; but the startling events of the last two days, and especially of the last two hours, demanded that it should be convened earlier.

At one o'clock the President of the Chamber, Sauzet, took the chair. On the left bank of the Seine all the approaches were open, save the bridges of the Place de la Concorde, where strong detachments of cavalry were posted on guard.

Within the Chamber all was solemnity. About three hundred members were present. The opposition seemed joyous and confident, though anxious. The conservative party was troubled. The Ministerial benches were deserted.

At half-past one the President turned round in his chair, and kept his eye fixed upon a side door, as if expecting some one to enter. Suddenly a bustle was heard in that direction, and the Duchess of Orleans, in deep mourning, attended by her two sons and followed by the Dukes of Montpensier and Nemours, entered. The latter was received with marked expressions of dislike. The Count of Paris, garbed in complete black, was conducted through the crowd to the space in front of the President's chair; the Duchess followed and seated herself in a fauteuil upon the same spot. On each side of her was one of her sons, and behind her stood her brothers, the Dukes of Nemours and Montpensier. This position was subsequently changed for one more distant, but otherwise remained throughout relatively the same.

Being seated, the Duchess rose and bowed repeatedly to the assembly. At the same moment an immense multitude of National Guards and the people rushed in through the passages, and despite the shouts of the officers, "You cannot enter!" the space beneath the tribune was instantly and densely thronged. At the same time the public tribunes were invaded by a second body of the people.

For some minutes the greatest uproar prevailed. At length it comparatively ceased, and, in a moment of quiet, M. Dupin, who had accompanied the Duchess of

Orleans to the Chamber, ascended the tribune. The stillness was instantly as great as had been the previous agitation.

"The King has abdicated," said M. Dupin. "The Count of Paris is nominated as his successor and the Duchess of Orleans as Regent."

"It is too late!" shouted a man from the gallery of the people.

"The Count of Paris is proclaimed King by the Chamber and the Duchess of Orleans Regent!' exclaimed the President.

"No--no--no!" was the almost unanimous shout that now rose in the Chamber.

"I demand," cried M. Lamartine, "that the Royal family withdraw!"

The question was put, and the Duchess and her sons, after great hesitation, were drawn away to a side door, at the further end of the hall. At the same moment a new crowd of the people rushed in and took seats beside the opposition members, by whom they were welcomed.

"I demand to speak!" cried M. Marie. "By the law of 1842, the Duke of Nemours is Regent. How can the King abrogate that law? I demand a provisional government!"

"A provisional government!" cried M. Cremieux. "We made a mistake in '30. Let there be no mistake in '48!"

"A provisional government," said the Abbe Genoude, a Legitimist; "but it must be the will of the people!"

M. Odillon Barrot, who had been long expected, now entered and immediately mounted the tribune.

"The crown of July rests on the head of a woman and a child!" cried the great lawyer.

The Duchess of Orleans instantly rose, as if about to speak, but, at the urgent solicitation of those around her, resumed her seat.

"I call on the country to rally around this woman and this child," cried M. Barrot, "the two-fold representative of the principles of July, '30!"

The voice of the speaker was drowned in shouts of dissent and of "Vive la Reforme!"

"I dissent from the opinion of M. Odillon Barrot!" cried the Marquis de la Rochejacquelin. "If he is right, the people are nothing!"

"Order--order!" cried the President, putting on his hat, but he was at once induced to remove it.

At this moment another vast crowd burst into the Chamber, garbed in a style so heterogeneous as to be grotesque--some with blouses--some with dragoon helmets on their heads, some with weapons and many with flags.

"Down--down--down with the Throne!" was the terrible cry of this infuriated mass.

"I demand that the sitting be suspended!" cried M. de Mornay.

"There can be no session at such a moment," said the President, putting on his hat.

"Off--off--off with your hat, President!" cried the populace; and several of their muskets were at once pointed at the President. The hat was removed.

The scene was chaos!

"Beware!" shouted M. Chevalier, editor of the Historical Library. "Beware how you make the Count of Paris King! A provisional government we must first have!"

"What right have you to speak?" shouted a man. "You are not a deputy!"

"In the name of the people, silence!" roared a terrific voice that drowned every other.

It was the voice of Ledru Rollin.

Many of the deputies now withdrew, and their places were filled by the people. The Duchess of Orleans sat calmly amid the uproar, and the Duke of Nemours with equal calmness stood behind her chair.

"The throne has been tumbled from the windows of the Tuileries and is now burning in the Place de la Bastille!" cried M. Dumoulin, who commanded the Hotel de Ville in July of '30, displaying the tri-color flag.

"No more Bourbons! Down with the Bourbons! Down with the traitors! A provisional government!" shouted the people.

"Aye, a Republic!" cried M. Chevalier.

Cremieux, Ledru Rollin and Lamartine were at the same time in the tribune.

"In the name of the people, silence!" again roared the awful voice of Ledru Rollin.

"A provisional government!" shouted one of the people.

"You shall have a provisional government!" exclaimed M. Maguin.

"In the name of the people--in the name of the people of Paris in arms," again began Ledru Rollin, "I protest against this King and this Regency. The constitution of '9 demands the will of the people to fix a Regency. Yet the law of '42 makes the Duke of Nemours Regent, and now it is the Duchess of Orleans. I protest against it all! I demand a provisional government!"

"Question--question!" shouted M. Berryer. "A provisional government!"

"In 1815," continued Ledru Rollin, "Napoleon abdicated in favor of the King of Rome. The King of Rome was refused. In 1830, Charles X. abdicated in favor of his grandson. The grandson was rejected. In 1848, Louis Philippe abdicates in favor of his grandson--the Count of Paris!"

"Question--question!" again vociferated M. Berryer. "We all know those histories!"

"In the name of the people," continued Ledru Rollin, "I demand a provisional government, named by the people--not by the Chamber--but by the people!"

Tremendous shouts followed, and M. Lamartine, who had stood beside Rollin in the tribune, now took his place amid renewed shouts.

After an eloquent speech on the same side as his friend, he concluded by demanding a provisional government, with an appeal to "the people--the entire people--all who by the title of man have rights as men."

While Lamartine was yet speaking, a violent knocking was heard at the door of the Chamber, which was forcibly burst open and a vast crowd rushed in.

"Down with the Chamber! Down with the Deputies!" shouted the populace, and muskets were instantly leveled at Lamartine, and, also, at the Royal party.

"It is Lamartine! it is Lamartine!" was the cry of terror that rose from his friends.

The muskets were lowered.

The Duchess and her party were at once withdrawn from the Chamber by a side door, and having first retired to the Hotel des Invalides, next fled to the Rhine; the Duke of Nemours fled to Boulogne and thence to England.

"Silence--silence--silence!" shouted the President, violently ringing his bell. But the uproar only increased. "I pronounce this session closed!" cried the President, and putting on his hat he instantly left the chair.

Here ends the Chamber of Deputies.

A large number of the members withdrew with the President, but the opposition remained, and with them the people and the National Guards.

After the noise incident to this departure had subsided, the venerable M. Dupont de l'Eure, a gray-headed old man of eighty, was, by unanimous acclamation, placed in the President's chair. Lamartine still remained in the tribune, and repeatedly strove to make his voice heard, but in vain.

"In the name of the people, silence, and let Lamartine speak!" at length was heard in the thunder tones of Ledru Rollin, rising above all other sounds.

Silence for a moment being obtained, Lamartine exclaimed:

"Citizens!--a provisional government is declared! The names of the members will now be announced by the President!"

Lamartine then descended from the tribune; applause and uproar succeeded.

"The names of the members nominated for a provisional government I will now read to you," said the aged President, rising and displaying a paper.

The following names were then read, and were repeated as they came one after the other from the speaker's mouth by the reporters in loud tones: Lamartine, Ledru Rollin, Arago, Dupont de l'Eure, Marie, Georges Lafayette; all were received with general approbation.

"The members of the Provisional Government must be conducted by the people to the Hotel de Ville and installed!" cried a voice from the crowd.

"Let us adjourn to the Hotel de Ville, Lamartine at the head!" said M. Bocage.

Immediately Lamartine, accompanied by a large number of citizens, withdrew. But a great multitude still remained upon the benches and in the semi-circle of the Chamber.

"Citizens!" cried Ledru Rollin, "in nominating a provisional government you perform a solemn act--an act which cannot be performed in a furious manner. Let me once more repeat to you the names you have chosen, and as they are repeated, you will say 'yes' or 'no,' precisely as they please you; I call on the reporters of the public press to note the names and the manner in which they are now received, that France may know what is here done."

The names of Dupont de l'Eure, Arago, Lamartine, Ledru Rollin, Cremieux, Garnier Pages and Marie were then read out, and all, except the last two--which were received with a few negatives--were confirmed by unanimous acclamation.

The names were then engrossed in capitals on a sheet of paper and borne around the Chamber on the bayonet of a National Guard that all might read for themselves.

"I have one more word to say," cried Ledru Rollin. "The Provisional Government has immense duties to perform. We must now close this meeting, that the Government may be able to restore order--stanch the flow of blood, and secure to the people their rights."

"To the Hotel de Ville!--to the Hotel de Ville!" responded the people in a tremendous shout. "Vive la Republique!--to the Hotel de Ville!"

Headed by Ledru Rollin the excited multitude withdrew, and at four o'clock all was as silent in the Chamber of Deputies as if not a voice had resounded or a footstep had echoed within its walls for centuries. In the distance, however, could be heard the repeated shout:

"Vive la Republique!--to the Hotel de Ville!"

# CHAPTER XXIII.
# THE SACK OF THE TUILERIES.

Scarcely had the carriages conveying the Royal family disappeared on their flight toward St. Cloud, when the whole mass of the populace poured as with one simultaneous purpose into the deserted palace. The Palais Bourbon had already been sacked; a like fate might be supposed to await the Tuileries; but the Tuileries belonged to France, not to the House of Orleans, and a certain respect was observed for everything but the insignia of Royalty. For these was shown no regard. The throne itself of the state reception-room--that throne on which sat Louis Philippe for the first time, as King of the French, ere the Tuileries became his throne--was torn from its base, and, having been hurled first in derision from the windows into the court, was borne in mock triumph on the shoulders of men, who shouted that now the throne was indeed supported by the people, to the Place de la Bastille, and there consumed to ashes. In the courtyard, in the Rue de Rivoli and on the quays, huge fires roared, fanned into fury by a hurricane of wind, and fed by richly carved furniture, gilded chairs, canopies, pianos, sofas, beds, costly paintings, splendid works of art and the Royal carriages glittering with gold. The magnificent tapestries of the Gobelins were borne as streamers, in frantic fury, along the boulevards; mischievous gamins were frolicking about in the long scarlet robes worn upon Court occasions, which they had filched from the Royal wardrobe; the escritoire of the King, the key having been found in a tea-cup, was ransacked, and private letters, books and the garments of ladies were strewn about the court and gardens of the Tuileries. The cellars of the palace were soon filled with the insurgents; but they declared the wine bad, as it never remained long enough in the cellars of kings to get good! Destruction, not pillage, seemed the order of the hour, and to guard against robbery the people took upon themselves the arrest and punishment of offenders. The walls bore the menace, "Robbers shall die!" In several instances the threat was carried into immediate execution, and bodies, suffered to lie on the spot upon which they had been cut down, bore on their breasts the label "Thief!" in terrible warning. Sentinels also stood at the gates, and no one was allowed to leave the palace without rigorous search.

In the apartments of the Duchess of Orleans, the table was found spread for the dinner of herself and her children; upon the table were the little silver cups, forks and spoons of the young Princes, and on the floor were scattered their costly toys. The latter were gathered carefully up by a workman in a blouse, and as carefully concealed in a corner. The former, together with all jewels and other valuables found in the apartments of the Duchess, were deposited in a bathing-tub, on which a workman seated himself as guard and suffered no one to approach until the aforesaid valuables could be conveyed by a detachment of the Polytechnic School to the Government treasury. The story runs that, on the night succeeding the sack of the Tuileries, the conquerors chose a king and queen, and that, in the palace hall, was spread a banquet composed of the viands found in the Royal kitchen and the wines found in the Royal cellars. The queen, who was a soubrette more noticeable for beauty than for cleanliness of person, garbed in Royal robes which she well became, and with a coronet upon her stately brow, was seated in a chair of state and received the most extravagant homage from her willing subjects, while groups of gamins, in the long crimson liveries of the Royal household, boisterously frolicked before the sans culotte court amid roars of merriment.

# CHAPTER XXIV.
# A MEMORABLE NIGHT.

Generally, the rogues throughout Paris, intimidated by the awful, immediate and certain penalty for crime, forsook, for the time, their calling. A man who attempted to fire the Palais Royal was shot at the Prefecture. Another, for a like attempt on buildings in the Rue Monceau, met a like fate. In the Rue Richelieu lay the bodies of two thieves, each with a ball through the breast, and over the aperture the word "Thief" on a label. In like manner were eight more robbers executed at once on the Place de la Madeleine. A woman of the street wrested a bracelet from a lady's wrist; she was instantly seized by the bystanders and shot. But for this summary punishment of malefactors by the people, dreadful that night would have been the state of Paris, without laws to enforce or a police to enforce them. It is true the Chateau of Neuilly was sacked and burned, as well as the splendid villa of the Baron Rothschild at Parennes; but both were supposed to be the property of the King. It is true, also, that some rails on the Northern Railway were torn up, and a viaduct between Paris and Amiens, and another between Amiens and the frontier of Belgium were demolished; and that the railway stations at St. Denis, Enghien and Pontoise and the bridge at Asnieres had been destroyed; but all this was done to prevent the concentration upon the citizens of Paris of additional Royal troops.

A workman entered a house and demanded bread. Meat and wine were offered him. "No," was the reply, "bread and water are all I want."

Yet such was the scarcity of food that horses were killed and eaten at the Hotel de Ville, on the third day of the Revolution.

"Arms--arms!" shouted a band of workmen, entering a house on the Rue Richelieu. The proprietor, alarmed, shouted for help. "Do you think us robbers?" was the indignant reply. "Give us your weapons!"

The weapons were given and the band retired; on the door they wrote, "Here we received arms!"

At five o'clock, on the evening of the 24th of February, a proclamation to the citizens of Paris, issued by the Provisional Government then in session at the Hotel de Ville, declared the Revolution accomplished--that eighty thousand of the National Guard and one hundred thousand of the people were in arms--that order as well as liberty must now be secured, and the people, with the National Guard, were appointed guardians of Paris.

The effect of this proclamation was magical. Never was Paris so well protected as on that night of the 24th of February, when, filled with barricades, she had no police and was guarded by her citizens.

And how was constituted the Provisional Government whose power was thus implicitly obeyed? It was founded by the people who obeyed it. This was the only secret.

From the Chamber of Deputies to the Hotel de Ville proceeded the members of the Provisional Government. They marched under a canopy of sabres, pikes and bayonets into halls stained with blood and encumbered with the slain, and there, at a small table, while the conflict between the two Republics had already commenced, within an hour had they organized their body by the nomination of Armand Marrast, of "Le National," Ferdinand Flocon, of "La Reforme," Albert, a workman, and Louis Blanc, the editor and author, as Secretaries of the Government; their first official act was to issue a proclamation to the people.

The scenes witnessed the night which succeeded in Paris will never be forgotten by those who witnessed them. Patrols promenaded the streets, the men of the barricades slept upon their weapons, beside their works, and through all that night ceaselessly toiled the press to spread over all the world the news of the great events of the three past days in Paris.

Upon the door of an edifice situated in the Rue Jean Jacques Rousseau--a street which was filled with barricades of immense size and strength--was posted a printed placard, "The Provisional Government," lighted by a single lamp. Entering the door with a vast multitude, and ascending the dark and winding staircase, you found yourself in a large room, dimly lighted and crowded with armed men.

It was the editorial apartment of the office of "La Reforme."

At a large and massive table sat a dozen persons most industriously employed in writing. Around them, looking on, rose the rough, stern faces of the men of the barricades, seeming still more rough and stern by reason of the shadowy light; in the hands of all were weapons.

"A copy of the names of the members of the Provisional Government!" was the incessant demand of these armed men, a demand which the dozen writers at the table were unable even by most indefatigable industry to supply as fast as made. And as fast as the demand was satisfied, the armed men would hurry away, only to leave room for the crowds constantly entering.

"A copy for the Hotel de Ville!" cried one.

"A copy for the Place Vendome!" shouted another.

"A copy for the Palais Bourbon!" screamed a third.

"Are there no printed copies left?" asked many.

"They were gone long ago--twenty thousand copies," was the reply. "You will see one at every corner. The demand was not expected. The printers have just gone to sleep. They had not rested for fifty-two hours."

"Will 'La Reforme' appear in the morning?" asked another.

"Perhaps so," was the answer. "But all the people are worn out--writers and compositors. Here is your copy of the names."

"Many thanks. Vive la Republique!"

With this shout, in concert with the same which constantly issued from a hundred lips, the citizen folded up his precious document, and carefully depositing it in his cap hurried off to communicate its contents to his comrades of the neighboring barricade.

In another apartment of that same edifice were a large number of the Republican party connected with "La Reforme."

"The Provisional Government is now in session," said one. "They will, doubtless, make immediate provision for departments of State so important as the post-office and the prefecture of police. Early to-morrow a proclamation----"

"To-morrow may be too late," interrupted a large and muscular man. "The post-office is more active than ever to-night. Every moment couriers are arriving and departing. That powerful instrument remains in the hands of the foes of our cause! Who may estimate the injury, the irreparable injury which they may this night accomplish by its means!"

This man was Etienne Arago, brother of the great astronomer, and, for sixteen years, celebrated as one of the boldest members of the Republican party, as well as one of the bravest men in Paris.

"And the prefecture of police," observed another--"the present utter derangement of all its functions may lead to most serious results. Already those foes of freedom, Guizot and his colleagues, have been suffered to secure their escape from the just indignation of an outraged people. Delessert, the Prefect, has also fled!"

The man who said this was Marc Caussidiere, a well-known Republican.

"Citizens!" cried M. Gouache, "this state of things must continue no longer. In the name of the people, I demand that Etienne Arago immediately assume the charge of the post-office, as its director, and that Marc Caussidiere fill the position of Prefect."

This demand was confirmed by acclamation, and committees for the installation of the nominees into office at once accompanied them to their respective departments.

The immense edifice of the post-office was surrounded by people, and its numerous windows were flashing with lights. Within the utmost activity seemed to prevail, and without couriers were leaving and arriving every moment, and mail coaches were dashing up to discharge their burdens, or, having received them, were dashing off.

"In the name of the people, entrance for Citizen Etienne Arago, Republican director of the post-office!" shouted one of the committee.

Instantly a passage through the immense crowd in the courtyard was cleared by the National Guard, and the director entered with his escort.

"In the name of the people, Citizen Dejean, you are dismissed," said Etienne Arago, entering the private cabinet of the Director General.

"And who is to be my successor?" asked the astonished Count, rising to his feet.

"In the name of the people, I am sent to displace and to succeed you," was the answer.

"But your commission, Monsieur?"

"Is here," pointing to the committee.

"Before I resign the direction of this department," said the Count after some hesitation, "I must ask of you for some record of this act, bearing your signature, to be deposited in the archives of the office."

"Certainly, Monsieur, your request is but reasonable," answered Arago, seating himself in the official chair. And writing a few lines to which he affixed his signature, he coolly handed the document to his astonished predecessor. It contained notice of his own appointment by the people, in place of the Count Dejean, dismissed.

The Count read and folded the paper, and having made a copy of it, which he laid carefully in his porte-monnaie, he placed the original on file among the papers of the day belonging to the department. Then, courteously bowing, he took his hat and cane and marched out of the building.

# CHAPTER XXV.
# THE PROVISIONAL GOVERNMENT.

In the Hotel de Ville, closely closeted, sat the Provisional Government of France. Over that stern old citadel, over the dismantled Palace of the Tuileries, from the tall summit of the Column of Vendome, over the Hotel des Invalides and in the Place de la Bastille is seen a blood-red banner, streaming out like a meteor on the keen north-western blast. Eighty thousand armed men invest the Hotel de Ville, and wave on wave, wave on wave, the living and stormy tide eddies and welters and dashes around that dark old pile. All its avenues are held; its courts are thronged; ordnance frowns from its black portals and against its gates; drums roll- -banners stream--bayonets glitter; and from those tens of thousands of hoarse and stormy voices goes up but one shout of menace and command:

"Vive la Republique! Vive la Republique! No kings! No Bourbons! Down--down forever with the kings!"

And upward to that dark old pile of despotism, as to the temple of Liberty herself, are turned those tens of thousands of swarthy faces, dark with the smoke of battle, yet livid with excitement and exhaustion--and as they realize that within those walls the question of their fate and that of their country is then being settled- -that from that night's counsels in that vast and ancient edifice are to flow peace and prosperity, and freedom and plenty, or else all the untold terrors of anarchy, civil war, bloodshed, violence and strife--what wonder that the sitting of the council seemed endless and their own impatience became intolerable--that all imaginable doubts and fears and absurd apprehensions took possession of their inflamed imaginations?--that at one time the rumor should fly, and win credence as it flew, that the Provisional Government were consulting with the friends of Henry V.--or again, that they were considering the question of a Regency--and that under such influences they should roar and yell, and thunder for admission at the gates, and burden the air with their shouts?

"No Bourbons! No kings! No Regency! Death--death to all kings! La Republique! La Republique! La Republique!"

At times, in terrific concert, would the thousands of uplifted throats roar forth the chorus of that startling canticle of '92:

> "Vive la republique! Vive la republique!
> Debout, peuple Francais! debout, peuple heroique!
> Debout, peuple Francais! Vive la republique!"

Then the song would change and the mournful notes of the "Death Hymn of the Girondins,"--"Mourir Pour la Patrie"--would swell in wild yet solemn cadence on the wintry blast:

### DEATH HYMN OF THE GIRONDINS.

By the voice of the signal cannon,
France calls her sons their aid to lend;
"Let us go," the soldier cries, "to battle!
'Tis our mother we defend!"
To die on Freedom's Altar--to die on Freedom's Altar!
'Tis the noblest of fates; who to meet it would falter!

We who fall afar from the battle,
Lone and unknown obscurely die,
But give at least our parting blessings
Unto France and Freedom high.
To die on Freedom's Altar--to die on Freedom's Altar!

'Tis the noblest of fates; who to meet it would falter!

And thus all that terrible night, even until the morning's dawn, thronged those men of the barricades around the Hotel de Ville, and all the night, even until the morning's dawn, calmly continued those men of the Provisional Government of the French Republic, amid menace and mandate, uproar and confusion, in their noble, yet arduous work. At midnight a proclamation of the Provisional Government was read by torchlight to the excited masses by Louis Blanc, from the steps of the Hotel de Ville, declaring for a government of the people by itself, with liberty, equality and fraternity for its principles, while order was devised and maintained by the people--which served somewhat to allay their apprehensions and distrust. This proclamation appeared in all the morning journals, and was placarded all over the city the next day.

That day was Friday, the 25th of February. But still the Provisional Government remained in session, and still the armed masses of the barricades, in congregated thousands, rolled in tumultuous billows around the Hotel de Ville. At length the populace, exasperated by impatience, hunger and sleeplessness, with brandished bayonets rushed into the very chamber of council, with furious cries, and with threats which were well nigh accomplished. Again and again, at the entreaty of his colleagues, did the brave, the eloquent, the wise Lamartine present himself upon the steps of the Hotel de Ville to assuage and quiet the rising tempest. Again and again, throughout that fearful day, did he come forth, single-handed, to wrestle with violence, turbulence, anarchy and strife; and again and again, beneath the magic of his eloquent tongue, the storm lulled, the tempest ceased. Again and again, throughout all that fearful day, were the acts of that noble Government matured and sent forth. Proclamation followed proclamation, and no branch of society seemed forgotten.

The names of the members of the Provisional Government were again published. Caussidiere and Sobrier were confirmed in the police department, and Etienne Arago in that of the post-office. Merchants of provisions were recommended to supply all who were in need; and the people were recommended to still retain their arms. The Chamber of Deputies was dissolved, the Peers were forbidden to meet, and the convocation of a National Assembly was promised. To all laborers labor was guaranteed and compensation for labor. At noon the garrison of the fort of Vincennes was announced to have acknowledged the Republic, just as the people were about to march upon it. To insure order and tranquillity, the Municipal Guard was disbanded, and the National Guard entrusted with the protection of Paris under M. Courtais, the commandant, who was ordered immediately to recruit twenty-four battalions for active service. All articles pledged at the Mont-de-Piete, from February 4th, not exceeding in value ten francs, were ordered to be returned, and the Tuileries was decreed the future asylum of invalid workmen. An attack on the machinery of some of the printing offices was checked by a proclamation.

General Bedeau was appointed Minister of War, General Cavaignac Governor of Algeria, and Admiral Baudin to the command of the Toulon fleet. On the part of the army Marshal Bugeaud and on the part of the clergy the venerable Archbishop of Paris gave in their adhesion to the Republic, while the entire press, Bourgeoisie and the Provinces hesitated not an instant. Indeed, from all quarters came in adhesions to the Republic. The Bonapartes were among the first. Barrot and Thiers also came, but too late to save themselves from contempt. Mr. Rush, the American Minister, the first of foreign ambassadors acknowledged the Republic. The son of Mehemet Ali was next. The Papal Nuncio succeeded, together with the Ministers of the Argentine Republic and Uruguay. Next came the ambassador of England; but those of Austria, Prussia, Russia and Holland awaited instructions from home--little dreaming of the news they were about to receive! The city of Rouen sent three hundred of its citizens as a deputation, with abundant supplies of arms, by the morning cars of the railway.

At about noon, the Pont Louis Philippe was destroyed by fire. Henceforth it is to be "Le Pont de la Reforme." And so with all other names. Royal is to give place to Republique, and "Liberte, Egalite et Fraternite" is to be again inscribed on all public monuments.

The children of citizens killed in the Revolution were declared adopted by the country. The civil, judicial and administrative functionaries of the Royal Government were announced released from their oaths of office, the colonels of the twelve legions of National Guards were dismissed, and all political prisoners set free. Every citizen was declared an elector, and absolute freedom of thought, the liberty of the press, and the right of political and industrial associations secured to all were proclaimed.

A warrant for the arrest of the late Ministers was issued by the new Procureur-General, M. Portalis, based on an act of accusation presented to the Court of Appeals. But all of them had fled. Guizot is said to have escaped from the Foreign Office in a servant's livery. When the people broke into his hotel, they found only his daughter, and retired. The other members of the Ministry are said to have leaped from a low window of the Tuileries, and to have escaped at the moment of the King's abdication. M. de Cormenin was appointed Conseilleur d'Etat and M. Achille Marrast Procureur-General to the Court of Appeals in Paris, in place of the refugees.

Such were some of the acts of the seven men constituting the Provisional Government of the French Republic, during their first extraordinary session of sixty-four hours--from the hour of four o'clock in the afternoon of Thursday after the dissolution of the Chamber of Deputies to the hour of four o'clock in the morning of Sunday, the 27th of February, when the people of Paris consented to retire to their homes. But during all of this period, night and day without intermission, every moment was the Hotel de Ville surrounded by tumultuous masses infuriated by suspicion, apprehension and distrust. For two whole days and two whole nights armed men incessantly inundated the square, the courts and halls of the Hotel de Ville. They insisted on giving to the Republic the character, the attitude and the emblems of the first Revolution--they insisted on a Republic violent, sweeping, dictatorial and terrorist, in language, in gesture and in color, in place of that determined on, moderate, pacific, legal, unanimous and constitutional. At the peril of their lives the Provisional Government resisted this demand. Twenty times during those sixty-four hours was Lamartine taken up, dragged, carried to the doors and windows or to the head of the grand staircase, into the courts and the square, to hurl down with his eloquence those emblems of terrorism, with which it was attempted to dishonor the Republic. But the vast and infuriated mass refused to listen, and drowned his voice in clamor and vociferation. At length, when well-nigh exhausted in defence of the emblem of a moderate Republic, he exclaimed: "The red flag has been nowhere except around the Champ-de-Mars, trailed in the blood of the people, while the tri-color has been around the world with our navy, our glory and our liberties!"

The furious and hitherto obdurate and bloodthirsty populace became softened-

-tears were shed, arms were lowered--flags were thrown away, and peaceably they departed to their homes. Never--never was there a more glorious triumph of eloquence--of patriotism!

It was on the morning of Sunday, the 27th day of February, that the Provisional Government deemed it prudent and proper for them to bring to a close their initiative labors, and once more, for the last time, Lamartine descended the steps of the great staircase of the Hotel de Ville, and, presenting himself in front of the edifice surrounded by his colleagues, announced to the vast assembly the result of their protracted toil:

Royalty abolished--

A Republic proclaimed--

The people restored to their political rights--

National workshops opened--

The army and National Guard reorganized--

The abolition of death for political offences.

With louder and more prolonged acclamations than any other decree was this last received. And, instantly, in accordance with this proclamation, the director of criminal affairs, on the order of M. Cremieux, Minister of Justice, dispatched on the wings of the wind, all over France, the warrant to suspend all capital executions which were to have taken place, in virtue of Royal decrees, until the will of the National Assembly, at once to be convened, should be promulgated on the subject of the penalty of death. The effects of this decree, as it sped on the lightning's wings, like a saving angel, all over France, may be imagined perhaps, but portrayal is impossible! Who can imagine even the joy, the rapture it brought to many a dungeon-prisoner, who was counting the hours that yet remained to him of life and preceded his awful doom, or to those who sorrowed over his untimely--perchance his unjust fate!

Leaning on the arm of Louis Blanc, the youngest member of the Government, the venerable Dupont de l'Eure, the eldest, accompanied by the other members, now appeared on the balcony of the room formerly called the Chamber of the Throne, but now the Chamber of the Republic! Lamartine then advanced a step before his colleagues, and in a brief and eloquent address proclaimed to that immense throng the existence of the Republic.

The announcement was received with, acclamations of joy, and shouts of "Vive le Gouvernement!"--"Vive Lamartine!"--"Vive Louis Blanc!" mingled with those of "Vive la Republique!" loudly rose.

From the Hotel de Ville, the Provisional Government proceeded in a body, despite the rain which fell in torrents, accompanied by the people, to the Place de la Bastille, there officially to inaugurate the Republic, agreeably to announcement.

At the appointed hour, the Place de la Bastille was thronged. The National Guard, consisting of two battalions from each of the twelve legions of Paris, together with the Thirteenth Legion of cavalry and two battalions of the Banlieu, were drawn up from the Church of the Madeleine to the Column of July. And, there, at the base of that column erected in commemoration of the Revolution which had made Louis Philippe King of the French, his downfall was commemorated, and on the ruins of the throne then established was now inaugurated a Republic!

During the ceremony of the inauguration, the "Marseillaise" was sung by the National Guard and the people, and, at its conclusion, about the hour of three, the troops filed off before the Column of July to the thrilling strains of the "Marseillaise" and the "Mourir Pour la Patrie" of the Girondins. The members of the Provisional Government, preceded by a detachment of the National Guard and accompanied by the pupils of the Polytechnic School and the Military School of St. Cyr, then descended the boulevards, followed by the whole of the military and civic array, who chanted the national songs. The effect was stupendous. Hour after hour the immense procession moved on like a huge serpent through the streets of Paris; and, at length, when its head was at the Hotel de Ville, its extremity had hardly left the Column of July.

It was night, on Sunday, the 27th of February, when the members of the Provisional Government, for the first time during four days, returned to their homes. But their work was accomplished. A Republic was gained, proclaimed and inaugurated!

# CHAPTER XXVI.
## DANTES AND MERCEDES.

It was a tempestuous night. The wind howled dismally through the streets of Paris, and the rain and sleet dashed fiercely against the casements. At intervals a wild shout might be caught as the blast paused in its furious career, and then a distant shot might be heard. But they passed away, and nothing save the wail of the storm-wind or the rushing sleet of the winter tempest was distinguished.

But, while all was thus wild, dark and tempestuous without, light, warmth, comfort and elegance, rendered yet more delightful by the elemental war, reigned triumphant within a large and splendidly furnished apartment in the noble mansion of M. Dantes, the Deputy from Marseilles, in the Rue du Helder. Every embellishment which art could invent, luxury court, wealth invoke, or even imagination conceive, seemed there lavished with a most prodigal hand. The soft atmosphere of summer, perfumed by the exotics of a neighboring conservatory, delighted the senses, the mild effulgence of gaslight transmitted through opaque globes of glass melted upon the sight, while sofas, divans and ottomans in luxurious profusion invited repose. To describe the rare paintings, the rich gems of statuary and the other miracles of art which were there to be seen would be as impossible as it would be to portray the exquisite taste which enhanced the value of each and constituted more than half its charm.

Upon one of the elegant sofas reclined Edmond Dantes, his tall and graceful figure draped in a dressing robe, while beside him on a low ottoman sat his beautiful wife, her arm resting on his knee, and her dark, glorious eyes gazing with confiding fondness into his face.

Mercedes was no longer the young, light-hearted and thoughtless being who graced the village of the Catalans. Many years had flown since then and many sorrows passed over her. Each of these years and each of these sorrows, like retiring waves of the sea, upon the smooth and sandy beach, had left behind its trace. No, Mercedes was not now the young, light-hearted and thoughtless girl she once was; but she was a being far more perfect, far more winning, far more to be loved--she was a matured, impassioned, accomplished, and still, despite the flight of years, most lovely woman. She was one who could feel passion as well as inspire it, and having once felt or inspired it, that passion, it was plain, could never pass lightly away. Her face could not now boast, perhaps, that full and perfect oval which it formerly had, but the lines of care and of reflection, which here and there almost imperceptibly appeared, rendered it all the more charming. In the bold yet beautiful contour of those features, in the full red lips, in the high pale forehead and, above all, in those dark and haunting eyes lay a depth of feeling and profundity and nobleness of thought, which to a reflective mind have a charm infinitely more irresistible than that which belongs to mere youthful perfection. There was a bland beauty in the smile which slept upon her lips, a delicacy of sentiment in the faint flush that tinged her soft cheek, and a deep meaning in her dark and eloquent eye which told a whole history of experience even to a stranger; while the full and rounded outline of the figure, garbed in a loose robe of crimson, which contrasted beautifully with her luxuriant dark tresses, had that voluptuous development and grace which only maturity and maternity can impart to the female form. In short, never had Mercedes, in the days of her primal bloom, presented a person so fascinating as now. She was a woman to sigh for, perchance to die for, and one whom a man would willingly wish to live for, if he might but hope she would live for him, or, peradventure, he might even be willing not only to risk, but ultimately to resign his life, would that fair being not only live for him, but love him with that entire and passionate devotedness which beamed from her dark eyes up into his who now gazed upon her as she sat at his feet. As for him, as for Edmond Dantes, his figure had now the same elegance, his hand the same delicate whiteness, his features the same spiritual beauty, his brow the same marble pallor, and his eye which beamed beneath its calm expanse the same deep brilliancy which, years before, had distinguished him from all other men and made the Count of Monte-Cristo the idol of every salon in Paris and the hero of every maiden's dream. Yet that face was not without its changes. Tears, care, thought and sorrow had done their work; in the deep lines upon his brow and cheek, in the silvery threads which thickly sprinkled his night-black hair, and, more than all, in the mild light of those eyes which once glowed only with vindictive hate or gratified revenge and in the softened expression of those lips which once, in their stern beauty, had but curled with scorn or quivered with rage could be read that the lapse of time, though it might, indeed, have made him a sadder man, had made him also a better one.

The husband and wife were alone. They still loved as warmly as ever, and, if possible, more fondly than when first they were made one.

Dantes stretched himself out on the sofa, and Mercedes, dropping lower upon the low ottoman at his side, passed her full and beautiful arm around his waist and pressed her lips to his forehead. He returned the embrace with warmth, and placing his own arm about her form, drew it closely to his bosom. Thus they remained, clasped in each other's arms, and thus they fixed on each other eyes beaming with love, passion, bliss, happiness unutterable.

"My own Edmond!" murmured Mercedes. "At length you are again with me--all my own!"

"Am I not always your own, dearest?" was the fond reply.

"But during the week past, I might almost say during the month past, you have been compelled to be so often absent from me."

"Ah! love, you know I was not willingly absent!" was the quick answer.

"No--no--no--but it was hardly the more endurable for that," said the lady, with a smile. "Oh! the anxiety of the last three days and nights! Dearest, I do believe I have not slept three hours during the whole of those three days and nights!"

"And I, dear, have slept not one!" was the laughing rejoinder.

"But all is over now, is it not?"

"In one sense all is over, and in another all now begins. The monarchy is ended in France, I believe, forever. The Republic has begun, and, I trust, will prove lasting."

"And all the grand objects for which you have been striving with your noble colleagues for years and years are at length accomplished, are they not?"

"That is a question, love, not easily answered. That the cause of man and France has wonderfully triumphed during the past three days is, no doubt, most true. But this victory, love, I foresaw. Indeed, it was but the inevitable result of an irresistible cause. It was neither chance, love, nor a spontaneous burst of patriotism that, on the first day, filled the boulevards with fifty thousand blouses, which on the second won over to the people eighty thousand National Guards, and on the third choked the streets of Paris with barricades constructed by engineers and defended by men completely armed. The events of the last three days, Mercedes, have been maturing in the womb of Providence for the past ten years. It is their birth only which has now taken place, and to some the parturition seems a little premature, I suppose. This banquet caused the fright that hastened the event," added Dantes, laughing.

"You are very scientific in your comparisons," replied Mercedes, slightly blushing, "and I suppose I must admit, very apt. But tell me, love, is all over? That is, must you be away from me any more at night, and wander about, Heaven only knows where, in this dark and dangerous city, or Heaven only knows with whom or for what?"

Dantes kissed his fair wife, and, after a pause, during which he gazed fondly into her eyes, replied:

"I hope, I trust, I believe, dear, that all is over--at least all that will take me from you, as during the past week. France has or will have a Republic. That is as certain as fate can make it. But first she will have to pass through strife and tribulation--perhaps bloodshed. The end surely, love, is not yet. But France is now comparatively free. The dreadful problem is now nearer solution than it ever was. Labor will hereafter be granted to all, together with the adequate reward of labor. Destitution will not be deemed guilt. The death-penalty is abolished. The rich will not with impunity grind the poor into powder beneath their heels. Asylums for the suffering, the distressed, the abandoned of both sexes will be sustained. The efforts which, as individuals, we have some of us made for years to ameliorate the condition of mankind, to assuage human woes and augment human joys, will henceforth be encouraged and directly aided by the State. This Revolution, love, is a social Revolution, and during the sixty-four hours the Provisional Government was in session, in the Hotel de Ville, I became thoroughly convinced that the thousands and tens of thousands who, with sleepless vigilance, watched their proceedings, had learned the deep lesson too well to be further deceived, and that the fruits of the Revolution they had won would not again be snatched from their lips."

"And the result of this triumph of the people you believe has advanced the cause of human happiness?" asked Mercedes.

"Most unquestionably, dear, and most incalculably, too, perhaps."

"All your friends are not as disinterested as you have been, Edmond," said Mercedes.

"And why think you that, dear?"

"For six full years I know you have devoted all your powers of mind and body and all your immense wealth to one single object."

"And that object?"

"Has been the happiness of your race."

"Well, dear?"

"And now, when a triumph has been achieved--now, when others, who have been but mere instruments--blind instruments, many of them, in your hands to accomplish they knew not what--come forward and assume place and power--you, Edmond, the noble author and first cause of all, remain quietly in seclusion, unknown, unnamed, unappreciated and uncommended, while the others reap the fruits of your toil!"

"Well, dear?" said Dantes, smiling at the warmth of his wife in his behalf.

"But it is not 'well,' Edmond. I say no one is as disinterested as you."

"Ah! love, what of ambition?"

Mercedes smiled.

"Let me tell you all, love, and then you will not, I fear, think me disinterested," said Dantes seriously. "I should blush, indeed, at praise so little deserved. You know all my early history. I suffered--I was wronged--I was revenged. But was I happy? I sought happiness. All men do so, even the most miserable. Some seek happiness in gratified ambition, some in gratified avarice, some in gratified vanity, and some in the gratification of a dominant lust for pleasure or for power. I sought happiness in gratified revenge!"

Mercedes shuddered, and, hiding her face on the bosom of her husband, clung to it more closely as if for protection. Dantes drew her form to his as he would have drawn that of a child, and continued:

"I sought happiness in vengeance for terrible wrongs, and to win it I devoted a life and countless wealth. What was the result? Misery!--misery!--misery!"

"Poor Edmond!" murmured Mercedes, clinging to him closer than ever.

"At length I awoke, as from a dream. I saw my error. My whole life had been a lie. I saw that God by a miracle had bestowed on me untold riches for a nobler purpose than to make his creatures wretched. I saw that if I would be happy I must make others happy, and to this end--the happiness, not the misery, of my race--

must my wealth and power be devoted. To this end, then, did I devote myself, and to this end, for six years, have I been devoted--to make myself happy by making others happy--you among the rest, dear, dear Mercedes," he added, pressing her to his bosom. "And am I then so disinterested?"

"But why should you achieve triumphs for others to enjoy, Edmond?" asked the wife.

"You refer to the Provisional Government," said Dantes with a smile. "Well, I see I must tell you all, even though by the revelation I prove myself utterly unworthy of the praise of disinterestedness. I may tell you, love--you my second self--without danger of being charged with egotism, what I might not say to others. Our friend Lamartine is the actual head of this Government. I had but to assent to the urgent entreaties to secure that position for myself. These appointments seem the result of nomination by the people. Yet they are not!"

"And why did you refuse to head the Government, Edmond?"

"I am ashamed to confess to you that I feared to accept," said Dantes after a pause. "My own selfishness, not, alas! my disinterestedness, has kept me from the post of peril. Perhaps, indeed, I can do far more for the cause of my race as I am than I could by sacrificing myself for office and position; at least, I hope so."

"Is the position of your friends then so perilous?" asked Mercedes.

"Dearest, they stand upon a volcano!" said Dantes, solemnly.

"Ha!" cried the lady in alarm.

"Mercedes--Mercedes!" continued Dantes with enthusiasm, "I sometimes am startled with the idea that to me have been entrusted the awful powers of foreknowledge, of prophecy, so fearfully true have some of my predictions proved! The events of the past week I foresaw and foretold, even to minute circumstances and the hours of their occurrence. And now--glorious as is the triumph that France and the cause of man have achieved--I perceive in the dim future a sea of commotion! All is not yet settled. Within one month, revolution will succeed revolution throughout Europe! Berlin, Vienna, and Madrid, perhaps also St. Petersburg, London, and all the cities of Italy, will be in revolt. All Europe must and will feel the events of the past week in Paris. Europe must be free!"

"And our friends--Lamartine--Louis Blanc?"

"Within six months Louis Blanc will be an exile, and Lamartine--he may be in a dungeon or on a scaffold!"

"Ah!" exclaimed Mercedes, clinging yet more closely to her husband.

"But the cause of human happiness, human right and human freedom will live forever! That must be, will be eternal--as eternal, my adored Mercedes, as is our own deathless love!"

# CHAPTER XXVII.
# ESPERANCE AND ZULEIKA.

During the whole period of the memorable Revolution Zuleika never once saw her brother, though she was burning with a desire to have an interview with him on the subject that had caused the separation between her young Italian lover and herself. Esperance made his home behind the barricades, from the time the struggle began until the people finally triumphed; gun in hand, he fought as heroically as the most devoted workman, fearlessly exposing himself whenever the troops pressed his comrades in arms and always in the thick of the fight. Begrimed with dust and powder, his garments torn by bullets and bayonet thrusts, his hat battered and rent, he encouraged the people by word and example, constantly shouting "Vive la Republique," and contending for liberty with the bravery of a lion and a persistency that never flagged. He, however, escaped without a single scratch, returning to the paternal mansion utterly worn out, but altogether unhurt, proud of having done his duty as a man and a patriot, and of having sustained the glorious cause for which his father was working heart and soul.

As he was slowly and wearily wending his way homeward, he suddenly encountered M. Dantes and his friend Lamartine in the Rue Richelieu; his gun was on his shoulder, and in his tattered attire, with the dust and powder on his face and hands, he had the exact appearance of an insurrectionist and a barricader. He touched his hat in military fashion to M. Dantes and his illustrious companion, and was about passing on when his father recognized him and, ragged and begrimed as he was, threw his arms enthusiastically about his neck. M. Lamartine watched the Deputy from Marseilles and could not restrain an expression of astonishment at his singular behavior. M. Dantes smiled and, taking Esperance by the hand, said:

"M. Lamartine, you will, I know, make every allowance for me when you learn that this young man, who has been fighting behind the barricades with the people, is my son!"

The head of the Provisional Government instantly grew as enthusiastic as M. Dantes himself; he grasped Esperance's free hand and, shaking it with the utmost cordiality, exclaimed:

"Your son, M. Dantes! Let me congratulate you! Why he is a perfect hero!"

"I have but followed my father's teachings and done what he would have done had he been my age and unable to serve the great cause of human freedom in a more effective way!"

M. Dantes' eyes sparkled with joy and a faint shade of color appeared upon his pale cheeks.

"What is your name, young patriot?" asked M. Lamartine, his excitement and enthusiasm continuing to hold possession of him.

"Esperance," was the reply.

"Esperance--hope--the name is both appropriate and auspicious; with such heroic young men as you fighting for our cause there is, indeed, hope, and of the brightest and best kind!" cried Lamartine.

"Nay, nay," said M. Dantes, "do not flatter the boy; he has but done his duty."

"Believe me, I do not flatter him," returned Lamartine; "I have simply told him the truth; in time he will rival the devotion and achievements of his noble father!"

"Enough, enough," said the Deputy, modestly; "we deserve only the credit of executing God's will--we are merely instruments in His omnipotent hand!" he added, impressively.

"And such instruments are exactly what we need in the present crisis. God grant us plenty of them!"

The next morning Zuleika encountered Esperance on the stairway; she led him into the salon, and, when they were seated, said:

"My brother, I have a question to ask of you."

A shadow crossed the young man's brow, and he quickly asked:

"Is it about the Viscount Massetti?"

"Yes."

"Then I must refuse to answer!"

"But the matter concerns my happiness, nay, my very life itself; think of that before you finally refuse to answer my question!"

Esperance hastily and excitedly arose from his chair and stood in front of his sister.

"Zuleika," said he, in an agitated tone, "beware of that man--beware of Giovanni Massetti!"

"Beware of Giovanni, Esperance--and why?"

The young man began to pace the salon with short and nervous steps; his hands twitched convulsively, and his face had suddenly assumed the whiteness of chalk.

"Zuleika, Zuleika," he murmured, "I cannot, I cannot tell you why! It would crash you to the very earth and make you blush with shame that you had ever listened to the seductive tones of that doubly false Italian's voice!"

"But, Esperance," said Zuleika, "papa certainly knows all about Giovanni; if he did not altogether approve of his character and conduct, he would never have consented to admit him as a suitor for my hand!"

"A suitor for your hand, Zuleika! My God! has he then dared----"

"He has done nothing that an upright and honorable man should not do!" interrupted Zuleika, warmly. "He did not even call here until he had written to papa and obtained his full permission to do so."

"Zuleika," said Esperance, approaching his sister and taking her hand, "no doubt Giovanni Massetti has conducted himself in all respects toward you like a perfect gentleman, but, nevertheless, he is not fit to be my sister's husband."

"But papa----"

"Has been deceived, as have many others, in regard to the true character and standing of this so-called Roman nobleman."

"And is he not a nobleman?"

"Once more I must refuse to answer any question in regard to him. I can only tell you to beware and shun him as you would a venomous serpent."

"Esperance, I love him!"

"Love him!--you love him, Zuleika! Oh! this is, indeed, torture!"

The young man dropped his sister's hand and flung himself upon a divan. He was a prey to the most intense excitement.

Zuleika, deeply affected to see him thus, and remembering Giovanni's mysterious behavior, together with his strange and ominous words, when she had questioned him in regard to his quarrel with Esperance, felt for a moment shaken and uncertain. She also recollected that, at the time of the inexplicable difficulty between the two young men, she had heard rumors to the effect that a youthful member of the Roman aristocracy had abducted a beautiful peasant girl, in which affair he had been assisted by the notorious brigand Luigi Vampa; the matter, however, had almost immediately been hushed up and she had learned none of the circumstances. Could it be possible that Giovanni Massetti was the youthful aristocrat alluded to by the gossips and scandalmongers of the Eternal City--that he was the abductor of the unfortunate peasant girl? She could not entertain such an idea, and yet that abduction, in spite of all her efforts, would associate itself with her Italian lover in her mind.

She arose from her chair and, going to the divan, seated herself beside Esperance, determined to make a final attempt to draw his secret from him. Throwing her arms tenderly about his neck she said, in a coaxing tone:

"If any sound reason exists why I should not love Giovanni Massetti, and you know it, your plain duty as my brother is to tell me. Will you not tell me, Esperance?"

Instead of replying, the young man buried his face in his hands and fairly sobbed in his anguish. Zuleika was filled with pity for him, and, as she gazed at him, tears came into her eyes; but still bent on discovering the nature of the obstacle that had so suddenly loomed up between Giovanni and herself, she continued after a pause, in the same coaxing voice:

"Esperance, I am no longer a child and should not be treated as one. What I ask of you is only reasonable and just. If I stand on the brink of a gulf I cannot see, it is your duty to inform me not only of my danger but also of its nature. Am I not right?"

Heaving a deep sigh, Esperance replied:

"Yes, you are right, Zuleika; it is my duty to tell you all--and yet I cannot!"

"At least, tell me why you are compelled to maintain silence on a matter of so much importance."

"Did you question the Viscount?"

"I did."

"And what answer did he return?"

"Like you, he refused to answer."

"Ah! then he has some sense of shame left!"

"Shame?"

"Yes, shame! And what did you do when he refused to speak?"

"I left him."

"And you will not see him again?"

"Not until he has decided to tell me all."

"Then you will never put eyes upon him more; he dare not tell you!"

"Dare not! And why?"

"Because, did you know the depth of his infamy, you would spurn him from you!"

Suddenly a grave suspicion stole into Zuleika's mind and made her tremble from head to foot. Might it not be that Esperance had been as deeply involved in the mysterious and infamous affair of which he declined to speak as Giovanni Massetti himself? The thought was torment, and totally unable to restrain her keen anxiety to be instantly informed upon this topic, Zuleika gasped out:

"Were you not, Esperance, as guilty as your former friend?"

The young man leaped to his feet as if a tarantula had bitten him.

"No, no!" cried he. "I was innocent of all blame in the matter! Luigi Vampa----"

He abruptly checked himself and stood staring at his sister, as if in dismay at having unguardedly uttered the brigand's name.

But Zuleika said nothing. Giovanni Massetti also had protested his innocence, and the young girl knew not what to believe. Luigi Vampa? So then he had been a party to this mysterious and terrible business, whatever it was! And again she thought of the abduction of the beautiful peasant girl. Could that be the fearful secret? Yes, it must be. Luigi Vampa had assisted in that abduction, if report could be relied on, and the chief criminal had been a youthful member of the Roman aristocracy. Oh! it was all plain now. Zuleika shuddered and felt her heart grow heavy as lead, while a sharp, killing pang ran through it. Had Esperance been misled by Vampa and the Viscount? Had he discovered too late the infamy of the affair and challenged Massetti on that account? This was, doubtless, the solution of the whole enigma, and yet Zuleika hesitated to accept it as such. No, no, she could not accept it without further and more convincing proof! But how was that proof to be obtained? Neither the Viscount nor her brother would speak; it was evident that their lips were sealed; possibly an oath to maintain silence had been extorted from them under terrible circumstances--an oath they feared to break even to clear themselves from a foul suspicion. But Vampa? He might, perhaps, be induced to give the key to the mystery. Vampa, however, was far away in Rome and inaccessible. Zuleika made a wild resolve--she would write to the brigand and throw herself upon his generosity; then she decided that the plan was impracticable; her letter would never reach Vampa--it would be seized by the Roman authorities and might cause additional trouble by reviving a smothered scandal--and even should it reach the brigand, would he answer it? The chances were a hundred to one that he would not. At this instant an inspiration came to the tortured girl like a flash of lightning. Her father had known Vampa in the past, and, perhaps, still possessed some influence over him. She had heard the story of Albert de Morcerf's adventure in the catacombs of Saint Sebastian, and was aware that the brigand chief had released him from captivity without ransom at her father's simple solicitation. Would not Vampa answer her questions if M. Dantes could be influenced to write him and ask them? She had full faith in her father's power to get a letter to the bandit notwithstanding all the vigilance of the Roman authorities. Yes, she would go to him, tell all her suspicions without reserve and beg him to write the letter; it was hardly likely he would refuse; he could not, he must not. Thus resolved, Zuleika looked her brother full in the face and said, calmly:

"I see I torture you with my questions, Esperance, that for some reason best known to yourself you cannot answer them, and that it is useless to torment you further. But something must be done and that at once. I am going to my father!"

Esperance caught her wildly by the arm.

"You are mad!" cried he.

"It is you who are mad--you and Giovanni! I tell you, I am going to my father; if you are innocent, you have nothing to fear from any revelation I may make!"

With these words she freed herself from her brother's grasp and quitted the salon, leaving Esperance standing in the centre of the apartment as if he were rooted to the spot.

# CHAPTER XXVIII.
## CAPTAIN JOLIETTE'S LOVE.

In a small but cosy and elegant suite of apartments in a mansion on the Rue des Capucines resided Mlle. Louise d'Armilly and her brother Leon; as has already been stated, the celebrated cantatrice had retired from the boards in consequence of having inherited a fortune of several millions of francs from the estate of her deceased father, who, rumor asserted, had been a very wealthy Parisian banker; Leon had abandoned the stage simultaneously with his sister, who had invited him to share her suddenly acquired riches, for, strange to say, the banker had not bequeathed to him a single sou.

The immense inheritance had been a complete surprise to Mlle. d'Armilly, and for some time she had hesitated to accept it, as a condition imposed by the will was her immediate withdrawal from her operatic career, and the prima donna was as ambitious as gifted; but, finally, she had yielded to the persuasive eloquence of the notary and the earnest entreaties of her friends, canceling all her engagements, and with them abandoning her bright professional future.

The director of the Academie Royale demanded a large sum to release the artiste from her contract with him, and this was paid by the notary with an alacrity that seemed to suggest he was not acting solely according to the directions of the will, but was influenced by some personage who chose to remain in the background; the notary also paid all other demands made by the various operatic managers who claimed they would lose by Mlle. d'Armilly's failure to appear; these amounts were not deducted from the legacy, a circumstance that gave additional color to the supposition that the will of the deceased banker was not the sole factor in the celebrated cantatrice's good luck.

One evening, shortly after Paris had again quieted down, Mlle. d'Armilly was seated in the little apartment that served her as a salon, and with her was her brother Leon. The contrast between the pair seemed intensified in private life. Louise had that dark, imperious, majestic beauty usually possessed by brunettes; her figure was full and finely developed, her black eyes had the deep, intense fire of passion, and her faultless countenance, glowing with health and loveliness, indicated at once firmness, decision and caprices without number. Leon, on the contrary, was delicate and feminine in appearance; he had exceedingly small feet and hands, and a single glance at his strikingly handsome face was sufficient to convince any experienced judge of human nature that he possessed a mild and yielding disposition. The young man bore not the remotest family likeness to his sister, and it was difficult to realize that they could be in any way related.

Leon quitted his sister and, going to a piano that stood in one corner of the apartment, softly opened it and commenced lightly running his fingers over the keys; then he seated himself at the instrument and played an air from "Lucrezia Borgia" with brilliancy and effect that only a finished performer could attain. At the first notes Louise arose and approaching the piano stood beside the player, her eyes sparkling with appreciation and delight. So absorbed were the brother and sister that they did not hear a soft knock at the door, and only at the conclusion of the air did they realize that a visitor was in the apartment. Leon sprang from the instrument in confusion, behaving like a startled girl, but Mlle. d'Armilly, with perfect self-control, turned to the new comer and said, in a tone of mingled coquetry and merriment:

"So, so, Captain Joliette, your military career has accustomed you to surprising the enemy to such an extent that it has become second nature with you, and you cannot avoid carrying your favorite tactics even into private life!"

Captain Joliette, for it was, indeed, he, bowed and answered with a smile:

"You must allow me solemnly to protest against classing yourself and your brother with the enemy! You are, both of you, very dear friends!"

"Especially Louise!" said Leon, with a sly look and a pretty little ringing laugh.

"Leon, Leon, when will you learn wisdom!" exclaimed Mlle. d'Armilly, a blush mantling her visage, and adding to its voluptuous beauty.

"Never, I suppose!" returned her brother, still laughing. "But I am already well acquainted with the value of discretion and, therefore, will withdraw!"

As he uttered those words, Leon kissed the tips of his fingers to Louise and Joliette, and lightly ran from the salon. When he had disappeared the Captain folded Mlle. d'Armilly in his arms and kissed her tenderly upon the forehead.

"Oh! Louise," said he, enthusiastically, "I love you more and more every day!"

The former artiste gently disentangled herself from his embrace and, smiling archly, led him to a chair; then she sat down upon another at a short distance from him.

"No, no," said Joliette, warmly; "come and sit beside me on the sofa. Even Leon sees that I adore you, and all my friends in Paris are aware that I am seeking your hand in marriage. Why will you be so formal and distant with me!"

She arose and did as he requested; Joliette, seated at her side, put his arm about her waist. Louise did not resist, but still maintained an air of coquetry that was displeasing to the ardent young soldier.

"Albert," she said, in a low, musical voice, "do you, indeed, love me as you say?"

"Love you, Louise!" cried Joliette. "I would lay down my life for you!"

"Are you quite sure you love me for myself and not because of the resemblance you say I bear to the woman you once so ardently admired? What was her name?--ah! Eugenie Danglars!" said she, looking at him with a piercing gaze.

"Quite sure, Louise, quite sure. Besides, Mlle. Danglars has disappeared, has not been seen or heard of for several years, and, no doubt, is dead."

"And yet you do not mourn for her! How strange!"

"I never loved her as I love you, Louise. Eugenie Danglars was a capricious and eccentric girl, and had she lived would have been a capricious and eccentric woman. It was well for me she vanished when she did! But, by the way, another singular and inexplicable coincidence is that Louise d'Armilly, the name you bear, was also the name of Mlle. Danglars' music teacher. I cannot understand it at all!"

"There is no necessity for you to understand it. Anyhow, it is a coincidence, as you say--nothing more."

"Well, Louise, let us speak no further about either the resemblance or the coincidence. Suffice it that I love you, and you alone--that I love you for yourself."

"Your words make me very happy, Albert," replied Mlle. d'Armilly, and her full red lips looked so luscious, ripe and alluring, that Joliette could not resist the temptation to bestow a long, burning kiss upon them.

"Be my wife, then, dearest Louise," cried the Captain, "and I will prolong your happiness until death shall strike me down!"

"Ah! Albert, men are so fickle; they become infatuated with women and declare and, no doubt think, they could pass their lives at their charmers' feet; but possession dulls the lustre of the brightest jewel, and the devoted lover is speedily replaced by a careless, if not faithless husband, who, instead of making his wife happy as he has sworn to do, forsakes her side to bask in the smiles of sirens."

"It will never be so with me, my own, my love!" protested Joliette, kissing her again and again. "I swear it."

"I know the value of a lover's oath, Albert," murmured Louise, with a meaning look. "When I was the brightest operatic star of the day many of them were breathed in my ear, but they were 'trifles light as air,' forgotten as soon as uttered. Besides, should I consent to become your wife, you would be forced to leave me in France and return to Africa in obedience to the call of duty; the lovely women of Algeria are prodigal of their beauties and endearments, and under the spell of some subtle Arab enchantress you would either forget poor Louise d'Armilly altogether, or remember her only as a clog upon your pleasures and amorous delights."

"Nay, nay, you wrong me; among all the dusky sirens of Algeria there exists not one who could make me forget you for a single instant; they are brazen, shameless women, who love with a recklessness and boldness that can only disgust a Frenchman."

"But they can dazzle even a Frenchman, render him delirious with passion and, ere he is aware, weave a web around him through which he cannot break. My heart tells me you are as susceptible to feminine wiles as the rest of your countrymen, and that, perhaps, you have already had half-a-dozen love-affairs in Algeria."

"Oh! Louise, Louise, it grieves me to the soul that you can thus doubt me. Give me a chance to prove my love and you shall be more than satisfied that I can be loyal and true."

Mlle. d'Armilly gazed at him with a singular expression on her dark beautiful countenance; it thrilled him to the very marrow of his bones, and caused his arm that was about her waist to tremble violently; at that moment the former cantatrice resembled Eugenie Danglars more than ever; her breath, was hot and convulsive as it struck his cheek, and a faint suspicion that all was not right--that she was playing a role with him, shot across his mind for the first time; with this suspicion came jealousy, and, releasing her waist, he said, in a gasping tone:

"You have another lover, Louise, a lover you prefer to me--am I not right?"

Mlle. d'Armilly laughed a short, nervous laugh, and answered in a voice that seemed to mock him:

"I have had hosts of ardent admirers in my time. Do you refer particularly to any individual?"

"I know not; I am beside myself with passion for you, and the mere fancy that another man may have the first place in your heart is unbearable to me! But there is one conclusive way in which you can prove my suspicion--my jealousy--groundless; marry me!"

"Albert," replied Louise, with a renewal of the singular expression of countenance that had so agitated him, "I shall never marry any one; I cannot--I dare not!"

The young man was startled as if by an electric shock; he drew back and gazed at her with wide-opened eyes, speechless from astonishment.

After a brief pause, Mlle. d'Armilly continued, in a dry, hard tone:

"You do not understand me and I cannot expect you to, for I can neither tell you my motives nor lay bare my sad history to you; you must be content with my decision--I shall not marry!"

Captain Joliette, strong man as he was, could not control his emotion; he buried his face in his hands and groaned aloud. The young woman gazed at him half pityingly, half triumphantly; she felt compassion for her stricken lover, but, above all, gloried in the overwhelming power of her charms that could so subdue a manly, victorious young soldier and make him her helpless slave.

"Is there then no shadow of a hope?" at length asked Joliette, in a hoarse whisper.

"Not the shadow of a hope!" replied Mlle. d'Armilly, firmly. "You can be my friend, my brother, if you will, but never my husband."

The young man recoiled in horror at the suggestion that seemed to be conveyed by this permission.

"What do you mean by friend?" he asked, a cold shiver passing through him.

Louise laughed a short, nervous laugh, and, looking him full in the eyes, replied:

"You know what I mean. I love you better than any man I ever met, save one."

Captain Joliette slowly arose to his feet and stood staring at her, his passion and his scruples waging a bitter battle within him for the mastery. The temptress half reclined on the sofa, a miracle of seductive grace and voluptuous beauty. He moved toward her as if to seize her in his arms; then, suddenly checking himself, he asked, with a convulsive gasp:

"And that man--that one?"

"Was separated from me forever through the vile machinations of that mysterious and cold-blooded fiend, the Count of Monte-Cristo!"

"The Count of Monte-Cristo?" exclaimed the young man, lost in amazement.

"Yes, the Count of Monte-Cristo, who afterwards disappeared from Paris and has not since been heard of."

"You mistake; the Count of Monte-Cristo is in Paris now; he calls himself Edmond Dantes and is the celebrated Deputy from Marseilles over whom everybody has gone wild for some time past."

Mlle. d'Armilly's eyes flashed with fury.

"Then I will have my revenge upon him at last!" she cried. "I will amply repay him for introducing the so-called Prince Cavalcanti into my father's house and thus breaking off the match between Albert and myself."

"Albert?"

"Yes; Albert de Morcerf."

"Now, Eugenie Danglars, I know you and it is useless for you to attempt the denial of your identity longer!"

The young woman leaped up from the sofa, with terror pictured upon her visage, and, seizing Captain Joliette by the arm with a powerful grasp, cried out:

"And how, pray, do you know I am Eugenie Danglars?"

"You unwittingly betrayed yourself by revealing the names of Monte-Cristo and Cavalcanti. Besides, Eugenie, look at me well--I am Albert de Morcerf!"

With a wild cry the retired prima donna sank back upon the sofa.

"You Albert de Morcerf!" she exclaimed. "I cannot believe it!"

"But my mother, the former Countess de Morcerf, who is now the wife of Edmond Dantes, will vouch for my identity."

The young woman passed her hand across her forehead as if dazed.

"If you are Albert de Morcerf, you must despise me after what has taken place this evening," she said, bitterly.

"Despise you? No, I pity and forgive you."

"Albert," said she, softly, "come here and sit beside me on this sofa; I have something to say to you."

The soldier obeyed; when he was seated, he said:

"Eugenie, why did you tell me I could be your friend?"

"Simply because I have long suspected your secret and wished to ascertain the real nature of your feelings toward me. You not only resisted a terrible temptation, the most terrible temptation to which a young, ardent and passion-smitten man can be exposed, but by your honor conclusively established the purity and sincerity of your love. Oh! Albert, Albert, are you satisfied with my explanation and do you still think me worthy of you?"

"My own Eugenie, my happiness is far too great for words!" murmured the delighted young man, gathering his beautiful companion in a warm embrace and repeatedly kissing her ripe lips and blushing cheeks.

It was soon known throughout Paris that Captain Joliette and Albert de Morcerf were identical, and that Mlle. d'Armilly was in reality no other than Mlle. Eugenie Danglars, daughter of Baron Danglars, the once famous and opulent Parisian banker; the report also was current that Albert and Eugenie were engaged and would shortly be united in the bonds of matrimony. Another bit of gossip was to the effect that the former cantatrice's brother Leon was not a man but a woman; in short, the real Louise d'Armilly, who had loaned her name to Eugenie Danglars and assumed male attire solely for professional purposes. This story was speedily confirmed, for Leon soon vanished and in his place appeared a most attractive and fascinating lady, who very quietly assumed, or rather resumed, the name of Louise d'Armilly. Still another rumor was that the wealth so strangely inherited by the former prima donna was not a legacy at all, but a gift from the mysterious Count of Monte-Cristo, who had thus striven to make amends to the daughter for the misfortunes he had, while pursuing his scheme of wholesale vengeance, so remorselessly heaped upon the head of the father.

# CHAPTER XXIX.
# ZULEIKA GOES TO M. DANTES.

M. Dantes was sitting alone in his library, busily engaged in reading a favorite work on the subject of political economy, and from time to time making copious notes. It was after midnight, and the vast mansion on the Rue du Helder was as silent as the tomb; the lamp on the Deputy's table burned brightly, but a large metallic shade concentrated the light and reflected it upon the table, so that the other portions of the apartment were shrouded in almost complete darkness.

As M. Dantes read a shadow suddenly fell on the page of his book, and quickly looking up he saw his daughter Zuleika standing beside him; tears were in her eyes and a look of melancholy rested upon her countenance.

"Why child," said her father, in a startled tone, "what is the matter with you? You are weeping and seem very sad. Has anything happened to young Massetti?"

"Not that I am aware of, papa," answered Zuleika, in a low voice. "But, nevertheless, it is of him I wish to speak."

M. Dantes pushed his book from him, motioned his daughter to a seat and prepared to listen as she did not begin at once, but seemed to hesitate, he said, kindly:

"I am waiting, little one; proceed."

Thus encouraged, Zuleika summoned up all her strength and, with downcast eyes, commenced:

"Papa," said she, "in the first place let me assure you that this is no mere lovers' quarrel, but a matter of the utmost importance that demands immediate action."

M. Dantes knitted his brows.

"Has the Viscount been guilty of any impropriety toward you?" he asked, fiercely.

"No, papa, not toward me, but I fear he may have been guilty of impropriety, or, at least, of indiscretion, with regard to another in the past."

"A woman, no doubt."

"Yes, papa, a woman--a Roman peasant."

"I heard of some such thing while you were at the convent school in Rome, but dismissed it as a slander."

"There may, however, be some truth in it."

"But, now I recollect, Giovanni's name was not associated with the scandal; it was a mere inference on my part that connected him with the youthful member of the Roman aristocracy mentioned by the gossips."

"Perhaps I am unjust, papa, in reviving your suspicions, but Giovanni's strange behavior when I asked him the cause of his quarrel with Esperance and of the continued coldness between them, forced me to think there was something wrong."

"His quarrel with Esperance? Ah! now I remember, there was a quarrel, but I imagined it was settled, and that their relations were altogether friendly."

"They are enemies, papa, or seem to be, and that is not all--Esperance accuses Giovanni of having been guilty of some infamous deed."

"You have spoken to Esperance then on the subject?"

"Yes, papa."

"And what did he say?"

"He dealt in vague denunciations, and positively refused to give me any definite information."

"That is singular."

"But what is still more so is that both Giovanni and Esperance seem bound by some fearful oath not to disclose the dread secret in their possession."

"Bound by an oath?"

"Yes, papa; but why both of them should have been so bound, unless they were accomplices, I cannot see; I even went so far as to accuse Esperance of complicity, whereupon he grew as white as chalk and protested his entire innocence, and in his confusion uttered the name of Luigi Vampa."

"Zuleika, Zuleika, you certainly misunderstood your brother; he could not have mentioned the name of that man! Do you know who this Luigi Vampa is?"

"Perfectly, papa; Luigi Vampa is a notorious Roman brigand."

"Exactly, my child, and therefore could not possibly have had any dealings either with the Viscount or Esperance."

"But I am sure of the name, nevertheless. Esperance said Luigi Vampa."

M. Dantes was evidently startled; he arose to his feet and paced the library excitedly. Zuleika had expected this, and hence was not surprised. At last her father resumed his seat, and when he again came within reach of the lamp's rays she saw that his visage was even more pallid than usual and that he was not a little agitated. She waited for him to speak, and in a few seconds he did so.

"Zuleika," said he, in a tone of decision, "I will see both the Viscount and my son in regard to this matter, for now that Luigi Vampa seems to have had a share in it, close investigation is imperatively demanded."

"You may interrogate them, papa, but I am convinced in advance that you will derive no information from either of them. The strange power that holds sway over them you cannot break, but there is one thing you can do."

"What is that, Zuleika?"

"Write to Luigi Vampa!"

"Write to Vampa? Why should I do that?"

"Because I feel assured that he is in possession of the full details of the terrible secret, whatever it may be, and will communicate them to you if you ask him to do so."

M. Dantes gazed at his daughter curiously.

"What makes you think I have such influence over this Roman brigand?" he asked, sharply.

"Oh! papa, do not be angry with me!" cried Zuleika; "but I have heard how Vampa released the Viscount de Morcerf at your simple solicitation without a single franc of ransom, though he had previously demanded a very large amount from the unfortunate man as the price of his liberty. I have heard this, and the natural inference I drew was that, if the brigand chief went so far as to surrender his prey to you, he would certainly answer your letter and tell you all he knew about the matter that so closely concerns my happiness and Esperance's good name."

"I am not angry with you, my child," replied the Deputy, in a milder tone, "for I know how deeply you have this affair at heart. I will write to Luigi Vampa as you desire, this very night, and in two weeks at the furthest his answer may be expected, but to-morrow I will talk with Esperance and then will question the Viscount. Rest assured that this matter shall be sifted to the bottom. I know the extent of your love for Giovanni Massetti; I also feel confident that I am not deceived in him, and that he will be amply able to prove himself entirely worthy of your hand. I have seen too much of men, Zuleika, and studied them too deeply, to be deceived in reading character."

"Oh! thank you, thank you ever so much, papa, both for your promise, and your kind, encouraging words. I, too, have full faith in Giovanni, but still I cannot rest satisfied until his record is entirely and conclusively cleared. No one must have the power to breathe even a suspicion against the good name of your daughter's husband!"

"Spoken like a girl of spirit!" said M. Dantes, his eyes sparkling with enthusiasm and admiration. "Now leave me, and I will write to Vampa."

Zuleika kissed her father and quitted the library with a much lighter heart than she had entered it.

M. Dantes, by the exercise of his iron will, had managed to control himself in her presence, but now that she had gone he gave free course to his emotions. For a full hour he sat leaning on his writing-table, his frame convulsed with anguish, and his mind filled with sad forebodings. He did not for an instant doubt that both Esperance and the Viscount could clear themselves from any criminal or dishonorable charge, if they would consent to open their lips, but their silence and Zuleika's belief that they were bound by some fearful oath gave him great uneasiness. Besides, his son had mentioned Luigi Vampa's name, and the thought that the young man was involved in some complication with the Roman bandit sent a chill to his heart. He was convinced that whatever had occurred had been merely the result of the folly and headlong disposition of youth, but this was scarcely a consolation, for he well knew to what length young men sometimes allowed themselves to be carried, especially in what they considered a love-affair.

In addition, the more he thought of the half-forgotten Roman scandal, the more clearly its particulars returned to him. He remembered that a young and handsome peasant girl had been mysteriously abducted, and that eventually she had been brought back to her home by one of the shepherds known to be in league with Luigi Vampa and his band. She asserted that she had been carried off to the bandits' haunt by her youthful lover, who had passed for a peasant lad, but was in reality a nobleman. This was all M. Dantes could distinctly recall, though he was certain he had heard other details that had slipped his memory. At the period of the abduction, he now remembered, both Esperance and the Viscount were temporarily absent from Rome; then followed their return and the quarrel that had almost resulted in a duel, but had suddenly been patched up without apparent reason. Had Esperance and the Viscount been concerned in the abduction? That was a question that only they or Luigi Vampa could answer, and it was evident the young men would not speak. Vampa then must be made to speak for them; that was the sole course left to pursue, for the peasant girl had disappeared immediately after her return, and her whereabouts were a mystery.

M. Dantes drew writing materials before him and wrote his letter to the brigand-chief; it was brief, but to the point. When it was finished, it bore the signature, "Edmond Dantes, Count of Monte-Cristo." The Deputy placed it in the drawer of his table to go by mail the following morning, having first folded and sealed it. "Thomson and French, Rome," was the direction it bore.

# CHAPTER XXX.
# TWO INTERVIEWS.

The morning following the events detailed in the last chapter, as Esperance was in his dressing-room preparing to take a short stroll through Paris, Ali knocked at the door and signified that M. Dantes wished to see him at once in the library. As such a summons was something unusual, the young man immediately concluded that Zuleika had been in consultation with her father and that he would now have to submit to a close and rigid examination; he had expected such an examination, but, nevertheless, the summons filled him with dismay and he grew pale as wax, his limbs trembling beneath him and his hands working nervously; however, he braced up as well as he could, and with as firm a step as it was possible for him to assume walked toward the library. On the threshold he paused, and his courage so utterly forsook him that he was tempted to take refuge in flight, but the thought flashed through his mind that this would be cowardly, and, making a supreme effort to control himself, he entered his father's presence.

M. Dantes, who was seated at his writing-table examining a curious manuscript written in Arabic characters, looked up as he came in and fixed his eyes searchingly upon his son's countenance, noting its extreme pallor and remarking with manifest uneasiness the difficulty Esperance experienced in maintaining a firm demeanor.

Motioning the young man to a seat, he said:

"My son, I have sent for you on a matter of the utmost importance, and I sincerely hope you will see fit to tell me in all frankness whatever you may know in regard to it."

Esperance partially closed his eyes as if suffering intensely, bringing his teeth firmly together and compressing his lips. As he did not speak, M. Dantes continued:

"I have every reason to believe that the revelation I am about to ask of you will be exceedingly painful for you to make, but you must consider that your sister's happiness is deeply concerned and that, for that reason, no matter what may be your motives, you have not the right to maintain silence."

"I know what you mean, father," replied Esperance in an unsteady voice, "but, notwithstanding the pain it gives me to do so, I must ask you, nay, entreat you not to question me, for I cannot answer you!"

M. Dantes cast upon his son a glance that seemed to pierce him through and through; the young man quailed beneath it and again partially closed his eyes, while a faint blue shade was mixed with the waxen pallor of his visage. The Deputy, though he had made a profound and exhaustive study of men and their varied motives, though he was a skilled anatomist of the human heart and a ready reader of the human countenance, acknowledged to himself that this time he was completely baffled. Was it fear or guilt that Esperance exhibited? He could not tell; but it was abundantly evident that the young man was not acting a part, that he keenly felt the suspicions to which he was exposing himself by his inexplicable conduct. At length M. Dantes said, in a mild but determined tone:

"Esperance, my son, you can, at least, enlighten me upon a few points, and I request, nay, I command you to do so. Are you bound by oath to preserve silence concerning this matter?"

"I am bound by a most solemn oath!" answered the young man with a shudder.

"And is Giovanni Massetti likewise so bound?"

"He is!"

"I will not ask you who administered that oath to you or under what circumstances it was taken, although as your father I have a right to do so and to compel you to answer; neither will I interrogate you further in regard to the main question at issue, the complication in which you and the Viscount seem to be so hopelessly involved; but I insist that you inform me whether any guilt or stain of dishonor rests upon you!"

"Father," said Esperance, rising and lifting his right hand toward heaven, "I solemnly swear to you that whatever wrong may have been done, whatever crime may have been committed, I am entirely guiltless and that there is not the slightest stain of dishonor upon me!"

"I believe you, my son," said M. Dantes, in a tone of conviction, "and this un-equivocal assurance from your own lips removes the weight of a mountain from me. Now, tell me, is the Viscount Massetti as blameless in this affair as you are?"

"The so-called Viscount Massetti is a black-hearted villain!" cried Esperance, excitedly. "He is guilty of a foul and revolting crime, a crime that should condemn him to a life of penal servitude!"

"But may you not be mistaken, may you not be the victim of some delusion?" asked M. Dantes, anxiously.

"I am neither mistaken, father, nor the victim of a delusion," replied Esperance, positively. "The charges that I make against that miserable apology for a man I can fully substantiate should the proper opportunity ever be offered me!"

"Zuleika informed me that, while you were speaking with her upon this mysterious subject, the name of Luigi Vampa escaped your lips. Does that notorious brigand posses a knowledge of this unfortunate matter?"

Esperance became violently agitated and instantly answered:

"That is a question my oath forbids me to reply to!"

"So be it," said M. Dantes; "but I have written him and he will reply for you!"

"You have written to Vampa!" exclaimed the young man, with a terror-stricken look. "Then all is lost!"

M. Dantes smiled, and, rising, placed his hand on his son's shoulder.

"Esperance," said he, calmly, "if neither crime nor dishonor attaches to you in this affair, as you have sworn, you have nothing whatever to fear, and, besides, Vampa's disclosures may relieve you of some portion of your heavy burden."

"Oh! God!" groaned the young man, "if Vampa speaks how shall I be able to prove my innocence!"

"My son," said M. Dantes, impressively, "God, whose name you have invoked, will not desert you in your hour of need!"

Bowing his head in his hands and trembling like an aspen leaf, Esperance quitted the library with a convulsive sob, as if the last ray of hope had been withdrawn from his life and all was darkness and despair.

M. Dantes threw himself in his chair and for an instant was plunged in absorbing thought; then he arose and putting on his hat and cloak left the library; a few moments later he had quitted the mansion by a private door.

Closely muffling his face in the folds of his cloak, that he might not be recognized, the Deputy from Marseilles passed hurriedly from street to street until he stood before a massive building in the Rue Vivienne. He rang the bell, and, when the concierge appeared, said to her:

"Is the Viscount Massetti at home?"

The woman, a large, fat, lumbering creature, cast a sleepy glance, that was half-curious, half-suspicious, at him and answered:

"Yes, Monsieur; but he bade me deny him to everybody."

"He will see me, however, my good woman," said M. Dantes. "Take my card to him."

The fat concierge took the card and glanced at it; when she read "Edmond Dantes, Deputy from Marseilles," she stared at the famous Republican leader like one possessed; then, filled with awe, she hastened away and climbed the stairs as fast as her cumbersome legs would let her. She returned, panting and puffing, followed by the Viscount's valet, who, with much ceremony and obsequiousness, conducted the distinguished visitor to his master's apartments.

The salon into which M. Dantes was ushered was large and sumptuously furnished; evidences of wealth and luxury were visible on every side, while everything displayed the utmost taste and elegance.

"To what am I indebted for the honor of this unexpected visit, my dear Count?" said Massetti, rising from a handsomely carved, red velvet upholstered arm-chair, in which he had been indolently reclining, and coming forward to greet his guest.

"To a matter that concerns both of us deeply," replied the Deputy, in a meaning tone.

A shadow crossed the Viscount's handsome visage, but it was gone in an instant, and he said, with the utmost politeness:

"Pray be seated, my dear Count, and before proceeding to business refresh yourself with a glass of rare old Burgundy. Here, Stephano, wine and glasses."

M. Dantes sat down in an arm-chair precisely resembling that from which the Viscount had arisen; Massetti resumed his seat and the valet brought the old Burgundy and glasses, placing the decanter and drinking vessels on a small table of glistening ebony between his master and the Deputy. After they had duly drunk each other's health, M. Dantes said:

"I regret, my dear Viscount, that I am compelled to disturb you, but my business was too urgent for delay."

"You don't disturb me in the least. Pray proceed."

"You remember your conversation with my daughter just before you and she parted, do you not?"

"I remember it," replied the Viscount, coloring slightly and evidently growing ill at ease.

"In that case, neither preface nor explanation is necessary. I called to ask you a few plain questions."

The Italian was now a prey to singular excitement; he grew pale and flushed by turns, finally rising and pacing the salon in great agitation.

"Count," said he, abruptly, when he could command his voice, "you are a man of the world and a cosmopolitan, and, of course, you know that one often commits folly, especially when the ardent and uncontrollable blood of youth is rushing through his veins. With this explanation, imperfect though it be, I must ask you to rest satisfied, for it is utterly out of my power to give you any other, or to enter into the details of the unfortunate affair which has brought you here. I assure you, however, that I am altogether blameless in the matter; investigation will abundantly establish the truth of what I say."

"I will make that investigation."

"I regret that I can neither empower you to do so nor aid you in it!"

"What am I to understand by that?"

"Simply what I say."

"You are, doubtless, aware that my son makes grave accusations against you, that he accuses you, in fact, of a dastardly crime."

"Esperance is mistaken, my dear Count; I swear to you that he is mistaken and that I am as innocent as he is!"

"But Luigi Vampa may have a different tale to tell!"

"Luigi Vampa!" cried the Viscount, coming instantly to a dead halt, and a sudden pallor overspreading his entire visage.

"Yes, Luigi Vampa; I have written to him and in two weeks will have his answer!"

"For Esperance's sake, for my sake, for your daughter's sake, destroy that answer as soon as received and without reading it!" exclaimed the young Italian, wildly, his pallor increasing to such a degree that his face resembled that of a corpse.

"Should I be mad enough to do so," said M. Dantes, calmly, "with it all hope of your marriage with Zuleika would perish!"

"Oh! do not say that, do not say that!" groaned Massetti. "What would life be worth to me without Zuleika's love!"

"Then deserve that love by clearing yourself, by proving that your record will bear the light of day!"

"I have sworn to you that I am innocent! Is not that enough?"

"No," replied M. Dantes, coldly. "I must have proof to support your oath."

"Then you believe me guilty in spite of all! This is the worst blow yet!"

"It is in your power to completely justify yourself; at least, so you give me to understand, and yet your refusal will forever separate you from the woman you love!"

"You fill me with despair!" said Massetti, in a smothered voice, sinking upon a sofa. "I fain would reveal everything to you, but an awful oath of silence stands between me and the revelation."

"Then I must wait for Vampa's answer, and shape my course by that!" said M. Dantes, firmly.

"That answer will destroy both Esperance and myself!" replied the Viscount, in a hoarse whisper.

"We shall see," returned the Deputy, rising and resuming his cloak; as he stood at the door of the salon with his hat in his hand, he added: "I thought you all a man should be, Viscount, and that you would make Zuleika happy, but my convictions have been sadly shaken. I came here thinking that love for woman was all powerful in the heart of man, that it would induce you to speak, even in the face of an oath, perhaps violently and iniquitously administered; I was wrong; farewell!"

M. Dantes turned slowly and took his departure, leaving Giovanni Massetti on the sofa plunged in grief and dismay.

# CHAPTER XXXI.
## VAMPA'S ANSWER.

As the time for the arrival of Luigi Vampa's answer to M. Dantes' letter approached, Esperance grew more and more uneasy and serious; he spent the greater portion of every day from home, apparently for the purpose of avoiding his father and sister; when he returned he was moody, depressed and silent, and far into the night he could be heard pacing his chamber as if unable to sleep from excitement and anxiety.

Zuleika endeavored to comfort him, but all her efforts were fruitless. She, poor girl, was herself overwhelmed with her own distress, though she strove to bear up against it. Massetti had neither written to nor attempted to see her since their separation, a circumstance she could not reconcile with his protestations of ardent love for her, and this served vastly to augment her sadness and anguish, though she still believed in her soul that the Viscount was entirely innocent of the crime laid to his charge.

M. Dantes, who had plunged into politics deeper than ever since the success of the Revolution, was frequently in consultation with the Republican leaders, and many of them visited him at his residence and were closeted with him for hours at a time; but, though seemingly engrossed in State affairs, the Deputy did not lose sight of his son and daughter, or of the mysterious complication that Vampa was expected to make clear. Ali had strict orders to watch both Zuleika and Esperance, and to report to his master whatever they did when at home in his absence, but the faithful Nubian found nothing amiss, save that the young people seemed burdened with a sorrow he could not fathom.

At length, when the two weeks that it would take to hear from Rome had expired, M. Lamartine called one morning at the mansion in the Rue du Helder, and having finished his business with M. Dantes was invited by his host to remain to lunch. The repast was served in the salle-a-manger, Esperance and Zuleika partaking of it with their father and his illustrious guest. When the edibles had been removed and the party were taking wine at the dining-table, M. Dantes, suddenly remembering that he had an engagement, begged M. Lamartine to excuse him and remain with his son and daughter until his return, that would be in half an hour at the utmost. This arrangement effected, the Deputy arose from his chair, threw his cloak over his arm and was about to take his departure, when Ali appeared on the threshold of the open doorway, bearing in his hand a letter. Instantly divining that this was Vampa's answer, upon which hung Massetti's fate and his own, Esperance leaped to his feet and fixed his wild and staring eyes on the ominous missive as if he would read its contents through its folds. Zuleika retained her seat, but lifted her hands in terror and stared at the letter with pallid cheeks and blanched lips. Even Lamartine turned in his chair and, holding his glass in his hand, gazed wonderingly at the Nubian and the epistle. M. Dantes alone seemed unmoved, and his pale countenance gave no sign of the emotion struggling in his breast; he stood like a man of iron, and extending his hand took the letter without a tremor. It was enclosed in a curiously-fashioned envelope, evidently made by the writer himself, and bore the Roman postmark; the direction, written in bold, scrawling, but perfectly legible characters, read: "M. Edmond Dantes, Deputy from Marseilles, No. 27 Rue du Helder, Paris, France. Personal and private." This direction was in French.

Ali having retired, the Deputy calmly broke the seal and hurriedly ran his eyes over the missive. Esperance and Zuleika eagerly and breathlessly watched his countenance while he read, but it was as impassable as a countenance chiseled from marble; when he had finished he turned to Esperance and without a word handed him the letter. For a moment the young man trembled so he could not read; cold perspiration stood in heavy beads upon his forehead, and vivid flashes of red passed before his eyes like sheets of lurid lightning. What thoughts, what suspicions, what dread shot through his tortured mind in that brief moment, making it seem an eternity of suffering! At last, steadying and controlling himself by a supreme effort, he read the missive from which he had feared such terrible consequences. It was in Italian, and ran as follows:

HIS EXCELLENCY, THE COUNT OF MONTE-CRISTO:
 You ask me to answer

your questions, and I comply. Pasquale Solara's daughter,
Annunziata, was abducted, from her father's peasant-home by
Giovanni Massetti, known as the Viscount Massetti, who is, no
doubt, the person to whom you allude as now in Paris, for he has
disappeared from Rome. You are right in assuming that he had aid.
He was assisted by a young Frenchman, and that young Frenchman was
your son, Esperance. Annunziata suffered the usual fate of abducted
peasant girls, and was deserted by her dastardly abductor in a
fastness controlled by my band. When the abduction took place,
Annunziata's brother strove to rescue her, but was attacked and
killed by Massetti. Through my means the girl was returned to her
home, but she was miserable there and fled; she is now in an asylum
for unfortunate women founded at Civita Vecchia by the Order of
Sisters of Refuge, and superintended by a French lady, a Madame
Helena de Rancogne, who, as is said, was formerly called the
Countess of Monte-Cristo.[1] It is due to your son to say that he
was entirely misled in regard to the abduction of Annunziata
Solara, and is altogether innocent of crime or intention to commit
it. The whole burden of guilt rests upon the shoulders of the
Viscount Massetti, who, I believe, compelled your son at the
pistol's mouth to take a fearful oath of silence.
                              LUIGI VAMPA.


When Esperance had read this letter that so effectually cleared him, and was
such a fearful arraignment of the Viscount Massetti, he restored it to his father and
sank into his chair utterly overcome by the terrible excitement and mental strain
through which he had passed. M. Dantes forced him to swallow a glass of wine that
partially restored him; then, turning to M. Lamartine, who had been an astonished
spectator of this strange and to him incomprehensible family scene, he said:
    "My dear friend, you are amazed, and you have a right to be. This letter that has

caused my son and daughter so much emotion comes from a Roman brigand chief, no other than Luigi Vampa, whose name is notorious throughout Europe. You will understand its importance when I inform you that it conclusively clears my son of an exceedingly grave charge."

M. Lamartine arose and took Esperance by the hand.

"I heartily congratulate you," said he.

"And Giovanni Massetti?" asked Zuleika, in a tremulous voice.

"Giovanni Massetti is unworthy of my daughter's hand!" replied M. Dantes.

"Let me see that letter," said Zuleika, her cheek growing paler and her heart beating tumultuously.

Her father gave it to her. She took it and read each line with an intensity of interest that was painful to behold. When she had reached the end, her eyes suddenly lighted up and the color came rushing back to her pallid cheeks.

"Esperance," she said, facing her brother with an air of resolution beneath which he quailed, "Luigi Vampa has not told all! Something he has kept back, and that something you know. What is it? Speak!"

"Luigi Vampa has told the truth!" replied the young man, doggedly.

"Yes, but not the whole truth. What has he kept back?"

Esperance shook his head.

"He has told the truth!" he repeated.

"Did the Viscount Massetti administer the oath of silence to you?"

"He did."

"Then who administered that oath to Giovanni?"

The young man did not answer.

"There is some mystery about this complicated affair yet unexplained, and until it is explained I cannot believe Giovanni Massetti guilty!"

"Come, come, my daughter," said M. Dantes, soothingly, "your heart speaks and not your mind."

"My heart and mind both speak, papa," replied Zuleika, "and both say that Giovanni Massetti is innocent."

"Let him prove it then."

"I feel certain that he can and will."

"Well, well, child, go to Madame Dantes and take counsel of her. Only a woman can heal a young girl's love wounds."

Zuleika quitted the salle-a-manger, her countenance yet bearing the stamp of an inflexible belief and a fixed determination.

"Esperance," said M. Dantes, "your honor is unstained and you are restored to my heart. I thank God for the blessings of this day!"

"You are a true father, Edmond, as well as a true patriot," said M. Lamartine, "and I feel assured that your son will be worthy of you and of our beloved France."

&ast;          &ast;          &ast;          &ast;          &ast;

That very day Giovanni Massetti received an unsigned little note, written in a tiny feminine hand. It was phrased thus:

"I believe you innocent in spite of all! Prove to me and to the          world that you are so."

Enclosed in this little note was Luigi Vampa's letter to M. Dantes.

The next morning it became known that the Viscount Massetti had disappeared from Paris. Gossip assigned a thousand scandalous motives for his sudden flight, but gossip could form no idea as to whither he had fled. Zuleika[2] however, knew that he had returned to Italy to clear his name and prove himself worthy of her love!

NOTES:

[1] The exceedingly romantic history of Madame de Rancogne will be found in that fascinating and absorbing novel, "The Countess of Monte-Cristo," published by Messrs. T. B. Peterson & Brothers, a wonderful book that everybody should read.

[2] A full account, from this point, of the life and remarkable career of "Zuleika, the Daughter of Monte-Cristo," will be found in the brilliant, original, and absorbing novel just published by T. B. Peterson & Brothers, Philadelphia, in uniform style with "Edmond Dantes," entitled "MONTE-CRISTO'S DAUGHTER," being the Sequel to Alexander Dumas' famous novel, "The Count of Monte-Cristo," and Conclusion of "Edmond Dantes." "MONTE-CRISTO'S DAUGHTER" will be found to be of unflagging interest, abounding in ardent love scenes and stirring adventures, while

the Count of Monte-Cristo figures largely in it, and many of the original Monte-Cristo characters are also introduced into the volume, making it in point of brilliancy, power, and absorbing interest fully equal to its famous predecessors.

THE END.

### The Codes Of Hammurabi And Moses
### W. W. Davies

QTY

The discovery of the Hammurabi Code is one of the greatest achievements of archaeology, and is of paramount interest, not only to the student of the Bible, but also to all those interested in ancient history...

**Religion**    **ISBN:** *1-59462-338-4*    **Pages:132**

*MSRP $12.95*

### The Theory of Moral Sentiments
### Adam Smith

QTY

This work from 1749. contains original theories of conscience amd moral judgment and it is the foundation for systemof morals.

**Philosophy**  **ISBN:** *1-59462-777-0*    **Pages:536**

*MSRP $19.95*

### Jessica's First Prayer
### Hesba Stretton

QTY

In a screened and secluded corner of one of the many railway-bridges which span the streets of London there could be seen a few years ago, from five o'clock every morning until half past eight, a tidily set-out coffee-stall, consisting of a trestle and board, upon which stood two large tin cans, with a small fire of charcoal burning under each so as to keep the coffee boiling during the early hours of the morning when the work-people were thronging into the city on their way to their daily toil...

**Pages:84**

**Childrens**   **ISBN:** *1-59462-373-2*    *MSRP $9.95*

### My Life and Work
### Henry Ford

QTY

Henry Ford revolutionized the world with his implementation of mass production for the Model T automobile. Gain valuable business insight into his life and work with his own auto-biography... "We have only started on our development of our country we have not as yet, with all our talk of wonderful progress, done more than scratch the surface. The progress has been wonderful enough but..."

**Pages:300**

**Biographies/**    **ISBN:** *1-59462-198-5*    *MSRP $21.95*

## The Art of Cross-Examination
## Francis Wellman

QTY

I presume it is the experience of every author, after his first book is published upon an important subject, to be almost overwhelmed with a wealth of ideas and illustrations which could readily have been included in his book, and which to his own mind, at least, seem to make a second edition inevitable. Such certainly was the case with me; and when the first edition had reached its sixth impression in five months, I rejoiced to learn that it seemed to my publishers that the book had met with a sufficiently favorable reception to justify a second and considerably enlarged edition. ..

**Pages:412**

**Reference**    **ISBN:** *1-59462-647-2*    *MSRP $19.95*

## On the Duty of Civil Disobedience
## Henry David Thoreau

QTY

Thoreau wrote his famous essay, On the Duty of Civil Disobedience, as a protest against an unjust but popular war and the immoral but popular institution of slave-owning. He did more than write—he declined to pay his taxes, and was hauled off to gaol in consequence. Who can say how much this refusal of his hastened the end of the war and of slavery ?

**Law**    **ISBN:** *1-59462-747-9*    **Pages:48**

*MSRP $7.45*

## Dream Psychology Psychoanalysis for Beginners
## Sigmund Freud

QTY

Sigmund Freud, born Sigismund Schlomo Freud (May 6, 1856 - September 23, 1939), was a Jewish-Austrian neurologist and psychiatrist who co-founded the psychoanalytic school of psychology. Freud is best known for his theories of the unconscious mind, especially involving the mechanism of repression; his redefinition of sexual desire as mobile and directed towards a wide variety of objects; and his therapeutic techniques, especially his understanding of transference in the therapeutic relationship and the presumed value of dreams as sources of insight into unconscious desires.

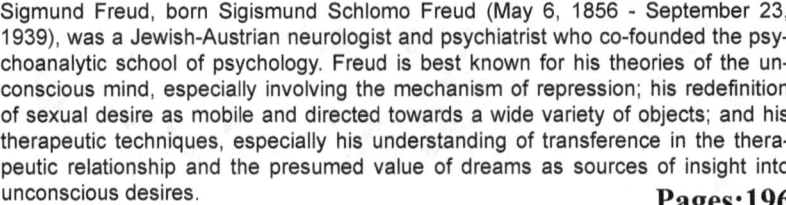

**Pages:196**

**Psychology**    **ISBN:** *1-59462-905-6*    *MSRP $15.45*

## The Miracle of Right Thought
## Orison Swett Marden

QTY

Believe with all of your heart that you will do what you were made to do. When the mind has once formed the habit of holding cheerful, happy, prosperous pictures, it will not be easy to form the opposite habit. It does not matter how improbable or how far away this realization may see, or how dark the prospects may be, if we visualize them as best we can, as vividly as possible, hold tenaciously to them and vigorously struggle to attain them, they will gradually become actualized, realized in the life. But a desire, a longing without endeavor, a yearning abandoned or held indifferently will vanish without realization.

**Pages:360**

**Self Help**    **ISBN:** *1-59462-644-8*    *MSRP $25.45*

**The Rosicrucian Cosmo-Conception Mystic Christianity** by *Max Heindel*  ISBN: *1-59462-188-8*  **$38.95**
*The Rosicrucian Cosmo-conception is not dogmatic, neither does it appeal to any other authority than the reason of the student. It is: not controversial, but is: sent forth in the, hope that it may help to clear...*  New Age/Religion Pages 646

**Abandonment To Divine Providence** by *Jean-Pierre de Caussade*  ISBN: *1-59462-228-0*  **$25.95**
*"The Rev. Jean Pierre de Caussade was one of the most remarkable spiritual writers of the Society of Jesus in France in the 18th Century. His death took place at Toulouse in 1751. His works have gone through many editions and have been republished...*  Inspirational/Religion Pages 400

**Mental Chemistry** by *Charles Haanel*  ISBN: *1-59462-192-6*  **$23.95**
*Mental Chemistry allows the change of material conditions by combining and appropriately utilizing the power of the mind. Much like applied chemistry creates something new and unique out of careful combinations of chemicals the mastery of mental chemistry...*  New Age Pages 354

**The Letters of Robert Browning and Elizabeth Barret Barrett 1845-1846 vol II**  ISBN: *1-59462-193-4*  **$35.95**
by *Robert Browning* and *Elizabeth Barrett*  Biographies Pages 596

**Gleanings In Genesis (volume I)** by *Arthur W. Pink*  ISBN: *1-59462-130-6*  **$27.45**
*Appropriately has Genesis been termed "the seed plot of the Bible" for in it we have, in germ form, almost all of the great doctrines which are afterwards fully developed in the books of Scripture which follow...*  Religion/Inspirational Pages 420

**The Master Key** by *L. W. de Laurence*  ISBN: *1-59462-001-6*  **$30.95**
*In no branch of human knowledge has there been a more lively increase of the spirit of research during the past few years than in the study of Psychology, Concentration and Mental Discipline. The requests for authentic lessons in Thought Control, Mental Discipline and...*  New Age/Business Pages 422

**The Lesser Key Of Solomon Goetia** by *L. W. de Laurence*  ISBN: *1-59462-092-X*  **$9.95**
*This translation of the first book of the "Lernegton" which is now for the first time made accessible to students of Talismanic Magic was done, after careful collation and edition, from numerous Ancient Manuscripts in Hebrew, Latin, and French...*  New Age/Occult Pages 92

**Rubaiyat Of Omar Khayyam** by *Edward Fitzgerald*  ISBN:*1-59462-332-5*  **$13.95**
*Edward Fitzgerald, whom the world has already learned, in spite of his own efforts to remain within the shadow of anonymity, to look upon as one of the rarest poets of the century, was born at Bredfield, in Suffolk, on the 31st of March, 1809. He was the third son of John Purcell...*  Music Pages 172

**Ancient Law** by *Henry Maine*  ISBN: *1-59462-128-4*  **$29.95**
*The chief object of the following pages is to indicate some of the earliest ideas of mankind, as they are reflected in Ancient Law, and to point out the relation of those ideas to modern thought.*  Religion/History Pages 452

**Far-Away Stories** by *William J. Locke*  ISBN: *1-59462-129-2*  **$19.45**
*"Good wine needs no bush, but a collection of mixed vintages does. And this book is just such a collection. Some of the stories I do not want to remain buried for ever in the museum files of dead magazine-numbers an author's not unpardonable vanity..."*  Fiction Pages 272

**Life of David Crockett** by *David Crockett*  ISBN: *1-59462-250-7*  **$27.45**
*"Colonel David Crockett was one of the most remarkable men of the times in which he lived. Born in humble life, but gifted with a strong will, an indomitable courage, and unremitting perseverance...*  Biographies/New Age Pages 424

**Lip-Reading** by *Edward Nitchie*  ISBN: *1-59462-206-X*  **$25.95**
*Edward B. Nitchie, founder of the New York School for the Hard of Hearing, now the Nitchie School of Lip-Reading, Inc, wrote "LIP-READING Principles and Practice". The development and perfecting of this meritorious work on lip-reading was an undertaking...*  How-to Pages 400

**A Handbook of Suggestive Therapeutics, Applied Hypnotism, Psychic Science**  ISBN: *1-59462-214-0*  **$24.95**
by *Henry Munro*  Health/New Age/Health/Self-help Pages 376

**A Doll's House: and Two Other Plays** by *Henrik Ibsen*  ISBN: *1-59462-112-8*  **$19.95**
*Henrik Ibsen created this classic when in revolutionary 1848 Rome. Introducing some striking concepts in playwriting for the realist genre, this play has been studied the world over.*  Fiction/Classics/Plays 308

**The Light of Asia** by *sir Edwin Arnold*  ISBN: *1-59462-204-3*  **$13.95**
*In this poetic masterpiece, Edwin Arnold describes the life and teachings of Buddha. The man who was to become known as Buddha to the world was born as Prince Gautama of India but he rejected the worldly riches and abandoned the reigns of power when...*  Religion/History/Biographies Pages 170

**The Complete Works of Guy de Maupassant** by *Guy de Maupassant*  ISBN: *1-59462-157-8*  **$16.95**
*"For days and days, nights and nights, I had dreamed of that first kiss which was to consecrate our engagement, and I knew not on what spot I should put my lips..."*  Fiction/Classics Pages 240

**The Art of Cross-Examination** by *Francis L. Wellman*  ISBN: *1-59462-309-0*  **$26.95**
*Written by a renowned trial lawyer, Wellman imparts his experience and uses case studies to explain how to use psychology to extract desired information through questioning.*  How-to/Science/Reference Pages 408

**Answered or Unanswered?** by *Louisa Vaughan*  ISBN: *1-59462-248-5*  **$10.95**
Miracles of Faith in China  Religion Pages 112

**The Edinburgh Lectures on Mental Science (1909)** by *Thomas*  ISBN: *1-59462-008-3*  **$11.95**
*This book contains the substance of a course of lectures recently given by the writer in the Queen Street Hall, Edinburgh. Its purpose is to indicate the Natural Principles governing the relation between Mental Action and Material Conditions...*  New Age/Psychology Pages 148

**Ayesha** by *H. Rider Haggard*  ISBN: *1-59462-301-5*  **$24.95**
*Verily and indeed it is the unexpected that happens! Probably if there was one person upon the earth from whom the Editor of this, and of a certain previous history, did not expect to hear again...*  Classics Pages 380

**Ayala's Angel** by *Anthony Trollope*  ISBN: *1-59462-352-X*  **$29.95**
*The two girls were both pretty, but Lucy who was twenty-one who supposed to be simple and comparatively unattractive, whereas Ayala was credited, as her Bombwhat romantic name might show, with poetic charm and a taste for romance. Ayala when her father died was nineteen...*  Fiction Pages 484

**The American Commonwealth** by *James Bryce*  ISBN: *1-59462-286-8*  **$34.45**
*An interpretation of American democratic political theory. It examines political mechanics and society from the perspective of Scotsman James Bryce*  Politics Pages 572

**Stories of the Pilgrims** by *Margaret P. Pumphrey*  ISBN: *1-59462-116-0*  **$17.95**
*This book explores pilgrims religious oppression in England as well as their escape to Holland and eventual crossing to America on the Mayflower, and their early days in New England...*  History Pages 268

www.bookjungle.com *email: sales@bookjungle.com fax: 630-214-0564 mail: Book Jungle PO Box 2226 Champaign, IL 61825*

**QTY**

**The Fasting Cure** *by Sinclair Upton*         ISBN: *1-59462-222-1*   **$13.95**
*In the Cosmopolitan Magazine for May, 1910, and in the Contemporary Review (London) for April, 1910, I published an article dealing with my experi-ences in fasting. I have written a great many magazine articles, but never one which attracted so much attention...*   New Age/Self Help/Health Pages 164

**Hebrew Astrology** *by Sepharial*        ISBN: *1-59462-308-2*   **$13.45**
*In these days of advanced thinking it is a matter of common observation that we have left many of the old landmarks behind and that we are now pressing forward to greater heights and to a wider horizon than that which represented the mind-content of our progenitors...*   Astrology Pages 144

**Thought Vibration or The Law of Attraction in the Thought World**    ISBN: *1-59462-127-6*   **$12.95**
*by William Walker Atkinson*                    Psychology/Religion Pages 144

**Optimism** *by Helen Keller*         ISBN: *1-59462-108-X*   **$15.95**
*Helen Keller was blind, deaf, and mute since 19 months old, yet famously learned how to overcome these handicaps, communicate with the world, and spread her lectures promoting optimism. An inspiring read for everyone...*   Biographies/Inspirational Pages 84

**Sara Crewe** *by Frances Burnett*        ISBN: *1-59462-360-0*   **$9.45**
*In the first place, Miss Minchin lived in London. Her home was a large, dull, tall one, in a large, dull square, where all the houses were alike, and all the sparrows were alike, and where all the door-knockers made the same heavy sound...*   Childrens/Classic Pages 88

**The Autobiography of Benjamin Franklin** *by Benjamin Franklin*    ISBN: *1-59462-135-7*   **$24.95**
*The Autobiography of Benjamin Franklin has probably been more extensively read than any other American historical work, and no other book of its kind has had such ups and downs of fortune. Franklin lived for many years in England, where he was agent...*   Biographies/History Pages 332

| Name | |
| --- | --- |
| Email | |
| Telephone | |
| Address | |
| | |
| City, State ZIP | |

☐ **Credit Card**            ☐ **Check / Money Order**

| Credit Card Number | |
| --- | --- |
| Expiration Date | |
| Signature | |

*Please Mail to:*   Book Jungle
PO Box 2226
Champaign, IL 61825
*or Fax to:*     630-214-0564

## ORDERING INFORMATION
**web***: www.bookjungle.com*
**email***: sales@bookjungle.com*
**fax***: 630-214-0564*
**mail***: Book Jungle PO Box 2226 Champaign, IL 61825*
**or PayPal** *to sales@bookjungle.com*

*Please contact us for bulk discounts*

## DIRECT-ORDER TERMS

**20% Discount if You Order
Two or More Books**
Free Domestic Shipping!
Accepted: Master Card, Visa,
Discover, American Express

www.ingramcontent.com/pod-product-compliance
Lightning Source LLC
Chambersburg PA
CBHW080901020726
47502CB00008B/2309